THE
REINCARNATION
LIBRARY

I REMEMBER LOVE

I REMEMBER *L*OVE

Mollie Hardwick

Æ

AEON PUBLISHING COMPANY

MAMARONECK, NEW YORK

First published 1982

Copyright © 1982 by Mollie Hardwick

This edition has been designed and typeset exclusively
for The Reincarnation Library.
All rights reserved.

Published with the kind permission of Mollie Hardwick

ISBN: 1-893766-23-3

Library of Congress Control Number: 00-134443

Printed and bound in the United States of America.

The Castle

YOLANDE AND JOSCELYN: 1464

Whatever befall, I never shall
   Of this thing be upbraid:
But if ye go, and leave me so,
   Then have ye me betrayed.
Remember you wele, how that ye dele;
   For if ye, as ye said,
Be so unkind to leave behind
   Your love, the Nut-brown Maid,
Trust me truly that I shall die
   Soon after ye be gone:
For in my mind, of all mankind,
   I love but you alone.

Anon

15TH CENTURY

$\mathcal{W}$e were very merry, that day of May in the rose-garden at Middleham. I remember the warmth of the sun as though it were upon my face now, and the carpet of daisies in the short grass that we three girls flattened with our skirts as we sprawled in a rather unladylike way, watching the fish in the little artificial stream that was fed from the marble fountain, tickling them sometimes and seeing them dart away, flashes of brown and silver. There were apple-trees and pear-trees in the garden beyond, and their petals were carried to ours by the soft wind, to settle in white and pink flakes on our hair and our dresses.

Three boys and three girls in a garden. Why were we there, and not at our lessons? Not because it was May Day, because we were not allowed to go rollicking off to the woods for May boughs as the country people did; Lady Warwick was not a strict guardian to us, but those were troubled times and we were not to be put at risk. (The other five, that is—I might have gone Maying myself, not being anybody of importance.)

I think we were on holiday because it was the Feast of the Apostles St Philip and St James. The boys in particular were glad of feast days, when they were let off the hours of study they had to endure otherwise: Latin, French, law and the sciences, music and history, taught to them by learned clerks and masters, and when the lesson-times were over

they were on their honour to keep their heads in great tomes like Frois-
sart's *Chronicles* and the *Government of Kings and Princes*. Richard was
always the last to lay his book aside: but then, he was a prince himself,
or next to one, being brother to the King.

Let me look back across time at the children we were, as though
a miniature-painter had caught us and preserved us with his skilled
brush and rich colours. The two Neville sisters, Isabel and Anne,
daughters of the Earl of Warwick, whose Yorkshire castle Middleham
was a small part of his vast estates. Both fair girls, both slight and
small-boned, Isabel with a proud high-nosed look like her father's,
already seeking for admiration from men's eyes (at eleven she was old
enough to be married, and a very desirable match with her inheritance). Anne, two years younger, had a softer air. She was gentle and
confiding and looked as fragile as the blossom drifting down on her
long, pale-gold hair, crowned with a silk plaited chaplet. Her high forehead was shaved at the hair-line, as Isabel's was, giving her the fashionable height of brow, and her eyebrows were plucked to a thin line, her
cheekbones high, her mouth bee-stung. I thought her the prettier of
the two. If she had been an animal, she would have been a white doe.

The two younger boys would have been puppies. Francis Lovell,
whom we called Francey, and Robin Percy, minded their masters when
they had to but lost no time in bounding out to play as soon as they
were set free. Apprentices in knightly conduct they might be, put
under Warwick's guardianship to learn the arts of ruling and of war, but
under all that weight of learning cheerful young things, brisk with the
confidence of the noble blood in their veins, Robin a sprig of Northum-
berland's line, Francey from sweet Oxfordshire. They teased us girls, as
much as they dared. But they never teased Richard Plantagenet.

What animal was he, thirteen-year-old Richard? Quiet, grave,
wary, desperately serious: I think perhaps he was like some creature of
dark forests in foreign lands, countries of which we knew nothing. The
Nevilles were some sort of cousins to him, and he was high in great

Warwick's favour for his seriousness and bravery. The younger boys outstripped him in growth and strength; he had always been delicate, a thin dark offshoot from the lusty blond Plantagenets and a most unlikely brother to the big golden laughing King Edward. But he bore his armour like a grown man when the boys went out to mock tournaments, tireless in practising the use of sword and dagger and battle-axe, a sound huntsman if not a keen one, his heart given to war: it was the way he could best serve the king-brother he worshipped.

Only a year before the time I write of, he, a twelve-year-old child, had been given the charge of levying troops from nine counties of the Realm. He was Knight of the Garter, Admiral of England, Ireland and Aquitaine, and lord of many manors. Above all he was a Yorkshireman, sprung from the House of York which had taken over the crown and the kingdom from beaten Lancaster in the struggle between the White rose and the Red—one who spoke with the northern tongue, who loved the wild and splendid moors and hills, the frowning castles and quiet abbeys.

And one girl, Anne Neville. I watched him, his eyes on Anne as she dabbled her hand in the water after the elusive fish, and knew that he would have caught the lot of them ruthlessly with his own hands if it gave her pleasure. He was not over-fond of the romances we took it in turn to read aloud—*The Story of Blanchfleur, The Troy-book,* the French tales of courtly love—but as far as they dealt with ladies and the gallant knights who lived to serve them, he listened attentively while the other boys furtively yawned.

Isabel grew tired of the fish. She woke her little dog, Dagonet, which had fallen asleep by her, and began to play with it. When it strayed away from her she looked round for something else to do, and saw me idle.

'Yolande, go and get your lute. I want to practise my new song,' she said imperiously. It was perfectly understood in her father's household that the rules of chivalry applied to girls as well as to boys.

A high-born lady must be courteous and humble to others, the great and the not-so-great, but Lady Isabel often let her tongue forget the if-you-please and I-thank-you. It was not for me to reprove her, the Countess her mother would do that sharply enough if she overheard. I went in and fetched my lute.

I was emphatically one of the not-so-great at Middleham, something higher than a servant, lower than an equal of the Neville sisters. It was a miracle that I was there at all, indeed, being the child of a Lancastrian, John de Clifford, Baron of Westmorland. He had become reconciled to the Yorkists, then turned from them and died in battle when I was ten. But that was no loss to me, for I never knew him. I was a bastard, born in his wild youth and brought up among the maids at his home, Skipton Castle. One of those waiting-women may have been my mother—I never knew. Bastards of the great were two-a-penny, and still are, I dare say, usually acknowledged and treated well.

I was not told why, after my father's death at Dintingdale, I was sent away from Skipton. My two half-brothers, whom I hardly knew, also vanished, because Lady de Clifford feared the Yorkists might seek them out and kill them. For a time I lived in a cottage with some peasant folk. Then a servant arrived and escorted me to Middleham Castle, of all places, a Yorkist stronghold, grander and grimmer than Skipton, a Norman fortress crowning a hill above the village, looking down fiercely on the water meadows and the rivers Ure and Cover.

At first I was lonely in wild Wensleydale, among strangers whom I had been brought up to think of as enemies. But Lady Neville sent for me and treated me with such gracious kindness that I never again felt like an alien, nor do I believe she ever told any of her household that my father was Black Clifford, known to Yorkists as the Butcher. Good lady, she was the perfect helpmeet to her brilliant lord, a constant star twinned with a blazing planet. God and Our Lady bless her, wherever she is today . . .

I cannot guess why she sought me out in the first place, or made me special companion to her two daughters. It may have been—though I think it was not—that my looks set off theirs; that would have been more her lord's way of thinking, proud of his girls' beauty as he was and set on splendid marriages for both. They were crystal-fair, white and delicate as windflowers, I as brown as a peasant, dark-skinned with eyes and hair the colour of an oaken chest, and as sturdy as they were slender. I thought I was very ill-favoured and would never look like a lady. My hair grew so low on the brow, in a widow's peak, that when I shaved it to give myself a beautiful bald forehead like theirs it immediately grew again in dark stubble, very unlovely, so I gave up and let it grow in short vulgar crisp curls like those between a bull's horns.

Playing my lute was not my idea of something to do out of doors on a May morning. I liked to ride out with my falcon, to practise archery and dance. My clumsy needlework had cost me many a whipping from the Mother of the Maids at Skipton, so that at Middleham I worked as much as possible on large canvases in which my awkward stitching would hardly be noticed. The lute, too, I found not natural to my touch; though I loved the music such instruments made I found my own attempts slightly painful to listen to, and I could see my feelings reflected by the Countess's raised eyebrows.

Obediently I plucked out the accompaniment to Isabel's song, a *chanson* of love in the French which was still fashionable in courtly circles, something about the pains of loving and the cruel darts sent out by a lady's eyes. Mid-way through she broke off.

'How very badly you play! I can't hear half the notes.'

'I'm sorry, madam. It's difficult in the open air.'

She pouted. 'It sounds easy when the minstrels do it. I wanted my lord to hear me sing tonight after supper. He's so seldom here I wonder he remembers what we look like. If he's not in London he's in York, or fighting on the Border. Fighting, always fighting. Will there never be an end to it so that we can all enjoy ourselves?'

'Perhaps it will end soon, now that King Henry's in the Tower,' Robin said. 'I wonder they troubled to put him there, a hopeless lunatic like him.'

'Poor man,' Anne said softly.

Robin laughed. 'Daft Harry of Lancaster! Too much of a saint to father a son. When they showed him French Margaret's babe he rolled up his eyes and said it must be the child of the Holy Ghost.'

'Holy Duke of Suffolk, more like,' Francey said.

Richard was not amused. 'That is no sort of talk. Henry of Lancaster was not our rightful king, but there's small virtue in mocking the simple and God-afflicted.'

'Oh, go to Paradise and be a saint yourself, Dickon. Just because you're brother to Edward . . .'

'His Grace King Edward,' Richard corrected stiffly. Robin went pink and was silent.

'Do you think our father will stay here long, Richard?' said Anne.

'I doubt it. His Herald should return soon with King Louis's answer to the French marriage proposal, and then he must carry the news to London.'

Isabel sighed. 'I wonder if Bona of Savoy is very beautiful. It seems sad that the King should have to marry a foreign princess when there are so many handsome ladies of England.'

Francey laughed. 'Including one who's only eleven years old and related to him? Come down from the clouds.'

'It's not impossible! Plenty of ladies are married at my age.'

'And old at twenty from child-bearing,' I reminded her, thinking of the contrast between her thin immature body and the huge frame of that young giant, the King. She tossed her head.

'You're jealous. I shall marry early, and so will Anne. Golden-heads never go begging, but brown maids must whistle for a husband. Besides, I am a great match. Who gets me gets a fortune in money and lands.'

'You may be rich in goods, cousin,' Richard said sharply, 'but you're as poor as a crow in charity.'

Isabel ignored him. 'I shall ask our father to look out for a golden man for me, then we shall have children as beautiful as the day and Queen Bona may turn as green as a leek with envy. Bona! What a name for a queen, like a dog's dinner.'

'Isabel.' None of us had noticed that Lady Warwick had appeared silently through the yew arbour and was standing behind us. She was tall and slender and firm of countenance, the fair hair that she had passed to her girls hidden under a high-pointed hennin, her face rather noble than beautiful. She had been Anne Beauchamp, daughter to that rich and powerful earl whose counsels had helped to burn Joan the Maid, and whose armoured effigy in gilded brass lay in the new, splendid Beauchamp Chapel at Warwick. At his death his title had passed to her husband, who was to make the name of Warwick even more famous. We young ones looked up to her, were a little frightened of her: except, I think, Richard. I loved her for what she had done for me.

She advanced on her elder daughter. 'I heard your last remarks, Isabel. They were forward, wanton, unbecoming on a noblewoman's lips. You will go to the oratory and say four aves before Our Lady's statue, and then return to your companions in a better frame of mind. Go, now.'

'Yes, madam.' Isabel left hastily, her head down. One did not argue with Lady Warwick. She surveyed us all. 'Have you nothing better to do than idle?' she enquired. 'Even on a Feast day it looks ill. Anne, Yolande, there is no work in your fingers. You lads would be better playing at cup-and-ball than sitting like beggars before a rich man's door. Do you suppose my lord ever sits thus? Find yourselves some occupation, pray. Get your horses saddled and ride abroad, or join the revels down in the Church meadow—anything but sit and gape like lords of Fool's Hill.'

Robin and Francey got to their feet and bowed, then left the garden as she had meant them to do. I glanced nervously towards my lute, hoping that my lady would not ask me to show her my skill with it, for she had a shrewd ear. But she said, 'So you were talking of marriage. I think you had best put it from your minds for years to come. And yet . . . Yolande, how old are you now?'

'Almost thirteen, madam.'

'So, we might begin to look round for you soon. With the kingdom settled and the wars over'—she crossed herself—'life will return to what it was before—not that one can remember *that* very clearly. Ten years since King Henry lost his mind first; nine since the wars began. The Wars of the Roses, save the mark—a pretty name for ugly times.' She looked towards the flower-beds where neat rose-bushes were not yet in full bud. 'Chop for chop, a see-saw tilting first one way, then the other, York up, Lancaster down, and next day the opposite.'

'But York won at last,' Anne said. 'And my lord father brought that about.'

'He did, child. Do you remember the day we got the news from Towton Field, that Edward of York was our King, French Margaret on the run, and Henry mad again?'

'Yes, madam. We were at Warwick Castle and you had Isabel and me brought down from bed. You said it was all our father's doing, and that he was the greatest man in England.'

'He was. Warwick the Kingmaker. And now a Queenmaker.' She broke into the rare girlish laugh which was part of her charm. 'Isabel was right, even though she spoke out of turn. "Queen Bona" sounds most outlandish. Perhaps the Council will discreetly suggest some other name as well.'

'Anne?' suggested my young lady. Her mother shook her head.

'Not lucky. The last Queen Anne died young of plague.'

'Isabel, then?'

'Queen Isabel was known as the She-Wolf of France. I think not.

Never mind. We were talking about your marriage, Yolande. I think we must find you some pleasant young country squire, and quite soon, since you're growing womanly. Would you like to live here in the North, or shall we throw out the net from Warwick?'

'Wherever pleases you, madam. But . . .'

'But?'

'I shall not like leaving you.' It was true. The Countess and her daughters were the only family I had ever known, since at Skipton I had belonged to nobody.

'That would be hard.' She smiled. 'Hard to get away from the Nevilles. We are here, there and everywhere. My lord owns more than half a hundred estates, a hundred manors and a score of castles, from Wales to Tees-side. So wherever you find yourself, we shall be difficult to avoid. Well, time enough to talk of that. Go in and get your work, and let me see your fingers busy.'

As I sat under a tree, stitching away at a piece of embroidery which was growing ever more grimy and blood-spotted, since I pricked my fingers so often, I thought of what the Countess had said. Once she had said a thing it was more than likely to happen, and soon. So before I was fourteen I might find myself mistress of my own household, chatelaine, wife.

Wife to whom? I would have to take whomever was chosen, but what did I hope for in a husband? So far I had not indulged in romantic dreams, for marriage was not a romantic business. A couple were brought together, for their mutual benefit, whether acquaintances, relatives or strangers, the legal business concerning finances settled; then they were wedded and bedded, and might fancy each other or not, as the case might be. Romance belonged in the old Courts of Love, when a knight might swear fidelity only to another man's wife, and as like as not nothing was done between them, since it was all an elaborate conceit made of flowery language, poetry and lute-twanging. So I would be as well off with one man as with another.

I thought of the men I knew. My adored Lord Warwick, awe-inspiring, almost too great to look up at, though he was always affable and kindly to me. My lady was clearly proud of him, loved him, even, if people so old could love. The knights and noblemen who came and went in Neville strongholds, loud-voiced, bristling with authority: I would not be chosen for one of them, since I could bring them no fortune nor political advantage. And the boys of my age? Robin and Francey were so young that I could only think of them as childish playmates below my years, while Richard . . . Richard was all but a man in his seriousness and intent. I should not like to be married to him if there were no laughter about it. His elder brother George, Duke of Clarence, was much handsomer, more like the dazzling young King. But George paid no attention to me. Why should he?

How ridiculous, to waste time on such thoughts. I would be lucky to get a husband at all, with my swarthy looks and all my riches an allowance from the Clifford estates, not to mention the drawback of being a Clifford at all.

As I thought, hardly aware of what I was doing, the embroidery was growing beneath my fingers. A lifelike, very large bee perched on a small flower. He was pleasant to work on because the yellow and brown stripes of his body made a relief from the endless monotonous greens of the foliage. For once I was sorry to be called in to change my dress for supper.

My lord was famous for the lavish banquets he laid on for visiting nobles; such dishes as peacocks and swans roasted, then put back into their feathers and powdered with gold dust; the King could do no better, from the wealth of all his lands, for Warwick owned almost as much as he. In his household, with no strangers present, he still liked to see a good hearty spread. As many as six oxen might be roasted to feed the vast numbers of his retainers, and any man was free to help himself to as much meat as could be crammed on the point of a dagger, and carry it away with him. His own people ate plainly and well, always.

We supped together, family and household, in the Great Hall, though at separate tables. I was honoured by a seat at the high table, where the Earl's family and a few of the upper domestics sat—the Comptroller of the household, for one. We were at our places when the Earl made his entrance: a lesser man might just have walked in, but he made an entrance.

Great Warwick! How shall I describe him? Tall and broad-shouldered, with the lean strong body of a soldier, equally at home in armour or court dress, like the supertunic of purple velvet trimmed with grey fur he now wore over a dark brown corselet, gold-figured, and a heavy gold chain over it. A fine head, the dark grizzled hair short, like the neat beard which outlined his strong chin. The high cheek-bones and pointed oval of his face showed the origins of his daughters' beauty, the prow of a nose was all male. And the glance of the dark eyes, sharp and all-seeing, was like the gaze of an eagle, or an heraldic lion.

It may be seen that I had an admiration for my lord bordering on idolatry, which the Church forbids us. But I was not alone in that.

The meal over, the family retired to the solar, the room behind the great hall which was theirs alone, not to be invaded by others without invitation. I stayed behind, prepared to go with the other maids, but my lady beckoned me to follow. Isabel and Anne moved to the table where a chess game was set out. Richard, Francey, Robin and the three other apprentices to knighthood melted away to occupations of their own.

The Countess waved me to a stool near her chair by the hearth, and to my surprise the Earl sat in his own throne-like chair on the opposite side. The solar was the best room in the castle, hung with painted cloths showing scenes of hunting and chivalry, and cheerful with flower-garlands brought in by the servants who had gone Maying that morning. Among the rushes strewn on the floor were scattered sweet-smelling herbs, and the burning logs in the hearth sent out a smoky, spicy fragrance.

'Yolande,' said my lady, 'since we talked in the garden I've given some thought to the question.'

'Madam?'

'Of your marriage. My lord feels as I do that an early betrothal would be a wise thing for you.'

I must have looked taken aback, for the Earl said, 'You see, Yolande, your position is a dubious one, even among our family. There will always be those who remember the legend that it was your father who slew mine at Wakefield. Nobody questions you here, but the name of Clifford is not the best heritage to own in a Yorkist kingdom— and a Yorkist kingdom this England is now, and will be all the stronger when the King marries and gets an heir. You understand?'

'Yes, my lord.'

'Now, I have an acquaintance by the name of Sir Thomas Cowley of Tarletondale, in Neville country. He owns a small manor and a few prosperous farms which bring him a fair income—not a king's ransom, but enough to keep his lady in trinkets.' He smiled: I knew that trinkets, to him, signified such trifles as gold and jewels. 'He also has a son, another Thomas, the only boy in the brood. So the estates will be his in time.'

'And his wife will be someone of consequence,' put in the Countess.

'So, Yolande, I think young Thomas would be a very proper match for you. Have I your consent to speak to him?'

My consent, indeed! As though the Kingmaker needed the consent of a girl so humble as myself. But it was courteous, and like him, to ask for it. Meekly I answered, 'Whatever my lord pleases.'

He smiled across at his wife. 'How easily matches are made when crowns are not in question. I wish my own daughters' matings were as simple.'

I knew that he wished nothing of the kind. He would delight in the manipulation of Isabel and Anne in the power-game that was as skilled and intricate as the chess-match the girls were playing as he talked, or the inter-weaving of the ribbons round a maypole. Yet per-haps it came nearer to the game of cards called Costly Colours, for the colours in the blazons of such brides and grooms would be costly indeed. As though he read my thought, he said, 'Tom Cowley will get a handsome dowry with you.'

'Thank you, my lord.' I felt that my part in the scene was played out; I rose, curtseyed, and left him. They had so little time together. When husband and wife are as close as they, minutes must be precious . . .

I lay awake only a little time that night in the chamber where the maids slept. My lord and lady had chosen for me. They were wise and rich and powerful, I only an attainted bachelor's bastard. An irreverent comparison crossed my mind—not my will but Thine. Well, no matter, if it were my lord's will it must be also *his* Lord's, and was not to be questioned.

So ended May Day, 1464. A more memorable day than any of us at Middleham knew.

I met Tom Cowley within three days. My lord, with his usual briskness, arranged matters so that the meeting might take place before he left us to ride south. Betrothals of very young people were common enough things and as binding as a marriage ceremony, if the two promised to marry before witnesses or exchanged vows in letters (if they could write, which was seldom). My lord was not a man to take chances, however. One cold morning, not at all like May, I was summoned to a chamber where my lord and my lady waited in state, with my lord's chaplain, Father John, and Isabel and Anne, all eyes. The thing was going to be done properly.

I had dressed in a gown of whitish-cream which I fancied made me seem less swarthy, though Isabel had said it made me look like a novice nun. As a maid, it would not have been proper for me to wear one of the charming little flower-pot-shaped hennins which hid the hair so effectively, but I had risked attaching a white gauze veil to the chaplet round my hair, the front gathering of it covering the brow-curls I hated so much. I saw my lady's glance flick over me critically, but I was not called forward to take off the veil.

Then we all waited. My lord, not noted for his patience, glanced repeatedly through the window, from which the winding uphill approach to the castle could be seen. Isabel began to whisper to Anne. I was half-excited, half-fearful. Sir Thomas was an acquaintance of my lord's;

he would be grand, haughty, and his son one of the glittering young men who went about in the train of the King and the Duke of Clarence.

After what seemed like hours there was a knocking on the door, and a steward ushered in two men. I stared and stared, then turned away in disappointment, for these were not the knight and squire we waited for. The older man seemed far older than my lord, red in the face (whereas my lord was weather-browned), greying of beard, and stout. His clothes would have looked very much in place in a cattle-market, though no doubt they were his best, and his thigh-length boots bore traces of mud. The younger was short, not much taller than Richard, and beyond that there was very little to notice about him. His face and hair were of no particular colour, and the liripipe hat with its jaunty tassel thrown over one shoulder was the only touch of fashion about him. Anyone more ordinary I never did see.

But my lord rose, and held out a jewelled hand.

'Welcome, Sir Thomas,' he said. Then I knew it was not a mistake, and these were no servants sent to say that their master could not come, but the knight himself and my promised husband. As the bowings and greetings and social talk went on I felt myself engulfed by a feeling of flatness. What I had expected to feel, I could not have said, but not this utter blank. When Tom Cowley turned to me and bent over my hand I saw that his face was almost hairless, like a girl's (or a pig's) and that his eyes, which were very pale, gave an impression of being pink. Into my mind darted a silly song, the last I would have wished to think of in the circumstances—

There was a lady loved a swine—'Honey, quoth she' . . .

'Your servant, Mistress de Clifford.'

His voice was rather high, and he spoke with a broad accent, as did his father. All of us had the tongue of the North, but in them it was sometimes so thick that the ear could scarcely catch its meaning.

'To business, now,' said the Earl, signing to Father John to come forward. Tom and I knelt in front of him and listened to a short discourse on the binding nature of betrothal and the great commitment of marriage, until my lord began to look out of the window again and tap impatiently with his fingers, at which the priest hurriedly brought the sermon to a close in a burst of Latin. Then Tom said, 'I, Thomas, take thee, Yolande,' and I answered that I likewise took him. When we exchanged betrothal rings his was so large that it immediately fell off my finger and rolled away across the floor, at which I was unable to repress a laugh, but managed to turn it into a cough.

'Eh, we'll need to get yon tightened up,' said Sir Thomas. 'Tha'rt a well-grown wench for thy age, mistress, but we'd not thought on t'size of a lass's fingers. Tha'lt ha' to go ringless for a while.'

'The jeweller shall see to it at once,' my lord said. 'Now, the document.' Solemnly we set our hands to a paper where it was written that we two were in the eyes of the Church and the law man and wife, but for the marriage ceremony, and that we were forbidden to have carnal dole with each other until that time. I thought this a very odd way of describing the act of going to bed together. Tom made a cross instead of signing his name, which hardly surprised me.

Then wine was brought and we all drank, and Tom and I were bidden to take a stroll in the gardens before dinner was served, so that we could learn to be pleasant with each other. Strolling was all very well, being pleasant quite another matter. Try as I would, I could not think of a single thing to say to my affianced except that the weather was a trifle chilly for the time of year. To this original observation he replied 'Aye', which word seemed to be one of the few he knew. Just as I was becoming desperate and running out of trite remarks, he said suddenly, 'Dost like sheep?'

'Sheep?'

'Aye.'

'I never gave much thought to them. I mean, there they are, all over the fells . . .' What in Heaven's name was I supposed to say about sheep?

'I'm reet fain o' sheep,' Tom said, obviously not resenting my ignorance. 'My feyther's got two thousand.'

'How . . . how agreeable.'

'I've getten yin o' my own.'

'Oh?'

'Aye. It were a runt. I browt it indoor and put it by t'fire. To save it deein', sitha. Didst ever rear a lamb?'

'No.'

'Ah. It's a fine great creature now. But t'others won't have it back.'

'How strange.' Even stranger, we were having a conversation, and that was something, if we had to spend most of the rest of our lives together. At least we could talk about sheep.

'It'll not be butchered. I'll breed from it this year, mebbe put it to t'ram come Pentecost.'

'Good.' Silence fell, but at least we had got somewhere. I escaped from him with an excuse, and joined Isabel and Anne where I knew I would find them, in the little pleasance where we used to meet by ourselves, without the boys. There I was able to open the floodgates of laughter, in which Isabel joined, though Anne only smiled and looked from one to the other of us as we giggled and gasped.

'What a clotpoll. Can it talk?'

'Not . . . oh, dear . . . not much.' I told them of our conversation, between snorts of laughter.

'I wonder if he shares his bed with the sheep?' Isabel said, wiping her eyes. 'It'll have to move up for you, when you're married. Will you take the outside or the middle?'

This sent me off again. Anne said gently, 'Yolande, he is kind. You must allow him that. Not many would rear a sick lamb and keep it from the butcher. If he is kind to it, he'll be kind to you, and that is much in a marriage.'

I sobered up. 'Anne, you're quite right, and I was wrong to mock at him, poor soul. It was only that I've been dying to laugh ever since I saw him, so like a—a p-porker.'

'Perhaps all your children will be piglets,' Isabel suggested, and we collapsed into mirth again.

But Anne said gravely, 'If you think him so ill-favoured, does it not make you sad to think you must go through life by his side?'

'What in God's name would be the use of being sad about it? I must do it, my lord has arranged it, and I daresay we shall do very well.'

Anne crossed herself. 'I hope so.' Her face was sad, as though a foreboding were on her of a loveless marriage for herself, and I knew that she was thinking of Richard, her sweetheart. Had we all known what lay in wait for all of us we could not have gone into dinner, as we did, with a good sharp appetite.

That was the last I saw of my affianced bridegroom for some time. It occurred to nobody, even the wise Countess, that there might be some merit in letting young people in our situation grow up together, or at least meet often and learn to know each other. The Lady Anne had an attachment to me, I was more use at her side than any-where else, and I would merit no place in Tarletondale until Tom was old enough to have his own establishment. I would not have wished it otherwise. I was happy at Middleham, I enjoyed the games and the hunting, and such special occasions as the household's journey to York for the Feast of Corpus Christi, to be entertained there by the city's dignitaries, fed on the finest food, even sea-fish caught on the coast and packed in ice so that they were fresh when they came to the table.

At Midsummer we travelled south to Warwick, which was truly the Countess's home and where, I think, she was happiest. The castle sat on a rocky prominence above the River Avon, and was the most beautiful place I had ever seen. Though it had been built as a fortress it more resembled a palace, stately and gracious where Middleham was grim and warlike. Peacocks strolled on its lawns, there were orchards of pears and apples and walls where peaches grew in sunshine—for sunshine there was in plenty, and warmer air than we had in the North. The little town was homely and friendly; sometimes we were allowed to amuse ourselves by visiting the market in the square and buying toys and ribands with our pin-money.

The Church of St Mary was as grand as any in York except the Minster, and I never tired of looking at the wonderful effigy of my lady's father, a sleeping knight in glittering armour, the faintest of smiles touching his craggy, clever face, and round the table-tomb small statues in niches, some of angels, others of members of his family, including my lord himself, the dead earl's son-in-law. My lady went often to pray for the repose of her father's soul.

The countryside round Warwick was lush and comely, very strange and charming after wild Wensleydale, with no mountains, only gentle hills; to me it was like a foreign land, all meadows and gardens and fat farm animals and people who spoke with a curious accent. There were boats kept at the Castle for sailing on the river, so that we were able to visit villages and churches without the trouble of riding to them. And at the Butts in the town I learned the craft of archery, and could soon out-shoot the boys, being tall and strong in the shoulders, as Isabel and Anne were not.

Alas, though I loved to shoot and take part in all sports, I was not pleased by my own growth and development. The more womanly I grew the sooner marriage would be on me, and I would have to leave the Nevilles and the life I was so fortunate to live. But there was no stopping time—changes must come, as surely as the bells rang to Evensong.

I could see the change in me reflected in the eyes of the older boys and young men of the household. I was sought out as a partner in the dance and invited to join in games, and though the manners of the apprentices in knightly conduct were without reproach (they had to be, or a report would go to the Earl, who was not tender with those who offended him) there were a few unseemly scuffles in gardens and on staircases with amorous youths who came off worst in the encounter. I knew it was not my beauty which drew them: how could it be, particularly now that my face had turned brown from the warm Warwickshire sun, because I had not heeded my lady's advice to rub fards and buttermilk into it to keep it fair. No, it was the shape of my figure in the tight-fitting dresses of the time, flattering the swell of bosom and hips, which earned me the favour of their attentions and them many a smart slap in the face.

And a slap was all they were worth, to me. Love was in the air, with so many youths and maids together, songs and sighs and vows and gifts of flowers, and much flaunting of long embroidered sleeves and the ridiculously lengthened pointed shoes which the boys affected. But I was untouched by the little winged god's arrows, though I felt there must be something wrong with me not to fancy at least one young man among those who wore the Bear and Ragged Staff that was the crest of Warwick. 'You're cold in the blood, it must be so,' said Alys my friend, who was as pretty as a rose and not above a few tricks the Countess would have frowned on. 'You're married, or at least betrothed, which is much the same, and a married lady may take a lover without shame. You should have been born a boy, since you care for nothing but sport.'

I answered, 'The kind of sport you and Meg and Cecily indulge in can lead straight to Hell—or a whipping at the least, if you get caught.'

'Cold, cold as Christmas. My Roger says you've an icicle for a heart.'

'Your Roger should know, being a past master of hearts—and other portions of ladies.'

It makes me smile now, to think how like grown women we talked, still children in years. Yet it had to be so when girls like Anne and Isabel were marriage-pawns from their birth, and such as I had no future but marriage or the convent. We had no childhood, no moppets to play with. I had been nobody's darling in my baby days, which may have been why I had no impulse to give out warm affection, except to my lady because she gave it to me.

Yet, on nights when the moon, like a great pewter plate, was reflected in the gentle Avon, and nightingales called, and linked figures moved among the shadows in the gardens, a strange pain plucked at my heart as though an unpractised hand fumbled with a lute-string: for Love and I were strangers, yet should be friends.

And now I come to an event which is not part of my own story proper, yet was to turn the current of my life, and the lives of countless others. I can only tell it as I heard it, from those who were at the scene and from my lady, who gave us a carefully trimmed version of it that left out her own burning anger.

The Earl was not with us that summer, but up on the Border, taming rebellious lords and taking their castles, then dealing with the nervous truce between England and Scotland. It seemed as though he held Fortune in his hand, she obeying him as readily as the soldiers of his private army. He had never been more powerful. Even the King's destiny lay with him. He had persuaded King Edward to give him full powers to make peace with King Louis of France (who favoured him greatly) and to sign a treaty for a marriage with Princess Bona, King Louis's sister. Warwick Herald, his messenger, had come back from France with a glowing account of King Louis's kind reception of him and the beauty of the princess. It would be a perfect match, people said, for the handsome popular King, twenty-two years old and the merriest bachelor in England, who adored beauty in women and could have seduced the holiest nun had he chosen. (Perhaps he did, for his loves were countless.)

But King Edward would not say yea or nay to signing the marriage treaty until he had laid it before his Great Council. My lord was impatient at the delay. As he rode to Reading on that September day he felt that his greatest hour was approaching. Two of the young squires who rode with him, Guy and Will, remarked to each other on the air of exaltation he wore, and the almost royal graciousness of his manner as he acknowledged the cheers of people who rushed to their doors to cry 'Warwick! Warwick!' as he passed in splendour on his great war-horse, a band of his red-jacketed soldiers following, the Bear and its Ragged Staff emblazoned on each, and the Bull of Neville couchant on the flying standard.

Reading town was all in a bustle. The King and Council in their midst, and the coming of the Earl, made them feel almost Londoners. As the Warwick train rode towards the gateway of the Abbey the press of spectators was so great that they had to be urged back with pikes, to keep them from being trodden down by the horses.

And there, in the vaulted Council Chamber, sat King Edward at the head of a long refectory table, round which his advisers were ranged. He greeted my lord with all kindness, as well he might—they were cousins, Warwick had been like a father to him since the killing of his own. On this day he looked more than usually splendid. His doublet and hose as royally blue as his eyes, his flame-coloured sleeves and collar worked with gold thread and pearls. He was a giant for our times, six feet four inches, red-gold of hair, with the complexion of a girl. Only his somewhat small mouth, which smiled so much, spoiled him for perfect manly beauty.

'So, let's talk of France,' he said. They talked. The Council were less confident than the Earl of King Louis's friendly intentions. My lord demolished their doubts. He was in Louis's councils, he had France in his pocket. King Edward sat and listened, smiling, playing with a jewelled pouncet-box which contained perfumed powder. At the Abbey one was frequently served by monks, to whom cleanliness was certainly not next to godliness. The gems glittered as he tossed the box from hand to hand.

One of the Earl's many blood relations, high in the King's favour, caught the steely Warwick eye across the table, and nodded slightly. It was time to speak.

'It can be no secret from your Grace that your subjects look eagerly to the day when you will give them a Queen. The House of York will then be strengthened so that none can challenge it.'

King Edward laid the pouncet-box on the table and regarded it as though it were some interesting, thought-provoking object.

'Yes, my lord,' he said, 'I do truly wish to marry.' Faces round the table relaxed. 'But it may be, perhaps, that my choice will not suit the liking of all present.'

Covert looks were exchanged. No one present had any objection to the French alliance. The King smiled broadly.

'Nevertheless, we will do what pleases us,' he said.

He was joking, of course, keeping them on tenterhooks. Warwick gave smile for smile. 'Whom has your Grace in mind?' he asked.

He looked from face to face, like a child with a naughty secret that will shock its elders. 'I have in mind,' he said slowly, 'Dame Elizabeth Grey of Woodville, daughter of Lord Rivers.'

There was a deadly silence; the elders were indeed shocked. But still they could only think of it as a far-fetched joke. The Archbishop of Canterbury took it upon himself to nip the frivolity in the bud.

'Sire, the Lady Elizabeth may be virtuous and fair, but she is not your match in blood—no wife for such a high prince as yourself.'

The King's fair eyebrows rose.

'Your Grace must know,' the Archbishop continued, confident of his ground, 'that the Lady Elizabeth is not the daughter of a duke or an earl, for her mother the Duchess of Bedford married a simple knight. What is more, she herself is the widow of a knight—a *Lancastrian* knight, Sir John Grey—and is the mother of sons by him. Such a lady can hardly be the wife of a great king.'

He prepared to sit down, conscious of the agreement around him. The King said flatly, 'I will have her and no other.'

Warwick's face was grim. 'I beg your Grace to change your mind.'

King Edward still smiled. 'Too late, my lord. I have already acted on my choice, since it was mine alone to make. The Lady Elizabeth and I are fast married.'

Those whose eyes were on Warwick saw the colour drain from his face, leaving only the mark of sunburn there, so that he looked like a man suddenly slain. He said nothing; nobody said anything, though the King looked round for comment. At last the Archbishop, his voice trembling, asked, 'When, and where, your Grace?' As well he might, since it would have been his office to perform the ceremony.

'Why, on May Day last, at Stony Stratford. Her mother and two witnesses were present—it was all perfectly legal. I saved a great deal of fuss and commotion, and the country a great deal of money, you must admit, my lords, so I see no need for this parade of funeral faces.'

Warwick said, in a voice of ice, 'Yet you permitted me to go on treating with King Louis. He believes—we all believed—you were content to marry Princess Bona. I fail to understand why my embassy was encouraged.'

The King shrugged. He must have known the answer; that he always acted on impulse, that with Elizabeth Grey it had been marriage or nothing, and that if she had been formally presented as a candidate for queenship the proposal would somehow have been talked down and he would have lost her.

But to my lord it was rank treachery and betrayal. The French treaty was no better than waste paper. He had lost face in France, where he was to have had such power. And, though he was able to hide his feelings enough to accept the new Queen in the world's eyes, what he felt for her was hatred, a hatred she heartily returned.

So was the tree of the House of York split as though by a lightning-dart, and brambles and cankers began to sprout among the white roses. And from that day onwards my lord seemed changed, as though a shadow had fallen on him that would not lift.

I *first saw the new Queen at her churching after the
birth of her daughter.* It was not the simple ceremony at
which a woman comes to church, decently apparelled, and
kneels before the priest to give thanks for her safe delivery.
The church was the Abbey of Westminster, the priest my
lord's brother, the Archbishop of York, and the mother wore
cloth of gold and a fortune in jewels. The psalm *Nisi Domi-
nus* seemed even apter than usual: *Lo, children and the fruit
of the womb are an heritage and gift that cometh of the Lord—
like as the arrows in the hand of the giant, even so are the
young children.* The newborn Princess Elizabeth was the
first arrow to be placed in the hand of the young giant
Edward, who would plainly be very happy to have his quiver
full of them, and their heritage would be a mighty one.

After the churching a great banquet was held in the
Palace of Westminster, with my lord representing the husband and father (which was appropriate enough, as he had
stood sponsor to the child). Gorgeously clad, he sat in the
throne-seat at the high table, a nobleman from Bohemia on
his right hand, silenced by magnificence. Both his brothers
were beside them, the Archbishop and John of Northumber-
land, Lord Hastings and his wife, my lord's sister Catherine,
with Lady Warwick, Isabel and Anne, and young Richard.
The two young ones seemed quietly happy. It was said in the
Household that they were to marry, and Isabel was betrothed

to the King's brother, George of Clarence, a piece of diplomacy that seemed to please everybody but the Pope, since they were cousins.

I sat at a lower table, with maids and esquires, Cecily and Meg and Alys and their lads, and we all fed on a multitude of dishes, the salted meats of winter, roasted geese, ducks, swans and hens and egrets, pies and brawns and potages, dishes bright with gold and silver powder and coats of arms, and the confections of pastry and sugar called subtleties. A great deal of wine went round. The young squire Will Heys sat beside me, plying me with glass after glass, until I ceased to care what I drank, and Will, unsteady himself, led me away from the table.

'Come and see,' he said, rather thickly. We walked, or staggered, across the hall, in the same direction that others were taking, towards an antechamber with the curtain at its entrance looped back. It was hung with tapestries. Against them Queen Elizabeth sat, like a figure from a tapestry, a glittering idol in her gown of cloth-of-gold, heavily embroidered, her newly maternal bosom almost bare, against it a gold chain bearing a white rose made of pearls and diamonds. Her beautiful brow was shaven almost to the top of her head, where the pale hair like winter sunlight began, and the tiny embroidered hat crowning it supported a veil of finest lawn. Her complexion was so fair that it might have been painted—but was not—her eyes like blue glass, and her mouth quite perfect. I could see why the King had been wild for her since the day she had waylaid him in a forest, all in widow's black, her young sons at her side. It was not witchcraft, as some had said, but the power of sex and the dazzle of beauty.

She sat alone at table, on a gilded chair. Before her, ready to hand her dishes at a sign, knelt her mother, the proud Duchess of Bedford, and her many sisters, humble as slaves. She said nothing to them, never looked in their direction, only towards the doorway where awed spectators were crowding, gazing at her seated in glory.

'When does Our Lady abdicate?' Will said in a loud whisper which brought him some shocked looks. 'She could hardly beat *that* show.'

'Oh, hush!' I pulled at his arm, and we made our uncertain way into a sort of cloister-passage opening on a lawn. The February air was cold, but I was glad of it after the insufferable heat in the hall and the reek of food. I sank down on a stone seat, Will beside me.

'Woodvilles!' he said. 'Woodlice, more like, under every stone. Sisters and brothers and cousins and aunts, all living off the King's favour, taking all the high offices and making all the rich marriages. Did you hear that Sir John has wed the dowager Duchess of Norfolk, and she not a day less than ninety?'

'I don't believe it. Nobody's ninety.'

''S true. Her great-grandmother was a water fairy.'

'The dowager duchess's?'

'No, the Queen's, of course. That explains a great deal. Did you see my lord's face at the meal? I'll tell you something, he'll give a bigger and better banquet in the spring, when meats are fresh, and there won't be a single Woodville at it. He hates them as much as they hate him, and my money's on him, the bear against the dogs every time.'

'Don't let anybody hear you say so.'

'Why not? I'm Warwick's man, not the Woodville Witch's. Listen! the dancing's started.' The music of flutes, viols and rebecks was floating to us from the hall. The tables were being cleared and the diners moving into the most joyous part of the entertainment—those of them who could still stand. Will pulled me upright.

'Dance, Yolande, dance!' He seized my hand and whirled me round until my head reeled and I fell heavily against him. We were both more than a little drunk, and when he caught me fast and began to kiss me I had neither the will nor the strength to resist. Indeed, I rather liked it. He was a big sturdy youth, comely enough in a beefy way, cleanly and full of life. I had never been held so long or so close by a man before, and I suddenly felt myself respond with a sensation quite new to me, of wanting to cling closer, to help the hands that were running over my body, and answer the lips that were searching mine. What might have been the end of it, there in the gathering dark, with only the light from a cresset over a doorway across the grass, I do not know. But a voice cut sharply into our amorous tangling, just as Will's weight was bearing me down to the stone seat.

'Mistress de Clifford! What are you at?'

Madam Agatha, Mother of the Maids of the Warwick household, stood over us. Her voice expressed clearly that she was in no doubt as to what we were at. Will hastily pulled away from me, while I straightened up and dipped a curtsey. She glared at me, tall and gaunt in her towering headdress. I had never been one of her favourites, perhaps because she was a fervent Yorkist, having been in her youth in the service of the King's mother, the Duchess of York, and looked on me as a Lancastrian cuckoo in the nest.

'My lady saw you leave the hall,' she said, 'and sent me to see that you came to no harm in such a press of people. I did *not* expect to find you huggling with a man.'

Will began, 'It was only that the hall was hot, madam . . .'

'But not so hot as your blood, Master Heys? or as this young madam's, whom I always thought virtuous, at least.' Thank you, I thought, for the "at least".

'I see it is not so. Shame on you. Go in now, and stay close until I find a servant to escort you back to Warwick House. I will see you when I return myself.'

Will and I shot apologetic looks at each other. Then he bowed and left us. I heard afterwards that Madam Agatha had reported him to my lord, who gave him a rating he would not forget in a hurry, then sent him to his personal chaplain for a penance, after which he was to work in the stables for a day, like a common ostler instead of a squire.

And I, after a miserable trudge through the dirty streets with a linkman walking before me to light my way, arrived at Warwick House in Newgate very cold and quite sober. Madam Agatha came to me as I sat on my pallet bed in the Maids' Chamber, alone because the others were still at the feast. She told me she had spoken to the Countess, who had agreed that my conduct had been unseemly, and that I should have a whipping. This she gave me with the switch she kept for the purpose. It hurt very much, but I would not let her see me weep, biting my lips as she laid about my shoulders.

'Stubborn,' I heard her mutter. 'Bad blood will out.'

I rounded on her, pulling up my shift. 'My blood is as good as any in the North, madam! John de Clifford was my father, Baron of West-morland, and he fought where he thought the best cause lay. Beat me, but keep your tongue off my family, if you please.' It was a bold thing to say and might have caused me more stripes, but she took a step back, startled; then, recovering, sneered, 'And one Rosamund de Clifford was a king's harlot. I suppose you are proud of that?'

'She was called Rosa Mundi, Rose of the World, for her beauty, and died in sanctity. I am proud of that. And *I* am not a harlot, madam.'

I was surprised when she half-shrugged and left me without another word. Perhaps I should have stood up to her before. I bathed my scored shoulders and got into my cold bed, unwilling to have to talk when the others came back. Any pleasure the day had held for me was gone, lost in pain and shame and anger with myself. Though I did not blame Will for what had happened, somehow I never liked him as much from that night.

Our stay in London extended into the spring. I took care to conduct myself well and get into no more trouble. At first the richness of life at Warwick House was enthralling. Everything was grander than at Middleham or Warwick Castle. The Earl's town mansion was one among many, but the finest of all. His gardens stretched to meet the wall of St Paul's cathedral close, and stood in the very heart of the City, a stone's throw from the Tower and the Guildhall, and so ringed with fine churches that you might say every word of an Ave in a different one, without walking out your shoes. The rich City companies, grocers and mercers and fishmongers and the like, had their halls here, and their private houses were on a scale with their riches. The shops of Cheapside provided a perpetual entertainment (so long as we avoided the butchers with their horrible spillings-out of offal into the gutter) and the display in Goldsmiths' Row, so much gold and silver and foreign coin, was enough to dazzle country eyes. I could never understand why these costly things were put openly on show, where any thief could snatch them and run.

Except that there was the New Gate, used as a prison, only a hundred yards or so from us—so close stood horror and splendour in London. Looking up at it, we could see pale faces at the little barred windows, from which bags hung down on long strings, so that the charitable passer-by might put in a farthing or more. Smithfield, only a little further, and a spot they called the Elms, which sounded rural enough—only that the Elms were huge elmwood gibbets, seldom empty. And near the gate of St Bartholomew's church, a wooden post, some eight feet high and three feet thick, charred all over with the marks of flame, and having iron staples and rings driven into it, to hold firm a writhing body. I could never look at it without a shiver.

There was in me a fearful dread of the fire. Not a day passed without death by execution, in some part of the City, for offences that ranged from stealing a loaf of bread or a bolt of cloth to poisoning and treason. There was always about Smithfield a terrible scent hanging on the air, a scent like roasting meat: which it was, but the meat was human. In those days (I think and pray it happens less now) the custom was not for the hangman to strangle the wretched victim mercifully before the flames took hold of him or her. It made my own flesh creep and my nerves cringe to think of such a horror, I who could bear the sight of blood without a qualm, yet who foolishly pitied the very logs in the hearth as they crumbled away to ash.

It seems to me that such fears, without reason in our own experience, are in all of us, come down from who knows what in our blood. Some fear snakes, shuddering at the sight of the coffin-worms pious men have carven among the bones of the stone effigies of themselves as cadavers, put below their effigies as in life to remind us of mortality. Some run to hide at the sound of thunder, some dream of pouncing lions and wake in a sweat. Since we live only once on earth, what memories can these be? Happy the man who died in his bed, or met the clean death of battle. Lady Isabel found out my fear, and brought it into conversation once when her betrothed George of Clarence was with us at Warwick House, as he often was these days.

'Yolande will never pass through Smithfield,' she told him. 'She fears they may be out of victims one day, and take her to keep themselves in practice.' They both laughed.

'No likelihood of that, with the times as they are,' George said, carefully selecting a sweetmeat from a silver dish. Since his boyhood he had shown a tendency to put on weight, and now at seventeen was distinctly portly, though still handsome in the same florid way as his brother the King. 'A glut of rogues and traitors. Be thankful for your sex, Yolande, at the least it will spare you the hangman's knife if you venture into crime.'

'She could be burnt as a heretic,' said Isabel maliciously, 'or boiled, for husband-poisoning. Don't you think that might be worse, Yolande?'

'I'm not a heretic, nor likely to be one,' I snapped, crossing myself. 'As for the other, Tom seems an unlikely subject for poison.'

'You never know. He might drive you to distraction, and then you would boil up some deadly herbs and slip them into his drink.'

'Is that the treatment I'm to expect?' George asked, lazily running his finger up and down her arm. She turned on him, laughing.

'You! The poor potion would drown in the quantity you put down.'

'True, very true, sweeting. Give me enough good malmsey and Death himself would hardly cause me a pang.' How sharply, long years afterwards, I was to remember that light remark of Duke George's! But then I welcomed it as a change of subject from death by flame.

'Do you stay long in London, my lord?' I asked.

'Oh, certainly, while *your* lord stays. My brother treats me like a puppy to be kicked aside.' His full mouth was sulky. 'He only cares for long-faced Richard, though *I* am his heir, providing that puffed-up wife of his continues to throw daughters. As she well may—they say some women have only girl-seed in their wombs.'

'She has borne two sons,' I reminded him, bringing a frown to his face.

'By another husband. My guess is that Edward can only get girls. Remember what he said at Reading, when he broke the news of the marriage? Somebody pointed out that the Woodville woman had two children already, and he said, "I'm a bachelor, but I have several myself." Now, I know much about Edward and his wenching, and I'll swear he never got a boy child, stallion though he is. So he would do well to treat me fairly—as your noble father does, my love, knowing which side his egg is roasted on.'

Isabel looked shocked. 'My father surely doesn't favour you for what he can get out of it? He would never stoop to that.'

George's blond eyebrows shot up. 'No? not because, when the nest of the Woodvilles is smoked out, Edward may take flight with them, and your father become a Kingmaker again: this time for me.' He smiled. 'King George the First—how does that sound? Very patriotic: a king named for our patron saint. King George for England. And his consort, Queen Isabel, second of that name. How do you fancy that, chuck?'

Isabel said uneasily, 'My mother told us it was unlucky, because of the . . .'

'The lady across the street?' We all knew the royal tombs in Grey Friars, Newgate Street, where Edward the Second's Queen Isabella lay with (they said) the heart of her murdered husband in a gold casket on her breast within the coffin.

'Well,' George went on, 'it was not so lucky to be a King Edward in those days, which may be an omen on the opposite side of the scales. And it was an Earl of Warwick who executed her King's paramour. A male one, I grant you, but the likeness is there. Perhaps Warwicks are born to bring down bad rulers.'

Isabel glanced uneasily round the great parlour where other young ladies of the household, maids in waiting and pages talked or played games of cards or pieces. 'Dangerous talk, George,' she said, 'people listen. People remember.'

He shrugged. 'And forget. No, I speak of no treason, only as others speak, when they say England has two kings, Edward and Warwick, and must choose between them one day, just as she must come down on one side or the other for an ally—Burgundy or France. Warwick is for France, my brother for Burgundy. A little rumour-spreading bird told me that neither was above using certain ladies as pawns in the game.'

Isabel and I exchanged glances. 'What ladies?' I asked.

'A child could see that, madam. Our little sister Margaret for Charles of Burgundy. My Isabel's sister Anne for anyone King Louis chooses.'

'Anne!' Isabel gasped. 'He would never . . . she's all but promised to Richard. Our father would not . . . use her.'

'No? What excellent comfits these are. I congratulate him on his pastry-cook. You know, if *I* were a confectioner I could devise a very pretty conceit; two sugar castles, two royal gentlemen in one, painted blue and decorated with golden lilies—in the other two pretty ladies, one in a dress of white roses, the other decked up in Ragged Staffs, with a tame bull at her little feet, and a king and a nobleman fighting over who should give which lady to which gentleman. And for how much.'

'How much money?' I asked, ignorant.

'Money? What's that between such players? No, power. My father-in-law to be is a great lord in his own country—in France, King Louis could make him a prince. Of Normandy, the little bird added.' He looked at us with sly satisfaction, waiting for our cries of admiration at his cleverness. But I felt a chill go through me. George was not a particularly clever person; I thought him rather stupid, compared with his brother Richard. Yet he had seen something I had not, from my place as an onlooker in the game. All women, it seemed, were only counters like the pieces on the chess-board Alys and Cicely were playing on, in the corner by a window down which raindrops streamed. A ploughman's daughter might be sold for the sons she would bring her husband, to be put to the plough when their time came, a merchant's daughter for her dowry, a nobleman's daughter for the lands and name she brought with her. And the daughters of kings, and near-kings— what fate might be theirs, sold for coronets and crowns? Better to be one like me, with no fortune and nothing on my shield but a bar sinister along with the checky gold and azure and fesse gules of the Cliffords. Better to be the wife of a dull knight's duller son with no more to bother my head about than how many lambs the ewes have borne or whether the harvest will be a rich one.

A gleam came into Isabel's eyes when George mentioned a possible princedom in France for her father. She had always been more given to worldly things than Anne, conscious of her position as Warwick's elder daughter, insistent on formal address from inferiors like me, pleased at the chance to dress up for a banquet or state occasion.

'I suppose,' she said, 'that Anne would not mind so much if they gave her to a handsome bridegroom. Are Frenchmen handsome, George?'

He laughed. 'King Louis most certainly is not. He looks like an elephant, with a great hanging nose and no chin. But if my little sister

Meg gets her Burgundian bridegroom, as the King wishes, she gets a fine strapping man, to judge by his picture. A trifle swarthy, perhaps; but personable.' His hand strayed towards the mirror set in ivory that he wore round his neck, and I knew that he was thinking of his own fair looks.

'Oh,' Isabel said thoughtfully. 'So they might pick one like that for Anne. After all, she's very young, and childish for her age, and Richard is hardly an Adonis . . . she would soon forget him.' Her face brightened. 'Oh, and I've been thinking. If Isabel is an unlucky name for a queen, I could take another—Anne, perhaps. I was given it as a second name, after my mother. Yes, Anne would sound very well.'

So she would steal her sister's name as well as see her married to a foreign stranger. I was beginning to think that Duke George and the Lady Isabel suited each other very well in ambition and hard-heartedness.

As it happened, we were not in London much longer. There was a round of courtesy visits, to Baynard's Castle, where the King's mother, the widowed Duchess of York, lived, and to the Erber, in Dowgate by the river, yet another Neville house. I for one was glad as we bade farewell to London, my heart lifting as we travelled North and I began to sniff the sweet air from the mountains, and look forward to galloping over the moors again, far away from the ugly sights and smells of the City.

It was bliss to be back in Middleham. I had a new horse, given to me on my birthday by my lord himself out of his generous kindness. I called it Brown Bailey: I forget now why, but I think it was some kind of a joking name. He was a gelding, swift, strong, gentle-mouthed, bigger than many maids would choose, but then I was woman-sized, full grown at fifteen.

There was a certain youth, Edmond Spiers, now with us for knightly training, in the place of those who had gone. He and I became friends since he was neither lecherous nor a despiser of women, and fonder of sport than learning. His family was wealthy, and he had many

clothes, far more than the boys usually brought with them. One day, as
we rode in Wensleydale, I said to him, 'I wish I could ride like you.'

'But you do—as well, or better.'

'I mean astride.'

He stared. 'Surely that's impossible for a woman.'

'If you think that, you know very little about the anatomy of
women, Ned. It has become the fashion to perch us up on this side-
saddle, that's all, and I find it somewhat ridiculous. A horse is meant to
be gripped between the knees, surely? Do you suppose the Amazon
dames or Queen Boadicea titupped about with both legs on the same
side of the horse?'

'But their skirts . . .'

'I never heard that the Amazons wore skirts. What I'm leading to,
Ned, is that I would like to try riding like a man, and wondered if you
would lend me some of your gear. A doublet, and breeches.'

Ned looked scandalized. 'Breeches are not proper wear for a
maid.'

'I'm sure you are going to remind me that the Maid of Orleans
was charged with witchcraft on that count . . . They would probably
have . . .' I switched my mind hurriedly from what they had done to the
Maid, and coaxed him. 'Ned, let me borrow something to ride in. We're
much of a size, and I'll take care not to be seen in the Castle.'

The upshot was that he loaned me a suit of leather and buckskin
which fitted me, with a few stitches, as well as if we had been twins. I
stuffed my hair into a cap and skewered it with a small dagger meant
only for decoration, but sharp enough. Among all the multitudes who
lived in the Castle one gangling lad would not be noticed. I used an
outside stairway to gain the mews, so that I was not seen indoors in
my male gear, and if anyone saw me saddling up Brown Bailey they
took me to be some newly-hired groom. I believe Edmond had something to do with it, too: he was a fast-growing youth, perpetually
starving, and as grateful as a dog for the scraps of spiced cakes and

puddings I smuggled out to him. I noticed that there were those who took care not to look me too directly in the face or engage me in conversation.

It was very early on a June morning, the Eve of St Barnabas, as I well remember, the sun not long up and the grass still sodden with dew, that I galloped back from Jervaulx Abbey, a favourite ride of mine, urging Bailey on with my heels (I would never use a crop on him) because I knew from the summoning bells that I would be late for Mass unless I speeded up. Folk were already about in the village, gathering round the Swine Cross, taking water home from the well and bread to the bakehouse. I urged Bailey towards a small gate that led into the courtyard by the mews just as a troop of horsemen entered the main gate. Something caused him to veer out of his way into the path of one of the outside riders; the horses' heads collided and as both neighed in protest Bailey reared and threw me.

I lay there, winded and shocked, on the straw-strewn cobbles, gasping up at my unusual view of the sky, with Bailey looking down at me, I swear, in surprise and reproach. Somewhere a voice said, 'Good Christ!' and as I tried to collect myself sufficiently to scramble up before hooves trampled me, a gauntletted hand grasped mine and pulled me upright.

Still clutching the rescuing hand I stood uncertainly, staring at a laughing face, brown-skinned and blue-eyed: the face of Joscelyn, my lord and love.

4

In that first moment I had no notion of how he looked—well-favoured or ill-favoured—only that I was shaken by something other than my encounter with the hard ground, and wished very much that I was not wearing Ned's second-best suit. My cheek was sore where the earth had scraped it and my hand was bleeding, but my pride was worse hurt. I longed to break away, and yet longed as much to stay; which was madness. And so I stood looking foolishly at this stranger.

'What's your haste?' he asked, still laughing. 'A message from the King, or a war broken out?'

'Neither.' I found it hard to get a word out. 'I was going . . . to Mass.'

'Take care your piety doesn't win you a broken head next time.' He clapped me on the shoulder, turned his horse and rode away towards the Castle, leaving me staring after him. Then I collected myself enough to take Bailey's rein and lead him towards the stairway that lay nearest to the Maids' Dormitory. There, to his surprise, I tethered him before rushing upstairs to throw off Ned's clothes and hide them in my bed before scrambling into my own and hastily washing the blood from my face and hand; one knee, too, was bleeding.

Mass had begun when I arrived in the chapel. Several heads turned as I hurried in. My face felt on fire with sore-

ness and shame, and I heard not a word the priest said, though I suppose I made the usual responses. Afterwards I told the others I had
fallen crossing the courtyard: which was true, though not entirely. I got
some odd looks from them, and Madam Agatha asked me whether I
didn't think I was too old to romp about like a tom-rig.

During the morning I managed to learn that the men-at-arms in
strange livery who swarmed about the Castle belonged to Sir John
Conyers, cousin-by-marriage to the Earl, from the castle of Hornby,
north-east of Middleham.

'I hope the visit will please my father,' Anne said, 'He has been so
sad and heavy of late. Isn't it strange, Yolande, that a man so powerful
should have need of friends? Yet I know he has. Perhaps Sir John will
raise his spirits.'

'Do you know this Sir John, madam?'

'Not I. How could one possibly know all one's Neville relations?
No doubt we shall see him at dinner.'

Sure enough, at the high table there sat by my lord's side a man I
recognized as my acquaintance of the courtyard. How could I not have
noticed that he outdid every man there? It may seem outlandish to
write of a man as beautiful, yet he was so, with a beauty that was all
masculine, all strength and lean hardness. He was young and fair-
coloured, his hair even lighter than the King's, almost silver where the
sun had bleached it, with streaks of darker gold, and his face tan-
brown, a merry face as he glanced from one to the other seated by
him, and I saw them laugh, a rare thing at Middleham these days. His
doublet was of almond-green, and plainly made.

Alys dug me in the ribs with her elbow and asked what I was staring at.

'Only at the strangers.'

'Lord, didn't you see enough strangers in London, that you gawp
at a lot of rough Yorkshire lads?' She glanced round the lower tables,
where men-at-arms and servants sat among our own people.

'I only wondered what was stirring.'

'Nothing, I daresay—just the Nevilles holding meetings against the Woodvilles.' She turned away. As soon as her attention was held I went back to looking at the man at my lord's right hand; but when he seemed to glance in my direction I hastily put down my head—as though he could possibly have recognized me at that distance, even with a hawk's eyes, which I guessed he had, being a hill-man. When the meal was over he went with his host and hostess into the solar, Anne and Isabel following.

Half the day seemed to pass before my restless wanderings about rooms and passages were rewarded by meeting the sisters as I came out of the long chamber called the Nursery, over the bakehouse. Two small slight figures came towards me, Anne in pale blue, Isabel in a darker shade, sunlight shimmering through their veils from the high windows in the thick wall, their long necks bending under the weight of their forked headdresses.

I said, 'Who is the stranger? All the maids are wondering.' (Which was not true.) 'Is it Sir John Conyers?'

'Not Sir John,' Isabel said, 'Sir Joscelyn. A cousin. He brought word that Sir John has raised a private army to join my father's banner if he decides to move against the King.'

'But my lord thanked him and said it was not time yet,' Anne added. 'They are all to go home again. So no war.' She sighed, and I knew she was thinking of Richard, who would range himself with the King against her father if things came to the worst. I was not so concerned with that as with my own interests.

'Do they go today?' I asked.

'No, of course not. That would be too inhospitable, since they set out from Hornby at dawn. I'm glad. It's good to have a young and cheerful gentleman at table. Sir Joscelyn even made my father laugh.'

'Why, Yolande,' Isabel said, 'what a colour you have, like a turkey-cock's wattles!'

'Thank you, madam,' I answered pertly, 'you might have said like a rose.'

'But it's not the least like a rose, and you should get Old Nurse to put some balsam on that wound on your cheek. Are you *sure* you fell down?'

'Yes, madam, I said so.'

'Take better care of your feet tonight. There's to be music and dancing in the Hall after supper, by my lord's decree, and we're to wear our best.'

I was only too ready to wear my best, to draw attention away from my face. The choice was not difficult, as I had only two garments for courtly occasions. One was a gown of soft silver-grey, kindly given to me by the Countess and made over to fit my larger form. I was grateful for it, but thought it more suited to an older lady. I chose the other, of a colour difficult to describe, somewhere between cinnamon brown and pale flame, worn over sleeves of dark blue, and cut with a low round neck. It made me look less swarthy, I thought. I covered my hair with a little cap of dark velvet, dipped at the front to conceal the low-growing curls I so much disliked. It was not very becoming but it would have to do. The polished steel of the mirror showed me a face I would willingly have altered in several particulars, but since it had pleased God to give me the one I had, I must be content with it. I bathed my cheek several times with rose water, but it still looked angry. There was no more to be done.

Supper was a statelier meal than dinner had been. My lord looked magnificent, a splendid gold chain round his neck and rings on every other finger of his hands. Again Sir Joscelyn sat by his side, wearing the same green doublet: evidently he had not come to Middleham prepared for formality. I looked and looked, tried not to look, and tasted nothing of the food, though it was Friday, fish-day which I liked best, and there seemed to be a hollow space somewhere beneath my ribs, almost an ache like hunger.

'Do you find custard tasty like that?' It was Ned's voice in my ear.
'What did you say?'

'I only wondered why you put salt on it, three times.'

'Stuff. How could I have done?' But when I tasted it, I found it vile, and pushed it away.

Cicely said, 'Yolande's spirit isn't with us. She saw a blessed vision on her way to Mass this morning, and is preparing herself for a sisterhood.' Half of this was so true that I thought she must be a mind-reader, but I saw from her face that she was only teasing me.

'Never mind what I saw,' I said. 'I may astonish you all in time, when I'm a holy abbess and you lot sinners on your way to Hell-mouth.' And I tossed back the remains of the wine in my cup, aware that at the high table the dishes were being cleared and my lord and lady had risen and were preparing to descend to the floor of the Hall. The dancing would begin soon, the musicians were tuning up in the gallery.

The music began. All took hands with those who were nearest them to make a chain: round and round in circles, then break up and rejoin, down the middle and spread out, curtsey and bow, and as the music went, into the hey or the pavane or passimezzo. A retainer of the Conyers band held my hand on the one side, a dark lad with a small beard; but I saw him eye me over and turn to the girl on his other side, Jacquette, whose fair plaits bounced as she danced. My other hand was held by Alys's Roger, who was more intent on measuring how near he was to her than keeping time in the dance. I caught sight of my lord, stepping out majestically with his lady, and knew that his mind was not on such frippery, but busy with great matters.

Then our chain broke, and we were standing facing each other, waiting to re-form as the rhythm changed. And I felt my left hand taken by a warm strong one: the hand of Joscelyn Conyers.

I was a star suddenly finding itself whirled close to the sun, a small boat pulled along in the wake of a great ship. I must have danced with my head turned, unable to take my eyes from his, that were blue and laughing. I know no way to describe the moment, only to say that it was as if half of myself had been away for a great stretch of time and had suddenly come back to me, or as if I had lain like Lazarus, four days in the tomb in grave-clothes, and heard a Voice, and risen to life again.

We danced down the length of the Hall, properly enough, considering that I was not looking where I was going. Then at the far end from the musicians' gallery I found myself drawn out of the chain and through a door the servers used, out into a stone walk hugging the outer walls of a turret. I had never been there before, and it was very high, a dizzy height; but I looked down steadily enough at the fells curving away from the huddle of the little town, and the shimmer of the Ure in the fading light.

We stood side by side, arms touching. I expected him to say something about the Castle, or the supper, even about my lord, but he was silent. Then he turned to me and touched, very gently, the wound on my cheek.

'Is it still sore?' His voice was musical and soft, deeply masculine with light tones to it, like a well-tuned viol.

'No. No, not at all.' My hand no longer hurt, nor my knee where the skin had been taken off. I was healed, like those who came to Our Lord: may He forgive me for the comparison.

'That was a nasty tumble you took. Were you not used to the horse?'

'Yes, he's mine. Unlike the clothes. I suppose that was how you knew me—by my spoiled face.'

He shook his head, smiling. 'I'd have known you anywhere.'

'And I you.' What was I saying? Was it in a dream? But the fresh wind from the valley was cooling my face, the stone of the balustrade cold under my hand. Far below, sheep were baaing, and somebody was shouting repeatedly to somebody else who was either deaf or a long way off. Such things were not a part of dreams. We had not been made known to each other, nor called each other by name, yet he was to me as familiar as a dear brother. Only I felt towards him something that was not what a sister feels.

'You go back to Hornby tomorrow?' I asked, as though I must know every second I might count on having with him.

'Yes. A lost errand, well meant. My lord Warwick sends my kinsman a message to stay quietly at home, until he and his men are sent for.'

'Sent for to fight against whom?' It was not a question a woman should ask, but he seemed not to notice that.

'For France against Burgundy. For Warwick and Clarence against Edward and Richard, Nevilles against Woodvilles. It will come to that in the end. Never mind; wars will keep. And you—you're a Neville?'

'No, a Clifford.'

'A wolf in the fold?'

'The sheep don't seem to fear me. They called my father the Butcher, but I never heard that he was any worse than other men, even in the getting of bastards like me.' I told him something of what had happened after my father's death, and how I owed thanks and loyalty to the family of Warwick. 'I am nothing, a dependant, a pensioner. And happy to be so.'

He nodded. 'I'm something of the kind myself, a younger brother's child. We're fortunate not to be more than very small pawns in the game, you and I. Hardly even pawns: more like chessmen almost too small to be seen on the board.'

'Yet you ride for Sir John?'

'I ride. I've no wish to see this land back in the hands of a poor holy idiot and a French shrew.'

'My lord calls Queen Margaret an evil bitch.'

'So I've heard. And so has she. I'll wager that somewhere in her household, somewhere in a chest in that little court in France, there's a wax doll with the Ragged Staff scratched on its body—hopefully.'

'Then the Queen's hopes are stillborn—my lord is well and hearty.'

'Curs have pulled bears down before now . . .' We were both silent then, looking out across the dimming landscape. Suddenly, from behind a dark cloud, the moon broke, almost full, a gleaming silver disc bathing us in her light which is like no other, and I felt my breath catch at the beauty of the face turned to me, the shadowed eyes scanning mine. Music floated from the Hall we had left, a stately basse dance with its melancholy minor cadence, a sadness that was pleasant too, and down in the dark trees by the church an owl cried. Joscelyn said, 'Take off your headgear—hennin—whatever they call it. Why will women wear these things?'

I took it off reluctantly, knowing the moon would show him no silvery fall of hair like Anne's, only my own dark mophead which was not even of a good length, being so taken up with its curls. *That* would turn his fancy away from me, if he had any. But he looked at it with the same kind, considering sweetness, and asked, 'Why do you hide it?'

'It grows so badly.'

'It grows like vine tendrils . . . And even by the moon your face is sun-browned.'

'I know, too well. I've tried lotions and washes and bathing in dew, but nothing does any good.'

Before I could reflect on the enormity of saying such things to a strange man he said softly, 'I like a nut-brown maid.'

And I knew that he was no stranger, that I could say anything to him without immodesty, and he to me. I leaned against his shoulder and his arm came round me, warm in that chilly evening air, in a tender closeness that was not lust nor the embrace of a brother, but something that was between us two who had met so short a time ago.

'Yolande,' he said.

'I didn't tell you my name.'

'I asked it. Do you note how well it goes with mine? Yolande and Joscelyn, two names from an antique story, of Arthur's court or King Pepin. They could have named me George or Dick, and you Meg or Kate . . .'

What else we said I cannot recall: only that we talked as freely as old friends, of light things, not of who we were and how brought up, as if we knew we had all our future for that.

Suddenly I found myself shivering, from cold or excitement or both. Joscelyn took my hand and led me back towards the Hall, where the music had changed to a lively hey. Just before we entered he said, 'Ride with me tomorrow, before we leave?'

'Yes.'

'At first light—in the stable-yard, at the place where we met?'

'Yes.'

Then we were among the others, part of a scene as rich in colour as a painting in a missal, blues and greens and reds and golds moving under the soaring timbers of the roof and against the tapestries on the walls. But I was only aware of them as a kind of dazzle, seeing nothing but the man at my side in his plain green doublet and the black hose that made his long legs look longer, the broad shoulders and the slender waist cinched in by a narrow belt of leather.

And at parting, when my lord had given the signal for the revelling to end: 'Good night, friends, and God keep you', Joscelyn bowed over my hand, and said, 'Tomorrow.'

I slept in fits and starts that night, trying not to turn too noisily or sigh from restlessness, so as not to disturb the others. At last the lancet window showed me a sky faintly lightening, and the first cock crowed. As silently as a ghost I rose and stole out of the chamber, having taken my shift from under my pillow and the robe I had worn last night from the rail where our clothes were laid, and a warm cloak—it was not mine, but I didn't care for that.

He was waiting near the stables when I led Brown Bailey out. There were many stirring, grooming and saddling horses, but I saw him at once, like a young sun-god, his bright head hatless. We exchanged the kiss of greeting and he said, smiling, 'Not like a lad this morning?'

'No, like a maid.' I had not wanted him to see me again in Ned's clothes. His own horse was a roan, sturdy enough to ride in battle he said, named Palamon, after one of the old heroes. We rode down by the river through the water meadows, dew-fresh so early, and I told him of the water kelpie, a fiend half woman and half horse, who slips out of the river unseen when children are playing on the bank, and takes them down with her to the depths, where her larder is.

Joscelyn laughed. 'Do you believe in her? A sound-headed maid like you?'

'Well. If I had children, I should watch them like a cat if they came to play where she could see them.' Then I felt myself going scarlet, I who had never given thought before to having children, all because I was with him I wished to be the father of mine. Joscelyn seemed not to notice, kindly, looking in front of him at the sun beginning to touch the hills into colour. A blackbird was singing its wild sweet song, surely a song of praise to Him who made it, and I saw that we were going down toward the forest of Coverham, where the river wound into Coverdale, and Coverham Abbey sat calmly by like a stately hen. The bell was not yet sounding for Prime, the first canonical hour of the day, we had set out so early.

I had thought of another story to tell him and thus keep my mind from the thought of children with hair like gold.

'Do they talk of the monk of Coverham where you come from, Sir Joscelyn?'

'Not in my hearing,' he said gravely. 'Is it another tale of frightening?'

'If you like to take it so. He was a very musical brother, this monk—I shall call him Anselm.'

'Why not? A good monkish name.'

'Well, one morning very early, about this hour, he walked out from the Abbey into the forest, having no particular devotions at that time, and heard a bird singing louder and sweeter than all the other birds. So he stood and looked up into the trees, and there he saw to his surprise that the singing-bird was blue. Now what bird is there of that colour in the forest?'

'The kingfisher?'

'Kingfishers don't sing. And they haunt brooks, not forest trees.'

'Your pardon.'

'So of course it was an enchanted bird. He fell entirely under its spell, and began to follow it as it went from tree to tree, always singing like an angel from Paradise. As he went he forgot the Abbey and the cell he'd lived in for—oh, twenty years—and his devotions and the brothers and the time of the next service, and wandered off through the forest until he was quite lost, and the blue bird had stopped singing and flown away. When he could no longer hear its song his mind came back to him and he felt a great guilt, and began to trace his way back to the Abbey through thorns and branches that fell across his path as though to stop him. At last he came into the open, and looked about him.'

'And . . . ?'

'And the Abbey was gone! No walls were left, only two arches and a little of the transept. So amazed with horror was poor Brother Anselm that he went away and became a hermit. And all this came of his following temptation.'

Joscelyn was looking thoughtful. 'When did all this happen?'

'Oh, I don't know. Nobody knows.'

'It seems to me it has not happened yet, since the Abbey still stands.'

This had never struck me before, and I was taken aback.

'Why, yes. So it must have been a vision, brought on by the guiltiness in his heart.'

Joscelyn reined in his horse and gazed at the towering Abbey, serene in its valley setting as a jewel in a ring. 'I wonder,' he said. 'There are some who can see the future.'

'But surely only witches and warlocks can do that, and this was a good man. Besides, how could Coverham Abbey ever become a ruin— or Jervaulx, or Bolton, or any of them, since they were built as strongly as castles to the glory of God?'

Joscelyn shook his head, his face more serious than I had so far seen it. 'Man can build, and other men pull down what they built. Even castles can fall in war.'

'But . . . there have been wars in our time, and no castles have been destroyed, or abbeys either, God forbid.'

'These are mysteries, my lady, these stories of yours. I only hope no truth lies in them that we can't even guess at. The sun is full up and the wind blowing—let's gallop!'

And gallop we did, my hoodless hair flying behind me in a tangle, the sharp morning wind blowing in our faces and our horses as full of exhilaration as we were. We rode until they began to tire, and slowed, and looked at each other and laughed for the joy of life and being young. Then Joscelyn sighed. 'We must go back, alas. My men can't leave without me, and you must be looked for by now.'

It was true. As we turned our horses' heads and began to climb out of the valley I knew that I had never wanted less to return to Middleham. We said nothing as we rode: there was no need, for each knew what the other was thinking, that we must part so soon after meeting. Something nagged at my mind, something that I should say, driven out of my memory by the joy of the past day and night and morning, but I failed to capture it, and did not try very hard, occupied with sideglances at him, attempts to fix his image in my mind's eye.

We rode up the Castle hill and into the courtyard, where his men-at-arms were milling about, saddled and ready to leave. One rode up and spoke to him, and he left me, with a word of apology.

Then I saw, at the foot of the staircase which wound up to the first floor, where the Great Hall was, a small, straight, stately figure with a handmaiden lurking behind her. I dismounted, went hastily to her, and curtseyed.

'Will you come to me in the solar, Mistress Yolande?' said the Countess, very coldly for her. I turned and threw one look back at the knot of men in Conyers livery, but there was no time to run to them and seek him out, even if she had not been standing still, watching me.

So this was our first parting, without a farewell.

5

There was an air of chill in the solar, despite the cheerful fire burning on the hearth. My lady sat in her high
throne-like chair, with only her elderly waiting-maid, Joan,
in attendance. She was not smiling.

'Mistress Yolande,' she said (and what had I done to
deserve such a stiff form of address?), 'since you came to us
I have treated you as one of our family, though God knows
you are not so. I thought I could trust to your honour and
your discretion as much as to my own daughters', but events
have proved me wrong.'

'Madam?'

'There was an occurrence in London, on the night of
the Queen's churching. You remember?'

'Yes, my lady, but . . .'

'Perhaps you thought Madam Agatha had not brought
word back to me of how she found you. She has a better
sense of duty than that, and I was not pleased. Yolande, I
never thought you to be a light wench. I knew you had been
punished, and so I said nothing. But yesterday, at Mass, you
rushed in as though the Devil himself were after you, bleeding in the face—why?'

'I fell off my horse.'

'Because you were not used to riding astride, in men's
clothes?' She gave a small tight smile. 'You were seen, and
word came to me. And this morning you were missing again

from Mass. I saw you, with my own eyes, return from riding alone with a man.'

I began to blush. 'Sir Joscelyn asked me . . .' That sounded as if I were blaming him. 'I said I would . . .'

'Never mind who asked, or what was said. Sir Joscelyn is an honest young man and my lord's cousin: I have no fear that he would lead any lady of my household astray. What concerns me is you, your modesty, the way you begin to conduct yourself, which is not seemly in a woman grown, and a woman betrothed.'

A cold shock went through me. I knew then what I should have told Joscelyn. I must have been mad—my brain gone with my heart. He could have seen the ring on the fourth finger of my right hand, but why should he? The Countess must have seen the dismay on my face, for she beckoned me to her and signalled that I should sit on the stool at her feet. She stroked my hair, and her voice was kinder as she said, 'I know you meant no wickedness, child. I should have seen a bad spirit in you long ago, if one had been there. But when a maid comes to your years her blood grows hot, like the blood of young mares in the spring fields, and she must be curbed for her own good. So I think it best to put forward your wedding: we shall have it next month.'

There was nothing I could say, nothing I could do but bend my head under her touch.

Lady Anne wept when I told her, so much that I feared she would make herself ill. I had been with her for so many years, friend and companion and sometimes protector, when Isabel's teasing had been unkind. She sobbed that I would go away to Tarletondale, never travel with her to York and Warwick and London again. 'Could my mother not have spared you for another year? That fat pink creature doesn't need you as I do.'

Isabel said tartly, 'I wonder he can take time away from his sheep to be a bridegroom. But the lambing season is over, of course, and the shearing not yet. What with this and what with that you'll hardly set eyes on him, my dear.' I knew that although she was sorry I was leaving them, she was thinking with private satisfaction of her own bridegroom-to-be, clever handsome George, with one eye on his brother's throne, and the difference between him and my rustic Tom.

When we met again I saw that he had grown an inch or two, but otherwise was the same blubber-faced creature he had been. He rather grunted than spoke, bringing back that silly song which had come into my mind when I first saw him.

There was a lady loved a swine: 'Honey,' quoth she,
'Piggie dear, wilt thou be mine?' 'Oink!' quoth he.

Once I had thought that funny. Now my heart was like lead and I could scarcely raise a smile at the wedding-jests I had to endure. For three Sundays the banns were read in the chapel, and each time I wished that something frightful and final would happen before the next reading, so that the wedding could never be. But the day grew relentlessly nearer, and at last it was upon me. I was awake when they came for me at dawn, ready to rise and put on my best robe, the cream one I had worn for the betrothal, and the wreath of flowers that signified my virginity.

The night before I had talked with Anne, alone. She called me to her in the embrasure where she liked to sit, at the window of a little round turret.

'Will it be the last time, Yolande? The last time you and I sit here together?'

'I think it must be, my lady.'

Her blue eyes searched mine. 'It's not only leaving me that makes you sad, is it? No, of course not. Then what is it? Do you fear the marriage bed?'

'Not at all. I should only fear it if my husband were cruel, and he is not that.'

'Is it that he is not of equal birth to you, a baron's daughter?'

'Why should that trouble me? I have no inheritance.'

'Then what, Yolande?'

I had not meant to say it, but I could not hold it back. 'I am in love. I fell into love like one who can't swim falling into a deep lake, and I am no more likely to get out of it. I loved him at once, and I shall love him for ever. Now you know.'

She nodded. 'The young knight from Hornby. I think I knew already. But how could love come so suddenly? I . . . I love Richard. But I always have, since we were children together. How can one love a stranger at first sight?'

'It sounds impossible, I know. Yet the moment I first saw him it was as if I recognized him, as if I knew him to be the one man for me in the world. And I think he felt it, too, though he said nothing: yes, I know he did. So little time together, but it was enough. I knew nothing of love before, I was scarcely a woman, but now I know it all, all its longing and pain. And I must marry another man tomorrow.' I began to weep. Anne took my hand and held it.

'I'm trying to think,' she said, 'if, even now, there might be a way—at least for you to meet him again and know better how he feels. When you were betrothed to Tom, how were the vows exchanged? I don't remember, but if you said "I promise to wed" then you could still get out of the betrothal but if you said "I wed thee" or "I take thee" then that binds you for ever.'

'I did say it. Father John told me what would be said, and I half-learnt it. So I damned myself out of my own mouth.'

Anne crossed herself. 'Don't speak of damnation. So, you're firmly betrothed, and if you were free, how do you know he is not betrothed himself—married, even?'

'I know. He would not have said—certain things—or asked me to ride with him, except honourably. Besides, I care nothing if he *is* betrothed or married—I would go through the world with him, any-where, anyhow, if he wanted me.'

'I begin to wonder if the man has not put a spell on you.'

'Only with his eyes.'

Anne sighed. 'If you feel so, you are lost. We are not free to give ourselves, Yolande. If my father chose another husband for me than Richard, I should have to take his choice. Can you not accept the will of God?'

'It seems to me more like the will of Warwick,' I said.

'Oh, don't blaspheme! You must pray, pray as hard as you can to be shown the right way, and freed from this enchantment which I'm sure comes from the Devil. Beg the blessed saints to help you.'

'Which particular saint or saints?'

'How should I know?' Even the gentle Anne was beginning to lose patience with me. 'Surely you have a favourite friend in Paradise.'

I thought, and came to the conclusion that I had not, never hav-ing been one to sit about communing with saints, as more pious girls did. There was St Alkelda, patroness of Middleham church, a Saxon princess said to have been strangled by two heathen Danish women. But I had seen her bones displayed in a stone coffin, and somehow I could only imagine her like that, instead of in glory, as she undoubtedly was. I shook my head, ashamed.

'St Jude!' Anne cried. 'He's the patron saint of the House of York, and he works miracles. He made me well when I was near death as a child, and preserved my father twice in battle. You *must* pray to him, Yolande. I would not advise you to if this were only a small thing, but your case is desperate.'

I thanked poor earnest Anne, saying I was sorry for my wild words to her, and I promised to beg for St Jude's intercession.

But when I knelt in the oratory that night, and lit a tall, costly wax candle to the great saint, my prayer was that he would bring my lost love back to me, and keep him at my side.

Tom and I were married in the Earl's private chapel. He himself handed over the purse of gold that was my dowry to Tom. Meg and Cicely attended me and Father John conducted the service, kindly slowing down his usual brisk delivery to suit Tom's difficulty in understanding the Latin, or, it seemed, even the English of the responses. At one point, when he appeared completely baffled by what the priest had asked him, a long silence fell in which I distinctly heard Isabel's muffled giggle. At last he got the solemn promise out, in jerks, prompted at every phrase by Father John.

'I, Thomas, take thee, Yolande, to my wedded wife, to have and to hold, for fairer, for fouler, for better, for worse, for richer, for poorer, in sickness and in health, for this time forward, till Death us do part, if Holy Church will it ordain: and thereto I plight thee my troth.'

I promised the same, adding the other promise which a bride must make, to be bonny and buxom in bed and at board. How joyfully I would have said the words had it been Joscelyn who knelt at my side instead of this plump youth whose clothes smelt strongly of the farm, and Joscelyn's ring that was taken from my right hand and put on my left, Father John holding it first over my thumb, saying *'In nomine Patris,'* then over the index finger, *'Et Filii,'* over the middle finger, *'Et Spiritu Sancti,'* and finally slipping it on to the third, the marriage finger, with 'Amen.'

The Earl and Countess provided the wedding feast, and a splendid feast it was, of every kind of fowl and meat in season, and fish brought packed in ice. There was no great set-piece of confectionery, such as had been made for some royal lady in France, a sugar castle in the rooms of which small mechanical dolls acted out the consummation of the marriage, her pregnancy and the delivery of her son. Tom and I were not a grand enough couple for such triumphs of the cook's art.

I suppose that in a romance a girl pining for love and tied to the wrong bridegroom would have pined at the feast and eaten nothing. That was not my way at all. For one thing, it would have been very mannerless when so much care and money had been spent, and for another I had an extremely sharp appetite after the fasting ordained before the ceremony, and the long kneeling through the nuptial mass. So I ate heartily and drank as freely as I wished, aware of Anne's eye on me, slightly reproachful. Tom and I sipped from the loving-cup and kissed over the rim, our first kiss, at which I felt less emotion than when I kissed Brown Bailey's nose, as I sometimes did, on letting him out of the stable in a morning.

The feast went on most of the day. After that there was dancing, at which Tom fell over his own feet and lay flat on the floor like an unhorsed jouster, and his father hoisted him up roughly, telling him not to be a great clumsy knackhead. Early on in the proceedings I saw that my lord had left, and soon my lady followed, so that only the younger ones and the servants were dancing.

At last it was time to retire. As the custom was, I was led away by the maidens and Tom by young men, pages and squires and such. Isabel and Anne were not there. None of them could have been called sober, and I only wished I were in the same state, for in spite of what I had told Anne I was not looking forward to the rest of the night. It was not fear, more distaste for Tom and anger with myself. For if I had not been foolhardy enough to go riding in Ned's clothes in the first place, and in my own in the second, I would not now be married. But then I would not have met Joscelyn.

A sort of confidence sustained me—perhaps it was my newfound faith in St Jude—as the giggling girls undressed me and wrapped me in a warm cloak. As the first bride to be bedded at the Castle for years, I was the object of interest, speculation and envy.

'Tell us first thing tomorrow how it was,' Cicely demanded; I suspected that she knew pretty well how it was already.

'Jane and I have a wager,' this was Meg. 'If you throw a boy first she's to pay me two shillings, and I pay her the same if it's a girl, so mind you make it a lad.'

'I should doubt if it will have much to do with me,' I said. They chorused a protest.

'But of course it's the woman who makes the child one or the other! If you don't know that you've no business to be a wife at all.'

They led me ceremoniously from the bedchamber to another, from which a great noise of laughter and singing came. There, in a large bed, Tom sat propped up by pillows, his face very red against the white linen. 'The bride, the bride!' the groomsmen shouted, flinging back the sheets so that I might get in beside Tom, and giving him advice at which the maidens blushed, or pretended to. Father John appeared, and a respectful silence fell as he blessed us, and the bed, and the progeny which would be created there. Then he shooed them away, and they went, reluctantly, looking back in regret at missing the main event of the occasion.

They were not missing a great deal. As soon as the door shut Tom fell asleep and began to snore. I began to think I was reprieved for the night. But before long he roused (as well he might, with the noise he was making) and murmured, 'Well, to it, wife, eh?'

I had known what to expect, of course; maids were not brought up in ignorance. I had not known that it would take so long, or be so uncomfortable, or that Tom seemed to have very little notion of how to go about it, which was surprising in view of his farmyard experience. I had thought, earlier, of the excitement I had unwillingly felt in the arms of young Will, that night at the Palace of Westminster, and had hoped that something of the kind might help me through this night.

But it was not so. I was only aware of the man who was struggling to make me a wife as a large, hot, awkward sort of animal without an animal's natural grace, and the whole process, which surely should have been a natural and joyous mating, seemed to be no more than an undignified tussle.

But at last some sort of union was achieved. I said, 'There, that's done. Now do give over, Tom.' Obediently he rolled away from me and fell noisily asleep. And, because I was worn out, I slept too. Not once during the whole tedious shaming business had I allowed myself to think of Joscelyn, because the image of him would have been tainted by what was happening.

Only when I woke some time after dawn, and looked at the porcine face on the pillow next to mine, did I begin to weep as brides are supposed to do at the loss of their virginity. Only I felt not that I had lost mine, but that it had somehow been foolishly mislaid.

Which, as events proved, was in a sense true.

The next morning, early, we set off for Tarletondale. The extra horses Tom's father had thoughtfully brought were loaded up with wedding gifts of linen, household goods, and bolts of cloth, our bounty from the Earl and Countess. She kissed my brow and gave me her blessing, but I knew she was glad to see me go, poor lady. Anne wept, and even Isabel's eyes were moist as we said farewell; I wondered how Fortune's wheel would turn for them, and whether I should ever see Warwick's daughters again.

The manor-house that was to be my home was like the tiniest of cottages compared with the huge castles I had lived in, Middleham and Skipton, an old-fashioned wood-framed building with walls of wattle and plaster, so rambling and up-and-down that it looked as though each generation of yeoman farmers had added on to please himself. And yet it was warm, after the great stone chambers that struck chill into one's bones, and there was a proper hearth in the Hall, with a hole in the roof to let out the smoke, and the window apertures had glass in them. Sir Thomas liked his comforts and could afford them, rough as he appeared. I felt more cheerful from the moment I set foot in the place.

The farm spread out to the side and behind, so that it was hard to tell where manor ended and farm buildings began. Animals wandered freely about, hens coming indoors to lay if they chose, a pet lamb of Tom's was treated as a member of the family, and the farm cats were not banished to the barns, but brought their kittens into the house when the weather was cold to mingle, seemingly unafraid, with the dogs.

Tom's mother was waiting in the Hall for me to be presented to her, and I saw at once why she had not come to Middleham for the betrothal or the wedding. Only her head and her hands moved freely: her limbs were crippled and distorted by the disease they called gout in those days, though I believe the doctors have another term for it now. I had seen it often in peasants, but never before in a lady. Her face was chalk-pale and lined with pain, but her smile was sweet as she extended to me her gnarled hand.

'Welcome, daughter. I'm glad to see our Tom has picked from healthy stock.' As she looked me up and down I felt, beside her small-ness and frailty, like a great swaggering muscular bowman. 'You see we can do with some heartiness. Tom being as fat as butter, you should breed good sound children. Margret and Joan, come and greet your new sister.'

The two girls who came forward were barely into their 'teens. Margret was very like Tom, plump-faced with light reddish hair and almost colourless brows and lashes, Joan thin and dark and with a shrewish look to her. I knew instantly that she resented me, and from Margret's wary expression guessed that she felt likewise, or had been influenced by her elder sister to feel so. There was going to be no love lost here.

They greeted me with bobbed curtseys and the faintest of smiles, as befitting their brother's wife. Their mother told them to leave us, and they went instantly, eager to discuss me by the look of them. Lady Cowley gestured to me to sit on the joint-stool at her side.

'You've come from a grand place,' her voice warm and kind, less broadly Yorkshire than her husband's and son's. 'I went to Middleham once, as a lass. I used to ride all over the dales, then. But when I were not much more than your age *this* came upon me.' She looked down at her hands, lying almost useless on her lap. 'It got worse with each bairn, and with the last one I was taken as you see me now, and the babe died; a little lad, the only one I'd borne after Tom. So I'll never ride out again. But I mind Middleham well . . . This must be like a byre to you, after yon.'

'I like it very well,' I said truthfully. 'I'll settle down in no time.'

So I did, surprising even myself. I liked the smallness of the house, the clean farm smells, the astonishingly friendly animals, the absence of the ceremony and strictness that had prevailed at Middleham. The maids and farm servants were friendly enough, if silent, once they had got used to the idea of a stranger from a great castle joining the household; at first I think they expected me to rap out orders and treat them like dirt. I became quite skilled in the domestic arts, weaving and spinning, making cordials and perfumes from the herbs and flowers in our gardens; rosemary, lavender, lily for keeping the skin fair, featherfew for curing a fever, horehound for a cough, rose-petals dried—even a decoction of marigold and valerian which Lady Cowley said soothed her aches.

As for Tom, I hardly saw him except at board and bed. He was wholly taken up with farming, not only his beloved sheep but our small herd of cows and the acres of oats and barley. It came to me that, thick-headed and stupid-seeming as he was, he put into the farm what brighter men keep for affairs of state and scholarship, and I began to respect him more than I had once done.

But as husband and wife we became no closer, lying in the best bed of the manor, big enough to hold five. Tom asked little of me, seeming to seek me out now and then out of courtesy or duty. And neither Meg nor Jane had the best of the wager, for neither boy nor girl child resulted from our bridal night or any that followed.

he two years that followed at the manor of Cowleys had the sameness, to me, of beads on a string or letters on a child's criss-cross row. Days passed, weeks and months, with little difference: sowing time, lambing time, shearing, harvest, killing and salting-down. Epiphany, Christmas, Passiontide, Pentecost. I was not discontented, pleased enough to have plenty of work to do, unlike some ladies with idle fingers. Only I felt, somewhere in my mind, that what I had thought to be a bright and beautiful dawn in my life had passed, and the sky turned to a dull cloudiness that would last till twilight.

My best satisfaction was what I was able to do for Lady Cowley. It seemed unbelievable that she, so gentle and uncomplaining, should be almost disregarded in the household. Sir Thomas's eye wandered past her at table, neither he nor Tom addressing her or asking her advice on anything. To them she was no longer part of their life, being helpless. The two girls seemed in a conspiracy together to avoid doing anything to make her life pleasant. Joan could read, and might have found time to entertain her mother, but never did, while lumpish Margret sat sewing at the same piece of stuff whenever she was in her mother's sight, a yard of dull tapestry with unsightly end-threads at the back, hardly uttering a word.

So my poor lady's life was a matter of being dressed and humped downstairs by two brawny servants, left to sit about all day in the same parlour, humped upstairs again at night.

I said, 'You would be better with a daybed down here, madam, to save you the pain of being carried.'

She looked startled. 'Oh! But . . . I couldn't lie away from my husband.'

'I doubt Sir Thomas would reproach you, madam. Are you restless at night?'

'Aye. I don't sleep much, nor does he, he says.'

'Well, then, he will rest better and so will you, and there'll be no more jolting you up and down the stairs. Leave it to me. You'll see how well it will work.'

So it did, and after everybody had said their say about the near-wickedness of separating man and wife in their sleeping, and the unheard-of situation of the mistress of the house having a bed downstairs, they had to agree that it saved work and trouble. As I pointed out to them, it was not all that many years since a whole household would all lie higgledy-piggledy in the great hall of a castle or manor, the lord and the lady along with the lowest serf, so there was nothing novel about a crippled person sleeping below, with servants within call. From this time she seemed in less pain, or perhaps her mind was less fretted, especially since on fine days I had her carried out into the herb-garden to sit under a tree among the sweet scents and enjoy pleasant sights, the sheep on the hill-slopes and the young horses rolling and playing in their field.

When I could, I took my work out and sat with her, and we would talk. She was to me the mother I had never known, and I think I was closer to her than her own daughters, for the ones who had married seldom travelled back to see her. We talked of many things, the state of the kingdom and the rumours of risings against the King. She loved to hear of the great ones I had seen, and their ways, and of how the young dukes Gloucester and Clarence looked, and the beautiful Warwick sisters; even of my own growing-up. One day she said to me, with no preparation, 'Our Tom isn't your choice, is he?'

I thought before answering. 'I had no choice, madam. The Earl and Countess were good enough to find me a husband.'

'Aye, aye. But there was another first? Don't start so, I know you were a maid. But when you look at Tom, you see another. Isn't that so?' She turned my face towards her, and I felt a blush rising.

'Yes, madam. You're very wise. But he was not a lover, only . . . someone I rode with once.'

'And ride with still, in your dreams?'

'Yes, may Our Lady pardon me. But not in the way of lust, and meaning no disloyalty to Tom. It is something . . . as though I knew him from another time and another place. As though he and I were one soul. Oh, never fear, I shall not see him again.'

'Who knows, in these troubled times?'

'If I should, you may trust me.'

'I wonder.' Her eyes, set among lines of pain, seemed to see beyond me. 'Love's sorcery is very strong. I know, I remember. There were two paths. If I had taken one, and held another man's hand along it but for a mile or two, matters might have turned out different. Better or worse, who knows? But I'd have had to defy my parents, and I was too weak. Now you are strong, Yolande, strong in every way.'

'Strong enough to resist temptation, I hope.' I felt the better for having been able to talk of Joscelyn, if only as sparingly as this. But it made me think how strange it was that he should still be in my mind, his face, his smile as clear before the inward eye as last time I saw him, his voice as merry. I, with as many tasks as there were hours in the day, to have time to think and dream of one who had long since forgotten me. Perhaps Lady Cowley was right, and there was sorcery in it. I had made the wrong prayer the night before my wedding, and now I was being punished by guilty thoughts.

One thing was very evident to me: Joan and Margret were very jealous of my closeness to their mother—not that they seemed to care for her, but that I had put their noses out of joint as the young mistresses of the house. I knew they whispered about me, and once I heard Margret, under my window, say loud enough to be heard, '. . . great brown mare', and then giggle.

They had subtle little ways of annoying me. One night I found a snake in my side of the bed, gently writhing between the sheets. I screamed for Tom, who came over and looked at it.

'Nowt to skrike about,' he said, 'yon's nobbut a slow-worm,' and he picked it up and threw it out of the window, where I hope it landed safely, for it was a harmless thing, but enough to frighten me. Another time I took up my embroidery and found that a piece of work I had just finished, and was particularly proud of, not being much of a seamstress, had been carefully unpicked. I was angry enough to seek out the girls, together as they usually were, eating apples on the lowest branch of an orchard tree. I held out the spoiled work.

'Is this your doing, either of you?'

They exchanged looks, and Joan smiled slyly. 'Nay, why should it be?'

'Because I can think of nobody else in this house who would do such a thing. Well? What about the truth?'

'Told you.' She bit into her apple again. 'Must have been Daft Alice.' Alice was one of the kitchen-maids whom the other servants supposed to be wanting in the head, though I suspected that in fact she was deaf, not daft, after I had called out to her when her back was turned, and seen that she hadn't even known I was there.

'Alice would not dare. Shall I ask your mother to judge on this?'

Joan shrugged, and Margret copied her. I turned my back on them and went into the house, where I set my poor work up on its frame again and began on the wearisome task of stitching it all over again, every leaf and flower and beast.

The next offence was graver. One of Lady Warwick's wedding gifts to me was something I greatly prized, a little Book of Hours. It had been lettered and illuminated by a young monk of Coverham Abbey, no great scribe or artist, yet the work was so lovingly and painstakingly done, and the tiny pictures set in the capital letters so innocently charming, that I never tired of taking it up.

The picture I came back to most often was of St John the Apostle with his eagle. The bird might have been a rather overfed sparrow, but the saint's face and hair reminded me, with a sweet painfulness, of Joscelyn. The complexion had a brownish glow, as though Our Lord's young friend had been out in the sun, and the hair lightly touched with gold leaf, just as my love's had looked in that early morning light.

I took the book out one day, after I had worked hard on the farm and needed some kind of rest and refreshment. The capital, and the picture of St John, had been cut out of the page in a neat square with a sharp knife.

For a long moment I looked, feeling a hot rage surging up through my breast and throat into my brain. Then I marched into the parlour where Lady Cowley was lying on a couch, half-asleep because the day was rainy and cold. She started up at my entry.

'My lady,' I said, 'your daughters have done me an injury.'

'What—injury, Yolande?'

'Not the first, but the worst. A precious book of mine has been riven, utterly spoilt. It was a wedding gift, and I treasured it, and now the best of it is gone, by the hands of some who hate me, Joan and Margret.'

She was sitting up, very pale. 'Can you prove this?'

'Look.' I whipped the book out of my skirts, open at the mutilated page.

She looked at it, long and sadly. 'And they did this?'

'Yes. No one else.'

'No. I saw it. Jealous and wicked; my own girls.'

'I intend to punish them,' I said steadily. 'Have I your leave, lady?'

'What you choose, Yolande,' she sighed. 'They deserve it, but I have no strength. Do what you will.'

I went to look for them, the book in the big pocket of my apron. It was an hour before supper, and I found them in the room they shared, combing their hair, whispering at the looking-glass, a pair of snakes far more dangerous than the poor thing which had writhed in my bed. I advanced on them and pulled them apart, throwing Margret to the floor and Joan over a stool. Then I pulled out the book and waved it at them.

'You did this—one or both of you. You took a knife to something I prized, and I am angry. Why?'

Joan pulled a lip at me. 'You've no place here. We hate you. You sit in our mother's lap and get the plums. Why should you have pretty books and sit conning them, while we live like scullerymaids? I've watched you swooning over the handsome saint, so I thought I'd cut him out and chop him up. I gave him to the swine, didn't I, Margret? Fed him to them, and they ate him with the swill.' Her eyes were ablaze with malice, and Margret was laughing. I darted at her and got her, unprepared, in the grasp of both my hands. Then I sat myself on a truckle-bed and pulled her across my knee, while Margret squealed and she flailed at me with her fists. But she was small, though wiry, and I had command of her with my left hand, while with my right I pulled off her shoe and yanked up her skirts and beat her soundly about the bum as she shrieked and wriggled and tried to bite me.

'There,' I said, between breaths, 'so should your mother have beaten you, long ago, but she was too weak, poor soul, and so you were both marred—and this—is the first time—you've been brought to book.' With that I laid on heavier than before. 'Now I am here, your mother's surrogate, and each time you offend—like this—this will be your reward.' With that I flung her to the floor, where she lay crying and screaming. Margret had run off. After a moment Joan picked herself up and scrambled to her feet, glaring at me as no decent maid should glare.

'Devil!' she spat. 'I'll be at evens with you, never fear!' With that she was away like a rat to its hole.

After that the girls ceased to persecute me. But their sullenness caused even their mother to lose her patience and threaten them with a beating from Sir Thomas unless they spoke more civilly. It seemed to me a strange thing that my life should be linked with a pair of sisters so different from Anne and Isabel Neville. One night I dreamed that I was back at Middleham, or Warwick, for places in dreams are seldom quite themselves. In my dream I was happy and free, running from room to room like a child, dressed in velvet and jewels, searching for something or someone it was very important that I should find. And then, far away, a harsh sound came to me, louder and louder: Tom's snoring. Then I knew, even in my dream, that it *was* a dream, and began to weep bitterly for the loss of my happiness. When I woke fully there were no tears on my face, as I would have expected, but the feeling of sorrow and loss remained with me.

Are our dreams the shadows of things to come? For one August morning, not two weeks later, as I helped our maids with the spreading of newly-washed linen on the lavender hedge, I saw a single horseman approaching along the lane that led northwards. We had few visitors, so each one was an event. I shaded my eyes, the sun being in them, and my heart leapt, for as he drew nearer I could see that the device on his scarlet jerkin was the Bear and Ragged Staff.

I went forward to meet him. He doffed his cap.

'Is the mistress of the house at home, dame?'

'Lady Cowley is indoors.'

He pulled a paper out of his scrip and handed it down to me. 'Then will you take her this, and I'm to wait for an answer.'

I read the writing on the outside. It was in a hand I knew.

'This is not for Lady Cowley, but for me, Mistress Thomas Cowley. And I see it comes from Lady Warwick.'

He grinned. 'It's a marvel to me how scratches on paper can mean so much to folk. Aye, it's from my lady.' I saw him eyeing me, no doubt wondering how anybody important enough to be written to by a countess could appear in a humble stuff gown with an apron round her waist and her hair hidden in a cloth. He was not a man I knew, and spoke with a southerly accent. I read the letter: it told me that Anne had been taken ill with a fever, and was continually asking for me. Would it be possible for me, out of kindness, to come to her, if my household could spare me? It might only be for a few days, until she came properly to her senses. 'The Lady Isabel is gone and we have great company so that I am constantly called for.' That sounded like unusual disturbance of mind for the calm Countess. The letter ended with an assurance that nobody else had caught the fever so I need not fear infection, and with courteous messages to Sir Thomas and his lady.

I told the messenger to go round the kitchens where he would be given some ale; he went with alacrity. On my way back to the house I read the letter again, and a strong desire swept over me to go to Middleham; not merely for Anne's sake, but from the craving that had remained in me ever since I had visited there in my dream.

I read the letter to Lady Cowley, afraid that she would tell me my duty lay at home. But she took it from me, studying with admiration the words formed by so great a person, and the seal which bore the Bull of Neville.

'I think,' she said, 'you must go, Yolande. Poor Lady Anne needs you more than you're needed here. And it's an honour to be asked, when all's said. Go now, while you've the man to guide you.'

'The work . . . the running of the house . . .'

'It got done before you came, and it'll get done again. Margret and Joan will have to stir their stumps and set about it—not that they'll do it as you do. Never fear, we'll manage. Get into your best gear and be off as soon as you can. I'll tell the men when they come in from the fields. Go, now.'

I ran upstairs as if I had Mercury's feathers on my heels, changed into suitable clothes for riding, packed a parcel of others to take with me, and skipped down again, relieved to see that Tom was still absent. Not that I feared he would scold me or try to stop me; I simply wished not to see him, now that the vision of Middleham had risen in my mind. Lady Cowley kissed my cheeks. 'God speed, daughter. I'll miss your bright face. Come back to us when you can.'

I rode north with a far merrier heart than I had ridden to Cowleys. Brown Bailey seemed to know his way, and to be glad to be going home. The sunny August fields of crops, waiting for harvesting, lay on each side of us like banners spread, the messenger whistled, anything from soldiers' camp songs to *Angelus ad Virginem*, and I felt as light in the saddle as a bird. We rested for ale and bread at an inn and reached Middleham a little before supper-time. My heart rose as we rounded the bend of the river and saw Middleham's battlements appear, towering above the huddled houses and the crouching church, against a sky as blue as Mary's robe.

As we drew nearer I became aware of movement and activity around the Castle. There were men-at-arms on guard at every entrance, others pacing the battlement look-outs, as though keeping watch on all approaches, and a party of armoured riders were leaving the great gateway. My escort drew level with me, having kept a respectful distance throughout the journey, and taken his refreshment apart at the inn.

'What's all the stir?' I asked him. 'My lady Warwick wrote that there was company.'

He laughed. 'Company, aye. No less company than the King.'

'The King! But he never visited us before that I remember. Why now?'

'Well, it's not for me to talk, dame. But the word is that my lord put a bit of persuasion on him to visit, and ain't eager to see him leave. We brought him up from Warwick by night marches to keep the thing quiet. Very pleasant he was about it, not like a prisoner, but we all guessed what was what.'

'But what *is* what? Has Lord Warwick turned against the King?'

'You don't hear much in Tarletondale, it seems. The country's upside down, Woodvilles against Nevilles, the Duke of Gloucester with the King, His Grace of Clarence with my lord—you know the Lady Isabel's wed now, Duchess of Clarence?'

'No.'

'Aye, in France, they say, t'other week. Robin of Redesdale's up in arms—that's Sir John Conyers, you know.'

I knew.

'And there've been heads off, Lord Pembroke's for one, along with his brother. I saw it done, at Northampton. Did you ever see a beheading? Well, I've seen a lot worse in battle, but it's no pretty sight to watch a man go to his death in cold blood, as you might say, with a confessor at his side and the headsman one of your own comrades, a fellow with a strong right arm . . .'

I let him prate on, wishing that he had done some prating on our journey, so that I could have absorbed all these changes. There I had been buried at Cowleys, never stirring from the circle of household duties, knowing nothing, but for the occasional rumour that had come by way of travellers. Isabel married at last, and civil war broke out again; not this time between York and Lancaster, but between York and York, two white roses fighting on one branch, two cousins, King and Earl, ready to spill each other's blood. My lord of Warwick loved power, he was proud to be called Kingmaker. Why should he not make himself King, or as good as?

The Castle bustled with a sense of excitement, people hurrying with cloths and dishes, flagons and loaded trays. My guide had left me, but a gentlewoman of my lady's appeared to greet me and take me to Anne.

A small antechamber had been prepared for me next to hers: they had been very sure that I would come. I washed in water scented with rose-leaves, changed my gown, and tapped at her chamber door. Grizel, the old woman who had been nurse to the sisters as long as anyone could remember, opened it.

'Thanks to Our Lord you're here, madam,' she said, half-whispering. 'She's asked for you so often, over and over again. "Fetch Yolande, fetch Yolande." There was none other would do, Lady Isabel gone away, my lady too busy with high matters to sit by her, poor lambkin, and she wasting with fever yet talking, ever talking. She's quiet now, first time for hours. See where she lies.'

I knew the girl in the bed for Anne, but only because she was so familiar to me. The delicate paleness of her face was turned to a dusky red with the fever, her lips encrusted, her beautiful fair hair a greasy tangle on the pillows, her eyelids puffed up horribly. I took one of her hands, which was clenched as though with pain, and said, 'Anne.'

Her eyes gleamed through the swelling, but I realized that she neither saw nor knew me, and the hand stayed clenched. Grizel said, 'She'll not be able to speak to you. Her poor mouth's dry as a bone now. At the beginning she retched and purged, saying she was first hot and then cold, and that her sight was dim. Then the fever came on her, and she began raving as though a devil possessed her.'

'How long has she been like this?'

'Three days and more. My lord's physician Master Ralph has bled her, but it did no good.'

'That I believe. Has she any pain?'

'Aye, a great deal, here.' She drew back the sheet and prodded Anne's swollen body below the ribs, causing her to wince and moan. I covered her again.

'Let her be. She is poisoned.'

Grizel crossed herself. 'Jesu! Who would do such a thing?'

'I said nothing about anyone giving her poison. Such an illness as this can come about by taking bad food or drink. Has anyone else here suffered the same?'

'Nay. The family are well . . .'

'I mean anyone in the Castle who might have taken the same food. Go to the kitchens and ask, Grizel. And bring me back fresh mustard-seeds ground into a paste, and comfrey and lovage from the herb-garden. Run!'

The poor old creature was past running, but she made what haste she could. I sat beside Anne, listening to her harsh breathing and moans. It came to me that a great Providence had made me mistress of a house and a farm these two years, the one who was supposed to know everything domestic, to whom everyone came with ailments or wounds. I had cleaned and bound up a ploughboy's leg after a blade had cut it, brought an erring servant-girl through premature labour and saved her child, doctored everything from the bites of horse-leeches to strange swellings on the bone, for which, alas, my remedies did little good. Some of the old wives' cures that had been practised at Cowleys seemed to me loathsome and foolish: boiled mice, powdered lungs of hogs, newly-killed pigeons tied to the patient's feet. I knew, as one does know these things by instinct, that I had a sort of gift to tend the sick (perhaps because I was born under the sign of Pisces), and it satisfied me to make people well, or better, by the use of the plentiful herbs that have been given to us.

Among the many illnesses at Cowleys had been two cases with just such symptoms as Anne had. Both women had fallen ill at once, and one, an elderly servant, had died within two days. The other I dosed with comfrey and lovage powdered in apple-wine, till slowly she lost her fever and recovered. Meanwhile I had searched the larder and found the remains of a joint of meat turned green and purple with corruption; I knew it had been the poisoner. I would not have foul meats served at my table, but greed seeks out forbidden things for its satisfaction, and the two sufferers had only themselves to blame.

Grizel returned with the news that a cook-maid had been taken ill in just the same way, but she was a stout healthy wench and was recovering. So I was right, and something corrupted had been mistakenly served to Anne, and finished by the girl.

I began to treat her, first with a mustard emetic to get rid of the poison, then with spoonfuls of the herb decoction. Within a few hours the fever began to ebb, the livid colour to fade. As the swellings round her eyes went down she began to look her fair self again, and drank thin watered wine eagerly. The first word she spoke clearly was 'Yolande . . .'

'Yes, my dear one.'

'I wanted you. How did you come here?'

'On my horse,' I said, 'because they told me you were asking for me.'

'I've had such horrible dreams . . . visions . . .'

'Well, I am not a vision, and now you are almost well the others will not trouble you again.'

'Was Master Ralph here? I thought I saw him. But my eyes were so strange, everything looked double, or seen through a mist.'

'He was here, yes, but I told him not to return. Now be quiet, and take another sip of this.' She obeyed like a child, and like a child she looked, so slender and small in the bed. Long after nightfall I left her side and undressed and lay down on the pallet-bed, after sending Grizel off to her own place. But first I lit a candle, on the branch above Anne's prie-dieu, and spoke to St Jude for her fragile life.

I slept uneasily on the narrow couch, waking to find the long candle still burning. I half-sat up to look at Anne. She lay on her back, her hair spread about. In the candle-shine I saw distinctly, unmistakably, the outline of a gold crown encircling her head. So clear was it that I sat bolt upright to see it sharper. As the light changed it vanished, and soon afterwards the candle went out. I lay awake, thinking and wondering what the portent meant. Would King Edward's queen die, and would he take Anne instead? I thought of him, and her, and Isabel married far away in France, and Richard—where? My man-at-arms had said 'with the King'. So, was he here? Suddenly, in a maze of changing pictures, knights and battle-scenes, the half-dying Anne and Richard as a small grave boy, I fell asleep.

Though I seemed to have slept for a night and a day it was only sun-up when I woke, warm sunshine filling the room through the lancet window, and Anne breathing quietly, herself again but for the state of her hair and the sharpness of her cheek-bones. Rather than wake her I dressed as far away from her bed as I could, splashed my face at the basin, and went softly out of the room, through my own chamber where I never troubled to look at myself in the glass. From the corridor beyond a staircase wound downwards on the outside of the Castle. I think of it now, old woman that I am, and how fearful I would be to try it, with no handrail, only the slippery stones underfoot and the lichened wall by which to steady oneself; but I never thought to do that, flying down lightly, glad of the open air and the sun after the stuffy sick-chamber, as steady as a roe-deer on the crags. Down in the moat ducks were quacking, the soft whinnying of horses rose from the stables. A man in a red coat was walking by the willows at the river-side, his dog at his heels. I was free for the time, Anne was going to be well, and my heart sang.

I reached the end of the flight, near the entrance of the Great Hall, and came face to face with Joscelyn.

It was as if time froze for an instant as we stared at each other. Then he opened his arms and I ran into them, feeling, as they closed round me, that I had come home.

He held me tightly, as though he would never let me go. Then he put me at arm's length, his eyes searching my face.

'They said you were married and gone away.'

'I was—I am—but I came back to nurse . . . oh, no matter. And you? I never thought to find you here, but I have had no time to think since I arrived.'

He took my arm. 'Let's find a more retired place. Up those steps there's a turret where one can't be seen.' We climbed up to a little round tower which served as a look-out point, fortunately without a sentinel. We sat on the ground and began to talk, as though we had both been enclosed in a silent order for years. I found myself telling him of Cowleys, all the things I had been able to say to nobody else, and he recounted what had been happening in the world outside: how the split between the King, the Woodvilles and Lord Warwick had widened like a deep sword-wound, and how England had become virtually Warwick's.

'My cousin John and I set to in the North and did valiant work, though I say it myself. Then we marched south and met some King's troops near Banbury, Lord Pembroke at the head of a band of Welsh pikemen. They fought like wildcats, but our guns and arrows were too much for them, and when Warwick's men came up to back us we finished the little Welshmen off, poor devils. Well, that's warfare . . . And Pembroke and his brother lost their heads after.'

'I heard of that. It seems strange and ugly to think of my lord having people beheaded. He was always so kindly to me.'

'You were not a traitor to him. The velvet glove comes off when a kingdom is at stake. Now he has the chief piece in the game in his iron fist.'

'The King—he would not take *his* head off, surely?'

Joscelyn shrugged, smiling. 'How can I say, lady, what Warwick would do? But no, I think not. There are other ways, such as the way King Edward dealt with poor daft King Henry. But King Edward is not a Henry, but a smooth, shrewd fellow: I almost said knave.' Joscelyn laughed. I thought he would be a match for any man, king or pikeman. I studied him as he sat, cross-legged and easy, like a soldier by the warmth of a camp-fire after a day's combat, and reflected how strong he was: a fighting man, an armed knight who wore the leather and steel of the battlefield as naturally as the silks and velvets of courtly life. He had shed blood, often. His firm beautiful brown hands had killed with the sword, his bright blue eyes had watched men die. What of it? That was the condition of war, the war that had been going on since I was a child. I could not have loved a clerk, I did not love the simple farmer who was my husband. But I did love Joscelyn Conyers.

He caught me watching him, and I knew that our thoughts went along together. I would always know that; as though his breast and mine were joined by an invisible cord. Perhaps that was what was meant in the Scriptures, the silver cord that should not be loosed until the last day of life. He put his hand on mine.

'You trust yourself with me, lady. Is that wise?'

'No. Something beyond wisdom. Something more than I can reason out. You must think me very bold. But from the first moment I knew it would be like this. I am not a maid any more, but a wife. Yet I am yours.'

He nodded. '"I am my beloved's, and my beloved is mine." You see, I was thinking of the Scriptures too.'

I said, looking into his eyes deeply, '"My beloved is white and ruddy, the chiefest among ten thousand. His mouth is most sweet; yea, he is altogether lovely. This is my beloved and this is my friend, O daughters of Jerusalem."'

And that exchange was our marriage ceremony, the strangest one old Middleham had ever seen. We sealed it only with a long kiss, yet it bound us closer than any nuptial Mass or ceremonial bedding. Then we took hands and went down from the turret, talking softly and easily, as we would always talk, as though we two were truly one.

On the way towards Anne's chamber after parting from Joscelyn I met Gilbert, my companion from Cowleys, on his way to guard duty. He gave me an enormous wink, and passed by, singing loudly enough to have got him a summons to my lord's presence, *My little pretty one, My little bonnie one, She is a jolly one, As ever I saw.* I have never heard the light song since without remembering that hour of time.

Anne was much better, looking almost herself, able to eat a mash of fruit, propped up on cushions. I sat by her and talked of this and that, nothing of Joscelyn, but she was eager to know if I had heard anything of Richard. I had, though I had no intention of telling her how.

'He is entirely for the King, fighting and commanding troops like a seasoned general. The King has made him Chief Steward of all Wales. Nobody knows where he is now, but doubtless about his brother's business.'

'And he only sixteen,' Anne said fondly. 'Do you think he might come here now that the King is my father's prisoner?'

'What, to besiege Middleham? Not very likely. But he proves himself to be the man he promised. You'll do well if they let you wait for him.'

'*If*. And if they let him wait for me . . . Clarence is my lord's ally, and safe, but Richard—might he not be called a rebel?' She shivered. 'My lord had the King's father-in-law beheaded. Richard might go the same way, even though my lord brought him up from a child. Do you think that could happen, Yolande?'

'Richard is strong. We must wait and see which way the cat jumps.' I was repeating what had been said to me, though she was not to know that.

A gracious note from the Countess was brought to me, thanking me for the good I had done to her daughter, and commanding my presence at a banquet that night. If Anne were well enough she too must attend. But she shook her head, making a face.

'The last banquet nearly killed me. It was a fast day, and we had eel pie among other dishes. I know it was that, for I feel faint when I think of it. I like eels, or I did, and I chose that though I could have had honest fish, more fool I. A mercy others had more sense, or we might all have been poisoned.' I forbore to tell her that one poor cook-maid had greedily eaten from the pie that had come down almost untouched, and had died of it, in spite of the remedies I had given Grizel for her.

So I went to the banquet alone, yet found myself not alone, for Joscelyn melted out of the crowd to be at my side and steered me to a place at table beside him, so that we were able to share dishes and even a wine-cup, which made it a love-feast indeed. But even in this happiness my eyes were drawn to the high table, where tonight there sat only my lord and my lady and the King.

I had seen him in London, from a distance, never so closely. His size would have distinguished him among an army, for he was many inches taller than any man present, even Joscelyn. He was in his prime now, twenty-seven years old, big-built, his short waving hair an imperial red-gold, his face a comely oval, with a strong nose and a small, ever-smiling mouth. It was plain to see why women were said to fall swooning at his feet if he so much as let his gaze rest on them, and why his bastards far out-numbered any children he might ever have by the Queen. I could see a likeness to George of Clarence, but none at all to small dark Richard. Here was truly the Sun in Splendour, the mortal image of the badge he had chosen for himself on the morning before a victorious battle, when he looked heavenwards through a thick fog to see the sun trebled, brilliant rays streaming out from it like the glory round a saint's head.

And he was playing his part—the part of a king, not a prisoner. He had a gracious smile for everyone, even the server who held out the silver bowl for hand-washing. When he turned to the Countess, his look was as devoutly admiring, almost desirous, as though she were a young maid he was wooing. To the Earl his demeanour was amiable, frank and friendly, with just a touch of the respect due to an older man. All this was plain to see even without hearing a word of the conversation.

Joscelyn said, soft and clear against the great buzz of talk at our long table, 'He has his path mapped out. My lord may think of him as a prisoner, but when he wishes to go, he will.'

'I can well believe that.'

'Your eyes are still on him. Do you admire him so much?'

'No woman could help it. But I would never trust him as I would my lord.'

'I believe you love that man.' His voice was gently teasing. My look told him the answer to the real question, but I said, 'Yes, I do, as a kind father and the greatest personage I ever saw.'

'Good. I approve that, for so do I. I would die for him, and if the King plays him false, as I think he will, I would willingly turn my sword against *him*.'

'Hush! you speak treason.'

'In Warwick's house one can only speak treason against Warwick.'

I think it was then I began to fear for Joscelyn, a fear that was never to leave me, for single-minded loyalty takes no care for itself, and there was an air of danger around us, a threat which came from one source, that splendid form on the dais, garbed in royal blue sewn with many pearls and wrought with silver thread. Edward the Enchanter, Edward the thorned White Rose, smiling and sinister.

My lord looked less sunny than his guest. He smiled little, and I noticed his fingers stray often towards the magnificent neck-chain of uncut emeralds that he wore on state occasions, as though his mind were troubled. After the banquet there was no dancing. Joscelyn whispered to me that the King would not be pleased at that, since he liked nothing better than to show off his skill and grace, and take hands with any beauties there might be among the company. Instead of the dance the royal prisoner was entertained by a concert of music. The tables were cleared, the throne-like chairs brought down from the dais for the three great ones to sit in the body of the hall, while the musicians and four singers took their places on the dais.

I understood very little of what they sang, for it was mostly in French and Latin, but it was plain that most of the canzonets, villanelles and ballets dealt with love; with sighs and kisses, the exchange of glances, despair and desire. No music had ever sounded so sweet to me, since I heard it with my eyes on my own love. Indeed, it seemed I had never truly listened to music before that night.

We were not together, for at the end of the banquet another of the Conyers party drew him away to talk, so that when the music began he was at the opposite side of the hall. As it happened, I sat, still in the seat I had occupied at table, a little to the fore of the three thrones. Looking across at Joscelyn I became aware that the King's attention was straying from the musicians. While keeping an attitude of rapt attention, his eyes were wandering interestedly round the company, or as many of them as he could see, examining faces and, no doubt, forms. Here and there I saw a blush rise and a smirk begin. All my friends had married and gone—Cicely, Meg, Jane and the rest— but other pretty maids had taken their place, young noblewomen aged anything from eight years upwards. And the King was weighing them up with his expressive amber eyes, as a farmer does cattle at market.

At last they came to rest on me. Now it was my turn to blush, but not to smirk, for he was hardly likely to linger on one so swarthy when it was well-known that his taste favoured such gold-haired white- skinned beauties as the Queen, and I was not so grandly attired as many there, having put on the only gown I had brought with me, the coral-coloured one I had worn on the unforgettable evening when I had danced with Joscelyn; it was two years out of fashion and crushed with travel. But, as the royal gaze held mine, it became clear to me that he was not surveying me critically, but with invitation.

I looked away, then, irresistibly, back at him again. This time he sent me a dimpling smile. I answered it, in a fashion; there was nothing else I could do.

Half-way through the concert the musicians were allowed to rest and take refreshment. Wine was brought to the King and his host and hostess. He spoke to them both, glancing round the hall; my lady looked faintly displeased, as I had often seen her look, but obviously agreed to whatever request he had made. She called up her gentle- woman, Catherine, who had taken the place of old Joan, and gave her some instruction. Catherine swiftly made her way round the company, speaking to one here, another there—and I realized that they were all women. As she spoke, they left their places and moved to where the King sat. She reached me.

'Mistress, the King has commanded that the ladies of the house- hold be presented to him. Will you follow the others?'

Again, I had no choice. I saw Joscelyn looking at me, and gave a slight shrug which I hoped he read rightly. As I stood awaiting my turn to be presented, I marvelled at King Edward's cleverness. As each lady curtseyed to him, he raised her graciously by the hand and spoke with her. But to the older and less well-favoured he gave only a greeting: the young pretty ones he kept longer, smiled on more warmly.

When my turn came I made my deepest obeisance. He raised me until I could not help looking into his eyes, and being aware of the witchery in them. It was not every day one met a king, and I felt a certain pride, but a sort of fear as well.

'Your name, madam?' he asked me, his voice as soft as the purr of a cat. I told him my name, and Lady Warwick said somewhat sharply 'Mistress Cowley was one of my household until her marriage.'

'Ah. And which of the gentlemen present has the joy of being your husband?'

'None, your Grace. He stays at home, at our farm.'

My hand was still in the warm grip of his; I felt his fingers move inside my sleeve and pause on my wrist-pulse. It was an amorous trick which must often have served him well. I grew even more scarlet than I was already, if possible, and tried to withdraw my hand, but he kept it, still gazing, with that conquering smile, until Lady Warwick broke in to introduce the girl waiting behind me. As I returned to my place I felt as the bird is said to feel which has encountered the eyes of a snake, overcome against its will.

When the concert was ended (and the music in the second half of it seemed not so sweet as in the first) I hung back, placing myself so that Joscelyn would pass close to me as he left the hall, and praying that he would not be detained by the man who was talking to him. Talk, talk, how men talk—far worse than women. A resolution had formed in me, something so daring that I wondered at myself, yet my heart would not let me go against it. There was a thing I had to do that night.

He saw me, and bade good night to his companion, and joined me. I led him out through a little door into the courtyard, the great door being bolted and heavily guarded, giving thanks silently for the warm August night that let us escape from the eyes and ears of others.

A young slip of a moon hung in a sky that would not darken entirely, pin-points of stars twinkling against its velvet, and one calm white planet, Love's lady, Venus.

Joscelyn took my hands and smiled down at me, a question in his eyes.

'So, my mistress. So many blushes for a king?'

'No! I blushed because he made me feel like a fool, standing there handfast with him, when everyone could see he was not captivated by me, but only wished to make it known that he could have any women he liked at the beck of a finger. Arrogant young cockerel!'

'Hush. Too many ears about . . . Why should he not be captivated by you?'

'Need you ask? Look at my hair and my complexion—'

'Willingly.'

'Oh, I know you—you have strange tastes in women, I thank God. But *he* likes them fair as the day, I've heard, not brown.'

'I think,' Joscelyn said, 'King Edward is like a man who loves roses. He fills his garden with white ones, then sees a red bloom, and fancies that better; a rose of Lancaster, in fact.'

I looked away from him, then, boldly, back. 'I have something else to say to you. Come to me tonight, Joscelyn.'

He was silent for a moment, and I thought I had shocked him, so I said, 'Do you not love me enough?'

'Courtly love is one thing—cuckolding a man is another.'

'No need to think of that; Tom cares more for his sheep than me— yes, even the ones with foot-rot or the bloats. He wouldn't give a farthing if I bestowed myself on the King, and all the world knew it.' (How little *I* knew then, poor love-struck idiot!) 'For one thing I've borne him no children, nor even lost any in the womb. I believe myself to be barren. So, you see, it would be quite safe . . . Oh, now you think I'm shameless.'

Joscelyn's look was more grave than any I had yet seen him wear. He kissed me on the lips, very gently. 'I think you to be an innocent, my love, a sweet bold innocent, a married maid it would be my joy to teach. If . . . are you quite sure this is not a game you play to test yourself, like children daring each other? I never knew a woman yet who would dare as much, except in coquetry. Or lust. But this is not lust, is it?'

'No. I can't tell what it is, only that I must belong to you, now, before it's too late.'

I thought he was going to refuse me. But at last he said, 'Well, I will come. Tell me where you sleep?'

'Next to Lady Anne's bedchamber.' I described it, how it was up a winding flight of stairs away from other rooms, and said that he was to come when midnight had struck. And he kissed my hand, with a promise, looking older and more thoughtful than I had seen him, as though I had laid some heavy charge on him.

My room was quiet. I looked in at Anne, to find her sleeping naturally, and Grizel snoring on the pallet-bed. If she woke I would hear, and go in to her; meanwhile I put up the latch on the door. Then I washed, and let down my hair and put away the coif that had proclaimed me to be a wife. I sat and waited, feeling the beating of my heart shake me, praying silently that all would be well; fearing more than I had ever feared anything that he would not come.

Down below, at the entrance to the Great Hall, was a miracle of clock-making, a huge dial on which each hour bore besides its number the position of the stars in the heavens, the sun and moon being in the centre, and round a platform above it leaden knights rode on chargers, brightly-coloured and gilded, revolving every time the hour struck. Now they were going on their longest ride, the midnight hour, and the deep clangour of the chimes would be heard all over the castle. Not in the far corner where I was, the south-looking tower, but I sensed the time by instinct. I remembered that clock from other summer nights in the past, when I had lain awake and heard dogs bark as the clock struck, and the shout of passwords when the guard changed on the hour. I could hear them now.

Then all was quiet again. My heart began to sink. He should be with me, and he was not. Only a deaf man could have missed the striking of that clock. He might have fallen asleep. He might have been enticed into a game of cards. But surely he would not, knowing I waited, hardly daring to breathe in case the noise of my own breath drawn masked his approach.

I heard a sound; somebody was in the corridor outside. My heart gave a wild jump and I unlatched the door, aflame with joy.

There, his face illumined into planes and shadows by the light of the candle he held, stood the King.

He towered over me like a tall pillar, looking even taller for the bed-robe he wore, a dark crimson trimmed with ermine. As I stared at him with my mouth open from shock, he said pleasantly, 'What a pretty welcome—uncoiffed and waiting behind the door. I like a ready dame.'

I began to stammer something, but he was in the room, the door shut behind him, looking me up and down like a hunter surveying with satisfaction a stricken deer.

'I never mistake a lady's glance,' he said, 'or a warm moist palm. Among a bunch of weeds, one lovely flower. So I lost no time in answering your signal. It was child's play finding out where you lay, once I'd tracked down the Lady Anne's chamber. How is she, by the way?'

'Much better, sir,' I said, as though this were a commonplace conversation.

'Good. Then we have some leisure to enjoy each other.' He gave me a dazzling smile and spread his arms, from which I backed away, feeling if possible a greater fool than I had done at the presentation.

'But sir, your Grace,' I said, not knowing too well how one addressed a king, 'I never gave you any signal—any invitation. How could you have thought so—your Grace?'

His shapely eyebrows rose. 'I tell you, I never mistake—and I know coyness when I meet it. Shall we end this little game?' He went to the door that led into Anne's chamber and examined the latch, then shot the bolt across. 'If your patient wakes, you must go to her—suitably clad. These things all help to smooth the path of love.'

By this time I was not only confused but desperately anxious: not because I was afraid he would rape me, for something told me he would never stoop to that, but because of Joscelyn, and for fear that refusal would turn the King's charm to anger, and I had no preparation for meeting royal wrath. He was regarding me curiously, still smiling.

'A married dame, and so shamefaced? Well, well. Or is it all a lady's device to inflame a lover's blood?'

I had a sudden thought of his fabled wooing of the Queen, when she was Lady Grey, strolling in a forest with her two small sons, beautiful and piteous, and wondered whether he had instantly proceeded to lay her on the green turf, having dismissed the boys to play. The picture aroused in me an impulse to laugh which became more and more hard to resist, until I struggled between it and cold fear of what rage that might arouse in him—as surely it would in any man, their pride being what it is. And then a gentle knocking came to the door.

The King spun round, his hand on the jewelled hilt of the dagger at his belt. Before I could speak the door opened, and there stood Joscelyn.

He took in the scene, and his face grew very grim. He bowed.

'Your pardon, sire. And yours, madame.'

'You mistook the door?' the King enquired ironically.

Joscelyn did not look at me. 'I did, sire.'

'No,' I said. 'Sir Joscelyn came here by appointment. We had . . . matters to talk over.'

Then there followed an awful silence, during which the figure of the King seemed to grow taller and taller, and his look change from blandness to a complete expressionlessness more alarming than a frown. I was aware of the strong sweet perfume that hung about him, some costly blend of civet and distilled flower-waters.

At last he said, very levelly, 'Sir Joscelyn. Of what house?'

'Conyers, sire.'

The King must have known very well that this was the surname of the man who called himself Robin of Redesdale, who had caused such ferment up and down the country fighting Yorkist troops, but he showed no flicker of interest, only surveyed us both, Joscelyn tight-lipped and angry, prevented by the sacredness of the royal person from breaking out as he would have done at finding any other man in my room, I shaking at the knees while scolding myself for weakness. King though he might be, he was only a prisoner in the castle and had no say in what any of his host's household might do.

It seemed hours, rather than seconds, before he said, 'I will leave you to talk over these weighty . . . matters.' Then, magnificently, he turned and stalked out, ignoring Joscelyn's bow and my low curtsey (which was not easy with trembling knees).

I turned to Joscelyn, ready to throw myself into his arms with relief. But his eyes were cold, and he made no move towards me.

'So,' he said, 'what a puppet-show it was. You thought His Grace mocked you, you blushed prettily, you denied all to me, and I find him in your chamber by appointment. What I fail to understand is why you invited us both at the same time. Are you so hot for a man that you secure yourself against the risk of losing one by summoning two? Or did your memory slip? If I'd come to you at eleven I might have been the fortunate one.'

'No! How can you think such foul things? It was all as I said. But you're jesting, and that's unkind.'

'I am not jesting, Yolande. I should have known you for a light-skirt when you offered yourself to me tonight. Even before that, now I think of it.'

'I am *not*! It was because I loved you as soon as I saw you—because I seemed to know you . . .'

His look was cold scorn. 'And wanted to know me better? Did you tell the King that story? Of course, and he believed it, and came running to add you to his bag of easy conquests.'

'I said nothing to him, nothing at all. How could I have done, in front of all that company? And I'm not his conquest, I care nothing for him, only for you, oh, Joscelyn . . .' I caught at his hand, but he pulled it away, and the touch I had of it was cold.

'I thought you a true wench and a treasure,' he said. 'I might have known that one who would clap horns on her husband would do as much to me. A man may live to twenty-two years and still be a fool. Good night, lady—farewell.'

Before I could plead any more he was gone. I was alone, hearing my own gasping sobs, tearing the flesh of my hands with my nails, trying to kill pain with pain, until I could no longer breathe easily and my throat was sore with crying. It was a relief when I heard Anne's voice through the door, calling for me. I went to her and found her restless, wanting a drink. Grizel still slept, and soon Anne was quiet too. I sat by her side, watching the dancing shadow of the tapers on the walls, that made the figures on the tapestries dance too, a grotesque masque of figures and flowers and unicorns.

Not long after dawn had broken there was a clattering of hooves in the courtyard below, and voices, then the sound of horsemen riding away, and I knew without looking that Joscelyn was one of them.

8

I went back to Cowleys. And was welcomed as though I had been a ploughman who had taken a day away from the fields with a leg-sprain in which nobody believed. Joan and Margret pumped me at first for Middleham gossip: was the King as handsome as they said? Was it true that Lady Anne had been poisoned by an enemy of Lord Warwick's? Then, when they tired of my curt answers, they left off and began to tease me again, in sundry little ways not worth repeating. Tom grumbled that I had not been there for some farmers' gathering at which he alone had had no wife beside him. His father enquired after Lord Warwick's health but otherwise seemed hardly to notice that I had been away, and only Lady Cowley was truly pleased to have me back.

'But by the looks of you it's done you little good. Did you catch the young lady's fever?'

'No, madam.'

'Then they starved you, shame on 'em, or you caught a rheum in that chill old place. Never mind, you shall fatten and mend now, and we'll be as snug for the winter as mice in malt.'

But it was a chill winter, as chill as my heart, now that the only one I loved was gone thinking me false. Not that much snow fell, not enough to trouble Tom and the shepherds about the coming lambs, but there was much cold rain, and a dampness in the air that found its way to one's

bones, however high they banked the fires. Poor Lady Cowley suffered
the pains of hell, and even I lay awake with the ache in my legs and
shoulders, wishing that Tom were a husband to huggle up to, to take
and give warmth. But he was not, no more than he ever had been. Now
and then he would claim his rights in an awkward mating, and look at
me sideways for some weeks after to see whether it would bear fruit. It
never did, and I knew that he was beginning to be in dudgeon over it.
Going on three years wed and no child: that had been the purpose of
the thing. There would be no more Cowleys at the manor, unless Margret or Joan should wed a cousin of the same name. But neither had
had any offers, from men of any name at all.

Rumours came, from packmen and travellers who stopped in our
sheltered dale. The King was back in London, working to pull down
the powers Lord Warwick had gathered. George of Clarence was out of
favour; it was whispered that Lord Warwick planned to make him king
once King Edward was overthrown. Middleham was empty of Nevilles,
for my lady and Anne had gone to Warwick Castle to join Isabel. I wondered where in all this Joscelyn was, and my heart was not only cold,
but heavy as lead for him.

In January, a few days after Twelfth Night, when the mummers
who played the Three Wise Men had laid away their fine robes, and
the Star of gilt wire had been wrapped in cloth and stored for the next
year, Lady Cowley had a fall. It was no further than her own length, for
she tripped on a flagstone as she was trying to hobble out to the privy,
nobody having heard her bell. She lay for an hour and more on the
ground, out in a walled yard, before Nance her maid found her, soaked
with rain and groaning.

I was called to her where they had put her, on the floor of the parlour, a folded coat under her head. She had swooned with pain at being
lifted so I was able to examine her quickly and find out the injury. Her
left thigh-bone was broken, snapped clean. I sent for a straight stout
ash-stick to be brought quickly, and tied it to the leg with strips of linen

wound round and round, so that it should not move. I knew she came round as I was doing this, and suffered, by the clay-whiteness of her face, but she made no sound until it was done; then she opened her eyes, looking full at me, and said, 'I shall die of this, daughter.'

And die she did, not of the leg but of a heavy rheum on the lungs that set in. She was not an old woman, only a little over forty. I and the servants grieved for her (though glad she had been taken out of her pain) but her family did not, it seemed. Tom grumbled that the death would put paid to the festival of Plough Monday, when we were to have enjoyed all sorts of merry-making, the Plough Procession with cow-horn blowing, and the most comical lad in the district mumming as the Bessy, gowned and hooded in a fox's skin, dancing with skirts kilted up to show the bullock's tail sewn to his breeches. Now all this was not to be, and there were mutterings that the poor lady might have chosen another time to die, such as Maundy Thursday.

We were all about her when she died, as the custom is: her family, all but a married daughter too great with child to travel, and the servants. While she could still speak, after she had blessed us all and promised to intercede for us in Paradise, she pointed to her small jewel-box. From it her weak fingers lifted a necklet of blue carven beads with a small crucifix hanging from it, and a silver ring set with coloured stones.

'For Yolande,' she said, very low, but loud enough for all about the bed to hear. Her glazing eyes sought for me, and I rose from my knees and went to her, touching her hands. She smiled and held the things towards me, and, after a few minutes, died.

The women had scarcely laid her out in her best gown before Joan and Margret sidled into the room where I was stitching mourning-bands. Joan prodded Margret, who said, 'Yon should be ours.'

'What?'

'The necklace and the ring. Our mother promised us.'

'When—lately?'

They exchanged glances, and I knew that they had not been promised lately, or ever. I said, 'Your mother gave me them on her death-bed, and I must obey her wish. There must be other things for you to have.'

'Father's taken the box,' Joan said sullenly. 'Likely he'll give the best of the stuff to our Kate and our Joyce, them being older than us. We should have had the ring and the necklace.'

'We should have had 'em,' Margret echoed.

I could have given in, and said, 'Take them,' but I was not minded to do any such thing to please this sour pair. 'I shall keep them to remember your mother by,' I said, and went on with my sewing. They stayed, watching me silently. Just before they slipped out Joan turned and asked me, 'How did you make her give 'em you?'

'What do you mean?'

Joan gave her sharp giggle and they scampered off.

I put away the jewels, which were pretty but not worth much money, to wear when I was no longer mourning. The whole thing had left my head when, going into the kitchens one day, I came suddenly face to face with Daft Alice. I may well have startled her, but surely not enough for her to blench and cross herself, and jump back from me. I beckoned her, and saw her cower.

'What ails you, Alice?' I shouted slowly, that being the only way to talk to the poor deaf thing. 'Why did you bless yourself? Are you afraid of me?'

Her lips moved in a sort of gibber, before she got out, in her flat, toneless voice, 'They say tha'rt a witch.'

'*What*? Who says this?'

She looked round nervously. 'T'others. They say tha put a charm on our missis. To get . . . yon.' She glanced at my hands, and the mystery fell into place. Joan and Margret had been putting it about that I had bewitched their mother. Anger boiled up in me, but it would not be policy to let it show, since witches were supposed to rave and curse at people. In a patient shout I told her, 'You must say this is untrue, Alice. Lady Cowley gave me the trinkets of her own will. This is a spiteful tale someone has put about. Do you understand?'

She nodded, but there was doubt in her pale eyes. From that time I began to see sly glances directed at me, and the witch-warding sign, two fingers pointed behind my back, and even in church they covertly watched me from behind clasped hands to see whether I was saying the same prayers as other people, or avoiding the holy names.

I was bitterly unhappy under such suspicion, having lost my only friend in the household, and that other one, so much more than friend, with the malice of those two little toads always needling me; not that I dared call them toads outright, for such poor harmless creatures were thought to be the Devil's playmates and the familiars of witches. Tib, the old mother of most of the kitchen cats, was uncommonly fond of me, because I never gave her blows or kicks, and nursed her on my lap when I was helping with table-jobs. But from the time the looks and the pointing started I kept clear of her, in case some fool should call her my familiar and stone or drown her. So my wretched life went on, through bleak January and February, day after day, while I longed for the soft willow catkins to dangle over the becks and the young lambs to be safe from snow. It helped my state to go up to the fields with Tom and do what I could for the lambs and their mothers; I thought it made him like me a little better, rather more than a yard-dog or the boy who scared birds, which was a grain of comfort among all that cold.

March came in like a lion, as the saying was, with wild winds and a bleakness worse than Christmas had been. But a bit of news came with it, from a travelling pedlar on the road early in the year, who called on us on his way westwards to Lancashire. The King was at York, he said, picking up provisions, and his men were scouring the countryside offering rewards for the capture of Lord Warwick and George of Clarence.

'The Great Rebels, they calls 'em. But none lets on to know where they are. Not at Middleham, for sure, not Sheriff Hutton, so it's hide, fox, and follow.' His shoulders shook. 'If you can lay hands on one or t'other you're a rich man, Squire Cowley, and no mistake. Gold, a purse of gold on each one's head, the Kingmaker's and boy George's.'

I felt a kind of shiver of excitement at that, as an enclosed nun might at rumours of the stirring world reaching her cell. And it was true: history and life were moving again, with the sap of spring.

I had caught my first bad cold of the winter near the end of March, and gone to bed early to snatch a few precious hours of rest before Tom should come up and start to snore and roll about. I took with me a decoction of dried horehound and hot water, and from the warmth of this and the welcome peace of having the bed to myself I was soon drowsy. I must have slept for an hour before a voice woke me, the servant Betty calling.

'Mistress, get up! T'maister wants thee in Hall.'

I dragged myself up from warm depths, asking sleepily what the matter was.

'Theer's a gentleman, come half an hour sin'. Summat to do wi' Earl Warwick.'

Confused, sleepy and full of my cold, I dragged myself out of bed and into my discarded gown and coif, and trailed downstairs, snuffling, too stupid to wonder who the visitor could be, unless it were someone offering us a reward for my lord's head, in which case I was not likely to be of much help. I heard low voices from the Hall, as we called it, though it was no more than a high-beamed parlour.

Two men sat by the fire, a flask of wine and cups between them. Both turned as I entered. One was my father-in-law, and the other was Joscelyn.

He rose from his chair and came to where I stood, unable to move, and bent his knee and kissed my hand. Sir Thomas was saying, '. . . my son's wife, Mistress Cowley.'

'Your servant, madame,' Joscelyn said, very formally. I knew that he had expected to meet me, had said nothing about our acquaintance, would say nothing. If it had been startling for him to see me a worn, winter-weary farmer's wife, with a red running nose, in a thick crumpled gown, instead of the willing lover he had left in the tower room, he showed no sign of it, nor seemed to notice my quickened breathing. For me, I felt the violent beating of my heart must be seen through my bodice.

He drew up a stool for me to join them by the fire, and Sir Thomas poured a cup of wine for me, which I drank thankfully.

'This is Sir Joscelyn Conyers,' he said, 'on t'run from King's troops. He asked about for any that might be Warwick's men in t'dale, and they sent him to me, as was reet. I've towd him he may bide wi' us as long as he likes. There's to be no clack about it, only that he's a cousin bound for t'south. I want thee to make him welcome.'

'Oh, I shall, sir,' I said, 'very welcome.' While he prattled on to Joscelyn about his long friendship with Lord Warwick, going into every trifle he remembered about it, and of my own connection with the Nevilles, I seemed not to look at Joscelyn yet looked at him all the time. He was leaner than he had been and there was a shadow of gold beard on the line of his jaw; his clothes were damp and muddied with travel. The bright look he used to have was a little dimmed: I liked him even better so, and longed to put out my hand and touch him. But all I could do was sit there, occasionally mopping my nose with a soaked kerchief, and ask him such things as where my lord and Lord Clarence were now.

'At Warwick Castle, I hope—they were bound there when I last heard. The Countess and the lady Anne are there, with the Duchess of Clarence, Lady Isabel that was, waiting daily for her heir to be born.'

Poor Isabel. So she was not to be queen after all. 'And King Edward?' I asked.

Joscelyn threw me a look that might have meant anything. 'Hot on the trail of all of us who were Warwick's men. He talks much of mercy, but I would be the last to expect much.' Suddenly he gave an uncontrollable yawn, and I realized that he was tired out. I left them to rouse the servants and give orders for a chamber to be made ready for him, with a good fire and plenty of sheets and blankets. Then I returned and said good night to him, assuring him that the soldier and page who were his companions were comfortably bedded down, and all three horses stabled. He thanked me with a weary smile which was as precious as gold to me, who had never thought to see his smile again.

My sleep that night was utterly deep and peaceful; when I woke my cold had miraculously almost disappeared. I put on a good dress of blue wool (not my best, for that would have given too much away) and a coif that showed some of my hair, and went downstairs to a day that seemed all brightness, in spite of the grey skies.

It was almost dinner-time, late morning, when I saw him walking in the garden. Tom, who had not been in the house the previous night, but up in the fields tending to a ewe who was having a difficult birth, was back with the flock, and Sir Thomas out with his bailiff. I ran out and caught up with Joscelyn, steadying my run to a sober walk as I approached him. He turned and smiled, a discreet polite smile as of a guest to his hostess.

I said bluntly, 'You knew you would find me here, and yet stayed.'

'Yes.'

'But why—after what happened, what you said?'

'Because I heard from a well-wisher that the King has taken a pleasant fancy to have my head. Not merely a Conyers head, but mine in particular. Now it seems to me that this fancy has much to do with a certain night when I met His Grace in a lady's chamber. Edward is not a cruel man, but there are matters that stir him up more than wars. Blows to his pride, for one.'

I began to see. 'You were there when he failed to make a conquest. Well, I did tell you! And it took the King hunting for your head to make you believe it.'

'Your pardon, sweet. I was a fool, I deserve hanging. I knew in my heart you were no wanton, but I was jealous-mad to find him there. I would go down on my knees and kiss the hem of your gown, if someone were not watching us with interest from a window. No, don't look. We must behave like courteous strangers. Show me whatever there is to see about the farm.'

We inspected horses, pigs, cattle in the shippon, Joscelyn asking questions as though he had never seen such animals before, and between questions telling me that he intended to ride on towards Warwick as soon as he and his men had dined, while the sky was still clear. I wanted to beg him to stay, take hold of him and plead, but I had to keep my demeanour calm for fear of watching eyes, even the dull incurious eyes of such men as were about the yard. And it would be of no good at all, I knew. If he said that he would go, he would, whatever I said, unless the hand of God intervened.

As it did. The clear sky grew darker, until it was the leaden grey that presages snow, and the air colder. As we began to make our way back to the house the first flakes fell.

So Joscelyn and the men Dickon and Guy had no choice but to stay, for snow in those parts fell heavy and lay in deep drifts, too high for riders to get through. It should have been a happy time, seeing him about the place, eating and talking with him, yet it was not. He was uneasy and restless, anxious to leave; and we both felt the stress of being constantly under the eyes of others, unable to exchange a word of our true feelings. Joan and Margret tailed about after Joscelyn, in their sly way, as though he could possibly want their company. Sir Thomas treated him with bluff friendliness. But Tom, I could see, resented him as a man handsomer, more learned, more noble in every way than himself—and more desirable to a woman. I had never thought he cared a pin for me as anything but a household chattel, yet now he looked askance at me and snapped at me for the least thing; very unlike his one-time amiable self. A feeling colder than the snow and frost outside crept into Cowleys, a feeling of evil; and though I dreaded the thought of losing Joscelyn's company, I longed for him to go and escape whatever danger might threaten him.

After three days the snow lessened and a bitter thaw began. I heard Joscelyn telling Sir Thomas that he would leave next day, unless the frost came back. A desperation grew in me to speak with him alone and tell him all my heart, just once, for the last time, it might be. I determined to bring it about, somehow, and when a woman makes such a resolve for love's sake, she keeps it. I got from the kitchen a shirt that had been washed for him, and took it upstairs myself, knowing him to be there in the chamber which was down a little passage and a few stairs.

He unlatched the door at my knock. When he saw me his face grew stern.

'You should not be here.'

'I brought your clean linen.'

'I thank you, but go now.'

'Only a word!'

'Yolande, don't put us both to the torture. You know how I want . . . it can't be. No, let me go.' He tried to shake me off, but I held him as a drowning person holds to a spar, and with a sort of despairing groan he let his arms go round me, and we clung together as though nothing should part us, his mouth on mine for only the second time in our loving. There was a flame of joy in my heart, and a longing that could not be satisfied then, yet for all that I was like a long-banished traveller come home at last.

Suddenly I felt Joscelyn's hold on me change. He raised his head sharply, listening. I heard nothing—then, the scutter of feet. I whispered, 'What . . . ?'

'Hush. You must go.'

'Was it *them*?'

'The wenches. I think so. Go!'

At supper I feared the salt beef would choke me, so tight my throat felt. Joscelyn seemed as calm as usual, talking with Dickon and Guy about the way they would take to Warwick, the safest houses on the way to make for. Tom described in great detail to his father the progress of the sick ewe. The behaviour of Joan and Margret puzzled me. They seemed in a plot to play some silly wooing game with Joscelyn. First one, then the other, would ask him a question half-smothered in giggles.

'Will you send me a fairing back from Warwick?'

'And me.'

Joscelyn answered politely enough. 'The times are not fit for sending messengers on ladies' errands, mistress.'

'Then will you cut off a lock each of your hair, to make rings with?'

'You could buy better rings than that from a packman.'

'Oh no, because your hair's finer than gold, isn't it, Margret. I like a yellow-haired man, don't you, Yolande?'

I said I had no preference one way or the other.

'Oh,' Joan said, 'that's strange, seeing as yours is so dun—you ought to like the colour that's opposite.'

'Get on with your supper,' I said sharply. 'Sir Joscelyn needs to sleep early tonight.'

At that they fell into a fit of stupid laughter, so that even their heedless father banged on the table for them to stop.

I slept little that night, thinking of the danger Joscelyn was going into once he left the shelter of our roof. He might be captured by the King's men, or run into a battle, or fall by the wayside in new snow. Staring into the dark, very still by Tom's side, I thought it unlikely that I should ever see him again, and my life stretched before me, emptiness. Perhaps the last sight of him I should get would be at dawn, when he left. Thinking these sad, bitter thoughts, I drifted into sleep.

When I woke, heavy and unrested, Tom was gone from the bed. Grey light filtered through the casement. I started up and looked out.

Dawn had broken, the men were about their work, and Joscelyn was surely gone. I dressed in a hurry, for once not noticing the cold, and ran downstairs. Peg, the old servant, was cleaning, sweeping up rushes from the floor in the Hall. I shouted at her, for she was nearly as deaf as Alice, asking whether Sir Joscelyn had left or not.

'Aye, an hour and more sin'.'

So nobody had wakened me, and he had left without a goodbye.

'Mistress.' It was Sir Thomas's voice, from the doorway, where he stood with Tom behind him. Both of them looked grim, Tom more surly-faced than I had ever seen him. 'Get out,' Sir Thomas told Peg, who gathered up her broom and basket and sped away as fast as her old legs would go. The two of them closed on me. I saw that behind them Joan and Margret were lurking, and I knew in an instant what was coming, though not the form it would take.

'We've been hearing things,' Sir Thomas said. 'About evil and for-nication, and all manner of ills, between you and yon knight.'

'*What*? There was nothing . . .'

'Our Joan and our Margret witnessed it, in the man's bedcham-ber.' For once he was talking like a gentleman and a justice of the peace, as he was, rather than in the country manner he affected. 'Lewd embraces and hugglings and fond words, not for t'first time. What hast to say to that?'

I could only brazen it out. 'Rubbish, twaddle. They saw a kiss of friendship—*not* in Sir Joscelyn's chamber—and made the worst of it. I only bade him God-speed, in case I missed his going this morning—as I did.'

'Friendship, between two who were strangers till two-three days sin'?'

'We had met at Middleham, briefly.'

'You never said that to us.'

'It was hardly worth the mention. I . . . hardly knew him at first, when he came here.'

Tom stepped forward, his look ugly. 'You knew him a' reet, wife. Well enow for kissing and more, and maybe well enow to lay a bewitchment on me that we should never have childher, for else why art barren, a healthy young lass? Nay, tha put the horns on me, for thy secret pleasure.'

'What secret pleasure have I had, since we've been wed? What pleasure of any kind, come to that?'

'Don't thee talk wicked!' Sir Thomas shouted. 'What about the time at Middleham, back in summer? Was it Lady Anne who called thee there, or him, yon pretty lad—tell me that?'

Before I could answer Joan had pushed forward Margret, who piped, 'She got our mother's jewels by sorcery, that we should have had.'

Joan added, 'She put a charm on Tom's ewe, and it died. I heard her.'

I ran forward to box her ears for the lie, and found myself gripped by the two men, my arms forced painfully behind my back until I cried out.

'You'll come wi' us before you do more harm,' Sir Thomas said. Between them they frog-marched me out of the house, across the yard, I stumbling and slipping on the cobbles in my cloth house-shoes, the girls skipping behind with cries of glee.

'Where are you taking me?' I managed to ask, ceasing to struggle because they were so strong, the two iron-handed men.

'Where you'll not get out easy,' Tom answered. They propelled me towards a barn where we kept hay stored. Now it had been all eaten by the animals kept through the winter, and would not be used again until the next haymaking. They thrust me into it and Tom whipped out a length of rope. I thought he was going to thrash me, but he tied it round my bent-back arms and my ankles, so that I was helpless.

'That's t'way they tie witches,' Sir Thomas informed me, 'mostly when they're swum in t'pond. Maybe they'll do that to thee, eh?'

Something other than my own fear was on me. 'Where is Sir Joscelyn?' I asked, afraid of the answer.

'On his way. Our quarrel's not wi' him, it's wi' thee, for robbing us of heirs, and I'd not take a man of Warwick's. Now, bide there, and say some prayers, if you know any but those to summon Owd Nick.' He pushed Tom out; my husband gave no backward look at me. But Joan and Margret ran up to me and began to pinch me, hard and cruelly, laughing all the time.

Then the barn door was slammed, and bolted from the outside.

9

Thus began the longest day of my life: I sometimes thought, the last. At the start of it I wished very much that they had let me break my fast before imprisoning me, yet perhaps it was better that I was so empty, because my mind was clearer. Somehow they had combined to put a charge of witchcraft on me, and they would not take it off lightly, even if I could offer any proof of innocence. It came to me now that this had been building up ever since my marriage, a slow resentment against me, from Tom, because I bore him no children and because he sensed, clod though he was, that I was not the jolly wife he had expected; from his father, on the first count and because he had been worked on by Joan and Margret; and from them, because they had hated me from the start, mostly from jealousy.

So, I was doomed, but to what? Witchcraft was a grim charge. Long ago, before my birth, the Duchess of Gloucester had been condemned to life imprisonment for it. But she had been noble. An ordinary person might be lucky enough only to have the Service of Commination read against him or her in church, and be made to do public penance. Or worse, set up in a public place and killed with the hurling of stones, rocks, or whatever objects favoured by those who came to jeer.

Or worst of all, burned. It happened, not so much in our own country as in France, to heretics and to those the

Church suspected of querying its doctrines. Joan the Maid had gone to the stake for hearing heavenly voices, among other offences (such as winning victories for France against England, for which my lord Warwick's wise and witty father-in-law had been one of her main accusers). My mind faltered away from the thought of burning. It must be the most terrible pain the human body could suffer. The executioner was supposed to strangle the victim before the fire took hold—but if the cord were not tight enough, or if his hand faltered . . .

I would not think of it. Instead I planned what I would do when they took me out and put me on trial. There would be no sacred oath I would not take to save myself. Our parish priest was a dim-eyed old man, but surely he would be convinced if I undertook to say every prayer in the Psalter on my knees before him, begging Our Lady for the gift of a child for Tom. I would do that, anything, for I was young and life was strong in me.

Yet, perhaps I was not meant to keep my life. Somewhere it had gone awry, when through my own folly I was bound to Tom before I had seen Joscelyn, my love and my liking, the one to whom my heart was tied. Then I had betrayed Tom by my words, though no other way. So for all that perhaps I must die, though it seemed rather unfair, measured against greater sins. At least I was being given time to think, to make my peace with God and pray for help; and that was something, when I thought of those who had been dragged from their homes to sudden death.

Before very long it began to be difficult for me to think clearly, even of such terrible matters, for I was too uncomfortable. I lay on the hard floor of the barn, nothing between me and the chilly earth. Over in the corner was a pile of hay. If I could have got to it I could have lain soft and warm, compared with the bed I had. But though I managed to roll over and propel myself a few inches, I could make no more progress because my bound arms got in the way. The rope was cutting into them through the stuff of my sleeves, and into my bare legs. Stiffness crept over me, and pain spread through my strained shoulders.

I was very hungry. A few yards away there lay a turnip, left over from food for the cows which had been taken from the barn to slaughter—as I might well be myself. It was old and mouldy-looking, but a few mouthfuls of it would have staved off the weakness I began to feel. And over by the far wall was a water-trough. The water would be stale now, but not too stale to drink. Now I knew what the priests meant by that particular Hell-torment in which the sinner lies unable to move, held down by fiends, with food and drink just out of reach . . .

There was little noise from outside. The yard was quiet at this time of year, and the barn lay beyond it, next to a piece of rough land. If I heard a human voice or footsteps I would shout, and hope that whoever answered was not under Sir Thomas's orders.

But no one came. Far off I heard squeals from the pig-pen—that would be our old boar, fighting again. Once there was a clatter as though of buckets, someone filling at the well. Through the high slit-windows I watched the light change through the hours, from early grey to something brighter, but never snow-light; and the drip of the thaw went on steadily, with an occasional slide of melted snow. So the travellers would not be hindered on their way, and at least I could be thankful for that.

I thought, hoped, someone might think to come and give me food. Surely the servants would have asked where I was, and one of them would take pity on me, even secretly. The women had always seemed to like and respect me. I had never put on airs, that I knew of, and had learned humbly and willingly the household skills they had taught me when I first came to Cowleys. But dinner-hour was surely long over, and my hopes began to fade.

As the hours went on I knew nothing but cold and aching stiffness. I prayed that someone would come, if only to take me to a different place, a different prison. Perhaps they meant me to die there, as sheep die in snowdrifts, and at least it would be a better death than the fire.

Somehow, even in the pain and the cold, I drifted into sleep. Or a kind of sleep, with visions coming before my eyes, seeming so real that I could have touched them if my hands had been free. And then I would start awake, and the misery would take hold of me again.

After the evening shadows began to fall I believe I swooned for a long time. When I came to myself it was quite dark in the barn.

But not silent. Tiny squeaks and scamperings told me that I was not alone; the rats had come out, and were moving, near me. I saw their eyes gleaming against the dark.

I was very afraid then. After the winter they would be hungry, and a hungry rat cares nothing whether its food be dead or alive. Already they were eating something—the turnip I craved, or some other vegetable scraps. If I had ever prayed in my life, I prayed then; and an answer came to me. Rats fear two things, other than dogs—one is fire and the other noise. At least I could make a noise.

I began to sing at the top of my voice, anything that came into my head: the whole of the Mass, chanted to made-up tunes, the ballad of Sir Cawline and the Elf King, *The shepherd upon a hill he sat,* and an old song of Robin Hood. Never was such a jumble of sacred and profane as that wild singing of mine. While I kept it up the ring of eyes came no nearer—as soon as I stopped, some moved. I wondered how long my voice would last until it cracked from hoarseness. But my only hope was to go on.

> When the nightingale sings,
>   The woods wax green,
> Leaf and grass and blossom springs,
>   In April . . .

If only I might have a drink to moisten my throat, that felt as dry as leather. How did the song go on? My memory seemed to be failing.

In April . . .

Then, before I could creak out any more nonsense, there came a sound I could hardly believe—the bolts of the barn door drawn back. As the door creaked open the eyes fled, the feet scampered back to hole and nest.

I asked quaveringly, 'Who's there?'

And Joscelyn's voice said, 'A friend.'

What I said, or babbled, I can't remember, but I do remember him soothing me with words as though I were a terrified horse, as he worked with his dagger on the rope that bound me. Some light had come in with him, for the night was starry, so that he could see well enough not to cut my flesh accidentally. He was swift and skilful, free-ing me within moments.

With freedom came a fearful, agonizing cramp through all my body. What with the pain, and the relief, I wept sorely, lying there sup-ported in his arms.

'There,' he said, as gently as a mother to her child, 'hush, love. It will soon pass. Bide your time. If I rub your wrists and your ankles the pain will go sooner.' And indeed, I felt it ebbing at the touch of his fingers.

When I could control my voice, I asked him how he had found me.

'By your sweet carolling, how else?'

'You could hear it—out there?'

'I should think they heard it in York. No, a lie—I heard it because I was listening for any sound that might lead me to you.'

'But how . . .'

'Never mind questions, now, sweetheart. Tell me when you feel you can move, and we'll get you on your feet.'

Slowly, painfully, I managed to bend my stiff limbs until I was sit-ting up, then kneeling, and with Joscelyn holding me tightly I stood at last. Supporting me, he made me take a step or two, moving even nearer to the door.

He said, 'Listen. We must be quiet and quick. My horse is tethered on the other side of the rick. There's light enough to see, and I shall not let go of you if your footing fails. Would you rather I carried you?'

'No—the cramp is going. I can feel my feet now.'

We left that dreary prison, moving very slowly at first, then faster as my strength came back. The house was in darkness; I guessed they were all in bed by now, but Joscelyn whispered to me not to speak, for safety's sake. At last, with an occasional stumble, we reached the rick, and there, tethered to a waggon, was the dark shape of Joscelyn's horse, Palamon the great roan. As though I weighed no more than a feather Joscelyn hoisted me up on Palamon's back, then mounted himself, holding me in front of him, while the horse stood patient, as though he knew he must not greet his master aloud. He seemed to know the way through the dark countryside. So we travelled on, my abused body comforted by the warmth and strength of Joscelyn. It was like a journey in a happy dream, from Hell to Paradise.

This was the story he told me, as we rode.

On the way southward from Cowleys that morning he had been troubled in his mind. Both Tom and Sir Thomas had been about when he left, silent and surly in their manner. Neither had taken a cup of ale with him, as was usual with a departing guest, and when, disappointed not to see me, he had given them a message of regards and felicitations for me, a strange look had passed between them. He was certain, then, that our unlucky embrace had been seen and reported.

He was glad to be on his way, yet uneasy. Of course there would be reproaches for me, and an ugly scene, perhaps a beating. It was not unusual for men to beat wives who had been caught straying, and he guessed that I was not the sort who would allow herself to be badly hurt. And yet . . . I had told him nothing of the witchcraft lies, but he had sensed something, so close were our hearts and thoughts. Now, making good going over roads freed from ice, he felt some force pulling him back, willing him to stop. But how could he, when they had been so delayed already?

It was decided for him. About noon young Guy's horse went lame. They walked it to the nearest smithy—fortunately in the village they were approaching—where the smith examined a foreleg, and found a sharp flint painfully wedged between hoof and foot. He took it out, but there was soreness left. Even with the help of a strong ointment he kept for such slight wounds, he said that the horse must rest for some hours, or even overnight, unless his rider wished to hire another.

The travellers exchanged glances. All knew that they might hire a horse easily enough, but when might it be returned? Joscelyn made up his mind; he told them that while Guy's horse rested he was going back to Cowleys for something he had left there. A jewel, one he prized. Dickon and Guy were to remain at the little alehouse that passed for an inn, and he would return to them there as soon as he could. They were not happy about it, but he was master.

And so he rode the long miles back, promising Palamon a rest and a feed at the end of the journey.

He reached Cowleys well before dusk, the going being mostly downhill. Neither father nor son was in the house, to his relief. An old servant, Ezra Wright, opened the door. Joscelyn sensed something strange in his manner, more than surprise. Sir Thomas and Master Cowley had gone to market and would be back soon, he said. And Mistress Cowley? She was ill, keeping her bed. Ah, Joscelyn said, that was bad news. He went out into the yard where Palamon was standing, found a groom, and gave instructions for the horse to be looked to, taking care to shout and generally make his presence known.

Ezra somewhat grudgingly offered him ale and food. While it was being prepared he went upstairs to search, as he said, for the jewel he had lost. To his great relief Joan and Margret were not in sight. For form's sake he went into the chamber where he had slept; then, much more quietly, tapped at the door of mine, and getting no answer looked in.

It was empty, the bed made. He had known that was what he would find. He returned to the parlour, cheerfully produced the thin gold chain with its pendant jewel which he had with forethought concealed in his pouch, and expressed joy at having found it, as it had been a treasured gift from his father. Then he dealt with the refreshments, ably enough, wondering what to do, anxious to leave before the men of the house came home, yet more anxious to find out what had become of me.

When he could delay no more he called for Palamon to be brought round for him, thanked Ezra for hospitality, mounted and rode away; only far enough to be out of sight of the house. Then, very inconspicuously in the gathering gloom, he rode back and tethered Palamon where he could not be seen, behind the high rick, and set out on foot, making for the domestic buildings at the back. In the kitchens there were lights and movements: supper preparing. Patiently, quietly he waited. And at last someone came out with a pail, crossing the yard near him. He recognized Daft Alice, whom he knew from the constant teasing inflicted on her by Joan and Margret.

When she was close enough he jumped out of the shadows and seized her, stopping her scream with an arm across her mouth. For all her struggles she was so small and light that he was able to carry her bodily away from the kitchens, far beyond the herb garden, for he knew of her deafness and needed to talk to her.

The poor creature quivered in his arms like a rabbit, sure that she was to be raped, murdered or both. When he stopped and set her down he held her firmly, but so that she could feel his grip was not cruel. It was not quite yet so dark but she could see his hair, that silver-gilt hair which distinguished him from other men. When he thought, by her trembling growing less, that she knew him for the knight who had been civil to her during his stay, he spoke her name, very loudly, close to her ear, and asked her to nod if she understood him. The hesitant nod came.

'Where is your mistress?' he asked, still loudly and slowly, so that she could watch his lips. 'Mistress Cowley—where is she?'

Alice stared at him, seeming to understand but too afraid to answer. He asked the question again, adding, 'I am her friend.'

At last the girl said, 'Locked up.'

'Where?'

'I mustn't say.'

'Yes, you must. Nobody shall know you told me.' He was beginning to despair of her stubbornness when she said, 'Out here.'

He surveyed the many outbuildings of the farm, stables, byres, pig-pens, dovecot, sheds used for one purpose or another. Only their outlines were visible; there might be people in some of them for all he knew. As he relaxed his hold on her Alice broke away and ran back towards the kitchens.

Joscelyn let her go. He would get no more out of her, and his only course was to reconnoitre as quietly as he could, like a spy sent out to the enemy's line. How long it would have taken him to find me who can say, if my desperate singing had not drawn him to the outlying barn. For the first time in my life I was grateful to rats.

We made slow progress on that winding way by night, Joscelyn sometimes stopping to rest Palamon from his double burden. 'Courage, old lad. When we find our beds, so shall you.' The sky was beginning to lighten when we reached the alehouse by the river where Joscelyn had left his men. Guy and Dickon, roused from sleep, stared unbelievingly at me, but Joscelyn promised to explain when we were rested. There were no beds in the room where they had lain, only straw to be spread for myself; and so I spent the first of many nights by Joscelyn's side, near yet apart, happier on that coarse straw, with his cloak over me, than ever I had been in a fine bed with linen sheets.

The next day we held a conference. We had days of travel ahead of us to Warwick Castle and safety, hard days for men and horses. And women? 'We'd no thought of travelling with women,' Dickon said, none too amiably. He was a hard-visaged soldier of middle age, well aware that I was a wife, and, I thought, not much convinced by Joscelyn's story about my false imprisonment (for what, he had not said; it was dangerous to mention witchcraft without knowing your hearer's views on it). But because he was a Conyers man and Joscelyn his captain, he could only accept. He pointed out that we should look a strange band, two men, a boy and a woman, riding so far with so few goods, and added somewhat sourly that my husband might have sent word out for me, even as far down the Wharfe as we had come.

I said to Joscelyn, 'Then we must be two men and two boys. We'll go by Skipton town, only a mile or two from here, and buy clothing for me so that I can ride man-fashion. You remember the morning when we first met?'

'When you fell off your horse,' he said, trying not to laugh.

'I can stay in the saddle as well as anybody. So, is it agreed?'

We turned aside into Skipton town, where I found it strange to see again the round towers of the Castle, and Barden on its height, and remembered my young half-brother, smuggled away to a shepherd family—where was he now? We seemed a family born to disguises.

We found my own disguise in the market square, at a stall which sold clothes ready made-up, obtained from various sources—a servant selling his master's cast-offs, a widow disposing of her late husband's clothes, mis-fitting garments, and such-like. Joscelyn said darkly that he hoped none of them had come from a plague-house, and that he didn't at all fancy my wearing dead men's clothes; but I answered that we must take a chance.

We bought some reasonably clean-looking and fresh-smelling things: a brown doublet, pleated in front, to conceal my bosom, a pair of good woollen hose, black, a thin cambric shirt, a cloak, a cap, and, best of all, a pair of stout leather boots reaching up to my thighs. Josce-lyn did the buying, on behalf of a mythical page of his. I noticed with pleasure how instantly everyone obeyed him, and how nobody dared question his word or bargain with him.

At the lodging we took that night I changed out of my woman's gear, which I rolled up in a bundle for disposal by the wayside. The new clothes fitted me passably well, better in places than Ned's had once done. I called Joscelyn to see me. 'Do I look like a Warwick's man now?'

'Like a very pretty fellow. Too pretty, still.'

'My hair. Will you cut it?' I sat on a stool and held out my locks, that flowed down past my shoulders now I had taken the matronly pins out.

He sighed. 'A pity. But I must.' With his sharp dagger, hurting me a little, he shore the hair off level with my ears. Curiously regretful (for I had never thought it one of my beauties) I watched it fall thick on the ground. 'A Bronze Fleece,' he said, 'worthy any Jason's voyage.'

There was a mirror in the best room of the inn, dark and small, but enough to show me my new self. I was surprised to find that I liked it better than the old one. Now that I was no longer supposed to be a woman the low-growing peak of my hair was not offensive, and the short curls that covered my head were actually pleasing. My thick dark eyebrows came into their own at last, for a pair of thin plucked ones would have looked ridiculous.

I presented myself to the three men. Dickon stared pointedly at my legs, on view for the first time, and I could see that he thought me a brazen piece, but would not say so for fear of Joscelyn. Guy whistled and said, 'Cock's blood! A miracle, swive me else.' Joscelyn took hold of his ear, hard and painfully, making him cry out.

'We'll not have any words of that sort in Mistress Cowley's com-pany. She may look like a lad now, but she's still a noble lady and under our protection. Keep your oaths to yourself in her hearing, and your conduct what a queen might expect from her henchmen. The old days of chivalry may be dead, but by St Bavon the thing itself is alive, and you'll remember it, friend Guy, or feel the flat of my sword.' At that they both looked sheepish. But from that moment I never heard a rough word or saw a coarse gesture from either, on that long journey where we were usually obliged to share sleeping quarters.

As for Joscelyn, he conducted himself like old Chaucer's gentle knight, giving no sign in the men's presence that we were anything to each other, and only when we were, rarely, alone, acknowledging by look or touch the great loving-kindness that was between us. I have only known two men in all my life that might be called the flower of courtesy; Lord Warwick was one, and my love Joscelyn the other.

A day came, when we had travelled as far as Cheshire, more than half our journey, when I discovered what I had dreaded, that it was with me after the way of women, just a month having passed since the last time. I was cast down with the thought of how I should deal with it, or continue to travel, wearing my masculine clothes. Then it came to me that I should tell Joscelyn, privately, and ask his help. Frankly he gave it to me, telling me to go and buy what I needed, making as little of the matter as though he had been a physician. To Dickon and Guy he said that I was not well and must ride gently and sleep alone until I recovered. Whatever they thought they knew better than to cast a leering look at me. Within four days it was over, without need for me to blush for it once. This thing is carefully not mentioned in romances of disguised ladies riding after their lords into battle. I wonder if the men who write such poems ever give a thought to such a dilemma?

The weather was now, at the end of March, so mild and spring-like that it was hard to believe in the melting snow and raw-cold we had left in Yorkshire. My heart rose to be back in fair Warwickshire, riding through the market-bustle of Coventry, past the fortress of Kenilworth, and at last into Warwick.

As we drew near to the Castle Joscelyn's eager look faded. 'Not enough guards,' he said.

Dickon nodded. 'That's so. But maybe my lord has them within, for defence.'

'It's not his way to stand siege. Guy, ride ahead and ask who's there—and put your cloak back so that your badge can be seen.' We watched the boy approach the sentry by the gatehouse that guarded the moat, reply to his challenge and talk with him. He rode back slowly, his face foretelling his news.

'They're gone, all of them. My lord, my lady, the Lady Anne and the Duke and Duchess of Clarence. Days ago.'

Joscelyn's face darkened with disappointment. 'Gone where?'

'I don't know, master.'

'Then go back and find out. No, I shall go myself.' We followed him, listening to him identifying himself to the sentry, and asking that he and his men might enter and take rest and refreshment. Without hindrance we rode across the drawbridge, past more sentries, up to the main gateway of the Castle, where, as Joscelyn again identified us, the portcullis was raised and we went in.

The peaceful castle I had known showed everywhere signs of dis-order. Garments and objects were scattered about the floor, half-packed chests and bales had been left behind in hasty flight; in fireplaces logs had burnt through and the fires remained unkindled. A soldier offered to find Dame Catherine for us. Lady Warwick's chief gentlewoman was in charge of the domestic arrangements, it seemed.

Within a few minutes she came down, a stately figure, grave-faced as she greeted Joscelyn.

'Quite true, sir, they are gone—almost a week ago now. My lord heard by his spies that the King has sent out commissions of array all over England, and is marching south himself at the head of twenty thousand men. Did you see nothing of his armies as you rode down?'

'We came by ways I know well, not by the high roads, madame. I heard his forces were mainly in the west, sent to cut off Lord Warwick from his lands there. So, fortunately, we missed them. But where has he gone?'

'To France—from any port he could reach. My lady begged him to leave her and the Ladies Anne and Isabel here, and trust to the King's mercy, but he would not. They had waited for him for so long, and then to be bundled out in such haste . . . And they were not fit to travel, especially poor Duchess Isabel, so near her time, and ill with it even on land. How will she do if there are storms, or seafights? Only one maid with them and she a wretched weak thing!' Dame Catherine looked near to tears, her face lined and heavy with sleeplessness. Joscelyn spoke to her consolingly, but I knew that he too was anxious. Then she recovered herself and sent for wine for us, saying that we should have supper later, after we had taken the usual bath which was offered as a courtesy to guests of distinction. All this time she had spoken solely to Joscelyn, only glancing at me and the two men in the background, without, I could tell, a flicker of recognition of the weather-browned, short-haired boy that was I.

Joscelyn dismissed with a word Dickon and Guy, who went with a hovering servant, then said to Dame Catherine, 'I must tell you, dame, that this youth is in fact a young lady. You would know her as Mistress Cowley of Tarletondale, who came to Middleham during the sickness of Lady Anne.'

The dame looked me up and down, legs, curly crop and all, and I could see that she was deeply shocked. No doubt in that moment she thought the worst of me and Joscelyn, possibly of all four of us. All she said was, 'Indeed.' But Joscelyn went on, 'I brought her away from her home, where she was in great danger, and she dressed herself as you see her for more safety in travelling.

She is a loyal friend and servant of Lord Warwick and his family, and hoped to share their fortunes. Now that is impossible I beg you to let her take refuge with you here, while I follow my lord to France, if I can.'

I could hardly believe that I heard rightly. Then I turned on him, and said loudly and violently, 'No!'

10

*J*oscelyn *looked as though I had thrown a stone at him.* Then he said, coldly, 'I think you have no choice. You surely understand you cannot keep with me, now that the journey is so perilous.'

'But I would have kept with you if my lord had been here.'

'He is not here, and the case is changed.' He glanced appealingly at Dame Catherine. 'Will you talk some sense into her, dame?'

Her tone had all the warmth of the sound of cracking ice. 'If Lady Warwick would approve this . . .' This strumpet, I was sure she wanted to say. '. . . your companion to remain here, she is welcome. I believe a convent would be a safer refuge.'

I said, 'I am not looking for a safe refuge. I came here to join Lady Warwick's household, and that is what I intend to do. And if you believe, dame, that I've ridden so many miles in man's gear out of some kind of wantonness, I advise you to try it yourself and see how it inclines *you* to amorous sport.'

A flush came up in her cheeks, and with an exclamation of disgust she turned her back on us and left the chamber.

Joscelyn said grimly, 'Yolande. If I were your husband I should beat you well for this. As I am not, I can only order you to do as I say. I shall leave here in the morning, when my horse is rested, and I shall leave without you. If you try to follow me the sentries will be told to take charge of you and hold you prisoner. Do you understand? Now I shall go and bathe, and I advise you to do the same—and to come to your senses.'

He stalked away, leaving me furious and wretched at the same time, ready to weep with bitter disappointment, but having to hold back the tears in the presence of the serving-maid who prepared a bath for me. Even so it was soothing to sit in the warm water with sweet essences in it; I had not felt clean since leaving Cowleys. The girl laid out for me a woollen gown of dark blue, a linen shift and a pair of velvet shoes.

'Dame Catherine sends you these, madame. What you travelled in shall be cleaned.' With clear distaste she picked up my discarded gear and carried it off.

Dame Catherine's manner warmed slightly to me when I appeared at table in the borrowed clothes. The dress was too short and too tight, but I suppose it made me look like a respectable woman. Joscelyn sat at the far end of the table from me, to avoid having to talk to me. We were a small company: Dame Catherine, a couple of senior gentlewomen, an elderly steward and Lord Warwick's chaplain, who had reluctantly stayed behind. The conversation was of general things, the chances of the King of France helping my lord with forces for invasion, the possibility that Clarence might yet be made king, the dangerous delicacy of Isabel, who might have to bear her child on the way to the coast or at sea. I began to be a little ashamed of myself for being so wrought up about my own concerns, yet my resolution was not weakened.

The meal was not finished when a servant entered and whispered to Dame Catherine. She asked our leave, and went out with him. When she came back it was with a grave face. 'A messenger has brought news of my lord. He took ship at Dartmouth—formed a fleet there—and sailed round the south coast as far as Southampton.'

'So,' Joscelyn said bitterly, 'I am too late.'

'Worse news yet, sir. The king's ships were there, and drove them off and took three of his. And Tiptoft the Butcher tried and hanged their crews, and impaled their quarters on pikes.' She crossed herself—so did we all. John Tiptoft, Earl of Worcester, Constable of England, was a learned man known for his extreme cruelty. My own father had had 'Butcher' tacked on to his name, but I think it was for fierceness in battle, not in civil execution: I hope so. Joscelyn's eyes met mine, and I knew what he was thinking. Any Warwick adherents who tried to follow their leader to France would meet the same horrible end if they were caught.

I saw him alone when supper was finished. 'What will you do now?' I asked.

He shrugged. 'Not go to Southampton, if I value my neck. I shall make for Yorkshire, by back roads, and join my cousin John—if he's not taken already.'

'And if he is?'

'Go further north—make for Neville lands nearer the Scots border.'

'And if you meet with the King's troops?'

'If, if, if! I shall turn a civil face on them and do my best to look like a travelling merchant, or attorney, or some such.'

'You? Have you taken stock of yourself lately? Do you think a young man in the flower of youth, with hair like the Sun of York and the body of a soldier, is going to pass for anything but what he is? Can't you see that the farther north you go the more likely you are to be recognized? Are you going to walk into a trap like a blind fox? And have I been mistaken in my judgment of you?'

For the first time I saw my strong, sure Joscelyn taken aback, and I almost laughed, so unlike him it was.

'If I am a blind fox,' he said, 'you are a lioness who has been disguised all this time as a tame mouse-catcher.'

'Thank you, says poor Tib.'

'So, out of your long experience of wars, what would you advise me to do?'

'Find a safe place and stay in it until the air clears. Things must move quickly—my lord will come back, perhaps with French help, his troops will meet the King's armies, and when you hear of it you can join him. Keep away from the north and open roads, and send no word to anyone that might lead to your capture, for the King has many on the watch for you, depend on it, with the grudge he holds, and if they catch you they'll serve you up to him with butter.'

After a silence he said, 'That seems good sense. And if I take your advice, will you take mine and either stay here or with a sisterhood?'

'No. I shall come with you. I said I would.'

He sighed. 'Yolande, do you want me to go on my knees to you or give you into Dame Catherine's charge to be locked up? If I'm to lead the life of an outlaw how can I trail a woman along with me? And leaving out that, what would become of your good name if it were known you had lived alone with me in such a way?'

I had begun to feel that I was arguing for my life before a judge. Trying to keep very calm, I answered, 'What has become of my good name already—after our journey? You saw Dame Catherine's thoughts in her face—without reason, God knows, but the world cares nothing for that. My husband would never take me back now, even if I swore to him on a piece of the True Cross that I never put a spell or charm on a living thing, and never lay with you. Joscelyn, I love you and only you. I never loved any man before, and I never will again. I knew that when I first set eyes on you. So, if you leave me, my life is worth nothing, and I may as well ride away from here in this gown and shoes and take my chance. I could beg, or pick cresses and sell them by the wayside . . .'

It was a blessed, glad relief when he broke into a great laugh.

'God send me to face King Edward's cannon rather than a woman's tongue! Well, take your victory. Tomorrow you shall put on your doublet and hose again and we'll ride together. Now are you satisfied, and shall I hear no more argument from you?'

'Only if you stop my mouth.'

He did, in the best way a man could. In his arms I asked, 'Do you love me as I love you?'

'I do, and ever will.'

We left next morning, parting from Dickon and Guy, who stayed to help in the defence of the Castle if it were besieged. Joscelyn would not tell me where we were going, only that it was to a place he knew. A horse had been found for me, a gentle but sturdy gelding, not so handsome as my dear Brown Bailey, having a coat of dark and light patches that Joscelyn said would blend well with the colourings of the forest, making us less noticeable.

'Are we going into a forest?' I asked.

'Into Arden. It was forest once, in the old times, but now it's well-wooded country with a village here and there.'

From the Castle armoury we took two good short swords, a hunting knife, and a bow and full quiver each. When I told Joscelyn of my skill in archery he asked satirically whether I had any experience as a pikeman or a gunner, but I knew he was pleased and reassured that I was not going to be a useless partner. We took also a length of fishing line and a rod, two blankets tightly rolled, a parcel of food and sundries to make our life easier. Palamon, when we loaded up him and my mount Johan, rolled an eye and arched his noble neck as though bidding us to put a packhorse to that sort of use, not his proud self. The old steward gave us each a purse of money from the store Lord Warwick had left, carefully writing down the sum in his account-book. Off we went, well-provided, watched by Dame Catherine until we were out of the courtyard and across the drawbridge.

'She thinks us up to no good,' I said. 'My lady will hear a tale and a half next time they meet.'

'Let her.'

The country we rode through was familiar to me, gentle and pretty, in sight of high wooded hills dotted with sheep on their lower slopes. The horses moved at an even pace, for Joscelyn said there was no hurry; we had not far to go. Sometimes we let them stop and turn aside to crop the hedgerows, sweet-scented with the wild flowers of April and the tender young leaves. I felt that we were starting on a pleasant pilgrimage, not a journey of escape from enemies. Joscelyn whistled, as clearly as the larks that rose from the meadows, soaring up to trill high above us. I said it was a wonder the sun did not burn their wings, and he laughed, answering that the hand that made the world was too skilled to create flammable larks. Young lambs played and skipped close to the pathway, running away with shrill bleats when their mothers called them; I thought of Tom and how fond he was of his sheep, and wondered if some day when I was old that would be the only thing I remembered about him. How happy a thought, if only the pleasant things in our lives were remembered, as they are by the inscriptions on tombs testifying to the dead person's virtues, with no mention of any vices they might have had. I said as much, idly, to Joscelyn: at first he made no answer, and there was a dreaming look in his blue eyes.

'I want no such inscription. When I am dead, put no Latin on my tomb. What will it matter to anyone that I was full of *pietas* and *virtutis* and all the graces? In any case they won't believe it, being human themselves. But, now I come to think of it, I believe I shall not have a tomb.'

'What do you mean? All have tombs.'

He shook his head. 'Some things in the future I see in my mind, but not that: *Joscelinus de Conyers, armiger, de comitiae Ebor* . . . and above an effigy in stone arbour, as much like me as like the next man, and a weeping cherub or two. No, it's not to be.'

'Don't say such things! How can you jest about it?'

'Why, does it trouble you, sweet? Stone crumbles and bodies turn to dust, and neither you nor I will care, then.'

'*I* might,' I snapped back, and he laughed, touching my hand that held the reins. A cold feeling had crept over me, in spite of the morning's warmth, and a memory of a curious conversation we had had on our first ride together, about the monk of Coverham who returned from chasing a magic bird to find his Abbey long ruined. Stone crumbles . . . I tried to imagine my own tomb. Would it be by Joscelyn's side? (for what he had said must be all fancy). Would there be a line of kneelers behind each, boys for him and girls for me? And would it describe me as *uxor dilectissima et fidelissima de Joscelini,* as I would wish? Only if Tom died before me.

'Come back,' Joscelyn said. 'The morning's too fine for tomb-talk. And look, there are the roofs of Henley.'

Henley-in-Arden had a long, straight street, a handsome new market cross, a guild-hall, a good church and some inns. It looked to me the kind of place where everyone would know his neighbour's business. I said so, and Joscelyn smiled.

'Not ours. We turn aside by the church, out of the public eye.'

The lane alongside St John Baptist's was narrow and rutted, overgrown with hedges, so that we had to ride single file. Soon we crossed a little stream, sparkling clear; Joscelyn told me it was called the Alne. The town had vanished behind trees, though so near that we could still see the church towers. Another church was before us, a smaller sturdy one, with a new tower. Joscelyn led me past it, a little eastwards, where a mount rose, crowned with the remains of ancient buildings, a dry moat at its foot.

'The castle of Beaudesert,' Joscelyn said. 'It was a de Montfort place once, three hundred years or so past, and later came to Lady

Warwick's family. It was burnt during a battle, put together again badly, and now it stands as you see it. The Crown owns it, but nobody cares to keep it up.'

'And so?' I wondered if he had plans for us to occupy the ruins.

'And so we ride on.' There were no signs of habitation around us, only meadows, until, behind a clump of high trees, we came to a tiny building that looked as old as the castle ruins. It was built of stone, with small narrow windows and a door studded with iron. Weeds grew up the wall and the wisps of birds' nests showed below the eaves. Joscelyn dismounted, and went up to it as though he had often done so before. He turned the great iron ring; slowly the old door creaked open. He looked cautiously inside, then signed me to come nearer.

'I thought the travelling people might have found it, but the crest must have frightened them off.' I recognised the armorial shield of the Beauchamps above the door. Inside there was darkness, broken by the sunlight the opened door let in, and thin slits of light from the windows. As my eyes got used to it I made out the shape of stone benches along a wall, a table and a hearth recess. Cobwebs hung from the low ceiling and draped the door. Inside there was a smell of damp, and the stuffiness of a place long shut up.

Joscelyn said, 'It shames me to ask you to live in such a place. But it's better than outdoors—soundly built, and not fouled, so far as I can see.'

'What is it? How did you find it?'

'What it is I can't say, only that it once belonged to the castle. An outbuilding, perhaps a cottage for someone who had no need to live within the castle walls. I found it when I came with my father to Warwick as a child, and I used to ride out with other boys and play at sieges in the ruins of Beaudesert. We used to take shelter in here from the rain and eat our food from that table.'

'It must be much newer than the ruins, to judge from the fireplace.'

'Yes—all the better.' He turned to me, taking my hands in his. 'Could you live here, sweetheart? In a place so small and rough? If it daunts you too much I shall take you back to Warwick, whether you will or not.'

A strange feeling had crept over me as I stood there in the half-darkness. It was as though the little building was becoming light and bright, as cheerful as though the walls were hung with tapestries and the open slits of windows filled with the jewel-colours of stained glass. I saw clean rushes on the earthen floor, and a fire of logs on the hearth, and the table spread with napery. Even when the brief vision faded, I knew that this place was my home.

So, indeed, it proved. Joscelyn seemed able to turn his hand to anything. Before we had been in the place ten minutes he had made a broom of twigs and swept it out, banishing the cobwebs and dust and a few skeletons of mice, and birds which had flown in through the windows. One of the wooden bowls we had brought as kitchen-ware served to bring water from the stream, a little tributary of the Alne, which flowed nearby, and with this we washed the benches and table. Joscelyn cut small branches and ferns to make a ground-covering, a green sweet-smelling carpet, and set me to gathering twigs and fallen branches for our fire. Seemingly without effort he climbed on to the roof and put in place some lead which had been broken off and slid into the guttering. So we were protected overhead. Then, he said, we needed more light. Because it was impossible to enlarge the windows without a mason's tools, he hit on the idea of removing a whole square stone that was already loose, so giving an extra window.

I watched him with unbelieving admiration. 'I thought you were a soldier, not a house-builder,' I said.

He grinned. 'A good soldier should be able to pitch camp anywhere. Besides, I like my comforts. We'll be as snug here as any in

England outside Westminster Palace. When I can get hold of an axe I'll make blocks to put in the windows of nights.'

But that night the sweet air came in freely, when I slept for the first time in Joscelyn's arms, and knew love fulfilled. He was unwilling to take me, saying that it would be hard to keep up the pretence of my manhood if I were big with child.

'I am barren,' I said, 'I know it. Tom was no stallion, but a doughty trier, yet in two years and more he failed to get an heir. There is no life in my womb.'

Joscelyn looked thoughtful. 'I wonder. The doctors talk as if it were always the woman's fault when she fails to quicken, or gives her husband daughters instead of sons. Some even think she has a secret lover when she throws twins, and that to my mind is twaddle, since my own aunt bore them, as staid and pious a lady as ever spent more time on her knees than on her back. So don't be too sure, my brown girl.'

But I talked and kissed him out of such logic, and so became his love indeed, and the happiest lady in Christendom.

The days passed, and the weeks, spring warming into summer, while we lived like the first Man and Woman before the Serpent came. Few passed our little house, which was on the way to nowhere, and when they did they saw nothing odd about a fair lad and a dark one hoeing a little garden, sawing up logs, or practising archery at a target Joscelyn had made from a round section of tree-trunk marked out in circles. We shot in earnest for our fresh meat, deer and hare, Joscelyn carrying out the bloody business of preparing them, while I did the cooking on a skillet we had bought. I was not very good at it to begin with, never having cooked anything in my life, and we had many a meal either burnt black or too raw. But Joscelyn never complained or scolded me; he was the best-humoured man I had ever known, and the most resourceful. Witness this: the second deer we shot was a large buck, young and glossy-furred. Dragging him home, Joscelyn confessed to an unwillingness to kill such a fine creature, but it was for food, not sport, and must be done. Then another thought came to him.

'Why waste the skin? True outlaws would use it.'

I felt a certain qualm at the processes this would involve. Joscelyn saw my look, and clapped me cheerfully on the shoulder.

'Never fear, I'll draw him into the thicket and you shall know nothing about it.'

'Are you sure you know how to do it?'

'I've seen it done—that should be enough. Give me the salt-jar.'

He removed the handsome corpse well out of sight, and I heard him sharpening his knife on a stone. I strolled off into the wood; when I came back Joscelyn was washing himself thoroughly in the stream, his jerkin off. He told me the hide was pegged out in a clearing, where the sun would dry it, covered with salt for purification.

We were favoured with a week of hot sunshine; at the end of it the hide was almost cured, ready to be hung on a tree near our little house, where we could keep an eye on it. When the cold nights came it would be our bedcover, and by then I would no longer have to wrinkle up my nose when I went near it.

So we lived off the land, busy from dawn to dusk. Joscelyn fished from the Alne where it widened and deepened, we gathered mushrooms in the dew-wet fields, and early berries from the trees. For other things, eggs and cheese and bread, we had to go into Henley. We did this separately, to be less noticeable, and I went more often than Joscelyn, because of his conspicuous hair, which drew eyes wherever he went, particularly among the women. Nobody paid attention to me, though I feared they would if my bosom became any more prominent; for now that I was leading something much more like a true married life, I knew myself to be growing more full-figured and womanly. I dared not have another doublet tailored, so had to manage with the old one we had bought at Skipton. I would so have liked to be beautiful for Joscelyn, and to have walked by his side like a lady, but instead I must look like his swarthy companion.

There were those who were curious about us, in the market and at Mass, asking who we were and where we lived, two strangers with no family ever seen with them. The priest asked us our names: Joscelyn told him we were John and Adam Burnsall, half-brothers from the North. Having said that he would say no more, turning questions aside or not seeming to understand them. I was most afraid of one who took an interest, a gipsy girl of a tribe that had halted in the Forest. She seemed fascinated by Joscelyn, appearing out of nowhere to lay her hands on his arm and glint her black eyes at him under her coin-edged veil, calling him pretty gentleman, handsome Gorgio, and begging him to let her tell his fortune, which he would not, shaking her off good-naturedly. At me she shot sour looks, saying I was false and double-dealing and would come to no good. One day, when we had gone into the town together for once, because we needed oats for the horses and other goods, I was disposing the sacks in the store we had made round the side of our house when I saw out of the corner of my eye a flash of movement behind me. And there she was, a thin swift-moving creature in a dress of bright rags, about to slip indoors.

'Hey!' I said, remembering to pitch my voice down. 'Get out of there.'

She ducked away in a series of mocking bobs. 'Spare the poor chy, good master, that means no harm, only to set eyes on thy handsome companion, else she dies of love, like the maid in the song.'

'Set hands on our goods, more like,' I growled. 'Now get off, will you.'

Instead she dropped down on the grass, ankles crossed, knees apart, surveying me. 'Don't despise the Romany chy too soon, young master, for she knows more than you think. She sees two fair donzels, and a tall fine chal with green jewels at his neck. And then a short rough-spoke lad, and sheep the colour of rocks, and two other donzels with tongues like adders. And they call out Witch, witch! And then she sees Golden-head on a black horse . . .'

'And I see a prating gipsy wench.' Joscelyn had returned from feeding the horses. The girl rose in one swift movement and ran to him.

'Don't be angry, beautiful master, and I'll tell thy future for a kiss—not even a piece of silver, just a kiss that costs nought.'

He pushed her away, though gently. 'None of us knows the future, nor should know. Leave us be, will you? There's danger in too much knowledge, and in telling it.'

Her red mouth was sullen. 'Danger, aye! And for pushing me off I'll not tell you where the danger is. One day you'll rue that you turned Mara away.' She raised her hand towards him, and to my surprise he seized it and held it fast.

'Don't make the sign, Mara! Don't ill-wish us, there's a good lass.'

'Then a kiss.' She held up her face, the bold creature. I could have slapped her, but Joscelyn bent his head and kissed her on the mouth. Then he took something from the pouch at his belt and put it into her hand. 'There. Go your ways.'

She looked in his face long and hard, before turning and running lightly away on dirty bare feet.

'What did you give her?' I asked coldly.

'A silver groat. It might buy us peace from her.'

'Or the kiss might.' I was far from pleased, thinking that even a slut in tatters and spangles might have more power to allure than me, lumpish in my fusty jerkin, with my hair as short as King Henry the Fifth's in his picture. But Joscelyn was not in a mood for female peevishness, I could tell. He sat down on a tree-trunk he had begun to chop into logs, gazing into the green distance of the forest glade, yet seeming to see nothing.

'Danger,' he said at last. 'I should have made her tell me where it lies.'

'As if she'd have told you anything true! They know nothing, these fairground strollers, only lying and cheating and nimming purses. But—do you feel there is danger for us?'

'It will come. How long do you think we can lie close here, like children playing at baby-house, in times like these? We've not seen the King's troops, no, but any day they may be on us. I should have gone back to the North and joined my cousin.' He forebore to add that it was I who had stopped him, and the knowledge made me wretched. 'If only we could get word!' he said. 'News of Warwick and Clarence, and the King. But this place hears nothing but untrustworthy rumours: Warwick is not at the castle, Edward is not in London . . . God send me a pedlar with a pair of sharp ears and a memory to match them.'

From that time Joscelyn became restless. I knew he had only stayed at Beaudesert as a temporary measure, until my lord needed him again. He had begun to be ashamed of idleness, of being away from any action there might be, and I knew in my heart that my happy time in the greenwood was nearly over.

But I was not to know how the news would come that would end it.

Every day we rode out, to exercise the horses and ourselves. Both Palamon and my Johan had put on weight during their summer of pleasant pastime. Usually we rode only in unfrequented places, where we would not be likely to attract attention, but one fine crisp morning in early September Joscelyn suggested that we ride south to the town of Stratford, where we might hear more than in sleepy Henley. He could no longer keep away from the chance of active service, even if it meant risk, as in this case it did.

Market day filled the streets of Stratford with people, carts and animals. I looked wistfully at the broad Avon, the same river we had boated on in the old days at Warwick. It would have been pleasant to take out a boat and row along aimlessly, under the swooning willows and past Holy Trinity church, between the ranks of swans. But Joscelyn had other plans.

The town seemed to have an inn to every four or five houses, all doing a brisk trade, to judge by the number of horses tethered and held outside them. Joscelyn settled on one, the Falcon, opposite the Guild Chapel and its hall. There were horses outside with the signs of war-training on them, and sharp-eyed sturdy men, crop-haired like soldiers. Joscelyn hurried me in.

In the house was more order than one would have expected from such a place. Servants were laying a long table with dishes and food. By the ingle-nook, where a brisk fire burned, a man sat, black-clad, with a cloak of purple about him. My heart seemed to miss a beat; for it was Duke Richard of Gloucester.

I had not seen him since the years when we were children together at Middleham, but I could not fail to discern the small grave boy of those days in the young man, still short-statured, slender and pale-faced, with a slightly hunched look to his right shoulder that came of handling heavy weapons at too tender an age. The face was lined now, with a look of illness in it. I reckoned that he would be no more than eighteen or nineteen, but he had the air of a man twice that.

'Gloucester,' I said to Joscelyn under my breath, 'Richard of Gloucester.' At the same moment the henchman at his side turned, revealing the crest of the White Boar on his doublet.

'Yes,' Joscelyn said, 'I remember him. On the King's side now. We will face this out.'

I walked up to Richard, made a formal bow, and said, 'My lord Duke.' The servitor moved to step between us, but Richard waved him back.

'I know your face,' he said to me. 'Have you a sister?'

'No, my lord. I am Yolande de Clifford.'

A lesser man might have shown surprise or disapproval; Richard merely glanced at my clothing and my hair. 'Time brings changes,' he said. 'You're a long way from Middleham, mistress.' Before I could answer he had made a sign that brought servants running with joint-stools, a jug of wine, and cups. Joscelyn remained standing. 'I am

Joscelyn Conyers, my lord,' he said, and I knew that he was giving Richard the chance to have him taken prisoner.

But Richard smiled the thin smile that was his nearest approach to jollity, answering, 'No matter. I forgive you.' I could have laughed aloud, it was so like his old self. He waved us to the seats and we drank, the wine tasting of nothing to me. 'Richard,' I said (for surely the only way through this thorny thicket was to remember that we had been as equals in the Warwick household) 'things have turned out very oddly for me, or I should not be here in this guise.' And I recounted, as briefly as I could, the tale of my mis-mating and the danger that had come on me at Cowleys, Joscelyn's rescue of me and our long sojourn at Beaudesert, saying nothing of that which was between us. He listened, taking in every word and registering it in that keen brain.

'Well,' he said at the end, 'well, well. And now that you have emerged from the greenwood shade, what do you propose to do?'

Joscelyn put in bluntly, 'I am Warwick's man, my lord. I intend to go north to join my cousin John.'

'I would think twice about that, Sir Joscelyn. My brother the King is in York. His men hold the county.'

'Then I must try to rejoin Lord Warwick, if I can learn where he is.' Very cool, I thought, talking thus to one so powerful, who was on the other side, but Joscelyn was not afraid of the Boar's tusks. 'Has he returned from France?'

A change came over Richard's face. From impassibility it seemed to sharpen until the long nose, long chin and thin mouth became like an axe-blade. Icily he said, 'You seem to have been short of news in your retreat. Lord Warwick is now King Louis's best friend. He is also bosom comrade to Queen Margaret, whom he drove into exile at the same time that he threw her husband into prison. He knelt at her feet a full quarter of an hour, while he begged her forgiveness for all his acts against her. And he promised to do the same, publicly, at Westminster after he had gained England for the House of Lancaster.'

Joscelyn said flatly, 'Impossible.'

'I am not in the habit of telling lies. The Queen and Warwick are allies. He has bought funds from Louis for an invasion, and sent runners to raise troops for him.' He paused, and it seemed as though a sort of furious light streamed from the livid paleness of his face. 'The great alliance has been sealed by a betrothal: his daughter Anne is to wed Margaret's son Edward.'

I could have echoed Joscelyn, and cried, 'Impossible.' How could Lord Warwick have sacrificed his delicate young daughter in this monstrous political game, his betrayal of the House of York and all he had fought for? He had broken with King Edward, certainly: but to join forces with Margaret, his old enemy, whom he had called an evil bitch (and the word had got back to her), this was beyond thought. In my early days at Middleham there had been a poem recited in his honour, in the Great Hall, that I had thought in my admiring love for him set out all that he was.

Richard, the Earl of Warwick, of knighthood
Lode-star, born of a stock that ever shall be true,
Having the name of prowess and manhood,
Hath been ready to help and rescue
King Edward, in his right him to endue.

And now, this. I pitied Anne, I pitied Richard in his grief and anger. I began to say so, clumsily, but he silenced me with a look in which I recognized contempt. He had forgotten the Yolande of Middleham, seeing now only a bold jig in male dress flaunting herself in a tavern with her paramour. Richard revered girls all sweet modesty, like Anne, the snowdrop maid: Anne who at fifteen was affianced bride to a young man she had been brought up to hate.

He was looking at Joscelyn.

'Well? Do you still intend to join Warwick?'

Joscelyn said, 'I must.'

11

A look of such anger blazed in Richard's eyes that it seemed he would strike Joscelyn. Then he said, 'A knight. A Yorkist born and bred. Your father served mine and saw him killed by Lancastrian swords in the hands of Margaret's men, and his quarters hung on the gates of York like meat on butcher's hooks. If you serve Warwick you serve the French queen, too.'

I said boldly, 'My lord Warwick was as much a father to you as your own. Think of that before you try to turn a man from his loyalty. What about your own motto, *Loyaute me lie?*'

'Be quiet. I'm speaking to Sir Joscelyn.'

Joscelyn said, 'My answer is still the same, sir.'

Richard got swiftly to his feet, the wine-cup beside him overturning and spilling a red stream over the table. I saw Joscelyn's hand steal towards the dagger at his belt, and was aware that a silence had fallen among Richard's men, and that they were eyeing us speculatively. If Joscelyn made a move towards their leader they would fall on us like wolves. But Richard said, clearly enough to be heard by those at the furthest corner of the room, 'It is not my way to take prisoners, even rebels, with no defence but their own weapons. Go, while you can, where you please, and take your doxy with you.' Then he strode through the silent company and disappeared up the staircase.

The spell was broken. 'Doxy, eh?' remarked a burly man in Gloucester's livery. 'And a rebel too. Let's take a look at her.' He seized me by the doublet and pulled me towards him, groping me grossly and painfully, while another man's hand tangled in my hair. I was terrified, a beast torn by hounds, their insults loud in my ears and their fingers invading my body. It can only have been for a moment, though it seemed an eternity, for Joscelyn laid about him right and left, striking blows that sent my assailants staggering back, until they left me and his arm went round me, holding me firmly. What he said to those men I was too shaken to comprehend, but his words were the most violent I had ever heard him utter—soldiers' language, crude and full of blasphemous threats of what he would do to them if one of them so much as approached me again. He was the tallest man in the room, and though dressed like a forester he had the unmistakable authority of a captain. They fell back for us as he half-dragged me towards the door.

He had no need to tell me what to do when we got back to Beaudesert. I collected together what few possessions were worth keeping, bundled them up, and buried the remains of our last meal and our fire. Joscelyn spread out a map he carried and brooded over it. I knew he was working out the position of the ports at which Lord Warwick might land, and how he would get there. When I saw that he had the two horses watered, fed, and ready I went out to him, pausing at the door to look back at the strange lonely little house where I had felt so happy. Castle adjunct or whatever it had been, to me it would always be a palace where Love had reigned as Prince. But Joscelyn never gave it a last look; such is the way of men.

'Where do we go?' I asked him, before we mounted.

'Warwick. I shall leave you there. No more words, Yolande.'

Indeed my heart was too heavy for words along the road that led to where the Castle's towers loomed. We entered the town after supper-time. There was a gathering of people in the market square, and laughter and music. We had to draw up our mounts because of the crowd. Outside an inn musicians were playing, three lads in motley. Their instruments were a shrill, loud hautboy, a rebeck and a cittern, and the noise they made was astonishing. We watched as they danced, capered, and acted out a masque of two shepherds wooing a maid cautious of her virtue, and a comedy of a jealous husband returning to surprise his wife with a lover. Then, when the laughter at their antics had died down, they laid down their instruments and sang, very seriously and sweetly, a French song, of one who begs his mistress not to withhold her charms, for they are as fragile as the petals of a rose, and will fade as soon; when the winter winds come there will be no roses left, only bare thorny stems, and her beauty will be no more.

There, among people grown quiet to listen, with the gold of sunset touching the old roofs of the square, I felt tears escaping from my eyes and rolling down my cheeks, splashing on to my doublet, welling out of me uncontrolled. The light made a glory of Joscelyn's hair like a saint's halo. He seemed not to look at me but very softly he said, 'Weeping never helped. And people will see.'

At that I conquered myself, and shut my ears to the sweet sadness of the song.

We came to the Castle. The news had reached them—even later news than we had heard. Lord Warwick had already sailed, had broken through the blockade set up by the Duke of Burgundy. Clarence was with him, and two powerful earls; King Louis was praying to all his saints and promising them rich offering in return for his friend Warwick's victory. He would probably land at Plymouth, in Devon, or nearby Dartmouth. So Joscelyn's destination was settled.

Dame Catherine was not pleased to see me. She must have hoped I would not return at all, but to receive me again, still in my immodest disguise, outraged her feelings almost beyond the bounds of politeness. Lord Warwick's worst enemy (and he had so many it would be difficult to pick out the worst among them) could not have laid the least charge of scandal to his name. Now I, so well treated by the family, dared to bring shame to his castle. When I was taken to the chamber she had set apart for me, up winding staircases and along dark corridors, I found there a gown and everything needed for a womanly appearance. I put it on, and hid my hair under a coif. This was the end of masquerading.

Thanks to her, my parting with Joscelyn was a formal one. After supper she called a page to light me upstairs, and another to conduct Joscelyn to his own chamber, which he had told me was little more than a cubby-hole near the guard-room, almost the castle's length away from mine.

We, who had been lovers and comrades, said farewell in the sight and hearing of half that household, face to face, unable to clasp or kiss.

'I shall be gone at dawn,' he said, awkwardly for him.

'Yes.'

'Towards Plymouth.'

'Yes.'

'And you promise me to stay here or go to some other place of safety?'

'I promise.'

Almost under his breath, he said, 'I shall find you again—that is my promise to you. Here, or somewhere; I know it.'

There seemed to be a tight band round my throat, so I nodded, and smiled quite cheerfully, I believe. Then I held out my hand, and he bent his head over it, bowing his knee as though I had been the Queen, and I said, 'God keep you.'

Autumn days were long at Warwick. I lived like a pensioner, Dame Catherine looking down her nose at me, the retainers hardly knowing how to behave to me. Sometimes I rode out on Johan, but never to Beaudesert. I began a piece of tapestry, the story of faithful Penelope and her long wait for Ulysses's return, beset by suitors bringing her gifts in hope of getting her love. It seemed to fit my own case, except that Warwick Castle was not overflowing with suitors, or indeed with lively company of any kind. The only excitement we got was the arrival of news, and that was eagerly awaited, as messenger after messenger appeared with fresh items. Lord Warwick was marching to Exeter, banners flying, distributing pardons right and left to all men except King Henry's 'capital enemies', whoever *they* might be, winning himself popularity along the way by forbidding his soldiers to brawl, and threatening them with death for robbery or rape.

One morning a breathless lad on a jaded horse rode into the courtyard, and the message he brought was relayed from sentry to sentry until it reached us within the walls. 'My lord is coming! His army is no more than two miles away, thirty thousand men. Lord Shrewsbury and Lord Stanley have joined him, and dozens of barons and knights besides, with their retainers. He halts at Warwick for rest and supplies.'

Then what a rushing to and fro there was, beef brought to the spit, the bakery in as much of a ferment as its own yeast, casks of wine opened, barrels of ale rolled out, every preparation made for tired and hungry men and horses. As the bright banners appeared in the streets, wending towards us, my heart beat wildly at the thought that Joscelyn might be somewhere beneath them, one of the armoured riders, and I stared hard at each black horse, looking for Palamon. But he was not there, the big-boned charger with the arched neck and a way he had of swinging his head from side to side as though in challenge.

My lord Warwick had never looked more magnificent. He had the air of a conqueror, a Kingmaker indeed, now that he was on his way to re-make poor doting King Henry. No one would have thought that he had so recently changed sides. He was forty-three years old now, with the authority of middle age, more than ever the rampant heraldic lion. He knew men, being one who never forgot a face, and was gracious in his greeting, unconcerned with what my presence in his castle might mean. I hardly dared ask him about Anne, but he spoke of her first.

'Your friend and playmate will be Queen of England, madame, and before very long, I would guess, the King's health being what it is.'

I ventured to ask what Prince Edward, her bridegroom, was like. He raised grizzled eyebrows.

'Why, personable enough. Fortunately he takes after his mother in looks.' (Queen Margaret had been a great beauty until anger and strife had lined her face. It was not surprising that the Prince did not take after King Henry, since he was popularly supposed to be the son of one of Margaret's lovers.) 'And very warlike in his ways and talk. If his sword could win back his father's crown alone, he would drive all the rest of us from the field.'

Poor Anne, I thought, and pitied her even more when I heard the gossip that young Prince Edward was a swaggering bully who enjoyed nothing more than talking of bloody deeds. I asked for news of Isabel. The Earl's look saddened.

'She was taken in labour on our voyage to France, with no aid but from my lady and Anne. Her boy was born dead. God send her better fortune with the next one. By now she should be in London, at The Erber, setting up house while Lord Clarence marches with me.' (Yes, there was cocksure George, near the head of the table, laughing very loudly over his wine.)

For the first time my lord looked at me with interest, struck by a thought. 'Would you not like to join her, madame, unless something keeps you here? She was very low in spirits last time I saw her, and company from one who was a girlhood friend might cheer her.' I wondered what my dear, single-minded lord imagined had happened to my husband, or if he even remembered to whom he had married me, and I came to the conclusion that such details simply did not interest him, not being concerned with affairs of state. But it seemed a very good idea to join Isabel's household, if she would have me. Whatever was going to happen in the realm would happen in London, and there I would like to be. I said so to my lord, who instantly called up a page and told the boy to summon one of his secretaries.

'I shall bid Isabel expect you,' he said, as though it were all settled, with no question of Isabel's feelings in the matter. Well, that was his way. I could see that the conversation had now come to an end, in his opinion, and hastily I managed to ask whether Joscelyn were with him.

'Young Conyers? No, indeed. All my northern leaders have gone ahead by the fastest roads to York, where Edward lies.' Having dashed my hopes so thoroughly, if unconsciously, he turned away from me with relief to talk to a man who waited patiently for his attention.

Within a day they were gone, my lord and his barons and knights and marching men, the horses and waggons; the Castle seemed so quiet and dull that I was overjoyed, not much over a week later, when a messenger from London brought me a letter from Isabel asking me to make all haste to her. 'For I long to talk with you, being alone here but for servants.'

Servants or not, Isabel was hardly alone, by any measure. The Erber was one of the great houses of the Nevilles, almost a palace, near to the river. It swarmed with people, and at the centre of it stood its mistress, Isabel, Duchess of Clarence.

She was more beautiful than ever in the maturity of wifehood, though so thin that her beauty was moulded by bones rather than flesh, splendidly dressed as befitted a duchess, very much the grand lady. She welcomed me with kisses and embraces, like a sister, and from that moment she hardly stopped talking, so that I was hard put to it to change out of my journeying clothes. How she talked! I heard every detail of her terrible labour aboard ship while a sea-battle raged in Calais harbour. I learned of the enmity of Charles of Burgundy to her father, and the great friendship shown to him by King Louis of France, the feasting and entertainments, King Louis's wily efforts to get the furious Queen Margaret to the point of a meeting with War- wick: 'and when they met at last, my father went down on his knees before her—picture that, Yolande! and knelt there for a whole quarter of an hour begging pardon for wrongs done in the past to her and the House of Lancaster. She was not willing to listen, but at last she gave in and agreed to Anne's betrothal to her horrid son.'

'*Is* he horrid?'

'A young beast.' She shrugged in a very French way. 'But that's neither here nor there, since the crown of England goes with the match.'

'Oh, Isabel! But she cared so much for Richard. Is that over, then?'

By the way she hurried on to the rest of her story I knew that it was not over—that Anne had been unscrupulously sold into a loveless marriage—and I wondered just how much love existed in Isabel's own marriage. She frowned when I asked after George.

'Well enough. But it would have been seemlier if my father had put *him* in Edward's place, instead of poor old daft Henry. Then I should have been Queen, not Anne who is much too timid and mouse- ish to enjoy it. *Il n'est pas toujours sage à propos les dames, mon père.*'

'But Edward is still king,' I pointed out. 'The struggle is not over yet.'

Within a few weeks it was over and King Edward had fled the country, sailing from East Anglia with his brother Richard and a few followers. England belonged to the House of Lancaster—and War- wick, Lord of the North.

London was a strange place that winter. One king in exile, another enthroned at Westminster, a poor feeble half-idiot, not very clean in his habits—one queen, Edward's Elizabeth, nursing her new-born son in sanctuary, another, Henry's Margaret, waiting to sail from France—two

Princes of Wales, Elizabeth's baby and Anne's husband . . . It was like some complex game of chess, in which nobody quite knew which pieces were which. And though poor Henry of Lancaster nominally reigned, by his side, living at the Palace of Westminster, was the man who had brought him out of prison and put him there, signing documents and giving orders because Henry was past such things.

And people were asking who is King—Henry or Warwick?

George of Clarence was now living with us at The Erber. He was not a contented man. Peevish lines had formed on the face so like his brother Edward's, his small mouth drooped, and when he spoke to his father-in-law it was none too respectfully. I heard him muttering to Isabel that he felt himself to be nobody in the land.

'He gave me my estates back, yes, and I sit in his Council. That's better than the case of Oxford and Shrewsbury, and Stanley and Tudor, those who helped to put him where he is. But is it good enough, when you think what I might have been?'

'He's not unfair, George. If Henry's heirs male are lacking, yours are to succeed. The Proclamation says that.' But Isabel sounded unconvinced.

George snorted. 'Henry's heirs male? He has none, as you and I know, and all the rest of the world. But Margaret's bastard son will have heirs male, being the French ram he is, now that he's firmly wedded to Anne. I'll warrant he bedded her before the candles were out on the altar.'

I thought of fragile Anne, and Isabel's dead child, and sighed.

When the Christmas season came, there came with it Duchess Cicely of York, mother of George, and Richard, and King Edward, the once-lovely Proud Cis, beautiful still in a haggard way and as strong-minded as became a mother of princes. Then I saw little of Isabel and George, they were closeted so much with her, and I knew they talked of George's grievances, and how Warwick lorded it over London, and what a thin crust of pastry lay over the Lancastrian pie.

The next thing in my story is hard to tell of because it happened so quickly I hardly had time to think. It was St Thomas's Eve, a few days before Christmas. Isabel was ailing with a heavy cold and cough; I had promised to stay by her until she slept, and she had sent her maids away, saying that they chattered and made her head ache. George, who disliked illness, kept out of sight, as was only too easy in that huge rambling place.

It was peaceful in the bedchamber, a small one she liked, on the river side of the house, looking out towards the dark Thames and the bobbing lights of boats on it. From All Hallows' church near by came a sound of singing, a sweet Advent hymn. I felt a pleasant melancholy, and poor Isabel, between her sniffs and coughs, looked more peaceful, less feverish.

A sharp, loud knocking on the door brought her upright on her pillows, startled. Before I could ask who was there the door flew open. A man stood there, a short squat figure I knew too well, and I felt myself turn cold with alarm, though the fire was banked high.

'So I've found thee, wife,' said Tom.

I stared and stared, and could get no words out. It was Isabel who asked sharply, 'Who are you, fellow? What's your business?'

'Tha's set eyes on me before, milady—when this woman and me were wed.'

Now it was Isabel's turn to stare, as she connected the stranger with the uncouth lad whose wedding she had witnessed, long ago at Middleham. It came to me that never once, since I had been at The Erber, had she questioned me about myself, asked what had become of my husband, why I was not at Cowleys. I believed now that she had never given it a thought, being of the same carelessly kind nature as her father, not giving to musing on other people's troubles. Now she turned her great eyes on me. 'You never told me,' she accused. 'I thought this . . . your husband was dead. I'm sure you told me so.'

Tom grinned. 'Nay, I'm wick enough. And I'm fain to see thou art too, wife, for I've a bone to pick with thee. But I'll pick it somewhere else.' He approached, seized me by the arm and jerked me to my feet. I think I screamed, Isabel certainly did. She leaned out of bed for the gold handbell with which she summoned her maids, but he snatched it out of her reach, and threw it down, jangling. Then he was pulling me, dragging me, through the door (which was strangely unguarded) and down a flight of stone steps, while I cried out and struggled, helpless against his brutal strength. Somehow we were out of the palace, in the street. I shivered in the cold air, and Tom laughed.

'Didst think I'd take thee whoam without women's company? See who's here.' From a cloaked dark figure by the door shot a hand that gripped my arm cruelly, sharp nails digging into the flesh, and a voice said, 'Well met, sister-in-law.' It belonged to my old enemy, Joan.

Between them they propelled me along the narrow street, little more than an alley, with a high wall on the farther side of it. Beyond it was another dark lane that must lead to the river, for the watermen's cries were growing nearer. I slipped in the mud of it, hauled humiliatingly between the two of them. Suddenly Joan said, 'I can't wait for it, Tom.' Stopping, she pushed me against the wall, and began to beat me, first in the face, hard stinging slaps on one cheek, then the other, then about the body, punching with her fists and kicking my legs, all the time making fierce low sounds of satisfaction, almost growls. And Tom laughed, more heartily than I had ever heard him laugh, enjoying my pain, holding me fast to endure her blows.

In those nightmare moments I felt a wild desire to have my hand on the hunting-knife I had carried in Arden—any weapon to attack them with, these two craven bullies who had me at their mercy. But I had nothing except my hands, and they were helpless. I screamed, but no help came. And when Joan had beaten me to my knees, she yanked me up again, and once more I was being dragged along, for miles, it seemed, though it may only have been hundreds of yards, until I managed to raise my head enough to see London Bridge looming up ahead. We must be near Old Swan Stairs. Were they going to pitch me into a boat? A party of men came towards us, laughing; I shrieked for help to them, but they laughed more, and passed by, no doubt thinking me a drunken slut.

'No help there, sister,' Joan crowed. 'Fie on you! Don't you wish to be with your fond kin, that couldn't wait to lay hands on you? Why don't you make a spell to get free, and fly away like a bat? Hey, look, Tom.' She grabbed my right hand and found with her fingers the ring Lady Cowley had given me on her deathbed. With one fierce twist Joan had it, and I thought my finger was broken. 'Now I've gotten it back,' she said, 'what was rightly mine, and Tom's gotten his wife back, and here we be.'

They had stopped in front of a house, one of a row. I realized that we were right on the riverside. Across the river the beautiful windows of St Mary Overie's shone like jewels; within they must be singing Vespers, and I remembered it was the Eve of St Thomas, and began to pray very hard, though whether to the Blessed Apostle or to the martyred Archbishop of Canterbury I could not have said.

Joan opened the door and between them they pushed me in. There was a rushlight burning, a small beam, but enough to dazzle one after all the darkness. Huddled on the floor, dazed and hurt, I waited for the next blow or kick. But none came; Tom gave a sharp cry, and Joan squealed. There were two men in the room with us, each grasping one of my captors. And the man who held Tom was Joscelyn.

As the scuffle broke out I managed to roll towards a wall, out of the way. Tom was cursing and Joan uttering high squeaks of pain and fury; Joscelyn and his man were absolutely silent, as though they had planned it all and knew exactly what they were at. Their dark struggling forms against that flickering light fought like fiends in a painter's vision of Hell-mouth. I saw that on the ladder stairs an old woman was watching, terrified. There was a flash of steel—a dagger in Tom's hand, menacing Joscelyn's throat. Then Joscelyn's arm came up and descended, and with an awful gurgling cry Tom slumped to the ground.

At that Joan shrieked outright, seeming to pull herself away from the man holding her, and was off through the open door into the darkness. Joscelyn shouted, 'Adam! after her!' His man disappeared outside. There were muffled cries, a loud oath from the man, then a long, diminishing scream, and far off a splash.

Adam came back, and nodded to his master. 'Done,' he said.

'How?'

'T'river.'

I sat up, shocked. 'Murdered!'

'Nay, mistress, fair fight. She lost balance and went over.' He held out his arm; bright blood was streaming from the wrist. 'She bit it through.' Joscelyn pushed him down on to a stool and demanded of me, 'Have you a linen shift on? Good.' Unceremoniously he pulled up my skirt and with his dagger sliced off a long strip from the hem; the dagger left a dark wet stain. With the linen he bound Adam's arm very tightly about the elbow, telling him to hold it up and let the blood drain back into the body. He must have done the same thing many times in battle. Then he turned to me and helped me to my feet. I smiled at him waveringly, holding gladly to his hand.

'How did you find me? It must have been a miracle.'

'No miracle, merely strategy. I'll tell you as we go.'

'Go where?'

'Back to The Erber. But first take a sup.' He produced a leather flask and made me drink from it, something very strong, malmsey, I think, then passed it to Adam, asking him, 'Are you fit to walk?'

'Aye, master.'

Before we left Joscelyn threw down a coin at the foot of the stairs where the old woman still crouched. 'For your silence, mistress. No calling the Watch, eh?' Then he led us out into the street, half-carrying me, until I proved that I could walk alone.

As we went (and how differently from my progress to that house) he told me, in his crisp matter-of-fact way, how my rescue had come about. A neighbour of the Cowleys at the head of Tarletondale, a man called Sutton, with a fair amount of land, a loyal supporter of Warwick, had mentioned during a parley of landowners at Hornby Castle that Tom Cowley had told him he intended to set out for London, which Sutton thought strange, the Cowleys being wholly dalesmen with no London connections. Joscelyn at once sent a spy, a discreet servant, to find out any gossip there might be at my old home.

He learned that Tom had found out where I was. Since my disappearance father and son had been intent on tracing me and bringing me to justice as an adulteress and a witch, egged on by the malice of Joan and Margret. Neither girl had found a husband, a lack which they blamed on me. A traveller to York brought word that I was with the Duchess of Clarence: at last they had what they wanted. All the servants at Cowleys knew, even the old priest: there was talk of a trial by water, and the old punishment for adultery, burning, which would neatly fit both my supposed crimes.

'So I set a watch on them,' Joscelyn said, as calmly as though describing the start of a summer day's hunt. 'When they left I followed them, with Adam here and a few others some way behind. They never knew we were there: too busy plotting. I tracked your late husband and the wench (a witch herself if ever I saw one) to the place where they planned to take you. And the rest you know.'

'Yes.' All so simple, the elaborate finding out of Tom's intentions, the ride of more than two hundred miles, with the chance of snow setting in, the timing of my rescue. I laughed with joy, and he understood, and laughed with me. I was bruised from head to foot, my face was scratched, I felt a black eye coming up and a tooth loose from one of Joan's buffets, and I had never felt more free and happy. 'My good angel,' I said, 'twice you have rescued me. When shall I rescue you?'

We were married during the Christmas feasting, on Holy Innocents' Day, in Isabel's private chapel in The Erber. She was there, still frail from illness and somewhat confused by the whole affair, and also present was Lord Warwick, as he had been at my first wedding. At Joscelyn's insistence we had gone to him and told him everything, every detail about the deaths of Tom and Joan and the house by Swan Stairs. Joscelyn made no case for us, no pleas or demands. My lord's dark eyes were inscrutable; he stroked his beard and regarded critically the heavy jewels in his finger-rings. Then he said, 'I will see to this. No questions shall be asked, or if they are, answered. It was an incident in the night; God knows there are many. The truth lies between yourselves and me. And, of course, our great and good King Henry.' At that I saw Joscelyn's lips twitch into the beginning of a smile, but he repressed it, returning levelly the Earl's grave gaze. They understood each other perfectly.

*O*ur happy wintering at The Erber was short. Soon Josce-lyn was spending much time at Westminster in council with my lord. The tide, he told me, was turning. The Duke of Burgundy, a bitter enemy to Warwick, was planning a league with the exiled King Edward. Queen Margaret, whose arrival in England with her son and Anne might have strengthened the cause of Lancaster, hesitated to sail from France. Noblemen of power were one by one leaving the Warwick standard: for, after all, he was not king, and poor Henry was only, as one chronicler put it, a shadow on the wall thrown by a candle. A king there was, and a strong one: Edward. And he was coming home.

Joscelyn was at Warwick with my lord, helping to raise an army when the news came. Isabel wept. 'We shall all be destroyed! George, I beg you do as your mother and I have counselled.' George looked sly: I think he knew very well what he meant to do. And I think my lord must have known, as he waited with his army at Coventry for the banners of Clarence to come to his aid. They never came. George of Clarence had joined Edward. And Louis of France had deserted Warwick too, having signed a treaty with Burgundy.

Now we got news daily. Edward was in York, he was marching south. Before many days he and his forces were in London, and the wretched Henry once more a prisoner in the Tower. Isabel's spirits soared, for at last she and George were on the right side and all was going to be well.

'And Anne?' I asked. 'How will she feel when she comes home to find her husband's cause a dead one, and England Yorkist again? Will she and her husband and Queen Margaret find themselves in the Tower, too?'

Isabel shrugged. 'Oh, I should think not. Edward is very good-humoured about these things. Really, our father might as well not have dragged us over to France last year and caused all this upset. Then I would not have lost my baby, and Anne would not have had to marry that young monster, and we could all have stayed Yorkist. I wish he had not been so impetuous.'

If she had not been a duchess, and as fragile as a windflower, I could have shaken her. 'Have you heard, madame, that he is now being so impetuous as to march on London to confront Edward, and that there will certainly be a very bloody battle within the next few days, since King Edward is getting ready to leave London and meet him?'

Her mouth was a round O of surprise. 'A battle? Oh, no, you must be mistaken. This is Holy Week, you know, and my father would not dream of fighting a battle at Easter.'

'What else can he do, madame? You know him. He would never bend the knee to Edward again—his great pride would not permit it. So they will fight. And that is why I must ask you if I may leave you for a time.'

'Leave me? But why?'

'To seek out my husband. We have not seen each other for a month, since he went to join my lord at Coventry. I shall take a guard with me, and send him ahead to find out where the army is.'

'Turn camp-follower? You must be mad. Are you going to put on doublet and hose again?'

'No, madame. It would not be seemly: I am with child.'

Isabel gasped. 'But I thought . . . you said that all the time you were married to that fat yokel you never bore, and that was what they held against you.'

'Indeed, I did believe myself barren, but it seems I am not.' It was a miracle, a wonder that had filled me with joyful awe ever since I had been certain of it; a sign that my love for Joscelyn and his for me was not sinful. That was why I had to go to find him, to tell him myself, not trusting such great news to messengers at such a time. Isabel embraced me, warning me tearfully against the dangers of travelling in my condition, which she knew all too well. Then she lent me the trustiest horse in the stables, and two men to guard me, one of them big Adam, who had been ill for weeks after the night of the deaths by Swan Stairs; it seemed that Joan's bite had turned into a poisoned wound, the doctors fearing at one time that he might lose his arm. Now he was recovered, and the best guard I could have had. He knew a way out of the City that was a different one from the route Edward's forces were taking, the direct road northwards. Instead we went east, touching the skirts of Essex, then cross-country by Hertford to where Adam guessed the Lancastrian army to be.

'Two days' march behind t'other, and coming from Coventry; nigh to St Albans by now, I reckon.'

That was where we met with their advance guard, just north of the cathedral town. We, going at a faster pace, reached St Albans before them. 'It's been twice a battlefield in our time,' Adam said. 'Lucky for Lord Warwick in '55, unlucky in '61. Wonder which it'll be this time. I was only in the last lot. There's the Clock Tower, see—they rang the alarm for battle there. Up yonder, beyond St Peter's, was the worst of it, so many dead they'd to pile 'em up in the churchyard, until there was time to cart 'em off, the noblemen that is, to the Cathedral. The rest's there still, under the ground. Men still turn up bones in the gardens.'

I shivered, and not because of the dank cold weather. My grandfather, Thomas de Clifford, had died at St Albans. Adam sent Peter, the other guard, to find me a room at the Fleur-de-Lys, a house where a king of France had once been kept prisoner. Then, leaving me by a welcome fire, the two went off in search of Joscelyn.

Tired with riding I fell into a light sleep, and dreamed happily, in spite of Adam's tales. I woke to a touch on my cheek; Joscelyn's kiss. He knelt beside me, cloaked and in half-armour. I held out my arms to him. His hair was damp against my breast, tightened by the rain into a tangle of curls, and his lips were cold. After a long embrace we both began to talk at once.

'You should not have come this far, mad wench. Don't you know there'll be a battle? It's no place for women.'

'It is, for me. How are you? Has it been hard going from Coventry? What are the chances? Does my lord know where Edward is?' And so forth, but I could hardly talk sensibly for looking at him and touching him, my husband, my spouse, my mate, who had given me the great gift of himself, and another besides.

When I told him he said nothing for a moment, so that I feared he was angry. Then he smiled his beautiful smile, and held me very tightly.

'You make me happy, wife—happier than I ever thought I would be.'

'Would you like it to be a son? Men always want sons.'

'Whatever God sends, son or daughter, so long as it is ours, it will be precious.'

'I thought I would always be punished, you know, for what I did; something terrible. The night before my wedding to . . . Tom, Anne told me I must pray to St Jude to be delivered from the spell of love you had put upon me. I did pray—but not for that; I prayed you would come back to me, and be with me always. So when I seemed to be barren I thought it a punishment.'

He crossed himself. 'Do you think the saints have no kindness for lovers? Now you see how blessed we have been.'

There was a bed in the room, a narrow couch with a rough fur covering. We lay on it together, silently touching, kissing, murmuring sometimes. I thought of St Jude's mercy to me, remembered that he was the patron saint of York: so which side would he support in the battle that was to come? His old servant Warwick, or young Edward, the Yorkist king? If saints had to follow the twists and turns of politics it must be very difficult for them . . .

I must have fallen asleep, for Joscelyn was saying to me, 'Love, I must go. We are only spared two hours before we march again. Take care of yourself and our child. I think . . . no man ever had a truer wife than you. Do you remember, I once called you my nut-brown maid?'

'I remember. Maid no more.'

'But mine. Always, as your prayer was. Let me go now, my heart.'

'But I shall see you soon?'

'When God pleases. May He keep you till then.'

He was out of my arms, cloaked again. With a last look back he went out, shutting the door behind him. The room had turned very cold; the fire burnt low.

And that was how I parted from my love.

I listened until the very last sound of the army's departure had died away, not wanting to venture out and see them go. Then, leaving word for Adam, who had gone part of the way with them, I walked down across the meadows to the Cathedral. It was a fine, soaring church, but plunged still in the mourning blacks and purples of Good Friday, the altars shrouded and the shrine of St Alban having only withered offerings around it. Later that day women would come to take away the palls and deck the church with flowers for Easter Day. I knelt by the shrine, for Alban was a soldier saint, and prayed, and thought, and dreamed, hardly knowing of what.

Dusk fell early, under such lowering skies. It was almost dark when I returned to the Fleur-de-Lys. I was glad to go to the bed I had lain on with Joscelyn, fancying that the air still held the scent of his rain-wet woollen cloak and the last tones of his voice before he went out of the door.

The Easter bells woke me, a joyful peal. I had slept all night, though there was no daffodil sunshine to greet Our Lord's rising, only dank mist, through which I could hardly see the houses on the other side of French Row only a few feet away. Downstairs servants laid out bread and ale for me. I asked for my men, and was told they had gone out very early. I asked for news of a battle; they shook their heads saying there had been a great noise, but far off, and nobody cared to find out what or where it was.

So I waited, watching the mists swirl and lift and form again, and people in their best clothes passing on their way from church, until at last the latch of the inn door lifted, and I knew it would be Adam who entered.

His face was so grim that I hardly needed to ask what I had to ask. 'Was there a battle?'

'Aye, lady.'

'And it went . . . well? Badly?'

'Badly. The fog was thick as porridge, no man could see another. They say there was some mistake about a banner—our ranks took Oxford's star for the Sun of York, and turned on their own side. And Edward was too strong . . .' He slumped down on a stool, his head on his arms.

'My lord?'

'Lord Warwick is dead. Killed as he tried to mount.'

'And . . . my husband?'

'How can I tell? So many dead, so many fled.' He called to a maid-servant, 'Bring me some ale here, I'm sick.'

The battle had been fought just north of Barnet, some ten miles south, very early that morning. I guessed that if Joscelyn had escaped he would have come back to where he had left me, perhaps hoping to make his way north. But I waited in vain, until long after noon. Then I summoned Peter.

'I am going to the battlefield to look for my husband. You come with me—Adam may stay until he is rested.'

They said I must not go, begging the innkeeper's wife to persuade me. But I went, the ten miles to the place where the smoke of battle tainted the air while we were still far from it, and fallen bodies began to appear, lying by the side of the road. It is amazing how soon the eye gets used to the sight of horrors. Severed limbs and heads, gaping wounds, the staring eyes of death, the bodies of horses stiffened in agony, corpses with arrows still sticking in them. I could never have imagined such slaughter, yet I was quite coldly orderly as I went about my task. I was looking for a golden head, as gold as that deluding banner which had helped to lose the battle. It was easy to see which of the dead had been noblemen, since they were naked, their armour and weapons having been plundered by soldier-scavengers. Some of them were still at it, and jeered at me.

I trailed all over that dreadful field, from Wrotham Wood to the outskirts of Barnet town, until dusk fell and the mists began to swirl again. But I did not find Joscelyn. At last Peter said, 'Come away, lady.' He brought our horses from where he had tethered them, safe from the plunderers, and we rode back to St Albans. It was still Easter Day, the bell in the tower by the Fleur-de-Lys ringing for the hour of Compline. I have forgotten how that day ended, or when we returned to London, or whether I felt much, or nothing.

I have lived long years since then. Years of such chequered history: Anne's young husband killed at Tewkesbury, the Lancastrian cause finished, the old King Henry murdered (they said) in the Tower, and

Isabel's George mysteriously dead, too, sometime before his brother King Edward. After that young, bitter Richard became King Richard the Third, with Anne at his side at last. Now they are all gone, and I lead a peaceful life in a Yorkshire dale, in Conyers country, watching my son John grow to manhood.

I am quite happy and contented. For I know that whatever happened on Barnet Field, I shall meet Joscelyn, my soul, my other self, again, somewhere: perhaps in Paradise, perhaps in another life, if we are granted one. 'I shall find you again,' he had said. 'That is my promise to you.'

BOOK TWO

The Way to the Red Room

MARGERY AND CLEMENT: 1538

A lightsome eye, a soldier's mien,
A feather of the blue,
A doublet of the Lincoln green—
No more of me you knew,
My love!
No more of me you knew.

This morn is merry June, I trow,
The rose is budding fain;
But she shall bloom in winter snow
Ere we two meet again,
My love!
Ere we two meet again.

Edmund's Song: Rokeby

I couldn't remember any more sins.

In the past week I had eaten the remains of a pie which should have gone to the poor, as all our household left-overs did; that was the sin of greed, gluttony. Envy? Madge Shotter's new plum kirtle had cost me a pang of covetousness, for I knew I should never get such a fine one out of Master Penny's pocket. Penny by name and penny-pinch by nature, they said of him, and oh dear, it was true, as I knew too well from keeping his household accounts. Why, he said, should he house a girl with book-learning and pay a clerk as well?

I could recall no sin of wrath, unless it was with the scullery-boy for stamping on a young mouse as it skittered across the floor, poor innocent. I had slapped his face smartly on both sides. I told the priest this, and I thought there was a smile in his voice when he said, 'Our Lord said that not a sparrow falls on the ground but his Father knows it. Should a mouse rank less than a sparrow? I absolve thee, daughter.'

I was surprised to hear such good sense from priestly lips; they were usually curt with me about such trivial things. I was encouraged to chatter on, though I knew small talk had no place in the confessional. 'I had a tame mouse when I was a child,' I told him. 'It was the gentlest little thing and knew me so well. Don't you think, Father, a mouse might have an immortal soul?'

He began to say something, then changed it to 'Your confession, daughter.' It was hard not to sigh, for I always disliked naming the sin I had no difficulty in remembering, and always left until the end. 'I have had carnal dole with a man who is not my husband,' I said, and waited for the usual sermon. But the priest was silent; I wished I could see his face under the shadow of the cowl which hid it. He was sitting in one of the choir stalls, I kneeling below, on the other side, so that behind the carving of the stall he was hidden from me except for the cowl.

At last he said, 'You sinned out of the lust of the flesh?'

'No, Father. I'm not sure what it is.'

His head moved slightly, and I could feel his gaze on my face, though I could not see it. His voice was gentle, not harsh as they usually were at this point, as he said, 'Would you like to tell me what you mean, daughter?'

'Ah. Well.' This was difficult and unexpected. 'I am concubine to a rich man, a merchant. My mother was his cook, and I was brought up in his house. He was taken with my looks and put me to school and bought me clothing. When I was fourteen my mother said that I was to go to his bed and be in every way to him as a wife, only that he would never marry me because he believed a wife could become a tyrant but a concubine never would. So I did. In the last plague my mother died and I've lived alone with Master . . . with him for two years, but for the servants.'

A faint but distinct sigh came from behind the carven wood. 'Do you love this man, child?'

'Love, Father? I'm grateful for what he gives me.'

'Love,' he said, stern for the first time, 'is what lies between Christ and His Church—between bridegroom and bride. It seems you know nothing of this.'

There was no reply I could make, since I had no notion what the holy man was talking about. My initiation into womanhood had been painful and had certainly not made me any fonder than I had been before towards Master Penny, and though since then I had put up with his embraces (if that was what they were) patiently enough, they did nothing to make me envy women in a state of lawful matrimony, since they must have to accept the same thing. Only they had their marriage-lines, and were not shunned and jeered at in the street as I was. That was all wedlock meant, surely: uncomfortable fumblings in bed two or three times a week, silent, greedy company at meals, and a great deal of hard domestic work to save him wages for extra servants. Where did love, and Christ and His Church come into it all? I rocked back on my heels, because my knees were aching, and waited for the usual grave remarks about the horrors of hell that waited for those living in mortal sin who could not receive the Sacraments, and the exhortations to forsake my evil way of life. How, I was sometimes pert enough to ask the priests, could I forsake it, except for starvation or a brutish existence among the harlots who herded together in their own quarter, on the outskirts of the town, under the city walls? (Once they had been kept outside the walls, but times were easier now for them.)

No reproaches came from the other side of the stall-bench. At last the priest said, 'Have you borne children?'

'No. I think Master . . . I think he is too old, or perhaps unable.'

'You must be thankful to God that you have none. They would have been conceived and borne in sin.'

'Yes, Father.' I could have told him that I had no wish for children at all, imagining them as little copies of Master Penny. But I thought that might in some way offend him. Hurt him, was the thought in my mind as I listened to him murmuring absolution for my other sins, though not for the great one. How strange that I should imagine a priest caring for what I said. They had always seemed to me to be of two sorts, cold-hearted woman-haters or sly pinchers of flesh and gloaters over naughty confessions. Perhaps it was because he was new and strange in Canterbury, and younger than most of the fathers of Christ Church Cathedral. Though not very young, to judge by his voice; not a boy only just out of his novitiate. When he blessed me perhaps I would see his face. I bent my head low as he spoke the blessing, then lifted it sharply, taking him by surprise.

The cowl slipped to the back of his head so that I saw him clearly. My guess was right. He was perhaps thirty years old, a good age to me, yet not chap-fallen as many of such years often were. He was pale, like most churchmen, his eyes dark, the lids drooping at the outer corners, giving them almost a triangular appearance. The long mouth looked to me as a poet's might, not fleshly yet not narrow-lipped or pinched, and there were little lines of thoughtfulness, or perhaps laughter, about it. The nose was large, a handsome prow, the chin oval, the ears coming to an elvish point, feathers of grey in the dark hair above them. Somehow I was glad not to see the tonsure that must make a bald spot on the crown. All this I saw in a flash, I who was not given to looking in men's faces for fear of seeing contempt there.

I got to my feet and scurried away, disturbed in my mind, partly by the unusualness of the confession, partly by shame at having tricked the father into showing me his face. To distract myself I climbed the worn steps to where a murmuring, exclaiming crowd of pilgrims stood or knelt around the thing all the Christian world came to Canterbury to see. The wonder of St Thomas's shrine always lifted my heart and took my mind off ugly worldly things. Above the heads of the worshippers it rose, a great ark-shape, all covered with plates of gold like the scales of a mighty dragon, the gold glinting out here and there but almost concealed beneath clusters of jewels. Diamonds and sapphires, rubies and emeralds, agates and cornelians, turquoise and onyx: and most precious and bright, pointed out by the finger of a golden angel, the Regale of France, the precious ruby as red as the saint's blood, given as a thank-offering by that King Louis who had been his protector. The duty-monk was telling the pilgrims the same stories he told every day, of the miracles shown in the windows above us which glowed like the jewels of the shrine.

'All these things were wrought by the power of the Spirit working through the blessed martyr,' he said, sounding wearily uninterested. 'Such of you good people who wish to partake of his holy protection may buy sacred badges and phials of St Thomas's Water as you leave by the south door.' There would be the usual rush, after the shrine had been sufficiently admired, to the stalls where the monks did a brisk trade in these lead badges which were turned out by the dozen, showing a mitred St Thomas on horseback, and small containers of what was supposed to be water infused with his blood. Since over three centuries had rolled away since the Martyrdom, we of Canterbury were not quite such keen believers in the power of this liquid as the trusting thousands who came on pilgrimage, innocently unaware that the saint would have to have held as much blood in his veins as there were drops in the River Stour that flowed through our city to provide such an abundance. But there, it did them no harm, poor souls.

When I had done looking at the shrine I went home, through the splendid Christ Church gateway rich with carven angels, along Burgate Street to the house of Master Penny. In sight of the door I was aware of a voice calling insistently, a cracked, feeble voice that yet would make itself heard. 'Mistress! Mistress!'

Behind me, hobbling as fast as he could, came an old man, long-bearded, in a rough homespun robe that somebody had tried to make into the semblance of a palmer's gown. The battered straw hat on his head was turned up in front and fastened with a shell brooch. I turned back and asked him what he wanted with me.

'Did I see thee just now in church, at the holy shrine?' That was what I thought he said, but his speech belonged to some other part of England, and I could scarcely make it out. I answered yes, I had been there.

'And dost live here, in this place?' I said that I did.

'Then tell me, of thy kindness . . .' he was almost choking with emotion, 'is it true, that they'll pull it down?'

'The shrine?'

He nodded, and a tear trickled forlornly down into his beard. I thought before answering. For months rumours had been coming to us from London and even farther north. The King had quarrelled with the Pope—he had ordered the beheading of Queen Anne Boleyn (a shocking tale which turned out to be true)—he had made himself Head of the Church and was paying himself wages in the form of treasures from small monasteries and abbeys which his men seized, turning the monks out into the world to fend for themselves. How could one believe such things, even of our King Henry Tudor whose temper was said to be as fiery as his hair? It was not wise to pass on rumours; even humble folk had gone to the gibbet for talking too much. But it seemed safe to give the old man some comfort.

'Never fear, sir,' I said. 'Who'd lay hands on it?'

'The King's men, the King's men.'

'Hush, sir. You don't know who hears . . . There have been tales of lesser shrines being seized, I know—but not Canterbury, never that.'

He nodded, trying to believe me. 'The Saint would protect his own, surely.'

'Of course. He would never let it be touched, a powerful saint like Thomas.' But I thought, all that treasure, jewels beyond price, sheets of pure gold, the ruby that glows in the dark. Fine rewards here for one with a conscience that twists and turns with his desires.

The old man was rambling on. 'I come every summer, you know, all the way from . . .' I couldn't catch the place he named. 'A stone's throw from Walsingham we be, and travelled there many and many a time, yet Our Lady never healed my poor old wife, or our Jack when he fell sick. And now all are gone, and I drag my old bones all this way for the health of my soul, by St Thomas's grace.' I thought that however healthy his soul might be his body looked very feeble, and I invited him to come home with me for a bite and a sup. He brightened at that, and went with me willingly.

Master Penny was not best pleased to hear that there was an extra mouth to feed in the kitchen, but it was considered unlucky to turn a pilgrim away, and with a sour glance at me he sent a groat to the old man by our servant Joan, before falling greedily on his own dinner. He never spoke to me at table, except to grunt a request for the salt or the bread platter or some such thing. I was not a wife, to be told how business had gone that morning, or what tales he might have heard about the town. I was only Margery, kept for his use, and because it looked more seemly to have a woman at board than to eat alone.

Not that I missed his conversation. I was content to sit, indulging my own hearty appetite and thinking thoughts which had perhaps been stirred up by the strange confession I had made that morning. Strange, because a priest had seemed to care about my way of life, instead of merely judging me. I looked across the dishes at Master Penny, fat, grey, balding, getting on with his dinner by the help of the teeth he had left. In himself he was not worth the stains that accompanied a state of mortal sin, the stares and flouts of neighbours, the drawing away of skirts if I should come close to one of them in the street or bargaining at a shop, the loud whispers which their speakers took care reached my ears—that I was worse than a whore, for Master Penny had bedded my mother before me, and it might well be that I was his own daughter, making us both guilty of the terrible crime of incest. I knew this was not true, my mother having talked much of my father, William Burgoyne, a servant in the house of the Roper family in St Dunstan's Street.

Soon after I was born he died of a sickness of the lungs, and so she settled for becoming cook and bedfellow to Master Penny.

Some of the wives who lived about us in Burgate Street and the Buttermarket were less harsh to me, perhaps because I bore myself modestly and flaunted no rich clothes—thanks not to my decency but to Master Penny's tightness of purse. After all, they reasoned (and this was said to my face) nothing was proved, I might indeed only be the man's cook-housekeeper, though he had no call to choose one so young or with hair that curled and danced like threads of tinsel in the sunlight, however tightly I strained it back under my coif (and I didn't try too hard) and a face of clear pink and white, like a new wax image of Our Lady.

I knew very well that my looks were comely, and was pleased enough to own them, even though they had got me nothing better than Master Penny, or were likely to, since I could bring no man a dowry, only a bad name. We may surely take pleasure in what the mirror shows, since it is none of our doing. I was thankful to have a mind that enjoyed small things, things that might go unnoticed because they come to us free and plentiful: the pretty shape and carving of the lute that hung on the wall, though never played because Master Penny had no musical skill and I had never been taught—this was always a delight to me to stroke as I dusted it. The flight of a blackbird pleased me as much as the soaring of a hawk does a huntsman, and the pinks and violets and such cottage flowers quite as well as any in the King's gardens at Hampton, great lilies and rare things brought over the seas. Not that I had ever seen them.

Through the window I watched our Nan pegging newly-washed linen on the clothes-line. The sheets leaped and danced against a bright blue sky with pearly clouds scudding across it, as though they rejoiced in their cleanness and the fresh air. The sight of them brought me a lift of the heart, such as I often felt at the sudden coming out of the sun after gloom and rain. Master Penny glanced up and asked me what I was grinning at.

'Nothing, sir.'

'Only fools laugh at nothing.'

'Yes, sir.'

'Then straighten your face.'

I straightened it, though the feeling of lightness and joy had not left me. To give it something more solemn than washed linen to dwell on, I went back in my mind to the shrine, all glowing with beauty as it would be now in the sunlight; unless the monk on duty had lowered its wooden cover back over it until enough pilgrims had gathered to make it worth his while to go over once again the story he told so many times a day. Would the Regale still shine bright, even in the darkness beneath the cover? Would the cluster of pearls with a statue of ivory set in it still keep the same soft bloom? From thinking of that I came to imagine a hood made of black or very dark grey velvet, its edge stiffened with wire and embroidered with pearls. How well it would set off the face and frame it! There was a picture I had seen of the late Queen Anne Boleyn wearing such a thing and appearing very handsome in it, though people who had been to her coronation said that she had little to commend her for beauty, only a pair of eyes black as sloes and a great quantity of hair. The hood would become me better, being light-haired and fair-skinned. But I would have to be an alderman's wife at least to wear anything of the kind, and that I could never be . . .

At this foolish, vain thought all the brightness fell from the day, for no reason. The washing was only wet linen, the sky had clouded over, and a discontent as sudden as my happiness had come over me.

What remained of my day, this day of summer? After the meal I would take myself to the kitchen and bake cakes and pies and fruit puddings for the week to come, pick the currants that remained on the bushes and make preserves from them, set fallen rose-petals to dry, for use later to scent the rooms sweetly, see to the spreading out to dry of the clean linen and the making of more soap, so much having been used for laundry.

By the time all this was done dusk would be falling. It would be time for Master Penny to read prayers with his household, all kneeling, and so edified we would go to bed, and either he would claim his rights of me or not. So the day, and the evening, and the night would be gone. And every daily span like it, until the last darkness of all.

Perhaps these melancholy thoughts still hung about me when the morning came, for I begrudged the time it took to swallow my breakfast cup of ale and piece of bread, I so longed to get out of the house into the sunshine, to visit the market stalls and talk to people—people who would not know me, some come in from the countryside with goods they had grown and spun. Nan walked a little behind me with her baskets, to carry whatever I might buy. We said little to each other, she envious of me and I taking little account of her, a sullen sharp-tongued creature that my mother would not have had in the house.

All the darkness fell away from me, swinging along Burgate, the cheerful sounds and sights of morning around me, Bell Harry Tower chiming the hour, the grey and gold of stone and the red of brick warming into life, everything seeming young and new, as I felt. Many of the stall-keepers called me 'maid', for I wore my hair loose with no cap or hood, only married women being entitled to wear those in the street. I liked to be called Honey-head or Golden-locks, and to see men's eyes follow me, while pretending not to see them. The cold eyes of neighbours, and the jeers, I ignored; it was that or invite a public brawl.

When I had bought all we needed, and Nan's baskets were full, I told her to go home and get on with preparations for dinner. She stared.

'And what are you to do, Mistress Margery?'

None of your business, I felt like saying, but instead answered that I had an errand in the town. She raised her eyebrows impertinently and flounced off; I wondered what tale would be told in the kitchen. I watched her short figure out of sight before I set off on my errand, which was nothing at all but to walk in the meadows by the river while the day was fresh.

I took the path below the bridge-house where the weavers work, soon reaching the Black Friars monastery. Monks were working in the gardens, sturdy bent figures, none raising his head as I looked across.

The river was narrow here, clear as it was not where it ran under the street, spoiled by filth and rubbish. In the hop-fields the poles were green-garlanded, ready for the autumn picking; apples were ripening, glistening red to tempt schoolboys. I loved this walk in spring, when apple-blossom and cherry-blossom lay over the land like a great veil of pink and white, and blackbirds sang in the trees like angels. They were quiet now, saving their small strength for the winter. I walked softly, looking about for what life there might be: a water-rat, swimming suddenly out of the reeds, a train of coots jerking their heads rhythmically as they passed by in neat formation, like King's ships.

I came to the woodland where a pool lies that they call St Radigund's Bath, and sat for a time on the river bank, watching the fish dart about like tiny silver arrows. Then, hearing the chimes of nine o'clock, I began reluctantly to retrace my steps. If I were away too long some household accident was sure to happen, and my absence blamed for it.

When I reached the footbridge that spans the river from the monastery I almost ran into two friars who had just crossed it, gazing about me as I was, not looking where I was going. One put out a hand to stop me from colliding with him, saying, 'Steady, daughter!' He was a stout, jovial-faced man, whose beaming smile saved me from feeling too foolish. I thanked him, begging pardon for my clumsiness, and would have hurried on but that I glanced towards his companion, and knew him for my confessor of the day before.

I saw in his eyes that he recognized me, and blushed, every word of my confession coming back to me in an instant. But the smile he gave me was sweet, with no hint of condemnation in it, as he said, 'A fair day for walking.'

'Most, Father.'

I would have moved on, but it seemed that they too were going back into the town, and they fell into step beside me. I wondered what we would talk about, or even if we were supposed to talk at all, having little experience of priestly company outside church walls. But the stout friar began to chat with the utmost readiness. They had, he said, been visiting a friend of the Black Friars, one who had been with them in a community in the county of Norfolk. 'But the King in his wisdom saw fit to disperse us and sell off the lands, not to mention filling his pockets from our coffers.'

I saw a warning look directed at him by his companion, but he went on unheeding. 'And so we bent our steps here, where they'll surely not trouble us. They call me Brother Ambrose, by the way, and this is Brother Clement.' He beamed, as though we were all meeting at some jolly assembly. I risked saying to the younger one, 'You took your name from the last Pope, Father?'

'I was fortunate enough to be given it. I might have been Swithun, or Remigius—or even Polycarp.' The smile was in his almond-shaped eyes, and the twitch at the corners of the long mouth; it made him look much younger and, if one dared think such a thing, quite charming. I thought the name Clement suited him, being gentle-sounding and pleasant, like his voice and looks. I said, bolder now, 'I wish they had called me after a saint with a pretty name, but my mother chose Margery.'

'That is not a bad name,' Clement said thoughtfully.

'Harsh and ugly,' I said, 'like nutmegs being grated.'

'No, no. It is from the same root as Margaret, which signifies in the Latin *Margarita,* a pearl, the name we give in English to the daisy-flower.'

I had not thought of this; my opinion of my name rose immediately. 'I shall like it better for knowing that,' I told him. There was a sudden sound from Brother Ambrose which in a layman might have been called a splutter of mirth, and he said something to Clement which sounded as though it concerned mules, but which I quickly understood to be concerning women, for the word I caught was *mulieribus,* which I knew from prayers. Clement answered in Latin, sharply, I thought, and a silence fell. We were crossing the bridge by the Weavers' House, back in the town again. As we reached the street Brother Ambrose said that he had an errand at St Dunstan's Church, and with a cheerful farewell was off, like a plump pigeon in flight.

I continued to walk by Clement's side, eastwards. Because we said nothing I had leisure to glance slyly sideways at him, aware of his height (I had not noticed that in the Cathedral), the straightness of his bearing and the squareness of his shoulders, altogether unlike many priests who stalked about like hooded crows, or scuttled like things that feared the light. Then, too, he looked about him, with a sort of eager interest, as though he were a stranger to the busy street scene; and I thought it a pity that a creature so alive should be condemned to the cloister. At least he didn't belong to an enclosed order, shut away from the world in silence; I was glad of that.

A cart being driven much too fast along St Peter's Street lurched on the cobbles as it came level with us, and veered towards us dangerously. In an instant Brother Clement's arm came round my shoulders, pushing me into the doorway of a fishmonger's shop. I felt a very curious sensation run through my body, as though the cart had indeed hit me and jarred all my bones—except that the feeling was not unpleasant, only disturbing.

'Clumsy ass,' said Brother Clement, referring not to me but to the drover. 'Forgive me for pushing you so rudely, daughter.'

'It was good of you,' I said; and then, perhaps because I caught the astonished eye of the fishmonger, who had paused in the middle of cutting up an eel, I, twenty years old, full woman, mistress of a household, felt a hot blush colour my face till it seemed to be on fire. I muttered something about being late and wanted at home, and darted past Brother Clement. Against all the noise of the street I heard him say,

'God be with you,' and fancied there was . . . in his tone . . . what? Regret, surprise?

As I hurried, needlessly, up the lane that led to Burgate Street I wondered why I had left him so suddenly. Surely there was no harm in walking beside a holy man, and he might have had much good counsel to give me, who was in need of it as he knew. Yet I had been afraid: of what, I could not tell. And yet again—how many 'yets' there were in this! I was sorry for leaving him, and the sun seemed less golden now that he was out of sight.

2

It makes me smile, even now, to think how ignorant I was, for all my twenty years and my knowledge of such things as the cooking of turkey-birds and the making of quince jelly. Nothing in my life had taught me the reason why, from that day, I was cursed with a wandering mind, with fits of dreaming and a strange impatience at the things which had been the stuff of ordinary life until then. If it had been springtime I might have blamed that, and dosed myself with flowers of sulphur, but who ever heard of such megrims in high summer? My brain and my fingers seemed not to belong to each other. One day I would bake a batch of cakes that came out sad and soggy in the middle, another day the damsons in the pie would go unstoned, causing Master Penny to curse as he jarred his few teeth on one. I who had so often scolded Wat the scullery-boy for neglecting to turn the spit failed to notice that he had dozed in the heat of the fire, letting the meat burn. And for the household accounts my mind had turned quite useless.

Master Penny glared up at me from the blotted and scored-out page he had been checking.

'This is all a mish-mash. Where are your wits, girl?'

I stared at him helplessly.

'Well? Cat got your tongue?' He made sounds of disgust. 'Off to the quack and get a sound purge.'

'I'm not ill, sir.'

He pushed the book across the table so hard that it hit my arm. 'Do this again and let me see it when it makes some kind of sense.'

I pored and pored over the wretched figures until they dazzled before my eyes. If they refused to come right this time I might well expect a beating. There was only one thing for it—to get help. When I knew Master Penny was out of the way I wrapped the ledger-book in my apron and ran to Doctor Lark, three doors away.

Whether he was truly a doctor of medicine I had no idea. He had no scroll displayed to show that he had qualified at a university, and I never heard him mention either Oxford or Cambridge. But he had a marvellous skill in curing aches, pains and fevers, and, I thought, a knowledge beyond other physicians. He never recommended (that I knew of) any of the horrible remedies so much used—dead dogs, infusions of spiders, dried, withered fingers from gibbetted thieves. I think he was too kindly a man to order such things—kindly, that is, both towards the patient and the creatures which must be killed to make the medicines. His house, though cleanly enough, smelt strongly of many cats; it was unwise to sit on any stool or chair in it without first making sure that it was not already occupied. He had a rat, pure white with eyes like pink jewels, that would lie curled round his neck, shaming the lawn of his collar with its pure snowiness. He called it Blanche, and it must have borne a charmed life, for I never saw any of the cats go near it—indeed, they seemed to avoid it with their eyes, as cats do when they prefer not to know about something. Nor did they pay any attention to the tame starling, Jack, which hopped about the house quite fearless, sometimes challenging Blanche for the envied position on their master's shoulder, where Jack would perch like a conqueror, turning aside now and then to bestow a beaky jabbing kiss on the doctor's neck.

It seemed to me very right and proper that such a man should bear the name of a bird, since he shared in the nature of dumb things enough to charm away their natural fears. Charm? Yes, I believe he used charms, both on animal and human, but not such amulets as gruesome things in small leather bags. Those who disliked him muttered that he was no better than a sorcerer, for he cast horoscopes, read the stars, and spoke of such mysterious and unlikely subjects as the life that he said existed in the things we call inanimate—stones, books, jewels, and especially furniture.

'For,' he said, 'was not this table once a living tree? And has it become dead, now that man's hand has fashioned it for his use? Who can say but that it rejoices in its new shape, in the skilled representations it bears of flowers and faces and such ornaments? Touch it gently, and it will warm to your hand; strike it, and you will be hurt. This book—its pages were fair flax growing in the field, its covers are the skin of animals; treat it well. May it not be wise, with wisdom it has learned? Or wicked, taught in vice by cruel or grasping hands? These pearls graced lovely necks and bosoms, whose beauty they have brought with them, and because they keep the life of the oyster that made them within their spheres, they know their wearer's sickness or health, joy or melancholy.'

So he would ramble gently on, to my pleasure but to the anger or laughter of those who thought him mad. I think he learned, just a little, to be quiet on these subjects when scoffers were about.

He scanned the mess I had made of the household accounts, and smiled his childlike smile that sat oddly on an ageing face. His skull was long, large in the brain-pan, pointed of chin, his nose short and up-tilted, his brow immense, fringed with grey wispy curls. He wore no beard, only a light moustachio, also grey. One would say he was a man given over to dreams and visions, but he had a shrewder calculating gift in his head than any clerk I ever met.

'Out of count here, Margery,' he said, 'sadly out of count. Were the sums beyond you? "One half-penny for lard. Bread 4 pence. Candles 6 pence. Boyes wages 2 pence half-penny." It seems simple enough to my eyes.'

'I know, sir. It was only that . . . My thoughts seemed unable to settle.'

'H'm.' He was lightly running a pen down the items and columns of figures, murmuring silently, then jotting down totals at the bottom. Over the round horn spectacles he glanced at me.

'Disordered spleen? Evil humours in the blood? A toothache?'

'No, sir. Only that I seem unable to think of one thing long, even long enough to add up.'

'Butterflies,' he said, 'are much the same, going from blossom to blossom for their sweets, yet they take no harm from it.'

'I should, sir, if I presented Master Penny with yet another botched sheet.'

'Yes . . . yes. There, that will do. Copy it in your own hand.'

'But he'll know—the page is spoiled . . .'

With a mischievous, triumphant smile, Doctor Lark took from his desk a tiny bottle from which he smeared the page and pressed it close to the one behind it, then handed it to me. It was impossible to see that the two had been joined. I said so, and praised and thanked him, then asked, 'What do you think is the matter with me, sir?'

He studied me with his head on one side, lights seeming to come and go in his almost colourless eyes.

'Nothing grave. Nothing for concern. It will pass; or it may not.' He picked up my left hand in his own long, cool, bony fingers, glanced at the palm and then at the back, plump and young and ordinary and nothing so white as a lady's. 'Do you feel nothing there, Margery?'

I shook my head.

'A cord goes from it to the heart.' He touched the third finger, which no ring encircled, and I could have sworn that a pang like the stroke of a dagger went through my breast, and that he knew it.

'There,' he said gently, 'take your book, child. Jane is in her parlour—she will be glad of a sight of you.'

I made my way up a little twisty flight of stairs, between walls of linen-fold panelling, to the room that was his daughter Jane's, hers alone, to ornament as she wished, to be alone in or to receive her few friends. Jane, eighteen years old, the only one of Doctor Lark's family to survive a terrible plague year. She had been sent away ahead of the others because of her delicacy, and when she returned to Canterbury it was to a home where neither mother nor sisters and brother were any more, for their bodies lay in a pit outside the city walls.

After that Doctor Lark took her from the school in the street where St Alphege's church was and taught her himself. It was better so, for poor Jane had the falling-sickness, the ailment which causes people to stare about them, then seem to swoon, or talk and sing in strange tongues before returning to their right mind. Jane had borne jeers and insults all her life, had been called Mad Jinny, pelted with stones and cries of witch, kicked as she lay senseless in one of her fits: such is the cruelty of children to each other.

So for the first time she was free of public shame, away from the taunts and blows, unseen by any but her father and the household when she fell, her father's only jewel. I had always been her friend, for Doctor and Mistress Lark had never been uppish about my mother's lowly status in Master Penny's house, or my own disgraceful one later. Indeed, Jane and I were both outcasts, each in our way, and sympathized with each other.

She was sitting in the window-bay, basking in the afternoon sunshine. When I entered she jumped up to meet me.

'Margery!' She flung her arms round me and gave me a bird's peck on each cheek, as her father had taught her to do because he admired the French fashion. She was altogether bird-like, small-boned and dainty, her straight brown hair soft as feathers, her plain little face having a comic look of Doctor Lark's. She was clever, far cleverer than I, able to write a letter in Latin and reel off verses of which I couldn't have remembered two lines. And she had another skill, one it did not do to talk about too much: the skill of divination. Her father had instructed her in the science of astrology, designing for her a wonderful chart which hung on her parlour wall, showing the constellations as figures of the people of legend whose names they bore: Cassiopeia in her chair, the warrior Orion waving his sword, captive Andromeda, the great dragon, Draco, which circles half the heavens, and besides these single planets and stars each with its own form and features, mighty Jupiter, the lady Venus, raging Mars, the dog Sirius. I had looked and looked at this chart so often that when I gazed up at the night-sky I fancied I saw them all, great bright shapes ever wheeling majestically above us and our little concerns. I spoke to them sometimes, reciting the beautiful mystic star-names Jane had taught me: Aldebaran, Delphinus, Vega, Boötes, Algol, Lyra. Only I made sure no mortal ear heard me.

I told Jane the reason for my visit to her father. She laughed.

'Margery become a scatterbrain? I can't credit that, in such a housewife as you.'

'It's true. Sometimes I feel half-crazed.'

'Perhaps you've crossed a fairy, who takes her revenge.'

'Then I wish she would take it some other way—the toothache would be kinder, nobody beats a person for having *that*.'

'Never wish such a thing on yourself—ills hear us, and come visiting.' Jane put her head on one side and studied me. 'Are you troubled? Have you some fear that frets at your mind?'

'Nothing like that. Only the fear of a beating for my clumsiness. Jane, will you divine for me? Look in your crystal.'

I was only half-serious: I asked because I wanted to get another look at the globe Jane kept hidden under a cloth worked in gold. It fascinated my senses, the thing of dark glass seemingly opaque, yet, when turned in the light from a window, revealing glimpses of depths changeable as an opal. Jane had told me that however long I gazed in it I would see nothing. Now she said: 'You know I would never use it except for a grave matter. We must not waste magic powers or our own strength—for strength goes out of me when I 'scry with the crystal, just as it went out of Our Lord when the sick woman touched His garments before He knew it.'

I was pleased to hear Jane quote Scripture, though I knew that such a dear good child could have nothing to do with evil, and I begged her pardon and asked her for some practical help for my wandering mind. 'You should eat fish often,' she said, 'not only on Fridays, for it nourishes the brain.' With her words there came to me a sudden vision of fish lying on a stall in their bloodied silver, and the strong smell of them, and for no imaginable reason I began to blush violently until I stood before my little friend with a face like an overblown cabbage rose. She burst out laughing and clapped her hands.

'I could venture what ails you, Margery,' she said, 'without the help of the crystal or the stars.'

'What? Oh, tell!'

'No. It would put you out, and may be only idle guessing. Did my father say nothing?'

I told her what he had said of the unseen cord between my hand and my heart. She nodded, and kissed me as I left.

Master Penny grunted when he saw the new page in the ledger, but made no remark, so I knew that he had not seen through the trick and was satisfied with the total. 'Mind your five wits go no more woolgathering,' was all he said. I resolved that they should not, and though it cost me many an aching head and more burning of candles than he would have cared for, stooping over words and figures, I made no more stupid mistakes from that day.

But I was still uneasy in my mind about my own state. I decided to go to confession for the second time in a week, knowing that Joan and Nan jeered at me behind their backs. Perhaps priestly wisdom would find out what fault I had in me.

Brother Clement was not to be seen, and I was glad of that, as I had been of his absence the last time. It was not good to tell one's sins to a person with whom one had even the least acquaintance, I told myself, forgetting those noble families whose confessor lived with them almost as a relative. Priests should not hobnob with lay folk, of that I was sure.

I was one of many penitents: the Devil must have been busy in Canterbury. I waited for some minutes, shutting my ears to the murmur of voices in the great soaring space of the choir, thinking, I suppose, of nothing in particular. Then the priest in the next stall dismissed his penitent with the usual hasty blessing and beckoned me. He was Brother Ambrose, my other acquaintance of the riverside walk; I was not very pleased by this, partly because I wanted to talk to someone unknown and impartial, but also because I didn't trust the fat, rosy-cheeked man with the worldly eye to judge such a strange disorder as mine.

Indeed, now that the moment had come I was suddenly unwilling to speak about it. I rattled through the usual list, impatience, lack of charity, the oath which I had let out when the butter-dish fell and smashed on the stone floor. At last I came to the admission of my mortal sin, which I so disliked making. I gabbled it as tonelessly as I could, as though it mattered very little to me.

Brother Ambrose bent forward and took a good look at me; I could swear I had cheered him up for the day. He began to ask me questions that any old gossip might have asked, having nothing to do with his priestly function. How old had I been when Master Penny took me into keeping? How old was he, then? Had he been continent until then or frequented other wenches? Had I maintained constancy to him, though not bound in matrimony, or had my fancy strayed to younger men? His words disturbed me increasingly, until, when he said, 'He must be a hot lover, this old merchant of yours, to keep such a pretty lass dancing to his tune, never looking askance,' I answered very sharply, 'That has nothing to do with my confession, Father. It is not modest of you to say such a thing in this holy place.' Surely such words were never spoken to a priest before at such a time, and I waited for him to rebuke me, perhaps to lay heavy penances on me.

But he only stared down at me, his face comically fallen, so downcast that I was strangely sorry I had spoken. In the silence that fell between us I guessed him to be a very simple, lowly man, a country fellow by his voice, drawn into the Church not from holy zeal but some other cause. I guessed too that he would not have chosen to live without women, and that his bold speeches sometimes won him the bed of one. Those who wanted to destroy our monasteries (it didn't do to name the King especially) talked large of corruption among the clergy, feasting and drunkenness, midnight whoring between nuns and monks; and everybody knew this was not all lies and slanders. Poor Brother Ambrose; he had thought me a hopeful case, and he was disappointed and ashamed of himself. I said hastily, 'Forgive me, Father.'

He smiled wanly. 'I should rather say that. *Peccavi.*' He crossed himself, then murmured the Absolution and signed my forehead.

It was not long after this that Brother Ambrose was brought into my mind again. Master Penny had a friend, Master John Tuke, a comfortable merchant like himself, as wry-built and wizened as my master was stout. Often he would drop in at supper-time for a cup or two of ale and some of my pie, his wife not being much of a cook, by the look of him. The two would sit nodding and gossiping like two old dames, over the fire or under the pear-tree in the garden, depending on the time of year. I was never invited to join them, as I might have been if my position in the household had been a lawful one, and I was only too glad of it, from the dull snatches of talk I heard.

But on that October evening it was evident that Master Tuke was crammed with news. Lantern in hand, he almost tripped over the doorsill in his hurry to get in.

'Have you heard the talk, neighbour Penny? All over the town, it is, brought by the Folkestone carrier, not an hour since—such a clatter never was.'

'He talks a deal of silly stuff, that fellow,' said Master Penny dourly, never one to show interest, though his ear was as sharp for tattle-tales as anyone else's. 'But come in, neighbour. I was about to sit down to my supper, as it happens.'

His friend, who knew this very well, eagerly accepted a place at table; I was glad I had baked extra that day. Being curious, I sat down with them to hear Master Tuke's tale, eagerly told between mouthfuls and sups.

'They're on the prowl, Master Penny, on the prowl for treasure!'

'Not mine, I trust. Though if they find any I'll be thankful for a share . . .' It was the nearest he ever came to a joke.

'No, no, neighbour, the Church's. Two days since, it seems, the King's man Layton went to Folkestone to take an inventory of the Priory there, with a band of men and Cromwell's servant Bartelot.' We in Canterbury knew all too well the name of Thomas Cromwell, once a soldier of fortune, then secretary to Cardinal Wolsey, long since disgraced and dead; afterwards worming himself into the King's confidence, become Privy Councillor, Master of the Jewels, go-between with foreign countries, royal secretary, having more power than the King himself, it was whispered. By his advice the King had broken away from the Pope and made himself Supreme Head of the Church in England. By his workings, poor Queen Katherine of Aragon had suffered divorce and banishment, and the Lady Anne Boleyn set in her place; and when the King turned against her he had once passionately desired, it was Cromwell who brought her to the Tower and the block. Now he was called Vicar-General in Spirituals, appointed to pry into abbeys and monasteries and find out good reasons for dissolving them and transferring their wealth into the King's coffers. So far his agents had not sought out Kent, but it seemed they were upon us now, like wolves on the fold.

'What they found at Folkestone,' Master Tuke went on, 'Denne didn't hear, but it was told to him in an alehouse that someone had sent private word to the agent, Layton, to go to the Abbey at Langdon and take the abbot by surprise. Which he did.' He paused to cackle heartily. 'He sent the men to surround the buildings and keep watch on every door and bolt-hole, so that the rabbits shouldn't run away.'

'Rabbits? What rabbits?' enquired my master testily.

'The monks, the monks. Then he, Layton, himself went to watch the abbot's lodging, skulking in the woodland beside to get a view of it before he began a-knocking—but none came to the door, not a soul stirred, only the abbot's little dog, one of these sleeve-curs they keep, jumped up and down behind the locked door, barking and howling.' He gave an imitation of the frantic dog, almost choking himself with laughter at his own wit.

'Yes, yes, let the dog be. What then?'

'Why, he came upon a pole-axe leaning up by the wall, and struck and struck at the door until it was smashed in, then set one of his men to guard it while he went round breaking in the other doors. Then out of one of 'em comes bolting the abbot's . . .' he glanced sideways at me, 'the abbot's gentlewoman, a very fine fat comely bird as naked as Venus but for her bully's cope that she was trying to fasten around her, but the men halloo'd after her so that it fell off and she ran before them in her skin, as brisk as any hare, pink as a rose.'

Master Penny muttered that it was unseemly, and beckoned me to go in case the tale got worse. I stayed where I was, being not in the least entertained by all this, and anxious to know the end.

'So,' Master Tuke refreshed himself with a draught, 'they caught her and Bartelot held her fast. Then out comes the abbot in naught but a pair of linen breeches, shouting sacrilege, and both of 'em are hauled up before Layton for questioning, after which he ordered the wench to be trussed up in the cope and sent off to the mayor of Dover, to be kept in prison for eight days. And I'll warrant she had a bustling journey of it . . . twelve lusty fellows to guard her . . .' He showed signs of going off into a fit of mirth again, but my master said, 'I want to hear no lewdness. What of the abbot?'

'Why, Master Layton brings him here.'

'To Canterbury?'

'Aye, lying tonight at Faversham.'

I felt a cold shiver go through me, as though the door had opened and let in a winter gale. There had been plenty of rumours of what had been done up and down the country, but folk will talk for talking's sake. Now the thing was moving nearer, turning into reality. I remembered what I had told the poor old man who had poured out to me his fears for the shrine. I would not be so confident now. My mind was disturbed, too; first Brother Ambrose had showed me how there might be corruptness in a holy-seeming man, and now came this ugly story. But I was sorry for the poor harlot, who had only been doing what so many do, but in the wrong place. Suddenly I was sick of the company of the two men: sick of all men. I excused myself and went to the kitchens.

Word was about in the streets next day that Layton and his prisoner would be in town before nightfall. I had meant not to go out when others did, our household and the rest who had had their ears pricked up from the first rumour, but curiosity is stronger than good resolutions. When the riders from Faversham reached Christ Church Gate I was there in the crowd, staring.

First came a stout-built soldier on a sturdy horse, the sort used for battle, wearing a broadsword at his side and a dagger and cudgel in his belt; they were taking no chances of attack by the King's enemies. Behind him rode a dozen or so more, looking sharply about them, then one who was plainly the royal agent Richard Layton. For a man in holy orders he had a full-fleshed, worldly face and clothes richer than any cleric might be expected to wear. His eyes were keen and roving: I thought of the wretched girl chased in her nakedness by his orders, and wondered whether he especially sought out females among the watchers with his restless gaze. As he passed through the gate a sort of sigh went up; behind him rode the prisoner, tied on his horse, his hands bound tightly behind him.

A man beside me said, 'Which is the sinner, eh? The bound or the free?' And indeed, the abbot's face was a comely one, the face of a man who has not led an evil life, and it was set now in harsh lines, as though he were prepared for any insult or abuse, and would scorn to show knowledge of either. As he drew near the gate I saw him raise his eyes briefly to its splendour of carven angels, armorial shields and saints in their niches, still immaculate in freshness and colour, for the gate had only been built in our King's reign. Would he ride out through it towards the gallows at Dane John, all for being caught out in a piece of folly? There were one or two boos in the crowd, and a cry of 'Whoremaster!' but he gave no sign of having heard, only swayed sideways as his mount slipped on a cobblestone; at which the guard behind him laughed and cracked the beast upon its rump, so that it lurched again. I saw women cross themselves as the prisoner passed from sight, and for the few grinning faces there were many solemn ones, and some angry. I saw a nun in tears, and another whispering earnestly to her.

Only a few minutes, I thought as I turned homewards. Yet part of Canterbury's history had been made that day, the day when Abbot Sayer of Langdon rode disgraced through her streets.

3

That night I was shocked out of sleep by a roar and chatter of voices in the street. For a moment I lay motionless, looking up at the soaring dark beams overhead, like the upturned hull of a ship, too snug and warm to move, half-wondering if I dreamed. But the noise was real enough, making my heart beat fast with alarm. Beside me my master lay huddled sunk in slumber, giving out whistling snores; he slept like the dead—a thing for which I should one day be more grateful than I knew then.

Slipping from the bed, I pulled a coverlet round my shoulders, shivering in the cold air, and went to the window. People were scurrying up Burgate Street, some with torches and lanterns, talking and shouting. I unlatched the casement and leant out the way that they were going. There, only a little distance away at the end of Burgate, I saw billows of thick smoke lit by flames. I turned and shouted to Master Penny.

'The Cathedral's on fire!'

Even he heard that, coming out of a fog of sleep to mutter, 'Whassat you say?'

'The Cathedral must be on fire—it can be nothing else. Get dressed quickly master—if the flames spread we may need to leave.' I was hurrying into my own clothes, or some of them—stockings, shoes, a kersey petticoat and woollen bodice, and a cloak over all—best be warm as well as decent. I ran through the house banging at the door where the two servant-maids slept, hearing them answer me that they were awake and about. There was no sign of Wat in the kitchen, where he slept, so I knew he had gone out already—trust Wat to be in at any scene of public clamour.

Everybody in Burgate Street seemed to be out of bed and out-doors, clad in an amazing motley of garments. I asked our next-door neighbour, who was bundling goods on to a handcart, where the fire was, but he only pointed distractedly and bade me get to safety. Instead I forced my way in the direction of Christ Church Gate.

Thanks be, it was still there, and the body of the Cathedral seemed untouched. The fire was at the end of the Precincts, where a handsome new building called the King's Lodging stood—or rather had stood, for the great dining-hall was almost a shell already, sur-rounded by a crowd of men with buckets and ewers dousing it with water, black shapes like dancing demons against the blaze. Within the Cathedral lights were bobbing, most at the east end where the shrine was, jewels of colour flashing up in the windows as many as in Joseph's coat, beautiful to see even in that hour of danger. I watched in fascina-tion, drawing nearer to see better. Suddenly I screamed as a piece of flaming timber came flying down at my feet, almost catching my gown, and at the same moment someone grasped my shoulder and pulled me backwards so sharply that I almost fell.

Gasping, I recovered my balance, and looked up at my rescuer. It was Brother Clement.

'You run a great risk standing so close, mistress,' he said sternly. I stammered some sort of thanks, watching him kick the burning wood from him and stamp on it with his sandalled foot, a brave and rash thing to do. As he turned back to me I let the hood of my cloak slip back, so that he could see me clearly in the flickering light. He knew me, I could see that, and in his strange almond-shaped eyes there was a look I could not fathom: surprise, could it be?

'We meet for the third time,' I said, thinking as I spoke that it was a silly, frivolous remark to make to a holy man.

'Yes,' he answered, still with his eyes fixed on my face.

'What are they doing in there,' I asked, 'running up and down with tapers?'

'Monks—and Layton's men—guarding the shrine. If the fire spreads it will be stripped and the jewels taken to St Augustine's for safety. God send it may not come to that. Of all the mad, wicked ploys, risking the shrine and human lives too . . .' He broke off, leaving me curious.

'*Who* are mad and wicked?' I asked. 'Do you think the firing was no accident, then, Father?'

He seemed about to answer, then tightened his lips and shook his head.

'Not for me to say. Be advised and go home now, daughter; this is no place for women.'

What prompted me to be so bold I had no notion, but I said, 'Will you walk with me, Father? I have only a little way to go, but the crowds frighten me and I'd be glad of company.' This was not true, and I was glad of the little smile he gave me, that warmed his austere face more than did the light from the burning building. 'Willingly,' he said, 'since there's nothing I can do.' I wondered what he had expected to do. The fire now seemed to be getting under control, the crash of falling masonry almost ceased. The King's Lodging was almost a shell, the coughing men flinging water on it were standing back, watching the flames die down. From somewhere two men approached leading huge mastiffs on chains, and went into the Cathedral through the west door.

'Watch-dogs,' my companion said. 'The shrine will be safe tonight; Layton has seen to that. Shall we walk?'

As we left the Precincts, moving slowly enough through the still-watching crowds, I knew more strongly than I had ever known anything that I wanted with all my heart to stay in Brother Clement's company. I told myself it was because he presented a mystery, a puzzle, which I needed to solve. There was something about him not like an ordinary churchman. He had called me 'mistress' when he pulled me back from the burning brand, as though he were accustomed to that manner of speech towards women, and besides . . .

And besides I knew now that he had been troubling my mind since our last meeting, only I had not been plain with myself that this was so, and I had to be rid of the man somehow. It was not right to be plagued with the thought of one so much out of my reach; a kind of madness, truly. With female cunning I kept silent, as he did, while we walked the few yards along Burgate Street, hearing the slam of doors as neighbours went back to their homes, the far-off shouts of those who still fought the fire; and above, through the dying haze of the fire's glow, the stars showed again their silver points of light.

When we were almost at Master Penny's door I said very humbly, 'Do you remember what I told you in confession, Father?'

I felt rather than heard him catch his breath.

'It is not for me to remember what goes on in the confessional,' he said.

'No, but you do, surely. Such as what I told you about my . . . state in life.'

I saw him glance up at the house-front, the stout door, the jetty of the upper storey, the solid merchant-face of it, and I knew that he remembered.

'Something,' he said cautiously.

'Well, then, will you not help me?'

'How, daughter?'

'Help save my soul. From the wiles of the Devil and the pit of iniquity. If,' I said wistfully, 'I were able to talk with one so truly good as you, and hear words of wisdom, I might come to a change of heart and learn to mend my ways.' I blushed in the dark for the hypocrisy of it, fearing that his silence meant he had seen through my falseness. Any moment now someone would come out of the house and my chance to hold him would be lost. Oh, speak, I silently begged him, say something for my comfort.

At last he said, 'If you are sure of this, daughter, then I will hear you and give you what counsel I can. It may be, who knows . . . it can do no harm.'

I could have laughed, for I knew we were both playing a game. But I kept a sober face. 'Where shall I come to you, Father?' hoping he would name the river-bank where we had met before, perhaps by St Radigund's Bath where at certain times otters played, and kingfishers darted in summer. But he said, 'In the Priory, there is a room where strangers and supplicants are received. Ask for me there at eight tomorrow.' He made the blessing sign and left me with my hand on the latch, unwilling to go in and shut him out.

There was a great to-do going on inside, Master Penny downstairs in his winter fur robe and nightcap, being fed hot gruel by Nan. I was no sooner in than he was spluttering to know where I had been and whether I thought I had leave to go running up and down like a fly-by-night. Nan, heating the rest of the gruel, turned her red angry face on me and muttered that they had given me up for murdered, with all the rabble in the streets. I knew she would have been only too pleased if I had been. I smiled sweetly at her as I unloosed my cloak.

'One of us,' I said, 'had to go out to see if the fire was near. We might all have been burned in our beds. Now I can tell you the danger is past.' And I described the firing of the King's Lodging as lively as I could, like a player on an inn-cart, until my master stopped glowering and listened as keenly as he had done to Master Tuke's tale. Only I said nothing of Brother Clement.

I said nothing of him next morning, either. Instead I told Nan I was going a little outside the town to see a farmer who had kept his late apple-crop so well that the fruit was fit to be used as though it were new-picked, and if I thought it a bargain I would buy some pounds and have them brought by waggon to Burgate Street. This was all true, the farmer's house lay just beyond the city walls.

The friar who let me in looked me up and down as if I were not the kind of stranger or supplicant he cared about, and showed me into the barest room I had ever seen. Its walls were of roughcast, not even whitened, the window an open square with a grill across it, high up on the wall, the air like ice. The only ornament was a large crucifix, the figure of Our Lord carved in such a way that one almost felt His pain, and saw blood where there was only wood. I wished I were somewhere else, for choice on the banks of the Stour under the golden autumn trees.

The door opened. Brother Clement looked very tall, thin and pale in his black cassock, and his greeting was grave. I wished even more that I had not been so foolish as to come to this place.

'Now daughter,' he said, 'you have much to tell me.' He sat, hands folded, very straight-backed on a miserable little stool, the only piece of furniture in the cell besides the one I occupied, feeling my ample curves overflowing its sharp edges. I opened my mouth, then shut it again. Whatever I had thought of telling him the night before, it had gone now. I could only stare at him, wondering why as he had entered the room a curious burning sensation had attacked my breast, as though a hot knife had touched my heart.

Perhaps he took my silence for shame-fastness. 'You wanted to tell me of your desire to mend your way of life,' he said kindly. 'Now, when did this good thought come to you?'

'Ah,' I said. 'Well, it was when I made confession to you the other week, Father.'

'Not before? In so many years?'

'Well . . . sometimes . . .'

'At what times?'

I struggled. 'The neighbours, the goodwives, look at me sneeringly when I go to market.'

'And you wish yourself as virtuous as them.'

'They, virtuous? A set of tattle-tales and jumped-up jades.'

'That is not a Christian view of your neighbours, daughter.'

'No.'

He sighed. 'So when people look sideways at you, you suffer only injured pride.'

This was so true that I could only shrug.

'You paint a dark picture of yourself, daughter,' he said. 'I think you grieve in secret, knowing that the saints in Heaven grieve for you. You are one who hides sorrow and shame under a merry outside. On fast-days I'll be bound you keep indoors and mourn more truly than any of these neighbours of yours.' He was willing me to agree to this, I knew, most earnestly trying to draw me into the kind of admission he had expected. I kept my eyes on his face, so strong-featured yet tender now, in the look he bent on me, and I thought how delicate and well-shaped were his ears, almost pointed where the dark hair swept over the tips of them, and how straight his brows. Because I couldn't tell lies to him, I said, 'We take little notice of fast-days in our house, Father. If we eat fish instead of meat it's only because it has come in fresh that day. And on my saint's day, the Day of St Boniface, that is, I went to the fair and saw a fine puppet-show and a white bear that danced, not that I liked the spectacle very much for I thought it had been tormented to make it dance, but you see I haven't been much given to godliness.'

Our eyes met and held, for a long time, it seemed. Then he said, 'I should not have guessed your patron saint to be the Blessed Magdalen. Why are you sullying your own image before me, daughter?'

I spoke the truth boldly, without thinking. 'So that you can know the worst about me and see me as I am.'

Brother Clement rose and began to pace about the cell. After a moment he turned and stood facing me; I could not read his look. 'I must tell you of two saints,' he said, as though he were in a pulpit and I his congregation, 'The holy St Francis held the Moon, the element of Water, even Death, to be his sisters. Yet he said, "To converse with women, and not be hurt by it, is as difficult as to take fire into one's bosom and not be burned. He that thinks himself secure, is undone; the Devil finding somewhat to take hold on, though it be but a hair, raises a dreadful war."'

I guessed he had learned this by heart, for my benefit, as a warning to me.

He went on, 'St Nicholas, visiting one of his abbeys in the guise of a palmer, found the abbot carousing in the company of a fair young maiden. But, knowing her to be the Evil One in fleshly dress, he took hold of her and straightaway she became a devil, horns, tail and all, and the beguiled abbot saw what pit had yawned before him.'

At this I was very minded to laugh, but for some reason found myself weeping instead, the tears rolling down my cheeks as though I had hurt myself badly. And the tall young priest who had been preaching to me so sternly was looking down at me with pity, or puzzlement, saying, 'Margery, Margery! Hush now, hush.' I reached up and caught his hand, so cool, smooth and strong, and heard myself saying, thick with tears, 'You preached at me, and I'm no devil nor ever did you harm.' Then I leapt up and ran past him, out of that cold place, aware of passing the grim-faced friar and heaving up the iron bolt of the door and hearing it clang behind me.

I bought some pounds of the farmer's apples, though they seemed to me poor shrunken things, fleshy enough but past their ripeness.

That night Master Penny would have me play backgammon with him, though my attention wandered often enough for him to rap me over the knuckles with the ebony rod he kept by him. It was tedious but soon done, for the game made him sleepy almost an hour before his usual time. When I asked whether I might sleep in the little chamber above the kitchen which I used when I was what he distastefully called unwholesome, he grunted that I was to do as I pleased. So I was free.

Free to use the back stair and the door to the garden: free to ask help from my only friends. A light still glowed in the upper room of Doctor Lark's house, the room built out over the street. The doctor himself answered my knock. He wore a long, rich velvet robe and a scholar's cap; on one shoulder sat Blanche, on the other Jack, their bright eyes unafraid of me or any visitor their master welcomed.

'Come in, Margery,' he said with his vague kind smile. 'I had half-expected you. Does the ledger still not balance?'

'Oh yes, sir.'

'But something else troubles you. We will wrestle with it.' He showed me into the upper room, warm and homely, apple-logs in the hearth sending out their fragrant smoke, sleeping furry forms entwined before their glow. I looked round, enjoying the fine curious pictures whose subjects I would have been hard put to it to name, the shelves upon shelves of books, the phials and alembics gleaming on a table in a corner, the mingling scent of chemicals and herbs and the sweet stuffiness of animals. Astrologers were said to have human skulls and stuffed caymans in their studies, but Doctor Lark kept no such horrid things.

'Jane is in bed,' he said, 'she was not well today. And you, child, have slept little—even the blue eyes of youth tell tales.'

I described the events of the night before, leaving out Brother Clement's part in them. The doctor nodded.

'I heard the commotion, but I knew the fire would not touch us,' he said calmly, and I believed him. 'This morning, they say, the worthy Layton ran about the town crowing that he saved the jewels of the shrine by his prompt actions. His masters should be pleased.' It was hard to tell from his tone whether he approved of Layton or not, but I rather thought not.

'I saw the Abbot of Langdon led in, bound,' I said. 'Do you think they'll let him go free?'

'What was his crime?'

'Lechery.'

'Ah, for that he may get off lightly. For disobedience, the penalty will be heavier, I fear.'

I knew he meant disobedience to the King, and would like to have asked him more closely what he knew. But the thing I had come to tell him lay heavily on me, and I was silent, sitting at his feet in the low chair by the hearth, where I had so often sat with Jane listening to her father's wonderful tales and wise discourses.

'Now tell me, Margery,' he said. I poured out the story it was beyond me to understand, hoping that he might.

'I am bewitched—I must be. On St Faith's Day I made my confession to a priest, a stranger to me. Since then I have thought of nothing but him, his face, his looks, his words. I have met him by chance twice, on purpose once.' I told of my meeting beside the river, and again in the Precincts, and of the interview I had so foolishly contrived that morning. 'I cared nothing for men before, sir, not a pin, neither for Master Penny, though he houses and feeds me, nor for any lad in this town, and there are plenty who ogle me. And yet I must turn brainsick for the sake of a strange man whom I *know* to be vowed to chastity, one who may never look at an honest woman, let alone one like me. This morning I behaved like a trollop, throwing myself at him, and much good it did me. If he were only handsome I might understand it—a bonny rosy-cheeked young fellow like Jem the carter. But . . . he's nothing much to look at, and yet when I look up at the stars I see him, when I lie awake in the dark I see him, I can never get away from him. *Am* I bewitched, sir?'

Doctor Lark looked down at me with kindly amusement. 'If love is a spell cast by Nature's witchcraft, yes. That being so, how can we say how it will strike, or whom our fancy will light on?'

'But—a priest!'

'A priest will do as well as any, when love is on the wing. And he, this enchanting priest, how does he view you, Margery?'

I stared into the flames, watching them leap and flicker. 'He was severe with me this morning, as he had to be. But I think . . . he speaks to me not quite as a priest speaks, but as man to woman. I only think so. I am so ignorant, sir. Will you help me?'

Instead of answering, he went to the fine carved court-cupboard and took out a casket. From it he filled his palm with gems, and came back to the fireside, where he sat contemplating them, stirring them thoughtfully with his finger. 'Garnet,' he said, 'for the banishment of sorrow. Emerald, for calming the mind; sapphire, too. Carbuncle, for night-fears. No, none of them.' He took a pretty light green stone between thumb and finger. 'The beryl, which helps understanding. And here the coral, which feels its wearer's passions and state of health.' He laid the beryl delicately in the cleft of my bosom (which I wore uncovered half to the nipples, as maids do, even though I was no maid), and put the piece of coral into my hand, closing the fingers round it. Then we sat silent, I feeling the coolness of the jewels gradually warming to my blood-heat, he gazing placidly into the fire. I thought that perhaps there was music sounding somewhere, but it may have been in my head.

Then he came and took the gems from me, and looked at them under the light of a candle-branch. Jack, cocking his head, seemed to look too. 'No disorder, no ill-health; all well-being,' he said. 'So, we must seek further.'

'How?'

'The crystal might tell us.'

'But that is . . .'

'Jane's. And Jane the only one who can read it. And she is in bed, as I told you. But Sleep is not our master, only our servant, you know; friendly Somnus, who gives us rest and dreams. I must leave you for a moment, Margery. Here, take some company.' He unwound the white rat from its place at the back of his neck and put it in my lap, where it stirred and looked around, its pink eyes like rose diamonds, then curled up, making a nest of my hands, with its tail wrapped round its delicate nose, its tiny flanks heaving against me, quite unafraid. I thought how strange it was that such magical men as Doctor Lark should live in our world of sin and evil, and how different things would be if such a man were to rule England, instead of the King who had ordered his second wife's dark head to be chopped off so that he could get an heir on his third wife. But then holy magical people seemed not often to get born into the royal house, judging by what I had heard of it, though I remembered talk of one of our kings they called Holy Harry for his saintliness, a poor soul our King's grandfather had turned off the throne and kept in prison; he, that grandfather, had been a red man like our King, a big laughing giant with a taste for women, though not for beheading them. I was not sure where I had heard this, since very little was said publicly about our King or anything to do with him . . .

Doctor Lark was back in the room. The rat Blanche raised her head and left my lap, leaping or gliding back to him again. Then I saw that behind him was Jane: Jane in a long white shift, not holding to his hand but standing motionless like a ghost. Her eyes were wide open, yet I knew she was asleep. Her father put his finger to his lips as I started to speak.

'Hush,' he said, 'we must be very quiet, not to startle her. It would harm her to wake suddenly.' He led the way to a chair in which Jane, without his touching her, sat, very straight and looking before her. He drew a small table alongside it, and placed on it something covered with a velvet cloth worked in gold. It was Jane's crystal.

He took off the cloth, then made a gesture with his hands at which her head moved, so that she looked down at the crystal. Then she turned herself and leaned forward, her elbows resting on the table, gazing into the opaline depths as I had seen her do at the rare times when she had 'scryed for me, her eyes still wide, unblinking. She was very pale, so pale that I wondered for a frightened moment whether just her spirit sat there. On her father's right shoulder the starling had put his head under his wing, as though he too slept.

Then Jane spoke, her voice low and without expression. 'The bear,' she said, 'the bear.'

I thought instantly of the unhappy dancing bear I had seen at the Michaelmas fair, but why should Jane see that poor thing, hobbling in its chains? I opened my mouth to ask, and received such a bright forbidding glance from Doctor Lark that it was as though he had clapped a band of steel over my lips.

'Holding between his paws a staff,' said Jane's dreaming voice. I saw that her father was scribbling on the ivory writing-tablets he kept at his belt.

'The castle. Searching. Up a twisting stair. Not in the little tower.'

I held my breath, afraid of missing a word, though nothing she had said made sense to me.

'Brown. A brown horse. But the saddle . . . empty.' Then there was a long silence, in which I could hear a cricket chirping somewhere by the hearth, and a wind beginning to rise, whistling through the narrow channel of the street.

Doctor Lark said, in a voice as soft as a wisp of smoke, 'Jane. What are you being shown?'

'Brown.'

'The brown horse?'

'No. A . . . I can't see. Silk? No, hair. A curl of hair—and a gold one twined with it.'

I began to shiver.

He asked, in the same ghost of a voice, 'Can you see the owner of the brown hair?'

A long pause. 'A lad. Square-built. But the face . . . no, that's

wrong. The face of a woman.' Her voice quickened. '*Now* I see someone. Gold hair, and—steel? A coat of steel?'

'Armour?' whispered Doctor Lark.

'Something . . . red. Cloth. Stitchwork. The bear.'

Here we were again, back to the bear which surely could not be
the one I had seen dance. I heard a sighing gasp, coming from myself.
None of this could have anything to do with my troubled mind, with
Brother Clement.

Doctor Lark asked, 'Jane, what manner of bear? Describe him.'

'Not . . .' she seemed to struggle for words. Then, 'He stands,
sideways. Wearing a muzzle. Between his paws a staff.'

Her father said, 'Yes. Now go back to the man in armour. What is
he doing?'

'Searching. Through trees, in a forest. No—up a stone stair. Sad,
troubled.' There were tears in her dreaming voice. 'Always searching
for the brown person.'

Doctor Lark made some signs in front of her face, as if weaving
invisible thread with his hands. She sat back in the chair, suddenly as
limp as a doll thrown down. He lifted her, gently supporting her round
the waist, and led her out of the room, leaving me very much per-
plexed. I knew Jane's powers to be real; but what had she seen that
could possibly mean anything to me?

The writing-tablets lay on the table beside the crystal where Doctor Lark had left them, the carved ivory cover thrown back. I picked
them up and stared at what he had drawn, three neat sketches: something like links in a chain—that would be the intertwined curls of
hair—the outline of a battlemented tower—and last, the bear Jane had
mentioned twice, a stiff formal creature drawn sideways, the right paw
resting on top of something that looked like part of a tree-trunk, the
other supporting it, a muzzle over the face. A staff, Jane had called the
tree-like thing. It came to me that this was not a living bear such as

could be seen in the menagerie at the Tower of London, or baited by mastiffs in the pleasure-gardens by London River, but a representation. Cloth, stitchwork, Jane had said, and red cloth.

And I knew, without knowing why, that the bear was white. Then before my mind's eye came a string of jewels, linked with gold, and I knew them to be emeralds; then a glimpse of fur, and a great ring on a finger. The vision went as though a blindfold had been pulled over that inward eye, but the shock of recognition was with me, and I felt the blood drain from my face as my heart began to beat heavily.

Doctor Lark was supporting my head, and I was lying on the ground. I tried to ask him why. He said, 'You swooned for a moment. It's nothing, it will pass. Take a sip of wine.'

I sat up, still trembling, but calmer for his soothing voice.

'It would have harmed Jane to let her see more, so I put her to sleep again. Tell me what you remembered when I was out of the room.'

'The bear, in your drawing, sir. It was on a shield—somebody's arms. I saw it hundreds of times over—at the same time—oh, what do I mean?' Another flash of light pierced my mind. 'There was something else, like it—a bull's head! A white bull . . . and a crown. And another thing that was not in your drawing, a string of emeralds which I think hung round someone's neck. There are emeralds among the jewels of the shrine, so I know how they look. Oh, what can it all mean—won't you tell me, sir?'

He was worried, frowning. 'I meant to help you, Margery, child, but I fear to disturb your mind too much. Do you truly want to know how I interpret what Jane saw, and what you are remembering? Truly?'

'Truly, sir. I must know.'

He sighed. 'Very well. The bear with the ragged staff is a part of the armorial bearings of Warwick. The bull's head you saw must be the Bull of Neville, and a Neville was once Earl of Warwick.'

'Not now?'

'Not now. The great Earl died in battle more than sixty years ago.'

'Then . . . what am I to him?'

'How do I know, child? It seems to me that someone from the past calls you, searches for you, as Jane told us. You are the brown person the man in armour sought for, still seeks. It may be the Earl himself, for love knows no degree or station, or another, one who sends out these images so that you may recognize and remember. A yellow-haired soldier—*don't* you remember, Margery?'

I shook my head, willing and willing that I should remember, but no picture came. 'Then is this soldier dead, like the Earl?'

'His body, yes, but not his soul.'

'I thought souls went to Purgatory, then Heaven or Hell.'

'Oh, Margery, Margery! How can we know the wonderful works of Our Lord with His creatures? For some souls one destiny, rest or a time for repentance; for others a return to seek what they lost before.'

I was glad to hear him mention Our Lord, for well as I knew Doctor Lark I had begun to be afraid I was caught up in the black arts. My head was aching very much, but I still struggled to think clearly.

'But I came to you, Doctor, for help in my bewitchment with Brother . . . with the priest. All this tells me nothing of him.'

The doctor's eyes were closed, and his face very weary. 'I can talk to you no more tonight, Margery; we both need rest. I shall think, and work, and hope for some answer. Now go, and come to me again in a week unless I send for you earlier.'

But before the week was up a change had come about in my life.

an came to me as I was preparing rabbits for a pie, an unusually pleased look on her face, for she knew something I didn't, and was glad to take me by surprise.

'We've a guest coming and Master says you're to dress a couple of fowls for supper.'

'Oh . . . But he says I was not to buy any more while they were so dear.'

'Well, now he says different. And you're to endor 'em.'

That really made me stare. Endoring was the painting of roasted fowls with a syrup of butter, saffron, egg-yolk and sugar, which gave a gilded effect and was much used in grand households. Master Penny disapproved of such expensive luxuries, calling them kickshaws and fal-lals, which was why we lived on a very dull and tasteless diet.

'What, is this for Master Tuke?' I asked. 'Since when has he deserved such fine dishes?'

'Not Master Tuke, but a proper gentleman, from London,' she said importantly. 'And you're to make a wine syllabub, and wear your best kirtle.'

'In that case you'd best wash your face,' I snapped, 'if you're to wait at table. The gentleman from London will hardly expect to be served by someone looking like an imp from hell.' Indeed, she had a smear of coal-dust on her cheek, but I was chiefly angry that she had tried to put me down with her airs and her orders.

'Nor hardly expect to find a cook's daughter playing hostess,' she flung back at me, 'and a doxy besides!' Then she backed away and out of the door, having felt the weight of my hands before after one of our scrapping matches. Still in a temper, I marched up to Master Penny's small parlour, where I guessed him to be; and so he was, counting out gold coins from a little box which he thought was a secret from me.

'I hear we have company,' I said without ceremony. 'May I know who, rather than having to glean it from servant-maids' talk?'

Usually he would have growled at me for sauciness, but for once he seemed quite amiable. 'Aye,' he said, 'Master Ralph Belstone—a new face to you.'

This was hardly surprising, as few people crossed our threshold except for Master Tuke.

'Is he a merchant, sir?'

'Why, no. A—a gentleman. Well to do. Of some importance.'

'Oh, indeed? In what way, sir?'

I thought a shade of awkwardness crossed his face. He said evasively, 'He moves in high places. See you pay him respect. He's to lodge here a week or so. Prepare the carven chamber for him, and lay the best sheets on the bed.'

Now I was really startled. The carven chamber was the best bedroom in the house. It had been slept in by Master Penny's parents, longer ago than anyone could remember, but he had chosen for himself (and for me) a smaller, less handsome one—out of mere meanness, I believe, because it took less fuel to heat during the winter and the bed was smaller. So the carven chamber stood empty, polished and dusted regularly, and the splendid coverlet, embroidered all over with scenes of hunting and court life, checked for moth. Now it was to be used; Master Belstone must indeed be of some importance. Puzzled, I gave orders for warming-pans to be put in the bed and the best sheets taken out of press, and a good fire lit in the hearth. The chimney had been unused for so long that it had to be raked out as far as Wat could reach with a pole, which produced a shower of soot and unpleasant things, including dead jackdaws. Downstairs the fowls were roasting, the syllabub prepared, another rabbit added to the pie I had been making, a good piece of brawn brought out and garnished with a rich sauce of mustard, and red wine poured into the silver flagon Master Penny would not ordinarily allow to be touched, much less used. What, no small ale, our everyday drink?

Master Ralph Belstone certainly had the look of one who moved in high places, if dress were anything to go by. He seemed to shine all over with the lustre of velvet, the sheen of satin, the gloss of rich fur and the glitter of gold-thread embroidery. His collar was of finest lace and I noticed how far his neck went on above it, long and unusually thick. For his face, it was quite unremarkable, but for a somewhat spoon-shaped nose. Round his neck hung a thick gold chain with a device pendant from it, which after much curious staring I found to be a rebus on his name, a bell set over a rock or stone.

That was the strangest supper-party I had ever made one of, no question. There was myself, grey-kirtled and in my best hood, anxious to seem as sober and respectable as I could, knowing that the guest knew my position in the household. There was Master Penny, straining himself to be polite, even charming, and Heaven knows it must have been a strain. 'Take some of this, sir, try some of that; more of the pie, another fill of wine—Margery, send the girl for more fruit and the hazel-nuts.' There was Ralph Belstone, visibly preening himself on the attention he was getting, living up to the great importance he felt himself to have. At first his manner with me was stiff, as though he knew all too well that I was not truly the mistress of the house, only of the master of the house, and might deserve no more courtesy than a cook-maid. But when, out of real curiosity, I asked him many questions about London life, he began to thaw, answering them at length.

Yes, he often saw the King's Grace, as sturdy and handsome a monarch as England had ever seen—ruddy of face and beard and big of limb, though somewhat corpulent now and no longer compared for beauty with his grandfather, King Edward the Fourth. It was said that his leg had not mended from a fall at hunting, and that an open sore in it still ran. For his spirits, he was as merry as a widower might be, though Queen Jane had only been in her tomb a little over a month; it must be his joy in the baby Prince that sustained him.

'It was told to me,' I said, 'that the King loved Queen Jane better than either of his two wives. Was she very beautiful?'

Master Belstone laughed shortly. 'Not a bit of it—the opposite, indeed. Cheese-faced, with a thin mouth and one eye larger than the other. No one could tell why the King favoured her above Queen Anne Boleyn—she who was no beauty either, yet had witchcraft in her face, fine black eyes and a mane of black hair, with a sort of ripe-plum look to her . . .' He looked hard at me as he said this, as though expecting me to show some feeling at his admiration of another woman, even poor dead Queen Anne. I gazed back calmly, being only interested in the royal ladies, not Master Belstone's opinion of them. 'Do you think the King will marry again?' I asked.

He shrugged. 'Who knows the King's mind? It may be that his zeal for the welfare of his subjects will lead him to take the hand of some suitable princess—suitable above all in sharing His Grace's opposition to the Bishop of Rome.'

'Do they truly name the Pope that now?' I asked innocently, knowing the answer but wishing to test this odd, pompous man. He gave me a cold glance.

'I trust he is given no other title, mistress—even in proud priest-ridden Canterbury.' At this Master Penny began to say something, stopped, and made some sign I missed. The men exchanged a look, and Master Penny went to his cup-filling as zestfully as before.

I could see them both getting flown with wine, the host's face reddening and the guest's voice growing higher, with a sort of cackling note in it. I felt the wine in my veins, being so unused to strong drink.

Something seemed to whisper to me that I should not let myself grow merry and loose-tongued in this company. I rose and excused myself, making a curtsey to both men. As I straightened up Master Belstone took my hand and kissed it. His lips were dry, hot, and strangely unpleasant. When I was out of the room I wiped the hand on my kirtle, washing it as soon as I could come to water and soap.

The next day the two went out together early, and remained away from the house until evening. I longed to know where they had been, and with whom, but when they returned nothing was said. We supped together again, this time with no stiffness on Master Belstone's part. Without asking, he talked freely of London topics—of the King's plan for a new palace so matchless that it was to be called Nonsuch, and a whole Surrey village was to be demolished to build it—of Princess Mary, daughter of the dead Queen Katherine of Aragon, tolerated again at Court because Queen Jane had befriended and spoken to her, but still in danger of her head because she stuck stubbornly to her Roman allegiance, being as fervent a Roman as her Spanish mother. I guessed from his talk that he was here, there and everywhere at Court and in any circle where he could pick up gossip or advance himself, though he seemed not to come of a distinguished family or to have any great position. The only hint I got of his connections was when he spoke two or three times of one he called my lord. I asked who this was, and got, again, a crossed look between host and guest.

'His Grace's chief minister,' Master Belstone said. 'Lord Privy Seal, Master of the Rolls, Chancellor of the Exchequer. Sir Thomas Cromwell. He has the King's ear above all others.'

'Yes,' said Master Penny. 'He has the King's ear.'

I remembered Master Layton, and the bound Abbot of Langdon, and things heard in the market-place, and suddenly the custard-pudding I was eating became of no importance to me, not even a plea-sure, for something else was overriding such small concerns. Again, having taken little wine, I said I must go to bed. This time my hand was

again kissed, and held a long time in the harsh dry hand of Master Belstone. Neither man seemed as flown as on the night before. It struck
me that they would have talked deeply, if I had not been there, and
were none too sorry to see me leave.

I went upstairs and took off my shoes, my best, with thick soles
and steel buckles, because they made a noise on the floors. After waiting a few minutes, making sure none of our people were creeping
about, I went downstairs again, shifting my weight from foot to foot
and moving as light as a fairy, I hoped. At such times a great creak of
wood usually betrays one but I was lucky, and thankful for my cat's-eye
sight in the dark. The men were talking loudly; there was a wide gap
between the old door and the wall, so that I had only to flatten myself
against the panelling to hear clearly all they said.

'So,' said Master Belstone's voice, 'we know who they are.'

'Do we?'

'To a man or so, neither here nor here. Does it matter?'

'Not overly. Why—do you want them?'

Ralph Belstone's voice was thick and languid. 'I should like to
have them—to play with. It might amuse His Grace.'

'How?'

A chuckle. 'He is pleased to see for himself how his enemies end.
In disguise, sometimes. Not that he can be disguised easily . . . A great
cloak and hood is best, with a huge body like his. It makes a pleasant
change from the hunt.'

'Monks,' said Master Penny, on a long swallow of wine. 'Creeping,
crawling monks, like so many snails on the face of the earth. I never
did like 'em. So their time is coming, their paws will be off the gewgaws at last.'

'Gewgaws, master? Is that what you call them, yet you'll be
pleased enough to get your own paws on one—or two?'

Master Penny spluttered. 'Two—is that possible?'

'It depends. On the other matter.'

'Whass tha'?' He was certainly the worse for wine.

'I think you know. The dove of Venus, the grey-kirtled Hebe.'

'Ah. Well, now. She's the comfort of me old age, sir, a good wench, a good wench. You'd not rob me of her, in all conscience?'

'In conscience or out of conscience, you know the bargain, Master Penny. A paramour for a pearl, on top of t'other jewel.'

A kind of groan. 'I'll consider it. Nay, I'm almost won over already. But the rest of the business, sir. You say you know their plans?'

'I told you. To cover the shrine and take them away by night. And the hatching of the plot at Christ Church, where I shall place my men when they arrive—good men, skilled at spy-catching, sharp at capture and none too merciful to the captured. There's many a monk will lack what God gave him when this play is over!' They both laughed extremely. Master Belstone said, 'They overshot the mark when the King's Lodging was set afire, and we may have them on some count for that. But I'll warrant you there'll be no lack of counts, with all the information we have and the authority vested in me—the sneaking cowls shall be downed, and if we catch their doxies with 'em so much the better sport, eh?' Then there was some muttering which I guessed to be lecherous, and put my hands over my ears. After that came more mutters, but to some purpose, I thought, for Master Penny said, 'Do you think . . . ?' and the other '. . . down from London tomorrow or the next day.'

I crept back upstairs as softly as I had come down them; so quietly that I frightened a mouse which flitted across the passage in front of me, squeaking, then, finding itself at a wall with no way of escape, huddled into itself, its tiny paws close to its breast, frozen with fear.

'Hush, little sister,' I said, 'I shan't hurt a hair of you. The other night I held a rat in my lap, as quietly as a babe, and if you will come to me you shall know this for yourself.' Then, not understanding why, I sank down on my knees with a sighing of skirts, seeing myself and the little creature dimly, by the light of the lantern we kept burning where the stairs divided, because there had been some dangerous falls at that place. Still in a sort of brief dream, I saw the mouse unknot itself and come towards me. I put out a finger and touched its soft trembling nose, and knew it trusted me. Then it was gone. I knew that I had worked magic in that moment, and that I was to learn something from this.

I made my way to the little chamber above the kitchen. For another night at least I might lie there without being sent for. My clothes off, I climbed into the bed and lay looking at the white purity of the moon through the little casement. My mind should have been in a turmoil, but it was quite clear and calm, as calm as the moonlight that touched my face.

They had told me nothing. They would have neither me nor anybody else know their plans. Yet, in those few words, spoken loudly in drink and not meant to be overheard, they had let me know their mystery. Master Ralph Belstone was an agent of Sir Thomas Cromwell, left behind, perhaps, by Master Layton as a spy in Canterbury. There was a plan to be scotched, a plan to save the jewels of the shrine from the hands of the King's men, a plan which might be centred on St Augustine's.

And Master Penny's part in this was that he had made an agreement with Ralph Belstone. He was to give some kind of help in return for a jewel from the shrine—two, if something else were agreed, the transfer to Belstone of me, to have for his paramour.

Now I must think in the quiet of the night. My thoughts went back to the strange hour in the house of Doctor Lark. I had tried to put it out of my mind, recoiling (though I felt so much warmth for him and Jane) from the visions the sleeping girl had seen—and I too—from the talk of the dead coming back to bespeak the living; from my very confession to the doctor of my sick-minded fascination with Brother Clement. I still felt all that, and shame as well, for meddling with such things; yet there had been magic, and I had felt it again, when I spoke to the mouse and it obeyed me. Perhaps I was a witch. I crossed myself three times at the thought.

In the future I would not meddle with divination, for it was dangerous. If the person from the past who sought me were to find me, would it be for my good? That person might as well be re-born in Ralph Belstone as in any other—a thought to make one shiver. What I had now to do was protect myself against any such assault, and especially against the bargain that had been struck over me.

Master Penny loved money, or he would not be thinking of selling me. He valued me deeply, not from sentiment but because as well as being a comely young woman to warm his bed, I had more sense and book-learning than most of my sex in my walk of life, and so saved him pounds a year in the management of his house and even in the keeping of the books for his clothier's trade. In a confidential moment he had mentioned to me that he had plans for buying a small mill further down the Stour, and producing paper, now so much in demand with the increase in printed books. One jewel, just one, from the magnificence that covered St Thomas's shrine, and that mill could be his. Women were cheap, mills dear. I could excuse him—just.

But to allow myself to be transferred to Ralph Belstone was out of question. For one thing, he could have no very high regard for me if I had taken his fancy in only two days, and for another, I hated the sight, sound and touch of the man. I resolved to waste no more time mooning over Brother Clement, but to watch the two of them at every turn, to save myself and what was of rather more value, the shrine.

To watch what, I asked myself, as the moon went behind a cloud and the pattern on the ceiling-beams changed. How should I know what they were planning, and how could I carry out any investigations without being noticed? How beautiful the moon's light was, turning the plain little chamber into a place of soft black velvet shadows and patches of pure silver; I looked at it so long that I fell into a kind of doze. I heard the bells chime one, though faintly, and the cry of a passing watchman.

I woke, or came to my full senses, with the knowledge of what I must do.

The monk who answered the supplicant's door in the monastic quarters of the priory of Christ Church was not the one who had received me before, but seemed no more pleased to see me. Asked for Brother Clement, he snapped that he was at his devotions and not to be disturbed.

'I beg you go and ask him to see me, when he is ready,' I said. 'I come on important business—the Prior's business.' He raised scanty eyebrows in disbelief, but went away, leaving me in the same cheerless room where I had waited on my last disastrous visit. I wondered why the Church, that could throw herself so heartily into the warm joys of Christmas and the white splendour of Easter, should need to show such a cold harsh face to us lay-people, and make her own sons live in poverty and bareness. Why could they not lead good lives and yet be merry and comfortable? A few clean thick rushes on the floor, a pleasant picture or two, a jug of bright autumn leaves and berries, would make all the difference to this place where those who needed help came to ask for it. The Miracle Windows in the Cathedral, now, they taught us great lessons while pleasing the senses, as those who made them intended, whereas cold plain glass would have done no good . . . I had just, in my mind, furnished the room and set in it windows that glowed and sparkled when the door opened and Brother Clement stood there.

I felt the betraying blush rise to my cheeks and the hot knife touch my heart; but this time I was strong, and conquered my lowest self. His face was grave, unwelcoming, even severe.

'How can I help you, daughter?' he asked, in a tone suggesting that he would like to be rid of me at the first possible moment.

'By listening to me, Father,' I said bluntly, and launched straight into the story of what I had heard the previous night, and what I guessed. As I talked the cold look left his face, leaving it alive, alert, intent. He heard me out, then paced a few steps up and down the room, silently. Then he faced me.

'You did well to tell me this. What made you believe I was the right person to hear it?'

'I don't know, Father. It came into my mind.'

'I salute you for your wit,' he said (and what an unpriestlike thing to say), with that sweet smile of his, warming my heart. Then he went to the door, opened it, looked up and down the corridor outside, and came back to me.

'This door has no lock, of course. We are not likely to have eaves-droppers, but ears may catch unwillingly things that will do them no good. Shall we walk in the cloister garden? In the open air we can talk safely.'

We strolled slowly up and down between the neatly-tended garden beds where lavender still showed its grey leaves and sad solitary roses drooped from leafless stems. To any watching we must have seemed deep in holy converse, but it was he who talked and I who listened.

To sum up what he told me, it was that among the brothers was a band dedicated and pledged to fight the forces the King would certainly send to pillage the Cathedral and take away the treasure. Any means were permissible—they might risk their lives, but must not put others' at risk unless it came to actual conflict. Someone, more hot-headed and foolish than most, had taken it on himself to set fire to the King's Lodging on the night of Layton's visit, and put the whole plan in jeopardy, for if Layton or any of his people had been killed there would have been an investigation which might have led to the disaster they were trying to prevent.

'There's not much we can do at present. Layton has made his estimate of the treasure. It will be reported to Cromwell, and that will seal its fate. But until we know the King's men are about to descend on us we can make no move.'

'How will you know?'

'We have a spy—a clerk.'

'And when you know—what will you do?'

He gave me an amused sideways glance. 'That would be telling all; three can keep a secret when two are away. What I ask myself is, what part your Master Penny has to play that makes him worth such a bribe?'

I shook my head. 'Money?'

'Cromwell has plenty.'

'Information?'

Brother Clement pulled a frail white rose from its branch and gazed at it thoughtfully as we walked. At last he said, 'The house where I left you on the night of the fire—is that Penny's?'

'Yes.'

'It stands almost square on to the eastern end of Christ Church, but some way off?'

I supposed it did.

'How many storeys has it? On how many floors are there rooms?'

'Let me see . . . cellars below, then kitchens, the buttery, and above the great parlour . . .'

'No, no, higher than that.'

'The best bedchambers, and the servants' above . . . oh, and the cock-loft.'

'The cock-loft?'

'The little room up its own stairs where we store stuff not often needed.'

He asked if it were much used, and whether it had a window. His eyes brightened with interest when told that it had, looking out towards the back. I only remembered with difficulty, as the place was dark and poky and the stairs twisted awkwardly. I think I had been frightened of it as a child.

He said, 'Margery, listen. When dusk falls tonight, will you go up there and make careful note of what you can see—what windows, what lights, whether people could be seen moving about? Everything, mind. And tomorrow—best not to come here again, or there could be talk.' He pondered. 'Will you meet me in the church of St Martin? There we shall be outside the walls and more private.'

I almost laughed as I agreed—it sounded so like a lovers' trysting. Then he said I must go, and at that I felt the same foolish pang I had vowed not to feel again. Almost not knowing what I said, I looked at the white rose in his hand and asked, 'May I have that?'

Surprised, he said, 'As many as you like. Pick them as you go.'

'No, I want that one.'

He held it out and I took it, our hands touching, sending a shaft of fire through my body, and our eyes locked. His look was grave again now, but not as it had been at first. He asked, 'What is your name?'

'Margery. I told you.'

'The other one.'

'Burgoyne.'

He shook his head as though puzzled, and suddenly left me, with an abrupt gesture which might have been a blessing or a dismissal. Looking round to see that no one watched I put the rose in my bosom. And it stayed fresh and fair for three days, though it had seemed to wither on the tree.

St Martin's Church stood high on a hill at the south of the city, as high as Bell Harry Tower. They said it was very old, old enough to have been a Roman temple at one time. That morning a fresh wind was blowing, bringing with it sweet smoke from fires of autumn leaves, and the scent of ploughed earth. I pulled off my hood and let my hair stream out, blowing across my face, covering my eyes and whipping into my mouth, making me laugh to myself, like an idiot. As I felt when I pushed it aside and saw the tall figure standing there, not a yard from me, though I had not heard his sandalled feet among the old gravestones. He was surveying me with an amused smile; in confusion I swept the wild hair back and held it so.

'It was better before,' he said, and again we were staring at one another like two cats about to fight; only fighting was not in my mind, or, I think, in his. He went before me to a long gravestone shaped like a shrouded body, and signed me to sit on it with him.

'I went up there at owl-light,' I said, 'and the floor was so covered with bales and boxes and old clutter that I could hardly get at the window, which is very high up. It was filthy, covered with spider-webs and dust, but I rubbed away some. And it looked right over to the eastern end of Christ Church, over the gardens and between two little buildings. There were lights in the windows, and I could see figures moving about on the greens.'

'Good. Excellently spied. I was right, then your Master Penny is hired as a look-out, and your cock-loft is the crow's nest. From there they can watch all comings and goings about the shrine, or rather Penny can watch, letting the King's man go back to London and tell his master all's well. They can get no nearer, you see, for the two prebendal houses between Burgate Street and the Cathedral.'

'But the other side,' I said, 'could they not watch from there?'

'Nothing near enough, all church land and buildings. No, they have the perfect spot, and a none-too-pious merchant to help them.'

'Will it not be "pull devil, pull baker", the first to let go loses the game?'

'Well thought, so we must not be first to let go. Will you do this for me, Margery? Watch Penny, whether he goes to the cock-loft at night, and what letters he writes to London. Can you make sure of seeing his letters?'

'Yes—I write some for him, to save him paying a clerk.'

'Good. Then look for any to this Belstone, after he has gone back. But I never asked you if you could read, let alone write letters . . . I believe I knew. That's strange.'

'What else do you know about me?' I asked boldly.

'Something, I think . . . a great deal. I can't remember. Yet how can I know anything?'

I looked round for something to draw on, and found it in a flat gravestone nearby, filmed with whitish dust from a stone that had fallen on it and broken. In that, with a small sharp stone, I drew as near as possible the outline of the heraldic bear; it came out quite well. He watched me, puzzled. 'Look at this,' I said when it was finished.

He studied it, not for long. 'A part of the arms of Warwick.'

My heart jumped. 'Is it, indeed?'

'Yes. A bear sejant argent, muzzled gules, supporting a ragged staff.'

'How do you know that?' I could hear the tremble in my voice.

'A man can hardly be trained up as a squire without learning something of heraldry . . .' He stopped short. 'I should not have told you that.'

'Why?'

'We are not allowed to talk about our life in the world.' He looked pale, and angry: with me, or himself? I felt a little pain of disappointment that my Bear had only led me to him in this present day, not to the past time Jane had seen in the crystal; but after all it was the living man I knew, the living man I was now sure I loved.

'Tell me,' I said. He sighed, then smiled, and seemed to shake something off, like a weight that had lain on his shoulders.

'Yes, I'll tell you, though I have to do penance for it. You shall know all I am and all I have been, Margery.'

I was no longer 'daughter' to him nor he 'Father' to me; we would never be so again.

5

This was the story he told me.

'I came of the family of Moyle, in the Stour Valley
southwest of Canterbury. My father was not the squire, only
a younger brother, but I grew up with the boys at the Manor
House as one of them, and was sent with them to the King's
School here, for some wit they thought I had, though God
knows it can have been little enough, for I cared for nothing
but riding and fishing.' He looked across to Bell Harry
Tower, beyond which lay the great school. 'To think I was
there, a careless boy, and now . . .

'When my father saw I was not meant for the University he sent me to Sir Thomas Boleyn at Hever Castle, to be
a page in his household and after that whatever Sir Thomas
chose to make me.'

'Boleyn?' I said.

'The same Boleyn. The Queen's father.'

'Then you knew her?'

'I knew her.' His voice was expressionless; I was afraid
he would tell me no more. But he went on, 'She was a few
years older than I, three, I think. I worshipped at her feet—
only a clod would not have done. She was just back from
France, where her father had been our Ambassador.'

'What was she like?' I tried to keep the jealousy out of
my voice.

'Like Beauty itself. Yet not beautiful, taking her feature by feature. Her eyes and her hair almost black, her skin browner than most English women's skins, a colour to set off pearls . . . she was shorter than you, only as high as my shoulder, I thought she looked like one of the Welshwomen I had seen in the Marches, but with a great lady's air and a pretty Frenchness to her voice. She was . . .' Suddenly he rose and flung a piece of stone he had been playing with far from him. 'I can't talk about her,' he said, sitting down again. 'The anger comes up from my heart and chokes me. I would like to fling him as I did that stone, into the uttermost depths of the sea, from the highest rock. I would like to see his thick red neck treated as hers was.'

There was no need to ask whom he meant, and I was silent. Even up there, among the graves and the silence, it seemed not wise to talk of the King. I knew then that there was more to Clement's fight against Cromwell's robbers than a desire to save the treasure. He was calmer when he spoke again.

'I was happy at Hever, even when Lady Anne had gone to Court. Sir Thomas was pleased with me and planned my advancement, seeing greatness ahead for himself and wishing to take his people with him. Young George Rochford, his son, was my friend, though I had no time to spare for his lemon-faced wife. But a little after Lady Anne became Queen, and our fortunes seemed made, a thing happened in my family.'

He paused so long that I thought he was not going to tell me what it was. Then, with an effort, he went on.

'My mother was a most pious woman. She had entered a convent at the age of ten, by her own wish. But while she was still a novice her elder sister died, being then betrothed to my father. It was a good match, joining two neighbouring estates into one—too good a match to let go. So, both sets of parents agreeing, my mother was taken from her convent and married to her sister's bridegroom. Everybody was thus satisfied, except the bride, who had been prepared to dedicate herself to chastity and found the whole condition of marriage loathsome.'

'Poor thing,' I said.

'It turns me cold to think of. What must my father have endured, as well as she . . . Well, her constant cry was that she must make amends by giving her children to the Church. Only my father would not have it; and my elder brothers, as they came towards manhood, proved to be such lusty lads as no abbot could ever have tamed, and my sisters a couple of merry giglots with as much piety about them as pigs in straw.'

'And you?'

'And I, the youngest, thought of nothing but wars and tournaments. Yet it came to me in the end. I was nineteen when my mother fell ill, saw her death not far away, and sent for me day and night pleading with me to take Orders and save her soul, for she had vowed me to God and would burn eternally unless I carried out her promise. In the end I did. All the others were married and the inheritance provided for. What did I matter? Fool! Fool! Fool!' He struck his fist repeatedly against the stone we sat on, and my own nerves jumped at the pain he must feel. 'I had no more of the priest in me than my horse. I gave what I could, but it was little enough, and here am I, at seven-and-twenty, less than half a man.'

I thought him about to weep, and in loving pity caught him close and so held him, for the first time. His arms came round me and we clung together. 'You,' he said against my shoulder, 'it was you who showed me what a wreck my life was. Margery, my pretty, my dear . . .'

There was nothing I could say; I rocked him against me and thought with anger of the mother who should have loved him more than to force him into a life that was not for him. And yet a part of me was exultant because I had found him out to be what he had not seemed to be, and so all the more mine.

After a time of that sweet closeness he drew himself away from me, smiling ruefully. 'Many a good-wife would have drawn off in horror at such a tale,' he said.

'I am neither good nor a wife, if you remember.'

'Yet to admit myself only a priest in pretence . . .'

'I am not all that fond of priests. I could never see why they should not take wives, and why they have to live so uncomfortably. A whole man for me, any day. It may be no bad thing if they should all be turned out of their nasty cells and made to do honest work.'

'Margery, Margery! a heretic?' But he was laughing, I was glad to see. For the first time we looked long at each other with joy at what we both now knew. He picked up a strand of my hair, still flying loose, and wound it round his finger, saying,

'With margerain gentle,
The flower of goodlihead,
Embroidered the mantle
Is of your maidenhead.'

'I wish it was,' I said, 'but my maidenhead's long gone, more's the pity. What a pair we are, a priest meant for a soldier and a thing neither maid, wife nor widow. You asked me what my name was yesterday—now tell me yours.'

'You answered me, Margery, and I answer you, Clement.'

'No, not your priest's name given at your swearing-in or whatever they call it—your own christened name.'

'Still Clement. My mother thought it had a good papistical sound.'

'I'm glad. I like it. So you lied to me about being lucky in your abbot's choice of it?'

'I lied. My whole life is a lie.'

'Not now.' I put my arm through his, leaning close. 'To each other we must be all truth, for ever.'

'For ever?'

'Yes, for ever.' It was on my tongue to tell him about Jane's crystal and what Doctor Lark had said, but I kept it back, in case it puzzled or distressed him, coming on top of his confession to me. I was already as tender of him as a mother of her child. Instead I said, 'When shall I see you and report what Master Penny does?'

'I will walk here every morning when I can. If you miss me, leave a note with the gate-keeper. Now we must go, and you shall set off alone, so as not to cause gossip. Go now,' he said gently, as I lingered, still close to him, willing him to kiss me, but he would not. To draw out the time I asked, 'Who wrote that verse you repeated?'

'John Skelton the poet, on a Mistress Margery Wentworth.'

'Will you write such a verse for Mistress Margery Burgoyne—to please her?'

He gave me the smile that warmed all his features, and especially his eyes. 'If you wish, and I'll say in it that Marjoram stands for blushes, in the alphabet of flowers, and that Margery has none, but is a pert forward wench.'

'You see—you *are* all truth to me.' And before he could escape me I kissed him on the cheek, a kiss as light as thistledown, and so ran away down the hill and back through Burgate home.

In the months that followed I seemed sometimes in a dream, sometimes more awake and alive than I had ever been. Sometimes, but not often, Clement was at St Martin's when I went there, but I felt that it would only increase his unhappiness if I were as bold with him as I had been. No formal word of love had been said between us, no promise made, nor could there be until some great change of fortune came about. I loved him too much to make his life harder, and I made myself be content, or as content as I could be, to see him briefly at these times, or, occasionally, in Christ Church at the great ceremonies of Advent and Christmas. Once I met him in the street, pausing to listen to the boys who sang for ha'pence the carol that was particular to Canterbury.

Welcome be ye Stephen and John,
Welcome Innocents every one,
Welcome Thomas Martyr one,
   Welcome Yule.

I wished him a merry and blessed Christmastide, and he wished the same to me, and that was all we could say, for Master Penny was with me. After we moved on he asked me, 'Since when did you consort with priests?'

'I hardly *consort* with them, sir' (how I wished I did). 'That was one of the Christ Church fathers who goes about the city on the Prior's errands.'

Master Penny snorted. 'A sneaking lot. Shun 'em.'

'Yes, sir.' And if only you knew what I do, I thought. All those nights when I crept up the little stair to the cock-loft, where I had seen my master creeping up earlier, or heard the creak of his foot on the old steps: how I found the floor in order where there had been chaos, a stool put up on a low chest, so that the watcher might have a more comfortable vigil; the once-dirty window-panes always clean now. Every now and then a letter was written to Ralph Belstone of which I usually contrived to get a sight before it was sealed—afterwards was too late, for the seal was engraved on his finger-ring. When an answer came by the carrier I tried to be about when it was opened, and make some excuse to draw him away from it after it was opened, such as pretending I heard a strange noise in the street or upstairs, then hurriedly glancing at it. But the letters were in such a spidery gentleman's hand that I could make neither head nor tail of them; only from their shortness I guessed that nothing much had been planned.

For all his dutiful watching Master Penny never saw anything untoward going on—no figures moving suspiciously, no laden pack-mules being led away. Nor would he, if he watched all night every night. I knew a little of what was going on, from things Clement had let slip, though he was as close as an oyster with me because of the danger of my knowing too much.

I knew, for instance, that figures did move about the shrine by night, though they came and went by no door that could be seen from our side. On the north of the great church, where the monastic buildings and the guests' quarters lay, a certain little door, so humble that it might have been for builders' use, led into the crypt, and through this dark forms came and went on soft-stepping feet, sometimes with barrows and chests. By the light of votive candles skilful hands were stripping jewels from the shrine, one by one, in such a way that nobody could see at a glance that there had ever been a jewel where now was a smoothly-applied piece of gold leaf or a cunningly-wrought enamel decoration. In this way, Clement said, they robbed Thomas to save for Thomas. I asked if the monks were not afraid of the saint's anger.

'Not at all. He was a wise, worldly man when he lived, and no doubt has not lost his wits by canonization. He knows—we all know—that the King's men will come; it may be days, or weeks, or months, but they will come and cart off the treasure. And when they come, they'll find less than they bargained for.'

I knew of something else that was being done, a grisly but necessary business. Above the lower part of the shrine was a timber chest, covered with gold plating damascened with gold wire and golden ornament, containing an iron coffin that held the saint's bones. In the crypt favoured pilgrims were shown the top of his skull, broken by his murderers' swords, set in silver: the great Archbishop still lay in his own Canterbury.

Now it was whispered (and not only whispered) that Cromwell's agents were under orders to get rid of 'rotten bones and dead relics' which encouraged superstitious worship. No relics in England had wrought more miracles than those of St Thomas. To kiss the broken skull would certainly cure you of anything you were suffering from, unless you were already marked for Heaven. His bones were treasures of a different kind from the jewels of the shrine, but treasures none the less. And so the pillagers would not find them.

Reverently, with many prayers, the worker-monks transferred the precious remains to another coffin, lined with silks and strewn with sweet herbs, and that was put into a deal chest so plain that none would have given it a second glance. And this was put . . . I may not say where, even now. Christ Church covers much land, and its walls are thick; let it keep its secret until the time comes to give it up.

In place of the bones they put those of a man long dead, unearthed in the cloisters. Perhaps he was a monk, a good man worthy of such an honour, perhaps a sinner. Nobody said; indeed they said as little as possible about the whole business.

All this need for secrecy constrained and bound me very much. I avoided the company of Doctor Lark and Jane, partly because I so longed to talk that I might not have been able to help myself with their sympathetic ears to listen, and partly because I was afraid their wisdom would find out my greatest secret, Clement. When Doctor Lark stopped me in the street and gently asked why I no longer visited them, I made some clumsy answer which cannot have deceived that wise man for a moment.

He said, 'A pity. Jane misses you. Could you not spare her an hour today?'

At that I weakened. I had no friends but them (and another, whom I dare not name). Both welcomed me as though I had never been away; we spoke of light things, the weather and a new herbal that had been published, the first to be written in English, and the health of the Lark animals. Only when I was leaving, Doctor Lark asked me: 'And has the searcher found his brown person?'

'I think so, sir. Such mysteries are beyond me, but I think so. Only . . . it's all such a tangle that I doubt it will ever be straightened.'

'All our life is a tangle. If here or there some threads lie straight and happy together, then we are fortunate.' I knew he was thinking of Jane, the pretty thread who remained from the sad tangle of his family life.

'I wouldn't wish it otherwise, sir,' I said.

It was a little after this, on a beautiful day in May, that Ralph Belstone came back.

I was gathering young mint and parsley in the herb garden when, looking down the alley at the side of the house, I saw an unfamiliar horse in gaudy trappings, and knew in my heart that he had brought nothing good on his back. I slowed down my gathering, to put off the moment when I must go in. When at last I entered the kitchen Nan and young Rebecca and Wat were all in a babel about the gentleman from London having come again, and the fine things we must buy for supper. As long as I could I stayed there, washing the sweet herbs and plucking the parsley sprigs from their stalks; anything not to have to go to the parlour.

But the summons came, as I knew it would. Master Belstone was there, stretched out in the one good chair that had a tall back and wrought arms, wine already on the table beside him, Master Penny standing before the hearth rubbing his hands. Belstone held out his arms to me.

'Margery, my chuck! What a sight for sore eyes. Come and welcome me.'

Instead I stayed at the other end of the room, dipped a short curtsey, and folded my hands against my farthingale like a servant waiting for orders. Master Penny frowned and the visitor looked surprised. I suppose he had expected me to be primed for his arrival, perhaps looking forward eagerly to my transfer from an old man to one less weighty in years. I thought that the court ladies must be a dowdy lot, if he preferred one who wore wooden pattens, an old linsey-woolsey gown, and a coarse hood over her hair. And indeed, he threw me a querying look, as though he wondered whether he were getting value for money—or something else, a jewel that didn't belong to him. Master Penny's face was glum. Gleefully I reflected that he might order me to change into my best and put on a charming aspect for the man to whom he was selling me, but the bargain was not yet complete, the jewel not yet snatched for exchange. I was so proud of myself as I fled out of the room and later sent a message by Rebecca excusing myself from eating with them. Perhaps now Master Belstone would think me too ill-bred to take up with. Later, as they supped, I listened to the chatter they made, the two of them and Master Tuke, who had got wind of entertainment and dropped in to share it, and thought that they were no match for me, one way and another.

Alas, pride goeth before a fall. Next morning my master sent for me, at a time when I was busy, and would not take no for an answer. There he sat in the little parlour where he kept his secret hoard of coins, Ralph Belstone with him, very heavy about the eyes from drinking.

'Give thanks to Master Belstone,' said my master, 'for your good fortune, Margery.'

'What good fortune?'

'You are to go to London, wench.'

I had empty hands for once, or anything in them would have fallen to the floor.

Then he told me, in a false sort of voice, that Master Belstone had been so struck by my natural graces that he thought me worthy of being trained in a noble household into the ways of the world.

'Trained for what?' I asked, 'since I am only a humble personage.'

'Who knows?' Master Belstone said airily. 'Fortune's wheel spins strangely.'

'It would need to, to change my condition. And I have no wish to go.'

'Don't talk folly, girl. Is it for you to toss gifts back in the giver's face?'

'If I don't choose to take them, yes.'

Ralph Belstone said, 'Come, think of the pleasure of telling your gossips and neighbours of how you're to be raised in life.'

'I have no gossips, and my neighbours care as little for me as I for them.'

'This is a surly wench, friend,' he said softly to my master, who sharply dismissed me. I was not spoken to again that day, and used the time to go and seek for Clement; why, I was not sure, perhaps only to see him for what might be the last time for weeks or months, perhaps to ask help from him in my plight. But he was nowhere to be found, and I got only blank or cold looks from those I asked. I even walked up to St Martin's, in the hope that some message from my spirit might have reached him and sent him to meet me there. But there was no sign of him, only a funeral party in progress. I stood aside from the procession and the burying, wondering who it was they laid in the earth and what sort of trials the person had endured, living.

That night I was not asked to sup with my master and his guest. I ate with the servants, seeming to take no notice of Nan's sniggers and Joan's and Rebecca's stares. The good food tasted of nothing, for my mind was troubled. I hoped the men would sit up late, but I had only just reached the bedroom when I heard Master Penny's footsteps coming up the stair.

I think I knew when he entered the room that this was not to be an ordinary night, when he would throw off his clothes, huddle into bed and instantly fall to snoring. (If he required anything besides sleep he would always doze first.) His face was grim, his hands behind his back, and he said, 'Strip naked.'

I stared. 'I was about to.'

'Not for bed-going, fool.' He pulled my hands away from the bodice I was unfastening, and himself pulled it off, then set to drag off my shift and farthingale, disregarding my cries and protests as I heard the ripping of good cloth. Anger must have lent him strength, for in what seemed like a moment my clothes were in a heap on the floor. What I saw in the glint of his eyes was not lust for a body he knew well, but anger alone. He threw me across the bed, where I fell face down, hitting my head against a post. Then I heard a swishing noise and felt the sudden dreadful impact across my shoulders of the bunch of birch twigs I remembered too well from my childhood. He had not punished me for years—now the fiery pain came rushing back, tearing my skin, descending again and again, all over my body, until I heard my voice rising to a scream as I begged him to stop. But he would not, until I had been punished enough. He was very strong, for an old man, stronger than one would have guessed.

When he left off at last, and I lay sobbing, he stood back from me.

'So you'd ignore my friend, and speak uppishly to me in his presence? You shall learn better manners, mistress, and soon. Would you flout me in my own house? Devil take me if I'll stand for it.' And so forth and so forth, as I had not heard him rail since he and my mother used to quarrel. At last he tired of it and pushed me out of the room, throwing my clothes after me, to lick my wounds, as he said. I suppose he hardly welcomed any more blood on his bed-linen.

The next day, rising sore and aching, I was told that I must leave for London that day, though I was unfit to ride.

I find it hard to put down the story of the three months after this, if indeed there were a story to it. What should have been a time of adventure and discovery to me, who had never left Canterbury in my life, was more like a term of slavery. I was taken by Ralph Belstone and the two servants who rode with him to a house in the City itself. 'My lady' was away, they said, but I was to become one of her household and learn her ways. Belstone left me there with hardly a word; I think he found me unpleasant to look at in my extreme discomfort from the beating, with a cut across one cheek and my face swollen with weeping.

The people of the house were very grand, even though they were but servants, and their speech was strange to my ears. I felt myself despised from the first, a country girl in a poor state. On the first night I begged the housekeeper, Mistress Pye, for some ointment for my cut back; when she seemed not to understand me, I unfastened my gown and showed her the stripes. She sniffed.

'Well deserved, I'll be bound,' she said. 'Ask in the kitchens— they're used enough to beatings.' So I was obliged to humble myself again to women who stared and laughed, and at last gave me a pot of unguent, which I laid on myself as well as I could, lying on a hard narrow pallet in the chamber I shared with three others. It was the most miserable night I had ever spent. I longed beyond longing to be back at home, in my own bed, even with the master who had lashed me so cruelly. And so I continued to long, through all that summer.

I found the next day that I was in the house of Jane, Viscountess Rochford. I had never heard of her, but soon learned her story. She was the widow of Queen Anne Boleyn's brother George, beheaded two years before by the King's command, on the charge of having carnal knowledge of his sister, along with other alleged lovers of hers. That in itself was terrible, but more terrible was the whisper that the wife herself had spoken as chief witness against him.

When I saw her, after her return from the country, I believed it. There was in her face such a bitter unhappiness as I never saw in any other—so much so that one might have thought her to be suffering with a gnawing illness. But she was not, only from being at odds with the world because she had helped to bring the axe down on the neck of her husband, and got nothing by it but askance looks, and the knowledge that Anne was dead, heaped into the same grave as her brother George—two brilliant Boleyns discredited and murdered. 'For the Queen never behaved ill with any man,' whispered my informant, the most friendly of the maids, Elinor. 'She had a quick laugh and a merry look for a man who admired her (and all did, only a few jealous of the power she had) and so stupid folk took her French ways for lightness, or said so. Poor lady, the King was mad for her until he bedded her, and then farewell love, because she couldn't bring him a son, only baby Elizabeth.'

My thoughts of the King were almost as bitter as Clement's, from all I had been told of him. What I saw in a glimpse of him as he rode in procession one day did nothing to endear him to me: a great square padded form with a great square head on top of it, seeming bald but for a few wisps of reddish hair seen from the back, tiny eyes and a little pettish mouth. He pleased me no more than the other famous sights of London, the Tower and the Bear Garden, Paul's Church and the river with its swarming boats, London Bridge that was both a bridge and a street, with houses from end to end (and the black rotting heads of traitors on poles at the Southwark side). I saw these things only when Lady Rochford was at Court, for she had crept back into royal favour, so far as to have been lady-in-waiting to the dead Queen Jane Seymour; the King had a sick dislike for any who brought the Boleyns to his mind.

Of me she took no notice. I had no place about her person, and was treated as a nothing in the household, being given almost menial work to do. I wondered and wondered why it was that I had been brought to her. It was not that Ralph Belstone wanted me away from my home in order to court me, for he visited seldom, and then never sought me out. I had no freedom to come and go, nor wanted it much, in the dirt and heat of London in summer, yet I felt like a caged bird, beating its wings. Only when we travelled to Rochford Hall in Essex and I was able to breathe country air again did I feel almost happy; that was a cheerless place too, as though that cold proud lady carried cheerlessness about with her.

And then, when summer was fading, we travelled south to Hever Castle.

My heart began to lift as we rode into Kent, as though the poor bird had suddenly found its cage-door open. The countryside was rich, mellow, apples rosy in the gardens and orchards, the villages small and clean, the people comely and civil, rosy too after the pale sickly-faced Londoners. When we came to Hever and its great moated Castle, the finest I ever saw, my heart grew lighter still, for this had been Clement's home, had known him in his youthful pride before he put on the sad unmanly robes of a monk. If only Time could have been in some magical way reversed, so that he was here again, free and young as I was, and love a thing that could be spoken of between us!

Yet all was a dream. The Castle was no longer a Boleyn home, for the King had snatched it as soon as the beautiful sister and brother were dead. Of his grace he allowed their father to live out his life in his house.

Sir Thomas, Clement's preceptor and lord, once a power in England, Sheriff of Kent, Treasurer of the King's Household, ambassador to France, Lord Privy Seal, Earl of Wiltshire—and now a broken old man, his body racked with agues as though the grief in his heart had seeped into his bones, his mind wandering. I knew, as one sometimes knows these things, that he would not live long, and indeed he was only a year from his grave. What he had been, it was impossible to tell—handsome as his son, perhaps, but now it was all gone and only gauntness remained. I was not supposed to address anyone above the rank of servant, yet I contrived to get myself sent on an errand which would take me to the chamber where he sat alone, most of the day. The Lady Alice, his second wife, was never seen, and I fancied neither of them had any welcome for Lady Rochford, who came to Hever only out of arrogance and a desire to irk them.

He sat alone at a table, among many books, under an ornamented plaster ceiling whose height made him seem a small man, though he had been tall at one time. His beard was grey and his grizzled hair thin, his head leaning wearily on his arm. He did not look up when I entered, so I went about fetching whatever it was I had gone for—some goblet or other, I think.

Then I approached him and said, 'My lord.'

He looked up languidly and I saw that his eyes were very dark, as his daughter's had been, but dull, like candles burning low.

'Pardon me, sir,' I said, 'but I lately met Clement Moyle, once of your household, and he wished to be commended to you.' Heaven knows whether I said it for the pleasure of speaking Clement's name, or because I thought it might somehow cheer him. Indeed, he did seem to come to life a little, showing even the flicker of a smile.

'Clement,' he said. 'Yes. Many years ago. A goodly lad that might have gone far, but that he . . . What was it he did?'

'Went into the Church, sir.'

'Ah, that was it. I forget things.' A spasm of bitter anger crossed his face. 'The Church! Prelates playing at politics, with stones in place of hearts. Men of God who serve the Devil.' I wondered if he were thinking of Archbishop Cranmer, who had once lived with the Boleyns and had crowned Queen Anne, yet done nothing to save her life because it suited his book that she should die; or of the terrible Thomas Cromwell, her chief enemy. I said nothing, hoping I had not provoked a collapse or fit in the old man, so strangely his face was working. Then he seemed to forget his anger and said very pleasantly, 'Clement Moyle. Yes, yes. And how has he prospered?'

'Well enough, sir. But he'd better have stayed with you.'

'So I think, so I think . . .' He looked at me directly for the first time. 'Do I know you, mistress?'

'No, sir. I came here with—Lady Rochford.'

At that the wandering look went from his face. He said very clearly, 'My daughter-in-law is a devil and no woman. Leave her, maid, or you'll rue it; she brings death to those about her. Leave her now, if you can. Are you one of her people?'

'No, sir, a woman of Kent.'

'Then go. I dislike to see fair faces spoiled.' With that he smiled at me, and I saw just a flash of the dark sparkling charm of the young Boleyns in their father's face.

I stood outside in the corridor, looking out into the sunny gardens. Something in the way he had spoken impressed me strangely. Perhaps it was my own nameless fear, perhaps a sort of conviction that came from the words of one near death, perhaps the new lightness and freedom of being out of London; but in those few moments I made up my mind to run away and return to Canterbury.

6

I came to my own beloved city on the morning of the ninth of September. The journey across more than half of Kent had been easier than I thought possible. I had asked in the kitchens of the servant who dealt with the bringing in of food-stuffs whether he knew of a carrier bound eastwards who could be trusted to take a valuable package for me to the town of Tonbridge, where I had an aunt. (I had none, of course.) I dared not mention Canterbury. A good, easy man, he suspected nothing, but told me of a carter everyone knew as Dick, who would leave from the inn-yard soon after dawn the next morning but one.

The night before I made my bid for escape I hardly slept, but lay, clothed up to my smock, waiting for the first light. When it came, I rose and silently put on my gown and shoes, picked up my few small possessions tied up in a kerchief, and crept from the room without disturbing any of the other maids.

Over the months I had saved nearly all the poor wages Lady Rochford allowed her servants. There had been nothing to spend them on, and there they were to help me when I needed them. Dick the carter was pleased with the fine morning, pleased to have a young wench to convey instead of a package, and even more pleased to be paid for it. At Tonbridge he set me down where I could wait for the waggon owned by his friend Ben, who travelled daily to Maidstone and back. Ben, too, was not displeased to give me a place among his goods, for a few pence, and though he had a keen eye for a maid and talked saucily, I found no quarrel with him.

From Maidstone to Canterbury was many miles, too far for a single vehicle to take me, and I had too little money to hire one. By slow stages I came to the village of Charing, high on its hill, walking part of the way, and stayed there the night in a rough bed an old cottager let me have. From there north-eastwards. I told varied stories to such as gave me a lift, transferring my legendary aunt from one place to another, and inventing tales which I was surprised to find those simple men believed concerning my reasons for travelling alone. And, most wonderfully, in all that journey no villain nor highwayman approached me, nor was I offered the slightest insult. Either I was under Divine protection or Kentish countrymen are an honest race.

At a late hour in the morning, when most folk were at their dinner, I came to the hamlet of Thanington Without, and for the first time in a quarter of a year saw the great towers of Christ Church, the sun glinting on the golden figure of Archangel Michael, high on the centre tower; I sat down by the roadside and wept for joy.

But when I came into the city by Wincheap I felt a strangeness in the air that chilled me. There were few people about, even as I passed through the Wincheap Gate and drew nearer the city's heart.

Then I found them. They were clustered in the High Street, and in the streets that led into it, crowds of citizens, some hanging out of windows, but most huddled against the walls, watching, as a great baggage-waggon drawn by four stout horses came out of Mercery Lane. It was all but too wide for that narrow little street, and the driver cursed loudly as he edged the cumbrous thing slowly out, while two tall fellows in leather jerkins forced the watchers out of its way. When at last the entire waggon was out, and the horses turned westwards, a strange sound went up, a groaning and sobbing noise such as I had never heard.

I turned to a woman who stood watching, stony-faced, silent, but with a grim look, and asked her what was happening.

'Where have you been that you don't know, mistress? The last of the treasure is leaving us.'

I must have gaped at her like a landed fish. A man beside me spoke up.

'They've been at their work three days. Chest after chest we've seen come out, as much as took six or seven men to carry, all loaded up and driven to London—and a slow journey I reckon, with all that weight up behind. Twenty-six waggons, there were.'

Others joined in, eager to tell what I did not know, some of them neighbours I recognized, who would once not have spared me a word. Three days ago Thomas Cromwell had come in person with his Commissioners, and a gang of sturdy men who had at once begun stripping the shrine. At first Prior Goldwell had protested violently, and some of the monks had struggled with the violaters, but had soon been overpowered and roughly treated. Laymen who had crept in to watch said that while the work went on the King's men sang and joked and swore, making lewd rhymes on the saint; and while some hammered away to dislodge the jewels and gold plate others went about destroying, by the King's special orders, everything they thought to be a relic. First went the silver-set skull of the saint (but I knew better), then his pastoral staff, silk robe and napkin, vestments of velvet, and after that the other relics of various holy people, such as St Sebastian and St Laurence—everything from skulls to hair shirts.

When they had done this they set to carry out the thing King Henry most required, the burning of the saint's bones. (I did not know, until it was explained to me, that he now hated holy Thomas because he had opposed his own King, and might set a bad example if folk were allowed to go on worshipping such a rebel.) The two coffins were broken open, and the old yellowed bones they held taken out to the Precincts, laid on a pyre, and burned, to howls of joy from the despoilers and tears from the monks and the people. One girl told me 'When I wept most bitterly, one of the fellows caught me round the waist and kissed me, saying, "Cheer up, sweetheart, for that rotten carcass was no saint but Bishop Becket, a rebel and traitor."'

I said, 'But . . .' then stopped, for though I knew the truth about the bones, it was not to be spoken of.

A stir and a murmur ran through the crowd as a man stepped from among those who watched the retreat of the waggon from the end of Mercery Lane, by the pilgrim's inn called the Chequer of the Hope. His rich furred gown marked him as a person of importance. A man in the crowd called out, 'Curst Cromwell!' and spat, then turned and disappeared before he could be set on by the guards. When I looked on the King's chief agent I thought how often what we are is written on our faces, for if ever I saw evil, greed and cruelty I saw them then. Close to him as I was, I could note every feature—the small dark eyes, darting from side to side, the large lumpish nose somewhat redder than the sallow cheeks, the tight-shut narrow mouth; and I crossed myself.

The people began to move away, as mourners do when a body has been laid in the earth; and I went, without a doubt that I had no choice, to Doctor Lark's house. I passed by Master Penny's without a glance, though I suppose I had had some thought of returning there, but now all was changed.

If I had been the doctor's own daughter and Jane's sister I could have had no warmer or more loving welcome. I was embraced, fed, rested, Jane's old nurse sent for to lay her special ointment on my feet, a brace of young kittens put in my lap, and a gem which the doctor said brought peace and calmness put into my hand, where indeed it lay very comfortable and cool.

There was much talking to be done. They knew I had been sent to London, though not where, and at last I learned why. 'There were eyes,' Doctor Lark said. 'Never ask how I know, but servants talk. Nan Pritchett saw you go up the cock-loft stair, and watched you in the mornings set off towards the Dover Road, though she dared not follow you; and when you listened to talk after supper Master Belstone guessed you were there, having an ear for a spy. So, because you could not be trusted, he had you conveyed to where you could do no harm, with a jailer who would have had no pity if you had rebelled.'

'I can believe that. Will she have me taken again?'

'Not now. Their cause is won, the shrine is down and the jewels safe in the Treasury.'

'They were short-sighted,' I said, remembering what I knew that others did not. 'They should have questioned me while they had me.'

'Never say that!' The doctor's voice was sharp, for him. 'Their questioning would have left you only fit to crawl, Margery. Do you not know yet what they are?'

'Fiends, sir? I thought so when I set eyes on Cromwell this morning, and in London the—the other one, riding in procession, more was the pity for his horse. Now I know why innocent folk have died, why Queen Anne . . .'

'Margery.' The wise grey eyes were stern. 'Hush, child, if you value your own life and ours. Now rest, and read, if you will, and think of your mercies, and of all things lovely and pleasant, and so shake off the influence of evil.'

I said that I would, and that I was sorry for my rashness. Jane kissed me, and went softly out after her father. I stretched myself on the pallet bed in her bedchamber, where the wall-hanging picturing knights and ladies in faded colours pleased me very much for some reason I could not name. I wrapped myself closer in one of the doctor's robes, fleece-lined and comforting, and in a moment was asleep, before I could even begin to think of what I had seen that day and what it meant.

It seemed only a moment, though it was some three hours, before I felt a gentle touch on my shoulder, Jane trying to wake me. 'Almost supper-time, Margery. You're to wear a gown of mine because we have a guest.'

'Of yours, pippin? Will it reach below my knees?' She was inches shorter than me, mere child-size.

'Alice has been working on it—she had not quite finished the sewing, and took it to pieces again to fit you.'

'My thanks to her, but what a coil to make me fine for supper! Leave me be, I shall do very well with a pasty and your father's books.'

But Jane, gently firm, insisted on my washing in sweet water and brushing out my hair with a powder made from flowers, then got me into the gown, which after all I was pleased to be able to wear, since it was of damask, in a delicate bluish tint, like lavender laid over with pearl, flattering to any complexion and particularly to a fair one, as Jane pointed out. Her father sent me a sapphire, dependent from a gold chain, with the message that it was to quiet the mind. I thought with gratitude what trouble they took to comfort me after a journey which had not been painful, even something of an adventure.

We went down to supper. I saw, as I entered, that Doctor Lark's guest was a man, reclining at ease in the best carved chair by the hearth. I could only see of him a pair of long shapely legs in green hose, and a slender hand holding a gilt pomander.

But as I let fall the latch and sailed into the room on a tide of blue damask, he rose swiftly and turned to me; and he was Clement.

Yet not Clement; for a moment, as though in a flash of light, I seemed to see another face behind the charming familiar one. And then whatever had been there was gone, and I was taking in the change that had come over the man I knew, for the friar had given place to an elegant young gentleman, clad in a good padded doublet of dark purple with slashed sleeves showing white satin beneath, breeches of the same cloth and stockings of green silk. The shock to me was great in every way but he had expected me and waited, smiling, until I recovered myself. Then he stepped forward and kissed my hand in the most courtly manner.

'Mistress Burgoyne,' he saluted me, at the same moment as I said tartly, 'And what am I to call *you,* gallant sir?'

Father and daughter had watched our meeting with wide pleased eyes. Now Doctor Lark led me into the room and sat me down, before pouring wine for all of us.

'We must talk before we sup,' he said, and indeed I believe we all talked at once, until he held up his hand and motioned Clement to speak.

What he told me, which they already knew, was that he had been a ringleader in the band of those sworn to protect the shrine and its treasure. The man Layton had spies, and soon marked him out, just as Belstone soon learned that I knew about my master's secret watch by night. They very soon found an equally accommodating householder at a point all too near to the quiet alley by which Prior Goldwell's men had been filtering out the treasure piece by piece, and word had been sent to London; but not before much that was precious had been rescued.

'So my work was done, all that could be done,' Clement said. 'None of us who had planned and laboured by night were anxious to die for it, as die we would have done, by the rope and the knife. Some of the brothers left silently, knowing their names had been taken, and I thought it best to do the same, and so I came to the house of Doctor Lark.'

'But how could you know him—or he you?' The men exchanged glances.

Doctor Lark said, 'I knew Clement a little from past days, when I taught his brother; he visited me when he first came to Canterbury. And then, you see, I had some interest in the safety of the treasure, for each jewel, to me, was a thing of power as well as of beauty, able to heal and comfort—or to bring ill fortune and destruction in the wrong hands.' He gazed into the fire, as though he saw something sad there. 'The Regale, now, the great ruby that was the shrine's glory—say what you saw of its fate in the crystal, Jane.'

Jane said, in her dreaming voice, 'I saw it set in gold, on the thumb of a man's hand, a thick hand with reddish hairs on the back of it, and three other rings. Then it was on a woman's finger, short and stubby, though a lady's, royal, I think. And then on a long white finger of a hand covered with jewels; and wherever it was, I saw a mist of blood.'

Her father sighed. 'That is what comes of wresting a fair jewel from a holy place. So I gave Master Clement here a little help, a word of advice, a few names, for the safe-keeping of the treasure . . . otherwise I was a mere bystander.' I knew that despite his modest words he must have been active in the plot, perhaps its brains, just as I knew by instinct that Jane had seen more than she said, and that the first hand had been the King's.

'So now what will you do?' I asked Clement. 'Is it safe for you here?'

He shook his head. 'Far from safe. Even in these clothes; there is *this.*' He lifted his velvet cap, and there, a pale island among the dark hair, was the betraying tonsure.

'But it will vanish,' the Doctor said placidly. 'I have a specific oil for growing hair on shaven heads. You have not said how well my garments become him, Margery. I was a tall sprightly lad enough in my young days, but I think they never became me half so well—nay, I'm sure of it.'

I felt a blush creeping up from the sapphire on my bosom to my brow. For Clement did look a most comely gentleman, and if I had admired him in his priest's gown how much more did I admire him now! His eyes met mine, reading my thoughts, and more. He said gently, 'The tonsure is all there is left of the priest, Margery. I took my vows for a mistaken reason, but I tried to keep them and do good. Now the Priory I served is coming to its end, and soon there'll be no more work in England for such as I was.'

'So . . .'

'So, when all this is over, I will send to Rome for a dispensation to free me of my vows. The King may have made himself Head of the Church, but there are things beyond his power.'

Nobody said anything. We were each shocked, in our way. I loved him, and now he would be a free man for my taking; yet I had also loved the part of him that had been dedicated, the spiritual part of him, the young priest who had spoken to me so kindly at my confession, and now that person was gone for ever. Doctor Lark, I think, knew for the first time that the business of rescuing jewels was only a small part of what was going on, which was the collapse of the old way of English life, the old Faith. He said, almost to himself, 'Can the King make saints, as he un-makes them; can he work miracles?'

And Jane turned suddenly pale, with that blankness in her eyes which meant the onset of one of her strange half-swoons, which often took her when she was troubled. I clasped her hand tight, willing her to recover. Her eyes cleared and she said in her usual tone, 'We must go in and eat, or the good food will be cold.'

We sat up late that night, talking of what we must do. Clement declared that he would lose no time in leaving the city. His presence in the house put his hosts in danger, for his face was well-known, and if he were to be arrested the odds were that they would be. 'I shall go home,' he said, 'to my father's house near Ashford. Nobody lives there now but my Aunt Cicely, who is almost a recluse, and her servants. I shall stay there until Brother Clement is forgotten and Clement Moyle lives again. All I need is a horse of yours, sir, and the loan of these garments, and both shall come back to you quickly.'

The Doctor said he wanted neither back, giving them freely and gladly. He turned to me, 'But for you, child, there is a home as long as you need one, and welcome. Jane, Margery must have the little chamber next to yours, with the painted wall.'

Jane shook her head. 'Father, she must not stay, though I long for her company. You don't know, Margery, what has happened at Master Penny's. He hates you now, spreading it far and wide that you robbed him of some fortune he should have had—but I can't think that true.'

I could. It was my guess that Ralph Belstone had gone back on his bargain with my master, because of the discovery that I knew of it, and so the old man got neither of his jewels. No wonder the thought of me rankled with him.

'And more,' Jane said. 'That fiery-faced Nan has got him to marry her.'

'Marry her? Never!'

'It's true. They said he did it to spite you, and now she peacocks about in finer clothes than you ever had, talking of you as though you were Queen Jezebel herself. The neighbours have it in store for you if you show your face about Burgate Street again—not that they love Mistress Penny, but scandal soon spreads.'

'Then I must go, and quickly. I endanger you, too.'

Clement said, 'No. How would you fare, a woman alone, in times like this?'

'I fared very well when I travelled from Hever. None molested me, or gave me worse than a wink or a saucy word.'

'That was good fortune, no more. You would take your life and your honour into the worst kind of perils. I forbid it, and that is enough.' He folded his arms and leaned back, the very picture of masculine dominance, and I rejoiced to see him think himself already so much master of me. Besides, I was only too sure that he was right; there was nowhere I could go, except where I intended to go.

'Then I shall travel with you,' I said.

As I waited for him to say no, it was as if Time stopped. We were again where we had been once before, in the same case. We were neither Margery and Clement nor the people we had been then, but all these, ourselves. It was a feeling more powerful than the glimpse I had had of time past, after Jane's crystal-scrying, when I had swooned; but now I did not swoon, only remained suspended with Clement in that moment, as though we were two spirits of air, out of our bodies.

'That would be best,' he said, breaking the spell; Time moved on. I thought, I sensed as if recalling a dream that had flown, that last time he had refused. So now the case was altered and we were living people again, Doctor Lark and Jane looking from one to the other of us, Clement smiling, holding my eyes with his.

It was very early in the morning when we rode out of Canterbury, Clement clad in yet more clothes that had been carefully stored for years in Doctor Lark's coffer, I very decent-looking in a frieze cloak covering me from head to foot, the property of Hannah, one of the family servants, who would be well paid for it, I knew, though not by me.

The morning was pearly and cool, the air brisk, as pure as though this were the first day of Creation. The fires of autumn blazed in the trees, scarlet, yellow and russet, some as fair as Danäe's shower of gold, sprinkling us as we passed. Houseless and penniless, knowing no more of what my future might be than a babe unborn, I was happy enough to have sung at the top of my voice, only it might have drawn attention from those who were just stirring to the business of the day.

As we rode through Wincheap Gate I turned to look back at my city, Bell Harry rising grandly over low huddled roofs, the walls the Romans had built still snugly enclosing all in strong arms, the twin towers of St Augustine's where the wreckers had already been, and the sadness of leaving touched me—but only with the tip of a wing, for I was riding with my love.

Our way lay along a lane which had the Stour as its companion, shining and dimpling out sometimes for long stretches, sometimes only glimpsed. Fat contented sheep browsed in the meadows, little knowing how soon their pleasant lives would end, in the slaughter that came with late September, providing dried salted meat for the winter. In the orchards bright apples still gleamed scarlet and green, and boys and maids on ladders were already picking them.

'I was born at this time of year,' Clement said. 'A little later, when the Virgin gives place to the Scales, but the whole month delights me, as they say one's birth-month does by nature. Is it so with you, Margery?'

'Yes, for I came to earth in May, under Gemini, and I love spring flowers above all things.' I thought to myself, and those born under Gemini, the Twins, search always for their mate, and are never happy until that mate is found. So, talking lightly and in our talk discovering each other, we came in the afternoon to the house of Clement's child-hood, sheltered under the green shoulder of the Downs near the little town of Wye. It was long and low, built perhaps a hundred years before, the roofs seeming to sag and curve in with their own weight, the dark red bricks of the walls softly clothed with ivy. Like everything else, it had grown wild; roses, still in bloom, rambled over the dia-mond-shaped window-panes, an ancient vine twined, all leaves and no grapes, round the pointed-arch porch over which a weather-battered crest bore initials, M twisted with what might have been a T or a C. In the tall trees behind the house were rooks' nests, and smaller nests of smaller birds under the porch-eaves and over windows.

Clement reined in his horse. He gave a long, low whistle, survey-ing the house. 'Is Aunt dead, then? By the looks of it nobody lives here but bats.'

'Smoke,' I said, 'coming from that chimney, look.'

We dismounted and tethered the horses. Clement pulled the iron chain which hung by the iron-studded front door. A melancholy clanging within the house followed, but no one answered the summons. As he pulled it again the iron decoration that formed its handle came off and fell to the ground. With the first oath I had ever heard him use, he gave the door a sharp push, to which it yielded. We stood in a dark, heavily-timbered hall, its ceiling-beams arching high above us. There was no fire in the roughly-built hearth, had not been for years, perhaps. A strong, unpleasant smell of damp hung in the air, seeming to strike upwards from the floor and inwards from the walls. I shivered. Clement said, 'A pretty place to bring you to. Oh God, if I had never gone away!'

'Was this where your mother . . . ?'

'Lived and died, and took my life with her, dying, for seven years, God rest her soul and forgive me for speaking against her when she thought herself in the right to do what she did. Never go against what your own inward self tells you is right, Margery, as I was fool enough to do.'

'No, Father,' I said meekly, and got a look so blended of anger and amusement that I laughed. It was good to hear laughter in that deserted place. We climbed the staircase, carefully, for the wooden steps looked unsafe, holding on to the carved figures of griffins and their like which ornamented the banister rail, themselves looking as wretched as their surroundings. The smell of damp now mingled with other things—long-lying dust, mice, something like stale grease, and a vague unpleasantness to which I could put no name. It came into my mind that Clement's aunt might very possibly be dead and her corpse undiscovered. I followed him, none too eagerly, along an almost dark landing.

'This door, or this?' He opened one, shut it again, and went on to the next. At that he paused and bade me to mind the step down.

We were in a long, low bedchamber, black-beamed, the plaster between almost as black, and the nameless smell that had been outside was ten times as strong. I fell back, but Clement, calling upon Our Lord, Our Lady and a number of saints to help him (I suspect he would have invoked devils if he had not been so well-trained) went to the triple casement and threw each window open, letting in late sunlight that had not been able to penetrate the grimy glass. Now I saw that a large bed, four-posted, took up much of the floor, and that tattered hangings depended from its tester. Clement stepped forward and began to rip them down, at which a faint chirping began which I hoped was not mice.

But when the rags were down, and the sunlight piercing through the motes of dust dancing in the air, we saw that the sound came from a person in the bed: the thin form hardly raised the covers, the face on the pillow was as gaunt as a *memento mori* carved under a tomb, of which it very much reminded me. But the dark eyes were alive, and the thin lips moved in twitterings of surprise and fear. Instead of a nightcap there was a hood of the old style, that had once been very fine.

Clement stepped back, 'Well, Aunt,' he said cheerfully, 'how long it is since we greeted each other. You find yourself well, I hope?'

If there were in all England a beggar-woman dirtier, more neglected, and seeming nearer death than Mistress Cicely Kempe, I should not like to have seen her. We stood by the bed, trying to breathe in as little as we could of the noisome air in the room; there was no need of words between us to settle what we must do. Clement said, 'She needs a doctor and perhaps a priest. Since I am a priest used to tending sick folk, and you have your womanly skills, I think we shall manage alone—yes?'

'Yes.' If the poor thing had been a leper, and yet Clement's aunt, I should have been just as eager to nurse her. We searched the house for servants and found none, only, in the filthy kitchen quarters, an old woman sunk in sleep beside the great hearth, where no fire burnt, surrounded by the remains of old food—stale crusts, eggshells, meat crawling with maggots, a chicken carcass and a lump of what may once have been cheese. She gave off, at close quarters, a strong odour of wine. Clement, grim-faced, shook her and slapped her cheeks until she roused. From her mumblings we made out that her name was Dorcas, that she was Mistress Kempe's only attendant, and that she knew nothing of any friends of her mistress's, or of any doctor who had been to see her.

Clement, controlling the anger I knew he felt, ordered her to get up and conduct us round the house. When she staggered he grasped her arm and frog-marched her up the stairs, from room to room, until she sobered somewhat and was able to show us where were such things as linen and clean garments. We were pleased to find a whole chest of these, clearly belonging to Mistress Kempe, stored so well that the moth had not got to them, and a quantity of soap balls, made long since but still fit for use, and lotions and scented distillations in unopened flasks. In the room that had been Clement's was a press that still held doublets and breeches, shirts and hose. He shook his head over them.

'Boys' gear, boys' gear. What hope is there it would fit me now?'

Yet, perhaps because of the hard life he had led for the past seven years, he had put on no flesh, only grown a little. When he came out of his room he wore breeches of leather and a plain shirt, discoloured with age, fitter for the work he had to do than what he had worn before. I put off my own good gown and donned a coarse woollen one I found with some that had evidently belonged to someone other than Mistress Kempe, and tucked up the sleeves. Then we set to work.

We set Dorcas, who seemed bewildered about the whole matter, to heat pans and fish-kettles of water over the fire Clement had kindled, and one after another brought them upstairs to the bedchamber, where he had made another fire. Then, between us (for the poor lady seemed past modesty) we washed Mistress Kempe from head to foot, clipped her hair, which was lousy, to a good short length, wrapped her in a warm robe and set her by the fire, where she sat round-eyed with wonder as Clement stripped the bed of its hangings and the filthy sheets and took them to burn outside. While Dorcas scrubbed and swept Clement fetched milk and fresh eggs from a nearby farm. With these, and some *aqua vitae* he had discovered, I fed Mistress Kempe, first by sipped spoonfuls, then by draughts as she grew more able to take the posset. All the time I talked lightly to her, of anything but the desecration of Canterbury, or of her own sad state. Gradually the look of animal fear left her eyes, and a faint colour crept into her face, which had been waxen-yellow.

When Clement came back after one of his errands, she spoke, her cracked lips moving with difficulty.

'Long . . . away.'

'Why, yes, Aunt. Many things kept me, or I would have come back sooner. You've been too long alone, but now that's over.'

'Ma-ry,' she got out, very slowly.

'She died, Aunt, your sister Mary—you remember? The angels have her now, fear nothing for her.' The eyes that seemed afraid of the light were fixed on me, puzzled. Clement read their question.

'This is Margery, my friend, Mistress Margery Burgoyne. She can cook and brew and sew, and do all you need. You shall not be cold or starved again now we are here. Try her with a little more broth, Margery.'

With careful feeding, good strong nourishing things, and warmth about her and the feeling of cleanliness, the lady who had been deprived and neglected within an inch of her life came slowly back to herself. Clement explained to me that the brain needs food from the body, or it loses its brightness and becomes dull like that of an idiot. 'Any lamp needs fuel,' he said. Now I found her to be cultivated and most pleasant in her manners, speaking as well as Clement and with something of his charm. She must have been sixty years old; her hair was pure white, her features delicately aquiline. Piece by piece, taking care not to tire her, we got out of her what had happened since Clement left to take Orders. The death of her sister, coming after a long and trying illness, had drained her of strength, and then her husband, many years older than herself, had also died. Some of the servants, lacking regular wages, had gone away, leaving her with only Dorcas and a kitchen-maid, who had also disappeared, taking enough valuables with her to warrant hanging if she were caught.

'And so it began,' she told us. 'I would sit here with none to talk to and every lively book in the house read. The only one of our family who came here was your cousin Gilbert, Clement, who had heard you were gone away and thought there might be pickings for him; but I misliked him very much and took to leaving the door unanswered when I knew him to be there. So, in time I answered to no one, and became as you found me. I was mad then—I would be dead now, if it were not for you two children.' She stretched out her thin delicate hands, one to each of us; I had pared and polished the nails to what a lady's should be.

It was very difficult for her to understand how Clement came to be there at all, and not in some monastery. The doings of Cromwell and the King's men had not come to her ears; we decided that it would only upset her mind to try to explain them. Clement talked to her alone, and though he said little to me I think he gave her some idea that he had never taken his final vows and was free to live as a layman again. I think too that somehow, without telling actual lies, he managed to convey this to Father Andrew, the priest from Godmersham who came to confess her (with many tut-tuts and fie-fies that she had gone unvisited so long), since no difficult questions were ever asked.

We had the house to rights by Michaelmas, or nearly. Everything that had rotted beyond repair was thrown out, the place cleaned from lofts to cellars as though a legion of friendly hobgoblins had been at work; but it was we who had scoured and polished, and the servants Clement had engaged.

He seemed to have plenty of money, considering that like all his Order he had taken vows of poverty. I asked nothing, and then in his own time he told me that his mother had set up a trust for him—not that she expected him ever to return to the world, but so that he could at some time make a handsome gift to the Church, or even purchase a high place for himself. He said that he had no scruple about using the money for other purposes. 'The Church has no need of it, for the Church is beyond help. She is dying at the hands of her own children. Why should I throw money into her coffin?' It was not for me to cross him. I had plenty to spend on good living for all of us—a housekeeper again, but with what a difference.

In the dark evenings we three sat in the best parlour, a long low room with a great hearth where a log fire burnt day and night. Mistress Kempe had a long memory and a lively turn of story-telling, unrolling the tapestry of her life before me; and I, who knew so little, listened gladly.

'I was born,' she said, 'while King Edward the Fourth still lived. I saw him once, on pilgrimage to Canterbury, when I was a little thing, and I see him now, clearer than Clement here. Oh, what a gallant he was, what a great tall ruddy-cheeked man, with a look in his eye that would make a holy abbess drop her beads—and all else, if it came to the pinch—there, I hope I don't shock you, child, but we used to be broader-spoken than folk are today. A little on the stout side, was King Edward, being too fond of the food and wine that took him off in an apoplexy in his prime, ah, dear. His Queen was with him, Elizabeth, and I thought her the fairest lady I had ever seen, like a lily, but proud and pettish. You can see her picture in glass in Christ Church Chapel of the Martyrdom, just like life, and the King's too, and the two little Princes, their sons. Alas!' She sighed, gazing into the fire.

'Why alas, dame?'

'You never heard the story? Well, I dare say young folk nowadays care nothing for old times. It was after King Edward died, and his brother the Duke of Gloucester became Lord Protector to the little King that was to be . . . I saw him too, Gloucester, on that pilgrimage, a very short slight young man to be brother to the King, dark-haired and with a lowering face; aye, and the other brother was there, George of Clarence, a handsome arrogant fellow—do you know, of all that band, he alone would have a sword carried before him in procession, as though he and not his brother had been king? Did you ever hear of such a thing? Well, he came to a bad end, Lord have mercy on him . . .'

'But the young Princes, what befell them?' I asked. She was inclined to ramble.

'Ah, my dear, nobody ever knew—except perhaps one, and those who did the work for him.'

'For whom?'

'Why, Richard of Gloucester, who lusted to be King himself. He had those poor infants declared bastards, and kept in the Tower of London. At first folk saw them playing together, sweet innocents, in the garden of their lodging, and then they were taken from the public view and seen no more. Never again.'

'Dead?'

'Foully murdered, they said, and by *his* hand.'

I was working it out in my head: Master Penny's household had not been notable for historical discussions. 'But Richard must have been their uncle.'

'So he was, and a cruel unnatural one.'

'And what became of him?'

'Why, he made himself King, and ruled two or three years, I forget which, and then met his death in battle, at some far-away place.'

'Bosworth,' Clement said, 'in the middle of England. Henry Tudor's men killed him—the present . . . King's father. And so we fell to the House of Tudor,' he added bitterly.

My whole attention was held by this, an old lady's tale of things past before even my parents were born. I said that I should like to see pictures of all these people, but neither Mistress Kempe nor Clement knew where there might be any, except in the King's palaces of White-hall or Windsor, and in coloured glass in the Martyrdom at Canterbury. But I dared not go back to Canterbury.

It became my amusement in those quiet pleasant evenings, to question Mistress Kempe about the royal people and the events of her youth, and to get her to draw sketches of them, so far as she remembered them, and the clothes they wore, which I thought were very much more graceful than the garments of our day—as I suppose one generation always thinks of those that went before it. Mistress Kempe was amused at my interest, flattered that a young person should listen so intently to her stories, and Clement said I was wise to study history, for it would help me to understand the present. 'This land is in a pretty plight,' he said, 'for throwing out its Plantagenet kings and letting the red Welshmen in.'

'But,' I said, 'King Richard was a wicked man and came to a bad end.'

'They all came to a bad end. The times were hard, but not so hard as these. And do you think a king who kills his nephews for political reasons wickeder than one who kills his wife for the crime of not bearing him a son?' His tone was savage; I knew he was thinking of Queen Anne Boleyn, and a pang shot through me of that jealousy I felt so unreasonably, since the poor wench was nothing now but bones in the Tower church, and Clement had in a way promised to be true to me. Yet had he? He had said something, that morning at St Martin's, to the effect that we must always be all truth to one another. Might that not mean only comradeship, since he had never spoken outright of love?

How I longed for him to speak of it, to perform it, when the happy evening was over and I lay in my wide bed that was far too big for one person, aching for his warmth, his lips, his arms round me, and the bliss I knew that union with him would bring. I used to pass the hours by saying over all the sad songs of lovers known to me (and there were not very many, so were often repeated), thus bringing myself the relief of tears sometimes.

O Western wind, when wilt thou blow,
    That the small rain down can rain?
Christ, if my love were in my arms,
    And I in my bed again!

Once, and only once, in my desperation I clung to him as we said good-night on the staircase, begging silently for his love and company. But gently, though with a strength I could not fight, he put me from him, saying, 'I am still a priest, Margery.' And so we carried our candles to separate beds.

Not the west wind, but the east, blew across the Stour valley that winter, bringing with it cruel cold and thick snows. We could no longer ride out along the pleasant lanes, only gaze out at the gardens cover-leted with snow, and throw crumbs to the poor birds which begged, their feathers puffed out for warmth, and the bright-eyed squirrels which sat up with their paws together, like little Christians. On holy days and the great festival of Christmas we went together to the Church of St Gregory and St Martin, whose great benefactor had been Mistress Kempe's relative, Cardinal Kempe. He had given the money for much of its fine buildings, and the music and processions which made it the admiration of the district, and had founded the Wye College.

But as we knelt there, Clement and his two ladies, we saw that faces around us were not as joyful as once they must have been. The destroyer was coming nearer, even here, and the glory of the time was marred by that knowledge.

Such was my winter. I hoped for so much from the spring, when I would surely see more of Clement. These grey cold days he seemed to be always shut up in the little library-room he told me his father had used, reading or writing. I rather wished he were not such a scholar. Mistress Kempe and I kept each other entertained, she glad enough to have young company, I pleased to be with such an amiable lady, ready to play the Old Times game with me as though the dead people had been dolls, and we children. I guessed she was not sure of how I stood with Clement, though she was too courteous to ask outright, and I longed to talk with her about it, but dared not in case she were horri-fied at my former life, and at his abandoned priesthood.

After the year turned I had a letter from Jane, brought by a carrier good-natured enough to step out of his way to Dover. It told me that Canterbury had been altogether stricken by the despoiling of the shrine, and that action was being taken against Prior Goldwell for having made away with several thousands of pounds-worth of jewels and plate belonging to Christ Church but not included in the inventory delivered to Cromwell's agent, and almost worse, he was accused of having murdered several monks and friars who had disappeared, Clement's name among them. I told him. His smile was secret and mischievous.

'Then I am dead and out of their way,' he said. 'All the better.' Standing beside him as he sat at his writing-table, I noticed that the tonsure had all but grown out, so much that nobody who did not look for it would see where it had been. I asked, tartly perhaps, 'How goes the shedding of the priesthood?'

'Well enough, well enough, but slow. Pope Paul's clerks are kept busy, with so many chicks squawking to leave the nest.'

I looked at his table, covered with papers, at the full ink-horn and the number of pens used and discarded, and wondered how much time it took to write a letter to Rome and receive an answer. But, like a good wife, I asked no questions. Wife, alas, if I had been! He spent much time in writing these days, very little in visits or entertainments. It was known that he was back, and living at Moyles, but he took care not to seek the company of those who might make trouble. His aunt worried about him, and confided in me.

'He was always one to be active. The life at Hever suited him so well, no dullness, Court life, plenty to sharpen his wits on, people of quality to consort with, while here there is nothing to do and only us rustics to talk to—not you, my dear, you must be all that makes this place tolerable for him. Poor lad, it's not his way at all.'

'He does occupy himself in writing, madam.'

'Writing? Tush, what kind of occupation is that? He never used to sit scrawling. What does he write, some learned book? Nature meant him for a soldier, not a scholar, that I'll swear, and if only my poor crazed sister had not bound him with her deathbed wish . . .' She rambled gently on, and I answered at random, but her words had put thoughts into my head. What did he write, indeed? I was filled with curiosity, but I would not ask him, and I would never spy on him as I had done on Master Penny. As the worst of the winter vanished and the roads began to be passable, the cheerful carrier who travelled from London to Dover and Dover to London called very often on us. I never saw what he brought or took away.

How quickly winter may give place to spring! It seemed that one day we looked out at a bare starved world and stone-grey skies, awaking to a pretty soft-hued morning, boughs tipped with buds, furry catkins hanging from the willow-trees, and birds courting their mates. Seeing it all I felt new-born, filled with a leaping joy that must have expression.

'Why, what's this?' asked Clement, as I ran full tilt into him, having leapt down the staircase two steps at a time. 'Where do you go so fast?'

'To the door, to be out in the air! Don't you feel it, the coming of spring?'

'I see it in your face.'

'Then come with me—come and walk on the Downs until the winter's all blown away!'

He smiled, and I knew I had won him over. 'I have a better thought. The horses need exercise as much as we, and the roads should be dry enough.'

It was like Paradise to ride out again, warm-clad, the light wind in our faces, the horses under us as blithe as we were to feel their freedom. We turned their heads towards the coast, sniffing salt in the air as we drew nearer to it. Even in those remote lanes and bridle-paths there were everywhere signs of new life. The first lambs, those that had lived through the snows, ran and bleated behind their mothers, a spindly colt staggered at the mare's side. Around farmsteads and cottages people were venturing out perhaps for the first time since Christmas. Those whom we passed close called or waved greetings to us, and we answered them cheerfully. Any new face was a friendly one to them, Clement said.

He told me we were riding through the Valley of Elham, and would soon be at the sea, which I had never seen in my life and could not imagine except as a kind of wide river. When we came at last to a place where the road sloped downwards, and no more hills or plains appeared before us, he reined in his horse, saying, 'There.'

I could see nothing, only a vast expanse of shimmering light that I took to be part of the sky. Clement watched me, smiling. 'There it lies, the sea.' I was silent with wonder, unable to believe my eyes, that so much water could exist without swallowing up the land. When he urged his horse forward and called me to follow I hung back in fear at first; then, ashamed of cowardice, slowly obeyed, amazed that the animal seemed not at all afraid, but paced sedately along beside Clement's.

As my eyes began to get used to the new wonderful sight I noticed not only silvery greyness, but many colours, dark blue and green, and the colour of sand. There were small boats near the shore, fishermen with nets—brave men to trust themselves on the great sea, thought I—and on the shore others were unloading their catches, spilling out bright wriggling fish like coins from a purse. Clement pointed out the buyers already waiting, eager to have the creatures in their first freshness. I remembered suddenly the morning in Canterbury when he had saved me from a lurching cart by pushing me into a fishmonger's. It was not quite the sort of encounter poets make verses upon, but he had touched me, and I had blushed hotly, and that had almost been the beginning of everything.

We had been riding for hours with only a meal of bread and ale. The salt air was making me hungry, and Clement too. He said he knew of a good inn near the church where we would eat and then turn homewards.

But, when the church tower was already in sight, a change came, a cold mist that dimmed the brightness of the sea and spread over the land. I could feel its beads on my face, already stung by the salt. Clement looked troubled.

'I had not thought of this,' he said. 'It will get thicker towards dusk, and we shall lose our way.'

'So what must we do?'

'Turn inland and ride quickly.'

We did; but the mist followed us. Soon it was difficult to see the ground under our horses' hooves, and mine stumbled once, giving me a fright. The sky was darkening. I trusted him utterly to get us back, but there were hazards beyond his control, footpads, the deep ruts in the earth that were now invisible to us, other things beyond my guessing. The same thoughts had been going through his mind, for he said, 'It should have cleared by now, but it gets thicker. Fool! to ride you so far. We're heading for the Forest of Lyminge, I think, and by the time we get there it will be dark—*if* we get there. Elham has an inn, but I remember no other.'

We rode slowly on, but never did countryside look so bleak (what we could see of it) or so entirely without human life, except ourselves. Suddenly Clement said, 'See! beyond those trees.'

I strained my eyes through the misty gloom until I saw it too—a faint rosy light. As we drew nearer a building took shape, the light coming from a window. Clement breathed a prayer of thanks. 'Whoever lives there will surely take us in.'

His loud, firm knock was answered by a man, youngish, short and sturdy. The ash-stick in his hand was, I felt sure, something to use on us if we proved to be thieves. Clement spoke swiftly before the stick could be brandished. 'We've ridden from the coast, friend, and can go no farther in this mist. This lady is weary and hungry, and our horses need rest. Will you, out of goodness, give us shelter?'

The man's suspicious look faded, and he smiled. 'Welcome, sir, you and your lady. It's poor thick weather for riding, that it is. We've fire and light, God send travellers no worse.'

'Amen,' said Clement, crossing himself. I fancied a curious expression crossed our host's face. He led us into what was clearly the living-room of the small farm; flitches of bacon hung from the ceiling, a savoury cooking smell flavoured the air, and the light from the brisk fire danced on the ceiling-beams, bright enough to read by if one had wished. By the hearth a young woman was seated on a low stool with something in her lap that I took at first for an infant, but then saw to be a lamb, so small that it must be almost new-born. She looked up and greeted us civilly, and bade the child beside her do the same. This was a girl about seven years old, round-eyed with wonder at the strangers, too shy to speak.

'There now, Mary, you take turns with the runtlet while I see to the lady and gentleman,' her mother said. The child took her place and began to feed the small creature with milk from a porringer, patiently trickling drop after drop into the pink mouth. I saw Clement watching this, with a look I had never seen before on his face, a tenderness I thought of as fatherly, and if my heart had been his before it was now doubly so, that a man should look thus at a child feeding a lamb.

Mistress Fagg, the farmer's wife, told us that the lamb's mother had died in giving it birth, and the shepherd had brought it indoors. It might be rearable or it might not, but they were doing their best for it as though it had been a Christian babe.

'"*Ecce Agnus Dei*,"' Clement murmured to me, so softly that Mistress Fagg must have had sharp ears to hear him, but she did, and I fancied the same look flitted across her face that I had seen on her husband's at the door. What an odd household were we come into, I thought.

Clement touched the lamb's tiny head lightly. 'If it lives, you must call it Agnellus, mistress. That is the Latin name for a little lamb.'

This time there was no mistake about her expression: it was one of wondering awe. Master Fagg, who had been tending the fire, turned sharply and stared at Clement.

'You know Latin, sir?' he asked, as though there were something miraculous about it. When Clement replied that he did, Master Fagg half-bowed to him, a clumsy, humble gesture which yet carried more than a courtier's obeisance. I saw him glance at his wife, then he asked, 'Do you come from London, master?' It seemed they both waited tensely for the reply. When Clement said that his home was at Wye, I thought they breathed out relief.

The little girl put the lamb, which was sleeping, in a basket by the hearth, and took up a doll which she began to nurse. To get a word from her I said, 'That's a fine babe you have there, Mary. What is its name?'

She looked up sharply at her mother, who, after a second's pause, nodded. The child, her head down, whispered, 'Mary.'

'Named for yourself?'

A violent shake of the head.

'Will you show her to me?'

The child burst into tears, clutched the doll to her, and went to her mother, burying her face in her skirts. As Mistress Fagg turned to clasp her I saw that she was pregnant. Clement—oh, so much cleverer than I!—rose and went to them, and put his hand on the child's head, saying gently, 'Trust me, Mary—I will do her no harm. Will you not show me her face?'

The fountain of her tears ceased to play, so kindly was his voice, and slowly she drew away the piece of blanket which covered the doll. Instead of the crudely-carved wooden puppet a farmer's child might well have nursed there emerged from the folds a small, sweetly smiling face, painted in colours as natural as life, a face of rose and lily, with painted golden hair; a skilfully-wrought, slender girl's form, one hand touching her body below the breasts as if something precious lay there.

Clement went on his knees, and I followed him and together we said an ave to the Blessed Virgin whose image we looked on.

'We hid her,' Master Fagg told us. 'They pulled the Priory to scraps for what they could get, a fellow they called Layton and his band. I heard 'em say all images not of gold or silver was to be burned—and that meant Our Lady there, for I knew she was of wood. So I slips into her chapel, while they were at their work otherwhere, and puts her in a sack I carried, begging her pardon, but 'twas to save her.'

'We thought it best to dress her for our Mary's moppet by day,' his wife said, 'lest that gang of rogues should come by again, but by night we crowns her.'

'It is almost night now,' Clement said.

Within the wide hearth-place, set in the wall, was a recess for the drying of salt, some inches deep with a pointed arch above it like a church window. Mistress Fagg took from a locked chest various things very carefully kept. On the image she put a blue cloak edged with silver thread, and a crown of stars made of gilt metal on its head. Then she placed it in the alcove and set in the hearth below it a jug full of such flowers as were to be had at that time of year—snowdrops, aconites, willow catkins, budding twigs. I never saw such a simple shrine, nor one so moving.

From the chest she drew something else, an object like a short rope of woven cloth, dun in colour, which had been wrapped in layer upon layer of linen. 'Our Lady's own girdle,' she breathed. 'The Prior used to show it to pilgrims as the most precious relic of all. He gave it to my man to keep, till the bad times be gone.'

Clement kissed it and laid it back in its wrappings. 'They will never be gone,' he said. 'It will be the new ways against the old, Pope against King, blood spilt in the name of religion, war instead of the Kingdom of Peace. We have seen the end of the faith St Augustine brought to Canterbury. You may keep to it, mistress, and I may, and all of us here, but the old Church of England has fallen and will never rise again. I was a priest and now am neither that nor a private gentleman.'

At that they fell to their knees before him, but he raised them up and gently bade them forget that they had ever seen him. 'The moon is up, we can be on our way.'

They pressed us to eat, which we did, though I for one was too disturbed to care about food any more. Then Clement blessed them, as they asked, and laid two gold pieces before the image of Our Lady, one to be put to their little daughter's dowry, he said. And so we rode away.

The moon was full up, all the mist gone, the landscape clear as at mid-day. It was long before Clement spoke.

'Now you see what that man has done, Margery. And for one family who hold to their faith there will be a hundred lost and bewildered, not knowing any more what to believe in, with no comfort in this life nor hope for the next. He has killed their souls.'

'But surely . . . he is Head of the Church, so there must *be* a Church.'

He laughed shortly. 'He? A tyrant, a fornicator, a miser, a murderer—a man who killed his innocent wife and his best friend Thomas More, Head of the Church? A pretty Head and a pretty Church! Oh, many a Pope has been no better, but they had authority and he has none. So, that poor rag you saw just now was no more Our Lady's girdle than your own is, and more relics are false than true; statues bleed red liquor mixed by a monk and speak with tongues worked from behind a curtain, but does that harm the faith of such as believe in them? There must be a special Hell kept for those who kill faith . . . Well, if I had doubts, I have none now.'

'Doubts, Clement?'

'About what we . . . about what I intend.'

I dared not ask what that was, for I had a faint, dreadful suspicion.

We turned a corner and saw before us the skeleton of a building, a hollow thing of empty windows, roofless walls and scattered stones. It had been a tall church, perhaps the Priory from which the image had been rescued, left pillaged and broken by the despoilers.

A pitiful sight, yet it was not so much the poor ruin, black against the moonlit sky, that made me shiver and catch my breath as a sudden, sharp memory of something of the kind seen, or spoken of, long, long before. Yet when, since such despoliations had only just begun? And why did I hear words in my mind: 'The Abbey was gone . . .' or 'is gone' and, 'It has not happened yet'?

8

I knew that something was beginning the day the two young gentlemen arrived from London. Sir Anthony Wyatt and Sir William Carew, said Clement, as each bowed low to me and Mistress Kempe; Sir Anthony pale-haired and high-nosed, with an aloof air, Sir William notable for a pair of dark brooding eyes and a small beard pointed like a dagger. Each had a single manservant in attendance and a fine horse glistering with good grooming. It was clear that they had not come for light chat or ladies' company, for they supped alone with Clement, while his aunt and I sat at our needlework.

We talked of small things, of a forthcoming christening at a neighbour's, of the new young greyhound Clement had given her, so pretty in its ways but difficult to house-train. Yet I knew we were neither of us thinking of them. Since her return to the world from her bed of famine and neglect she had lived less and less in the past, enjoying the visits of nearby ladies and discovering some Kempe relatives. One of these, another aunt of Clement's on the Moyle side, was much in London with her husband and full of Court gossip.

'They say the King's new wife, the Princess of Cleves, will never please him. He took a fancy to her picture, but found her nothing like. She says, poor simple creature, that after the candles are out he bids her "Good night, Sweet

Heart", and in the morning "Farewell, Darling", and that she thinks is the be-all and end-all of marriage. What will come of it, do you think?'

'Nothing that will fill a cradle. For the lady herself—the axe?'

'Oh fie! Yet, alas, it was so before.'

I had sworn to myself not to speak of her, but my mind kept returning to Anne Boleyn, and I asked Mistress Kempe if Clement had talked much of her during his time at Hever.

'Much? I never heard a lady so praised. I thought he would have turned lunatic when we knew that she was promised to the King.'

'Clement, lunatic?'

'Ah, you've never seen him smitten with love, child. I always believed he spoke for her hand in marriage, and either she, or her proud father, would not listen—and I tell you another thing, I think it was because he had lost all hope of her that he gave in to my silly sister's whim and took Orders.'

This came to me as a shock. Yet why had I not thought of it before? I must have shown my feelings, for she bit off a thread and looked sideways at me, consideringly. 'It would not have done at all, you know,' she said. 'Poor creature, she beckoned all men. It was said (though never repeat this, for your life) that young Thomas Wyatt had her before the King.'

Perhaps because I was troubled in my mind by the arrival of the two young men, this piece of gossip hit me like the strike of an arrow. For the first time I wondered whether Clement's love for her had not been only an ideal one. Perhaps she had taken him to her bed and charmed him so with her kisses and clippings that no other woman would ever do for him. I began to imagine it, the black-eyed black-haired girl, and him, and a dreadful ignoble jealousy overcame me. Better to be as I had been, feeling nothing for Master Penny or any other man, than this torture.

All that long evening I brooded over it. Clement and the visitors remained in the room he called his library, talking and talking. I made excuses for myself for crossing the landing, passing the door; I even saw a servant take in more candles, and heard the talk die down as she entered. But in one thing my mind was made up. I would not listen and spy, as I had on Master Penny's conference with Ralph Belstone. That, at least, was beneath me now. But I lay awake in my bedchamber on the other side of the house, listening for the slightest sound that would tell me they had broken up their gathering.

Next day they rode out together early. When they came back it was to take dinner with Mistress Kempe and me, she chattering away and nobody else saying very much. They said farewell to us indoors, courteously enough, but rather as though their thoughts were elsewhere. Clement saw them off in the courtyard. I was sneaking enough to slip out by another door, pretending to gather something from the garden border, and I watched as they mounted. Sir Anthony leaned down from his horse to shake hands with Clement and I clearly heard him say, 'He will hang in Hell.'

By the evening I had worked myself into a passion about it, or I would not have had the courage to march up to his library door, give a bold knock and walk in. He was sitting at the table, with something spread out before him that my sharp eye saw was a map, but not a map of countryside, rather of a building, with rooms and corridors drawn out. Instantly he rolled it up and pushed it away from him.

'Yes, Margery? What is the catastrophe?'

'The . . . ?'

'Is the house afire, or my aunt ill, or have thieves broken in? Otherwise you would not be here.'

'I came because I must know what the matter is between you and those men, and between you and me, Clement. You tell me nothing, not a word, you deal with me as though *I* were nothing, you shut me out like a leper out of a church, and yet I know you're putting yourself into some dreadful danger. I thought we were friends, comrades, if no more—what have I done to be kept outside your affairs?'

'Has my aunt sent you?' he asked very quietly.

'No. If she knew she would be angry.'

'*I* am angry, Margery. For your own good I have kept you out of my counsels—what right have you to force yourself into them? I thought better of you.'

'No right! You have given me no right! I am still what I was before, neither maid, wife nor widow, neither fish, flesh, nor good red herring. Folk used to stare at me and point, and so they would here if they were not too civil. I live on your bounty, and I thank you for that, but sometimes I think I'd rather tramp the roads, if you will make me neither your concubine nor your wife, either because your vows still bind you or because you think me not worthy, and so I have to see you running into mortal peril and not lift a finger or breathe a word to stop you . . .' With that I began to cry noisily, like a child, because the pale-faced stranger staring at me was not my gentle companion, and because I had spoken disgracefully to him. 'And I deserve whipping,' I said, choking on my tears and scrubbing my eyes with my fists.

He rose and set me down in a chair, then stood over me in contemplation.

At last he said, 'I shall not whip you. Never fear me, I am not angry now. You have shown me my own faults—will you forgive me? I can do nothing to make your state more honourable—Prior Goldwell has sent letters to the Vatican for me, but no answer comes. Oh, Margery! don't weep. Why must women weep?'

'I never did before, not to vex you,' I said, miserably conscious of my blubbered face and that I had no kerchief to wipe it. 'I have no care for my life, no care for myself, only I think I shall go mad if you keep secrets from me, when I *know* you to be in such danger. Do you think me a coward? I ran away from Lady Rochford's, I would run away again—with you—or do anything, be your wife, or your whore . . . What are those men to you, compared with me, your friend all these months? Are they friends—would you trust them out of all reason? You told me before, in Canterbury, about the treasure and the Saint's bones. Did I give you away then—did I run about the city telling folk? So why do you shut me out now?'

He left my side abruptly and began to pace up and down the room, and I was ashamed again for having said enough to make him desperate, as I could see he was when he spoke.

'Have your own way, then. Do you see this?' He thrust the map at me. 'This is a map of Whitehall Palace. Here a staircase, here the banqueting hall, the Privy Chamber, the jewel house, the counting chamber, kitchens, buttery—would you like to see all for yourself? No? Then you will question what I have to do with Whitehall Palace. It is this: I am to be let into it by the two men who left here today. And they, most curious Margery, are newly-appointed Gentlemen Pensioners to the King, drawn from all the noble blood in the kingdom to be his bodyguard, to rival the French king's. Now I am not in line for serving as one of them—it would be short shrift for me if I showed my face there, under my own name, but because there is such a great band of them, new at Court and not knowing each other well as yet, I shall be taken for one of them and no questions asked.'

I said, hearing my voice shake, 'Why?' But I knew the answer before he gave it me.

'To free England from the English Nero. To give our Church a last chance of life.'

'And to take life, to do it? You, a priest?'

'I took arms against evil when I became one.'

'But why you, Clement, why not one of these others?'

'Because they would be found out, and I, being known to none of them, can slip away.'

I felt as if a nightmare rode me. 'How will you do it?'

'With this.' He showed me the hilt of a dagger at his waist. 'A sharp blow in the neck—a trick I learned when I used to hunt. It kills instantly, and bleeds very little. There will be such a press round him, ushers and cup-bearers and servers, I shall not be noticed. The arras hangs behind him, under the canopy, and he wears his robe-collar low these days.'

'You must hate him very much.'

'I do, God forgive me.'

'For *her* sake.'

There was such hurt and rage blended in his face that I looked away. 'You had better go,' he said.

'I'm sorry to have pried.'

'Go.'

I was wakened next morning, out of a heavy sleep because I had lain awake most of the night, by my shoulder being violently shaken. Mistress Kempe stood over me, wild of look as I had not seen her since my first arrival at Moyles. 'Where is my nephew?' she cried. 'Where is Clement? What do you know of it?'

I crawled up from sleep, hearing her almost shout (and she was a soft-spoken lady) that his servant had found his bed empty that morning, his horse gone, and a letter addressed to her. She thrust it at me. It was very short.

> Good Madam-Aunt,
>
> Forgive me for taking no farewell of you, but I have sudden business and must leave at first light. Look to my affairs until I return, which will not be long, please God. Have no fears for me.

'But I *have* fears!' she cried. 'What can this sudden business be? And why did those two young men come here, if not to draw him away from us? I knew they meant no good. You, Margery, he talks to you— why is my dear boy gone?'

I lied to her, because I must. I said I knew nothing, that his friends must have brought him some message which he had not thought fit to tell us of, that he would surely soon come back, as he said. This quieted her, for she was too wrapped up in her own feelings to take any note of mine.

And for me, I thought of the dreadful words of Job's lamentation.

For the thing which I greatly feared is come upon me, and that which I was afraid of is come to me.

I was not in safety, neither had I rest, neither was I quiet; yet trouble came.

For two days after Clement had gone I could hardly sleep or eat. Every moment I feared a clatter of hooves in the courtyard, a knock on the door. We were some fifty miles from London, yet such news would travel fast: news of the violent death of the King. At any clang of the bell in the kitchen passage I felt myself begin to tremble like a frightened horse, so that I could hardly keep my voice steady when I spoke to Mistress Kempe. I knew that she noticed, yet said nothing that might bring our fear out into the open. The sudden barking of a dog set my heart beating wildly, and when at night sleep visited me for a few minutes, the least noise had me broad awake again, ready to leap out of bed. A fearful apprehension of disaster lay like a cold weight in my breast; now I knew indeed what it was to carry a heavy heart.

Mistress Kempe found me sitting by a window that looked across the courtyard, so lost in my anxious thoughts that her appearance startled me.

'What ails you, child? Did you take me for a ghost?'

'Oh, no, madam.'

'Yet your eyes seem to see them in every corner. Will you not tell me what you know? I fret as much as you, yet I think you have more cause . . . Margery?'

But I shook my head, determined to keep my awful secret from her.

And then it came—a single rider at the gate, in the courtyard, approaching the house, and I was on my feet and down the stairs even before the iron door-knocker sounded.

The cloaked, capped figure was not Clement, I had seen that from the window, nor was it any stranger. The face the wide cap had hidden was the face of Doctor Lark, set in lines of great weariness.

I gasped out some kind of surprised welcome.

'Margery, I have ridden hard. Will you take me where I can rest, and where we can talk in private?'

'Yes, yes.' I led him into a room at the end of the passage which was not frequented by the servants, then sent a boy to see to his horse, and ordered wine to be brought. When I returned he was slumped in a chair, gazing round him.

'So you still keep this as a music-room. My lady's virginals, and the old lute.'

'You know this house—I had forgotten.'

'I know it well. For three years I was tutor here to Clement's brother Robert. That is why . . . Margery, we must talk, quickly.'

'Yes, but take some wine first.'

He drank thirstily from the flask a servant had brought. I saw how much greyer and older he seemed since I had last seen him, and how his old look of abstraction was with him no longer.

'I have news,' he said. 'You know Clement's errand?'

'Yes. I made him tell me.' My throat was tight, as though a band of iron bound it.

'I had implored him not to go. It was in the stars, you see, in the stars, and I thought he would listen. But his letter came too late for me to stop him—the letter telling me what he planned to do. And so I sent a messenger to . . . to one who watches for me at Whitehall. Your eyes widen, I see; you thought I was only a simple medico and alchemist of Kent. But Margery, I was put on this earth to fight evil, and the greatest evil England has seen for many centuries sits on a throne in Whitehall.'

'"Sits"?' I echoed, hearing a knell in his words.

'Sits, still. Clement made his way into the Privy Chamber, and all went as he planned, nobody thinking of him but as one of the young men just come to Court. He drew near to the King, almost in the place he had intended. And then . . . Did you know the King has a jester, Will Somers, a misshapen sour-faced man, his best friend and adviser, almost a confessor? This Somers is always at his side, watching with black eyes like dead coals for anything that concerns his master; those eyes saw Clement and knew him for a stranger, and caught the glint of steel in his raised hand. He shouted and pointed, and the hunt was up. I say the hunt, for Clement had backed through the crowds before those about him knew whom to seek, and away down the back stairs he had used to reach the Privy Chamber. In the noise and confusion they missed the way he had gone. Yet his face was seen and known, and the King has sworn to have him taken.'

'Known? How known?'

'By one who was at Hever with him.'

We stared at each other. His face had the look of a death's head, and I felt mine must look so. This man was but a friend of Clement's, one who knew his family, yet he was moved to real fear for him. What of me, then, that loved him?

'What will they do?' I asked.

'The charge will be high treason—the gravest there is. Ask no more, child. He was a madman to risk this. It will be madness to come here, yet he will do it—I set Jane to the crystal and she saw him at this house.'

'Would you turn him away?' I cried.

'No, no. It would be useless to try. I have thought of a means . . . We must wait.'

'And Mistress Kempe, what must I tell her?'

'As little as you can. Better for her not to know. Now you must help me in what I have to do; smile and seem cheerful if you meet anyone.'

Clement came to us that night. I had thought my heart would stop when I heard hoofbeats, afraid that his pursuers had reached us first. He was haggard and begrimed, as though he had slept in a ditch, if anywhere, and his eyes were wild and haunted. I would like to have held him to me, nursed and comforted him, but I knew there was no time. When he saw Doctor Lark he shook his head as though in disbelief.

'I failed, doctor, I failed and the beast lives,' he said. 'You're come to reproach me.'

'No, Clement, to help you, for fools must be helped out of their folly by wiser men. Margery, make haste and fetch bread and wine, but keep the servants away, and if Mistress Kempe heard nothing, tell her nothing. We must act hastily.' And he, the man I had always thought a gentle dreamer, bustled about like any housewife, while Clement watched with something like a smile, that I was glad to see. When he had taken a little food and wine Doctor Lark said, 'Enough, no time for more. Come with me, and keep silence.'

He led us, candlestick in hand, to the chamber which in a grander house would have been a banqueting hall, but here was a handsome enough place with panelled walls, a long table for dining, and a great oaken press-cupboard, that I knew held all the best cups, plates, and cutlery of the household, as well as the fine silver salt which had been the pride of Clement's father. The room was scarcely used now, dust on the furniture, the floor bare of rushes. Clement looked wonderingly round, but I knew what we were to see.

Doctor Lark went to the press-cupboard and stood beside it.

'Your father showed me this when you were a child, Clement. He made me swear not to tell you or your brother of it, knowing the mischief of boys and fearing that either or both of you might be trapped here when he was away from home. He was told of it himself by his father, in case the wars between Lancaster and York turned the tide against your family. It was built for that, as a precaution, a hiding-place.'

Clement looked blank. 'The press?'

'Not the press. Watch me.' He bent and twisted the carving of a flower on one of the doors to the lower cupboards, then unlocked both doors and threw them open. Clement gasped. We were looking into the recess, a wide shelf dividing it, loaded with cups and plates of pewter, and behind—nothing, only a dark space. 'Show him, Margery,' the doctor said. I emptied the shelf, laying the plates and other things on the floor, then drew out the shelf, which was only perched on two wooden brackets. Now, by the light of Doctor Lark's candle, the darkness became the mouth of a passage-way with steps leading downwards, some three feet high and four wide. Shading the candle with his hand he stooped and entered the press, and we followed him, Clement's hand cold in mine.

At the bottom of the steps was a door. Doctor Lark pushed it with his shoulder in a particular way; as it opened we left darkness behind and entered light and warmth, and Clement exclaimed, 'Holy saints!'

The cellar-room was long, twenty feet or so, not wide, but spacious. And it was all red—the brick walls and ceiling painted scarlet, giving the feeling of being in the heart of a fire, unharmed. In the hearth opposite us as we entered burned a real fire of logs and sea-coal, glowing contentedly in the draught that came from the flue above, which led to a kitchen chimney. There was a table and two chairs, crockery and pans by the hearth, and, in the corner, a wide bed, made up with sheets and blankets.

Clement said, 'My grandfather Walter—he designed all this?'

'He was afraid,' said Doctor Lark. 'Afraid of the ebb and flow of war, which might make a man an exile who had been a Court favourite. Perhaps afraid of plague, and thinking he and his would be safe here from infection.'

'Safe,' Clement said wonderingly, 'safe!'

Doctor Lark looked from one to the other of us. 'Now,' he said briskly, 'all is well as it can be, Margery knows the way in and out, and but for daylight and exercise you have all you could wish. I must be back in Canterbury before dawn, and there I'll devise a scheme to get you clean away, Clement, God willing. This place is good, have no fear of it.' He took my hand and closed something within it. 'Something to calm the mind and induce placid thoughts. Good night, blessings on you; I shall be with you again.' And saying that this extraordinary man whom I had thought a star-gazer left us, letting himself out by the secret way, having carried out the whole of his errand without arousing any suspicion, even from Mistress Kempe, with whom he and I had taken supper, he chatting lightly of his time as tutor to the Moyle heir, the sad state of Canterbury, the situation of the planets for the coming month, a long account of the discovery of relics of Mary Magdalen and the disputes about them (of which I afterwards found I could remember not one word) and over all a scattering of references to Clement, implying that he was away on some important service.

When he had gone Mistress Kempe sat studying the chair where he had sat, musing. 'That is the wisest man I ever did know,' she said. 'I could almost think him a wizard.'

I answered, not wishing to start rumours, that he was only a learned doctor. But I was to find that for me and Clement he had woven magic.

9

Old Walter Moyle, too, had been a wise man in his building of the Red Room. It lay in such a way that no trace of it could be seen from outside, deep within the thick outer walls of the manor and underneath a small courtyard. By the side of it ran a little underground stream, dammed so that it could not undermine the fabric of the building, and emerging above ground out in the gardens where its source would not be questioned. The practical old man must have taken into account that water for drinking and washing would be needed by whatever fugitive lodged in the Red Room, and had even caused to be dug a deep well close by to serve as a necessary office. Logs were piled up on each side of the wide hearth which must have been there eighty years or more, bone-dry with age, and these were needed all the time, to make up for the cold which seeped in from an air-vent cleverly designed to look like a small drain covered by a grille, to anyone who noticed it in the courtyard, yet raised above the ground so that no standing water could get into it. On rainy days this was blocked off from inside by an ingenious sliding stone, and yet fresh air remained in the room.

I searched for old Walter's tomb in the church of Wye, and in the lonely little church of Our Lady at Eastwell, wanting to lay a tribute of flowers on it; but I never found it, and so he lay unthanked for the safety he had given to my love, and the joy we had in each other's company.

It was only possible to visit Clement at night, for fear of being seen by even one servant who might be suspicious. The household went to bed early, and we had no young skittish maids or men who might have stolen out for secret trysts. So, when I heard the last door close, I would slip silently down the stairs, carrying what Clement needed; food and drink, books to pass the time for him, candles and fresh logs (though of these I could only bear one at a time, and it angered him to see me with it, though I told him I was used to hard work and felt no strain, as a slighter woman might have done).

He bore confinement well, used to monastic discipline and the boundaries of a narrow cell. Only it irked him to have no exercise, except when I let him out very stealthily at night, and walked with him in the gardens keeping within the cover of trees and beneath the walls. If we had been seen, it would be thought that I had a secret lover.

And so I had, now; oh Clement, my dear heart! At last he was mine that I had desired so long. No more did I need to weep by night, but lay in his arms, knowing him now as a full man, not a priest (whatever the Pope might please to think of it) and myself for the first time as a true woman, neither cook's daughter and merchant's harlot, nor old dame's companion, but Margery, chosen of her beloved, free to enjoy him.

For we were free, in that strange beautiful dungeon. There we could love, or sleep, as we pleased, or talk as it was not possible in threatened England to talk in the open. I was not jealous now of poor Anne Boleyn, now that he was able to tell me that the boyish passion he had felt for her was shared by nearly every young gentleman at Hever, because her charm surpassed beauty, and her pretty French manners put a kind of witchery on men who had known no ladies but apple-cheeked English ones. 'She was like a young graceful doe,' he said, 'just as dark of eye and slender, and so Tom Wyatt wrote of her in verses with a sting in the tail . . .

Who list her hunt, I put him out of doubt
    As well as I, may spend his time in vain.
    And graven with diamonds in letters plain,
There is written her fair neck round about:
    'Noli me tangere, for Caesar's I am,
    And wild for to hold, though I seem tame.'

'Some things are not forgiven, Margery. Not a Caesar, but a Nero, had her judicially murdered, and I cannot forgive him that. Do you call this love? I call it chivalry.'

I said that I understood, and my heart was at peace about her.

He talked at length of his attempt on the King's life. 'It was folly, rank folly, I know. If I had not been so hot against him I should have known it then. I thought myself too clever, I and my poor dagger, with that bull's neck to pierce. And then to run, like a coward! I am ashamed of that, I can tell you—I was ashamed even as I fled down the back stairs in Whitehall. Oh, but the flesh is weak, and I knew what the penalty would be! Yet the martyrs suffered gladly, and so should I have done.'

I held tightly the body that I loved, saying, 'No, no, God forbid.'

'Life is very sweet, Margery, when one is young and a true love waiting . . . I blame myself, but not as I would once have done. We change, like the seasons, our needs alter, whatever the Church may say. Now I need you, and this time of peace.'

'But it must end, my dear.'

'Not in capture, I pray. What I hope for is to repay Doctor Lark by escaping scot-free.'

To try again, I thought, in some other way, less chancy.

'And if you should not escape?' I asked, envisioning an encounter in the night, an informer, the swooping-down of soldiers; all that would follow. 'Shall we not still be together, I being your accomplice?'

'Do you think so badly of me? I shall swear you knew nothing, nor my aunt—which is true—and Doctor Lark shall not be mentioned. I shall tell them I knew of this hiding-place and wrought all myself.'

'The food? The candles? The logs? The books? Do you think them idiots as well as knaves?'

He looked taken aback, Clement whom I had once thought a holy father and who was in reality a romantic boy. And so I laughed and kissed him, and learned all over again the lovely truths of Solomon's great Song which is not much dwelt on in church.

In all this I lost many hours of sleep every night. Mistress Kempe noticed my paleness and the heavy shadows under my eyes, though not, innocent lady, the new bee-stung look my lips had from so much kissing, and a sort of satisfied air, such as a cat has when she settles before a fire after feeding, her paws tucked under her.

'Why are you not sleeping, Margery?' my dame asked me. 'Do you pine for Clement? Be cheerful, for we should have known by now if any great ill had befallen him. Doctor Lark said he was gone on a mission, did he not? We shall hear soon, mark my words. Not that I am *quite* easy in my mind, sometimes . . .'

Poor soul, you would be even less so if you knew what I do, I thought, but said aloud that one could not help but be troubled in these times. Yet because I was young and hardy and full of joy in my love, I found it hard to pretend trouble—there was not the least need for Mistress Kempe to encourage me to be cheerful, and I even heard myself singing about the house as I had never done before, such ballads as *Heartsease,* a favourite of Clement's, whose taste lay not at all in the direction of holy ditties. Perhaps I had some notion that he might hear, so far below, so I sang

Where heartsease groweth I pray you tell to me;
That place who knoweth, his heart's desire hath he . . .

There was one strange moment in all my secret happiness. As I lay with Clement, warm in his arms under warm rugs, looking up through the air-hole at a spangled night-sky, wondering which stars were framed in it of all those music-named ones Doctor Lark had taught me, a sudden icy shiver went through me. Clement, half-asleep, murmured, 'What ails you, love? Cold?'

'No, not at all. I felt . . . it was as if I remembered—yet that's impossible.'

Courteously he shook off sleep. 'Tell me.'

'I seemed to remember us two being like this before—somewhere else . . .'

He laughed. 'In bed? Would that we had been.'

'But we were. Not only in bed, but hiding—pursued. The same, only not the same—I am not telling it well, but the feeling was so strange and so strong.'

'It was a dream, the kind that sometimes takes us on the edge of sleep.'

'It seemed not like a dream . . . Clement, have you never felt you knew me? That we had known each other long, many, many years, even though that could not have been?'

After a pause he said, 'I think I did, twice. It was the night of the fire at Christ Church, when we stood talking, and again at St Martin's. Not when I first saw you, when you tricked me into it in the confessional. I thought then your face was fair, but it was quite new to me. When we talked, there was something—your manner, perhaps . . . Who can tell?'

'Jane . . .' I began, then stopped. Somehow I felt it would be wrong to tell him what Jane had seen in the crystal, and how her father had interpreted it for me; as though that would profane some mystery. For if the souls of Margery and Clement had met in Heaven before our mortal birth (yet were there man-hunts and hiding-places in Heaven?) it was a thing not given to us to know.

He was asleep. I propped myself up and looked down at him, and thought how childlike and lonely a man appears in sleep, where not even his beloved can follow him.

*O*n a hot, airless afternoon in July I sat in the Knot Garden. A wilderness when we had come to the manor, Clement had set gardeners to pull up the weeds and replant it to its former state, a neat pattern woven in thyme and marjoram, betony and rue, sage and saffron, rosemary, mint, fennel and basil and a hundred more sweet-scented things, for all I knew. Their savours rivalled the stuffiness of the air, so close that I felt a headache beginning behind my brow. I wondered if Clement were half-stifled with it below ground, or if the coldness that was ever-present in the Red Room protected him from it. The house looked asleep, sunk in languor, not a sight nor a sound from anyone within. I wondered whether I dared go and let Clement out, to enjoy even half an hour of freedom. Surely it would be safe now, since we had heard no word of any pursuit; why should they come for him after so long?

I was on my feet, ready to go in and try at least to persuade him, when something wiser than myself told me that I was merely being selfish to think of it. Only Clement's worst enemy would lead him out in broad daylight for any suspicious eye to see. But oh, how long must he stay in that living tomb?

The heat and my own heavy thoughts must have sent me into a doze, on that bench, with my back against a young tree. I was far off in dreams when a voice called me out of them.

'Margery! Margery, do waken!'

A little creature all in green like a fairy was pulling at my shoulder with its small hand: I saw, only half-awake still, that it was Jane. Jane, in riding-clothes, and some yards away the sturdy tall maid Hannah, from whom my cloak had been borrowed when I rode away from Canterbury.

'Jane! Is it you?' We laughed and hugged each other, and I wondered aloud that the little thing could have ridden so far, yet she looked not tired, but rosier than usual and full of some excitement. I would have had her come into the house for some refreshment, but she said no, that must not be, we must talk out of doors.

'I am a messenger,' she said, 'of such good news! My father has the sneezing rheum too badly to ride, so he sent me, trusting nobody else to keep the secret—even Hannah knows nothing.' She glanced at the maid, who was strolling round the edge of the Knot Garden, examining the herbs as though she had never seen any before. Then Jane, crouching at my feet on a bank of sweet-smelling thyme, told me.

'Master Clement is to leave as soon as dusk falls, my father says. A ship is waiting at Dover, the *Gilliflower,* that will take him to France, and there a friend will be waiting to take him to shelter in his own castle—château, that is, which may not be altogether the same thing. I have a letter here,' she touched her bosom, 'that will tell him whom to look out for and what he must say. There! Wasn't that worth my ride?'

I tried to take it in, still stupid from my sleep. So soon, so sudden. I asked, 'And I? May I go with him?'

Jane looked surprised. 'Oh, nothing was said of that. But surely not. One rider might pass where two would be noticed—and it's known you left Canterbury together, for Master Penny has never ceased to pry and spy into anything that concerns you, and he found someone who had seen you in the crowd when the treasure was taken, and someone else who told him you had been at our house. Told him for money,' she added darkly. 'He would like to have had my father arrested for it, but people think so well of father that no one would do it. So you see, it would not be wise to ride together. Stay here with Master Clement's aunt, and be safe—after all, they hold nothing criminal against *you.*'

It was true; and when I went down to the Red Room to tell Clement to prepare for travel he said the same thing. I knew they were both right, but my heart was very heavy as I helped him to make his best clothes into a pack, and fetched money from the chest in his room, and whatever else I could think of to do that would pass the time until dusk, while Jane, upstairs, rested and chatted to Mistress Kempe of everything except the errand that had brought her to us.

Then the moment came. In the courtyard a horse was saddled and waiting, one that I told them in the stable I would use to ride with my friend a little way on the road back towards Canterbury. The fire was out, the glow of the walls faded into shadow. It was no longer a refuge for lovers, a place of joyful secret whispers, where two had learned each other and known love's delights. No longer this, just a cheerless, chilly underground chamber.

Clement put his arm round me, saying gently, 'Come.' I put up my face to him and we clung together in a long kiss, as long as eternity, as short as a heartbeat. It was almost dark, but when we drew apart I looked up at him still, not needing light to make out the features I knew so well, the strangely charming almond shape of the eyes, the proud nose, the lines at the corners of the lips that deepened so when he smiled, the chin pointed, with a small cleft that I had told him was Venus's mark. I had traced his face so often with my fingertips that I would have known it again by touch if I had been stricken blind, could have drawn it lifelike from memory if I had owned an artist's skill.

The door shut behind us; we climbed the steps and came out into the recess within the press-cupboard, then into the dining-chamber. I turned the carven flower to lock the panel at the back. Tomorrow I would go back and remove the books Clement had been reading, the cup and plate he had used, the candle-ends, and this, the story I have written of our love. Or perhaps not tomorrow, but later, when I was more used to the thought that I would not see him there.

We thought it wiser not to tell Mistress Kempe, even then, of his sheltering, though he would have wished to say farewell to her. The sooner he left the better. He leaned down from the saddle and took my hand in his gloved one, and held it.

'We shall meet in France. God keep you.'

'And you.'

I watched the three riders out of sight, two bound northwards, one to the south. Then I went indoors and sat at my chamber window, and watched the stars until they faded in the light of the dawn.

$\mathcal{I}$ am not writing this easily because the light is poor and my hands are very cold. The stone walls are so thick that the air is like ice, though I can see through the window-slit that the sun is shining. I have to think very carefully what I put down, because they will read it; soon. I suppose that is why they let me have paper and pen.

It was the day after Jane's return to Canterbury that the men came to Moyles. They said that they were officers of the King, and when I asked, surely, of Lord Cromwell? they laughed, saying that Cromwell had been beheaded weeks before, having fallen out of favour with the King over the Cleves marriage, and accused of treason.

They told me too that Jane's movements had been watched ever since the rumour got about that I had been involved with Clement's escape. When she was seen to ride out of Canterbury they went to Doctor Lark's house and questioned him about her, where she had gone and why.

'Questioned him?'

They glanced at each other and laughed again, but only said that though ill with a rheumy fever he had managed to tell them she had gone to Moyles. I knew, without telling, that they had made him speak not only by questioning. Then they said that they had come to find the traitor Clement Moyle, who was certainly hiding here (had they made Doctor Lark tell them that, too?). After that they searched the house as though they cared nothing whether they pulled it to pieces, calling in other men who had waited outside to help them. Poor Mistress Kempe, knowing nothing, was half beside herself, wringing her hands and crying, while I watched stonily, thankful to God that . . . there was nothing to find.

Then they questioned us, not as I feared they had questioned Doctor Lark, but so fiercely that Mistress Kempe began to look almost witless with bewilderment and fear. At length they accepted her innocence, for she was too elderly and simple to have fooled them with pretences. To me they said that if I would tell them nothing it would be the worse for me. I answered as I must, that I had not seen Clement since the attempt on the King, that he had not returned home or let us know where he was, and Mistress Kempe and the servants bore this out.

That pleased them not at all. They whispered together, and then bade me prepare to go with them.

'Where?'

'To Canterbury.'

I asked why, and they said I would find out soon enough.

On the journey I was allowed to ride with my hands unbound, though the rougher of the two officers had wanted to truss me up. The other pointed out that if I fell out of the saddle and injured myself so that I could not speak when we arrived they might be in trouble, so I rode free, and in time was able to shut my mind to the lewd insulting talk they bandied to each other about me and Clement, me and Master Penny, me and possibly themselves if they chose to turn aside from the road and share me between them. I supposed they would not do this, again for fear of reproof, and were instead amusing themselves by shaming me with talk.

But I looked about me at the trees and hedgerows, rich with late summer leaf, the cattle and the shorn sheep lying contentedly in the fields, the glint of the Stour where it ran by the road, the square towers of churches and the bulk of Chilham Castle, all the pleasant things I had seen first when Clement and I rode to Wye; and my mind dwelt only on them, and my happy memories.

In the courtroom they took me to an elderly justice who seemed not to know why I was brought before him. Then, a weary time after, as I sat between guards, Master Penny appeared, puffing, with Nan— Mistress Penny! That would have made me laugh any other time, behind his shoulder. He made a long speech which I suspected he had learned, since he was not given to talking above a few words at a time, saying how I had been dishonest and sly while in his household, had behaved suspiciously while the renegade priest had been about his evil works—so much so that I had had to be sent away into the care of a virtuous lady—and in my absence it was found that a valuable jewel, an opal, was missing from Master Penny's coffers and also four gold pieces, two Edward angels and two rose nobles, from his private store.

I spoke up, asking him to prove it. He gave me his bloodshot stare.

'How can I, since they're gone? Spent long since, no doubt.'

The justice nodded sagely. It was enough to declare the theft. I was put down as a thief. I saw Nan gloating over me, and the puffed pride in Master Penny's countenance at having got his revenge on me at last.

But it was not enough for the King's men. They took me from the courthouse to the West Gate, where in one of the two towers was a small room they kept for questioning. At that my blood did indeed run cold. Then they told me, smiling, that no rack was kept at Canterbury, or any other instruments such as were used in London against enemies of the Crown, but that they would do their humble best without such instruments to extract the truth from me about the escape of the priest, Father Clement.

I do confess I was weak enough to beg them not to hurt me, and when they did I cried very sorely. But I told them nothing of where

Clement was, since indeed I knew nothing. When they went beyond the point of pain-bearing I screamed out nonsense—that he was in Cathay or gone to the Indies the Spanish had found, or dead and in Heaven. I remember very little about the rest of that time, only being dragged up stone steps, and flung on to dirty straw in this room, which I now know is the city prison in the West Gate.

There are two other prisoners with me, a poor harlot too drunk to say what the charge against her is, and a foul one-eyed man who told me proudly that he had murdered three. I was lucky to have only them for company, the gaoler said, for sometimes the place was so crowded with villains there was no room to lie down.

I have lost count of the days. But after what seemed like only a few darks and dawns an important personage in a fur-trimmed robe came here today and read from a screed a great deal of stuff which all came to this, that I was a known thief, a woman of loose life, and an offender against the King's Grace in that I had assisted one indicted of high treason for the worst offence known to the law, an attempt upon the King's person, and for that I was condemned to be burned alive.

I am very afraid. So afraid that my limbs will not keep still but are in a perpetual tremble, and my teeth chatter against each other. At first the whore and the murderer jeered at me when I lay shaking, and then, when I got to my knees and began to say all the prayers I know, laughed aloud and called out lewd remarks. But I pray still, I pray, to the Holy Mother and all the saints, and to Clement, though he is only a mortal man and can do nothing for me that saved him. I am ashamed to find myself a coward. I hope I shall be brave when the time comes, and it comes ever nearer . . .

This morning the prison door opened and they pushed in one I knew. I scrambled up and threw myself into the arms of Doctor Lark. He was very pale, and more bent than I remember him, and I think he limped. He clasped me very tight in his warm embrace and touched his lips to my brow, murmuring to me as though I were a child.

'Margery, my dear, this is a grim pass you're come to. But here I am, you see, a friend with some cheer for you.'

I said, against his shoulder, that I thought they had killed him.

'No. No, I thank God. They took me up, but so many friends spoke for me, telling how I had healed them or others they knew, and how I was a simple soul who could have nothing to do with conspiracies, that they let me go in the end. And I accepted life, Margery my child; one must always accept life.'

'I wish I had the chance,' I muttered. He was silent, and I hoped for a wild moment that he had come to tell me of a reprieve. But he only held me, rocking me a little as a father might, and told me how they had frightened Jane into the worst swoon or fit she had yet had, which frightened them in their turn, and after that they left her alone.

'All is well,' he said, 'with Jane, and with others.' He looked at me meaningly and I nodded, knowing whom he meant. 'Jane has looked into the crystal.'

'And for me?' I asked; just, for that moment, bitter.

'Peace, and joy to come.'

'But sir, how can that be? Seeing what I shall have to bear.'

'Peace,' he repeated, then looked at the other two, but they had lost interest in our soft-spoken talk, and were sharing the drink some friend of the poor harlot's had sent in. The door was fast closed, nobody watching. Doctor Lark drew something from under his cloak and showed it to me. It was a tiny flask of some clear fluid, clear as water. But I knew that it was not water.

'Take it,' he said, 'tonight, and you will sleep well—very well. Pray first, your most earnest prayers for a bright awakening. Do you understand, Margery?'

I said that I understood, so weak with gratitude that I could have fallen at his feet. I put the phial in my bosom, feeling it against my heart, warm and comforting. For a little while more we talked before he said that he must go.

'Remember,' he said, 'peace and joy to come; a parting now, but another meeting in another time. This I can promise you, and I am no mean seer, as well as no mean doctor. Remember this, child.'

When he had left me I looked at the narrow slit that let in light, and saw blue sky. I have watched it all day, quite calm and happy, and now darkness is falling and I am ready to take my sleeping-draught, the draught that will spare me untold agony and bring me nearer to Clement: another meeting, another time.

Clement, oh, Clement. This I drink to you.

To us.

ED. *Here ends the story of Margery Burgoyne, found dead in the prison cell of the West Gate, Canterbury, two days before the date set for her burning on a charge of treason.*

BOOK THREE

The Romantic Young Lady

ROBERT AND AMY: 1865

Ho-ro, my nut-brown maiden,
Hi-ri, my nut-brown maiden,
Ho-ro-ro, maiden,
    For you're the maid for me.

Mo Nighean Donn, Bhòidheach

OLD GAELIC SONG

THE JOURNAL OF AMY PIRBRIGHT, JANUARY 3RD, 1865. LAMORNA TOWERS, SYDENHAM, SOUTH LONDON, ENGLAND.

I have written this on the front page of the handsome blank-leaved book Papa gave me for Christmas, and drawn some pretty sketches round it, so that I shall feel I have to turn to it every day and write something, however little. There is not much to put down at this time of year that is very agreeable, however. The house was full for Christmas, of course, all eight guestrooms, servants constantly running up and down the back stairs with cans of hot water, uncles and aunts and cousins everywhere so that one could never be private. I was so thankful for this old nursery which nobody uses now except me. Every morning I bribed Susan to light a small fire in the grate and add to the coals, and when I wrapped myself up in the afghan from the cupboard I was quite as warm as in my own room.

Indeed, I prefer to sit here even now they have all gone. It reminds me of when Letty was very small and I was older, but we still did our lessons together with Miss Tomkins. There is old Dobbin, the rocking-horse, with half his mane and some of his dapples gone, and the dolls' house. Some of the people who lived in it are still there, Mr and Mrs Brown and their children, with their shiny painted china heads and pink kid bodies, though nothing like as smart as they were, poor things; and the little bird in the gold cage. But he doesn't sing any more, his mechanism is broken. I always hated winding him up, from the time someone told me he was a real bird which had been killed and had clockwork put inside his feathers; I felt as though I were hurting him.

There is the toy theatre, I used to love making it work, though Letty never had much patience with it and broke the thing that draws the curtains. We used to entertain the family with *The Miller and his Men* and *Cinderella,* and a play I made up myself called *The Princess and the Raven,* in which poor little Letty always became too frightened to finish as the voice of the Princess, because I made the big black bird hop so realistically.

Little Letty, twenty-two years old now, with a baby girl of her own. They were not here for Christmas, because her husband Edward had promised to spend the holiday with his people in Surrey so that they could see little Amelia. It was nice that Letty called her after me.

It is getting very dark in here; there will be snow again before nightfall. Just now I wound up the musical-box that plays *The Bluebells of Scotland,* but after the first few notes it stopped. Fancy me, an old woman of twenty-seven, playing with toys still.

A nursery should have children in it.

I lit the lamp just now, to make the room more cheerful. It throws my shadow on the wall, huge and humped, like a witch's—only the hump is my chignon, piled at the back on my head in a chenille net. Mama says long hair is something I should be very thankful to have, and so I should, I suppose, having very little else in the way of beauty. If I press my nose against the window a sort of witch's face looks back at me—long and pale, eyes not large enough and a mouth much *too* large, and a forehead so high that it makes me look *clever,* dreadful thought. If I could wear a curly fringe to hide it I should look a deal better, but Mama says that would be terribly vulgar as well as being out of fashion, so I part my hair in the middle and scrape it back like everybody else's.

I don't think a silly little round lace collar at all becomes a long neck like mine. I shouldn't have been born to such fashions. Perhaps I shouldn't have been born at all, then Papa and Mama would just have had Letty, one perfect daughter, pretty and good-tempered and not given to fits of unreasonable gloom. I must confide to you, Journal, and I hope you won't think me a complete goose for it, that I sometimes hide away from everyone, just as I used to when I was quite small, up at the top of the attic stairs above where the servants sleep. It's very cold and has no carpet or American cloth on it, which makes me feel all the more agreeably wretched.

I can recite there, too, without anybody hearing me. I learned reams and reams of poetry when I was young—sometimes on the Sabbath when we were only supposed to read *Sunday at Home* or *The Good Child's Companion*—and never let them catch me at it. Not that anybody would have scolded, only I hated to bring a look of pain to Mama's face; Papa did see me once with the Works of Sir Walter Scott propped up in front of it, but he said nothing, I suppose because dear Sir Walter is still looked upon as respectable reading. So even now I can escape from being who I am, and make myself deliciously miserable with poetry.

> Where shall the lover rest
> > Whom the fates sever
> From his true maiden's breast
> > Parted for ever?
> Where early violets die
> > Under the willow,
> > Eleu loro,
> Soft be his pillow.

And

He turned him round and round about
  All on the Irish shore,
He gave his bridle-reins a shake,
  With 'Adieu for evermore,
   My love,
  Adieu for evermore.'

I wonder sometimes why I should be so moved by songs about parted lovers—seeing that I have never had a lover myself, parted or otherwise, in spite of all Mama's and Papa's efforts, and even dear unselfish Letty trying to pass on to me boys she thought too old or serious for her.

You would think, would you not, that a wealthy man like Papa would easily be able to find a husband for his elder daughter? With his great drapery emporium in Bayswater, and the new one he is opening at Eastbourne, not to mention smaller shops all over the south and the property he owns, he must be one of the richest men in England. All from starting off as a shop assistant in Clapham, when he was a boy of fourteen.

I am very proud of Papa. But he doesn't move in the right circles to get me married. The nobility don't mix with Trade, and there are not many families in Trade whose sons Papa would consider suitable, since he and Mama took so much trouble to have me nicely educated and taught etiquette and all the social accomplishments (not that I flatter myself I am much good at them, being naturally shy). A poor man, of course, would never do . . .

For Letty it was quite different. She met Edward at a tennis party, and he was charmed with her looks at first sight, and though he is a cousin of Lord Coulsdon and really very grand compared with us, he insisted on marrying her, whatever his family might say. The young men all flocked round her; she is that sort of girl, just as I am not. Yet (and this seems strange and a little sad to me) she was always the practical no-nonsense one, whereas I was dreamy and romantic, full of thoughts of gallant lovers rescuing beautiful ladies, and being married in a wedding-dress all roses and silver ribbons, since I was quite small. I remember a shopwalker from Pirbrights of Bayswater coming here to see Papa, and my being introduced to him (by accident, I'm sure) and falling desperately in love with his pale complexion and beautiful thick dark whiskers, though he *did* have a very unfortunate Cockney accent. Even Mama was quite cross at the way I went on about him, and Letty laughed so much that I was cured of it in no time at all.

So here I am, twenty-seven years old and on the shelf.

Well, Amy Pirbright, don't you think you ought to be thoroughly ashamed of yourself, putting down such things on the first page of your Journal? Come, think of your blessings, and remember the wise things dear Miss Tomkins used to teach us. 'Beauty and wit may gain us admirers, but goodness alone will acquire us true friends.'

There, that makes a very fitting end to today's writing.

FEBRUARY 26TH

I see that I have been putting down a great deal of silly stuff on your pages, dear Journal, such as that I went visiting with Mama, or that Papa kindly took me with him to Eastbourne to see the progress of the new shop, and it was so wet that the feathers on my new hat were ruined, or that our dog Carlo chased a rabbit in the gardens and caught it and brought it in unharmed, much to Cook's amusement. I am glad she let me beg its life. I wish I could have kept it for a pet. Carlo only cares for Papa and Frederick the coachman, and I would so like to have something of my own.

There, you see, nothing at all worth recording. So today I am going to take myself to task. I have already begun by offering myself to our Vicar as a Sunday School teacher and for such duties as decorating the altar with flowers, attending the Ladies' Sewing Circle where they make garments for heathens, and reading aloud to the sick. Most unmarried young ladies seem to occupy themselves in church work, so why should I hold off from it? except from laziness, a sin to which I admit freely. Do you not think this a good resolution, by which I shall make myself useful, improve my mind and my character, and please poor Mama, whom I often catch looking at me with an expression that says she wishes I were different?

We cannot live in a dream, even if we know clearly what the dream is about. And I do not, for I sometimes waken from deep sleep with a feeling of great regret, as though I had been somewhere very wonderful to which I would never find the way again, or met someone very dear to me, now lost . . .

I once tried to tell Mama about this, and she said that I should cultivate the habit of taking a brisk walk before bedtime, and drink less tea, as she had been reading that it frets the nerves if taken in excess.

I said, 'But I am not at all nervous, Mama; it is simply that I feel so strange when I waken from one of these dreams, or whatever one may call them.'

'I hope you have not been taking laudanum, Amy!' she said sharply. 'You know I have strictly forbidden it except in the case of toothache, ever since . . .' She did not need to go on; we both remembered too well the dreadful affair years since when one of the maids was found dead with the laudanum bottle beside her, after a regrettable affair of the heart. I assured Mama that I would never let myself turn to the use of sleeping-draughts. 'And,' I added, 'it is not that I need to sleep more, for I seem to lose myself completely, so that I hardly know where I am when I wake up.'

Mama sighed. Yes, I am sure she will be delighted when I tell her of my resolution.

MARCH 1ST

How I wish the Reverend Mr Burneside were a little less High! I know it is very fashionable to go in for Sung Mass and the Confessional and priests wearing birettas and all that, but I do find it something of a masquerade. And then for him to call himself Father Burneside, though he is not married, nor the curate, Mr Parker; and if they are vowed to celibacy it seems to me very strange that the young ladies who are church workers pursue them so *very* ardently with knitted mufflers and gloves, home-made confections, and invitations to tea. I confess (dear me! no joke intended) I never took any notice of this kind of thing when I used merely to attend church on Sundays, though Papa used to growl about it a little on account of having been brought up a Baptist and only changed to the Church of England because all the best people belonged to it.

I like the music, and the stained glass windows with their beautiful colours, and the words of the prayer-book, which are written in such musical and really quite Shakespearean English, and yet I feel there is something missing from it all. I wonder what? Perhaps it is that I am not truly spiritual.

It has not been altogether comfortable, so far, engaging in parochial duties. The younger ladies have not been at all amiable to me, and I don't need telling that it is because Papa is so rich and curates are notoriously poor. They need not have been afraid I should woo Mr Parker. All the pleasanter tasks have been taken by others, and I left with the visiting of what sordid cottages we have in the district. Some of the cottagers do not seem at all pleased to be visited, except for what one takes them, and even then I feel they would welcome bottles of beer more than the wholesome pasties and cakes we provide. I had a stone thrown after me the other day, and some remarks which I did not quite understand, but I am sure they applied to our living at Lamorna Towers.

And to me, alas; I distinctly heard one of the children shout, 'Old maid!' and 'Fright!' It was very hurtful.

The Sewing Circle is not very enjoyable, either. Miss Tomkins tried hard to teach me to sew, aided by an excellent maid Mama had at the time, but I never quite learned. The thread does break off so in the middle of a hem, and the knots I tie at the end of it seem so much larger and clumsier than other people's. And—now I am going to lose my temper, dear Journal—the whole business is boring, boring, boring! There I sit, surrounded by these pious ladies all tattling away in whispers, and my thoughts are neither with them nor the heathens but away in some distant country where nothing is like today in Sydenham, and I am a beautiful damsel riding through a forest with a gallant knight, my arms clasped about his strong slender waist, and there are bells on his horse's bridle and I know there is a dagger at his side to defend me if we are attacked, and in a moment he will turn round . . . but I can go no farther than that. I cannot see his face. Perhaps I saw it in that dream. I think of a hymn, and a verse:

> Time, like an ever-rolling stream
> > Bears all its sons away;
> They fly forgotten, as a dream
> > Dies at the opening day . . .

'Miss Pirbright!'

A lady in pince-nez is shaking me, dragging me back from the green forest and the warm body of the young man, and I could almost cry at the shock of it. I see her exchange glances with another lady, and I know they will say over the tea-cups that I am just a little simple.

As for reading to the sick, they seem to enjoy it no more than I do. Nine times out of ten they fail to hear me because they are deaf and I have a soft voice, and when they can they appear not to like what they hear. True, neither should I if I had to lie prone on a sick-bed and listen to long passages from *Lizzie Gray,* or *Some Leaves from the Life of a Working-man.*

MARCH 8TH

It would make me smile to look over that last passage if I did not feel so disgraced. Today I had to read to old Mrs Prout, who has so far shown no sign of understanding a word. It seemed to me to matter little what I read, so I gave myself the indulgent pleasure of reciting one of my favourite works, *The Lay of the Last Minstrel.* Judge of my surprise when the old lady suddenly sat up in bed with a sharp scream, demanding me to stop on the instant. I did so at once, of course. Though I offered to prepare a soothing drink for her, as she seemed somewhat agitated, she refused, and ordered me out of the cottage.

I had barely reached home when a servant from the Vicarage arrived with a message that his master wished to see me.

I was not prepared for the sternness of Mr Burneside's aspect (I will *not* call him Father) when I was shown into his study. He might well have been practising to assist at the Last Judgment. Without polite preliminaries, he asked me what work I had been reading to Mrs Prout.

'A passage from *The Lay of the Last Minstrel,*' I said, 'by Sir Walter Scott.'

His grizzled brows almost met in the middle. 'Will you favour me by repeating it, Miss Pirbright?'

'Happily,' I said, and began one of my beloved stanzas.

The way was long, the wind was cold,
    The Minstrel was infirm and old;
His wither'd cheek and tresses grey
    Seem'd to have known a better day . . .

And so on, provoking no reaction from him until I reached the lines:

> For she had known adversity,
>> Though born in such a high degree.
> In pride of power and Beauty's bloom
>> Had wept o'er Monmouth's bloody tomb . . .

The clergyman rose to his full height behind his desk.

'Stop!' he thundered. 'Did my ears deceive me?'

'I should not think so, Vicar, unless I am reading very indistinctly.'

'Did I, or did I not, hear from a young lady's lips a word which should not sully those of the meanest artisan?'

I must have looked blank, for he shook his head impatiently and ordered me to repeat the last lines. A silence fell. Feeling most uncomfortable, I asked, 'What is wrong, sir?'

'If you are not aware of the unspeakable vileness of the . . . the adjective *bloody*, Miss Pirbright, I am amazed and disappointed that your excellent parents have not given you a better education.'

'But Vicar, Monmouth's tomb *was* bloody, in a sense—at least his coffin must have been, for the executioner bungled the work and only severed his head at the third stroke, poor young man.'

He strode to the wall and turned the bell-handle. To the servant who answered he said, 'Show Miss Pirbright out. And, Miss Pirbright, from this day I would prefer you to take no part in parish activities. I have heard various other reports . . . Good-day.'

So, you see, I am an utter failure at Good Works. I told Papa of the incident, very shame-facedly, and he laughed loudly before straightening his face and saying, 'There, Amy, you weren't to know, I suppose, but some of your precious poets are a bit broad in their language. Never mind what the prosing old Puseyite pussy says, him and his incense and his frilly little lace canonicals. To thine own self be true, my girl, and it shall follow as the night the day, thou canst not then be false to any man. There's a bit of Shakespeare for you, and *he* used some funny words in his time, I'll be bound.'

I kissed him and thanked him for being so understanding.

But who *is* myself? Who am I, and what must I do with my life?

March 20th

I could paint, perhaps. I have always been good at sketching, flowers and faces and little scenes. I know that all young ladies are supposed to dabble in it, taking their sketch-books wherever they go, but I do think in all modesty I do it better than some.

I had a French drawing-master for a time. He did not think very much of my efforts; we never seemed to understand each other very well. But I am sure I have a little talent. I shall speak to Papa, who always lends a kindly ear.

Later. Papa was most patient. I think it is because he has made something of his life that he understands that even a woman might wish to be more than her Mama's companion, if she is not to have the fulfilment of marriage. I wonder, if I said I would like some hand in the running of Pirbrights, he would let me . . . ? But that is too fanciful, even though when we looked at the beginnings of the Eastbourne establishment I thought, just for a moment, that I might have been able to do rather better in setting out the furnishing and clothing fabrics, draping them over lay figures or against painted scenes . . . what a silly fancy, when Papa is so experienced in these matters.

'Do I take it that you want to be an artist?' he asked me.

'Not for fame and fortune, Papa; just to satisfy myself.'

He sighed. 'I suppose it *is* confounded dull for you, with Letty gone. Let me think.'

When he had thought, he said, 'There's Sir Edwin Bracegirdle,

R.A. Lives in Dulwich, just by the College grounds. Met him at the Sportsmen's Club, seemed a pleasant enough fellow. Want me to get you an introduction?'

I said that I did, excited by the thought of meeting so eminent an artist, once a shining light of the Pre-Raphaelite Brotherhood and now a highly fashionable painter of portraits and the sort of scenes people like nowadays, small children cuddling large dogs and making friends with robins. I thought he would be most unlikely to want to see anyone as obscure as me.

MARCH 23RD

But—oh dear, Journal, money talks! I do believe Papa's introduction would get me anywhere, except into the aristocratic *élite*. Within two days I had received a cordial invitation from Lady Bracegirdle to take tea, with a little note at the bottom saying that Sir Edwin would be most interested to meet me. We are to go tomorrow, I and my maid Sarah, for of course it would not be proper to go alone, even with Lady Bracegirdle's invitation.

MARCH 24TH

Oh, how am I to describe Bracegirdle House? Our own is very handsome, no expense spared on the furnishings—but compared with that, words fail me. It stands in an exclusive road on the edge of Dulwich Park, in its own massive grounds. On the outside it looks not particularly impressive, but once inside the eye is dazzled. Instead of an ordinary hall there is a kind of covered courtyard with a fountain playing in the middle, hewn out of black marble; pillars of white marble support the ceiling, on which are painted classical scenes. A bronze statue of a boy points the way up a short flight of steps with heavily-carved banisters to the magnificent drawing-room, with huge windows looking on to the gardens, its walls papered in a plush material patterned in gold . . .

You will think I was overcome with admiration at all this. I must tell you (for one should be quite frank with one's Journal) that I was not. I thought it too ornate, too heavily decorated; it seemed to shout 'Look how rich my owner is!' in a way that can only be described as vulgar. Perhaps my taste is very uneducated.

Lady Bracegirdle, however, was charming, elderly, most considerate of my shyness, and very thoughtful in not making me linger too long over tea before she conducted me to the Master's studio. Again, I cannot find words to describe what looked like an Arabian palace, rich with embroidered hangings and Eastern carpets, sculptures and draped couches and great paintings. Yet, after all, what was it but a workroom? I wondered whether, perhaps, the great man kept some plain humble apartment out of sight where the actual painting was done.

He was a little pompous, as one would expect of someone who owned such a house, and I had a suspicion that he expected me to drop my aitches. I found it hard to explain to him why I wanted to paint. The young ladies he is in the habit of meeting are no doubt in Society, or highly connected in the artistic world. But I stammered out something, distracted by his piercing glance and the most luxuriant curled beard I have ever seen. (I wonder if the use of curling-tongs . . .? But such a thought is unworthy.)

He listened politely, then asked me to show him my portfolio of drawings. He scrutinized each one carefully, laying them one on top of another in a neat pile, without speaking. Hours seemed to pass while he was doing this. Then, topping the pile with the last one, he turned to me.

'Young lady, you have a little talent. I could have made something of you, perhaps, if I had had the teaching of you . . . Who *did* teach you, by the way?'

I told him about my French master. He sniffed.

'I should like to know where the gentleman studied. There is no anatomy in your figures: they have flesh and features, but no bones or muscles. How do you suppose they stand, sit, or move at all? Just as well that you don't go in for studies of the nude, or we should have some laughable shapes. Have you ever drawn from a nude model?'

Unable to check my blush, but inwardly angry with him for deliberately trying to shake me, I shook my head.

'Then you should not attempt figure-drawing. Have you heard that Landseer is working on four great carvings in stone, the lions which are to surround Nelson's Column? Now, I suppose if you were given the task you would imagine lions—make sketches of what you could remember of pictures seen in books?'

'I believe I should go to the Zoological Gardens and study the living animal.'

Sir Edwin laughed. 'Landseer has done better; he has studied the *dead* animal. A defunct lion has been carried into his studio so that he might learn the construction of the beast's body in every particular— every hair, claw, muscle, tooth, whisker—and the result will be perfection in stone.'

I said that the air of the studio must be somewhat oppressive by now. The great man looked under his bushy eyebrows at me.

'That may be so. But artists must suffer to achieve perfection.'

I longed to say that he did not appear to have suffered a great deal himself, but bit back the remark as being too openly rude. Instead I asked him whether he would like me to take up the dissection of human bodies? for if so I would have to ask my Papa's permission. This time his glance was truly piercing.

'You're a pert young lady, Miss Pirbright—perter than you look. No, I shouldn't recommend such a drastic course. In any case, it would be unseemly in a female. But I would suggest that if you prefer not to attend life-classes, you should pay frequent visits to collections of classical statuary—the Elgin Marbles, for instance—and learn as much as you can from them. And another thing: don't you think your style a trifle old-fashioned?'

'How so, sir?'

'Your people—these boneless marvels that throng your sketch-book—they seem to come from the decade before ours, when my old colleagues Rossetti and Morris were painting nothing but die-away damsels pretending to be Queen Guinevere or Iseult or some other fictitious lady, squired by knights with soulful eyes and long legs who look as if they could do with nothing so much as a stiff dose of calomel. I assume you're a great admirer of the Pre-Raphaelite Brotherhood?'

'Not particularly, sir. I have seen very little of their work. Mama prefers landscapes.'

'*Does* she . . . Then why do you put these creatures of your brain into mediaeval clothes, or even clothes which look like those impossible effigies one sees on ancient tombs, women like Shakespeare's grandmother (I suppose he had one) and men wearing armour that I dare swear they never wore in their lives? They are neither graceful nor fashionable.'

I picked up the portfolio and turned over a few pages. He was right, the people moving in various romantic settings were dressed rather like Mr Rossetti's models. I thought myself that they *were* rather graceful, more so than we look at the present day, in our great unmanageable crinolines that distort our womanly shapes, and tight stays squeezing our waists into almost nothing, which cannot be healthy. I dislike the present styles very much, though one must wear them or look a guy . . . However, it would have been unseemly to mention such items as style to the great man, and I supposed he would not be interested in my views on rational dress for women. I merely said that the people in my drawings were figures of my fancy, and their dress must have come from pictures I had seen early in life.

He nodded, and a silence fell. I could tell that he had ceased to be interested in me, having been given the chance of exercising his superior knowledge of Art and venting a little sarcasm on me. I thanked him as earnestly as possible for his advice, and with no delay he rang the bell for me to be shown downstairs to where Sarah awaited me in the fantastic hall.

As we walked home I wondered whether it had been worth going to visit him, apart from the interest of seeing how such a distinguished man lived. Otherwise, I had learned nothing, only that I possessed less talent than I thought.

It is half an hour since I wrote those last words. In the interval I set up my sketching-block and let my pencil wander idly, where it would; I could not have said why, unless to convince myself that Sir Edwin had been right, and that my drawing was based on no firm foundation of study.

I could scarcely believe my eyes when the pencil began to move, taking my hand with it, in lines that formed a recognizable shape, not merely a straggle. I lifted my hand from the paper. Some force seemed to pull it down again and the 'drawing' continued, without any volition from me. This is quite true, Journal, though it may seem impossible. I can't say how long the process continued, for I ceased to try to control it, giving myself up to a sort of dream-state. I noticed that at some point the pencil raised itself and resumed drawing in another place.

At last it came to a stop, as a spinning-top ceases whirring. I looked down at the paper, and this is the strangest thing I have ever experienced or written down. There before me, quite clearly though not strongly drawn, were the outlines of two figures. One, the woman, wore a dress with a bell-shaped skirt, not so voluminous as crinoline, and reaching to the ground, with a tight neat bodice and hanging sleeves. On her head was what seemed to be a bonnet or hood with a pointed arched front, the peak over her brow. The man beside her (the pencil must have lifted to separate the two figures) wore a full-cut, rather burly over-garment, and under it an indication of another garment so long that short breeches must have been concealed by it; and on the head a wide, round cap with a feather. There was no shading, no indication of features, no detail of pattern or ornament.

I was still staring at the drawing when Mama came in quietly.

'Amy, dear. Still sitting in the old nursery? Isn't it rather gloomy? The crocus are out in the gardens. Surely you can't see to draw? What did Sir Edwin say to you?'

'Nothing special, Mama. I thought his house very fine and we talked about Art—that was all.'

'Oh. Well, I just came to tell you that we are to have company next weekend. An associate of Papa's from a Manchester house is bringing his family up for a few days. We shall have to be on our best behaviour, ready to show them London life, shan't we? I am really quite looking forward to seeing fresh faces. Don't strain your eyes, dear.'

I had hardly heard what she said, because I was still half looking, half trying not to look, at the drawing which I had done and yet had not done. The costume of the two figures meant nothing to me. We had only a few of Sir Walter's novels on the shelves in the library, and their illustrations were what I can only call very fancy, like those to the novels of Harrison Ainsworth.

I neither liked nor disliked what I had drawn, only wondered how they had come to be on the paper, and felt the air of the old nursery to be colder than usual.

APRIL 3RD

What a strange few days I have passed! Mr and Mrs Brearley proved to be very pleasant people, as ordinary-spoken in their Northern way as my parents in their London fashion. There is no having to live up to them, simple as they are. We all seem to drink a deal of tea and Mama and Mrs Brearley sit cooing over photographs of Letty's baby and the four Brearley daughters and *their* babies. The weather being fine and unusually mild for so early in April, we have taken them for drives to the Crystal Palace, so near to us, with all its wonders, up river from Charing Cross Pier to Richmond, to the Botanical and Zoological Gardens in the Regent's Park (I did *not* draw the poor shabby lions) and the South Kensington Museum. It has all been very agreeable and a change from our usual dullness.

It appears that Mr Brearley is the owner of Pratts Limited, a large emporium in Manchester; I had not realized he was almost as important in the trade as Papa (and as rich, surely, judging by Mrs B.'s furs and jewellery).

Mr and Mrs Brearley are accompanied by their son, Mr Arthur Brearley.

It is rather strange to have a young man as a house guest at Lamorna Towers; one who is not related to us, that is. How shall I describe Mr Arthur? He is two years younger than I, I heard his mama tell mine, very broadly built, with a healthy complexion one would not associate with the drapery line, but he tells me his hobby is shooting during the season at a nobleman's estate in Derbyshire. So he has good connections—I thought Papa looked a shade wistful as Mr Arthur talked of Lord Shawe, as though he too would like to be able to mention lightly such acquaintance. He—Mr Arthur—has a good head of hair and fine sidewhiskers, almost jet-black, and a cheerful expression; indeed, he laughs a good deal, more than we are used to in our rather quiet family. His manner to me is courteous, and he pays me a lot of attention—but then that would be expected of him, as I am his host's daughter.

We have talked a good deal, on our walks round the gardens, and as neighbours at luncheon and dinner. I find he listens to me very attentively, though I sense that it is better if I keep to light and popular topics. Letty's suitors, the ones she tried to divert in my direction, always had an air of painful duty, as though squiring me instead of her were a great bore, as no doubt it was, and even when they murmured some conventional compliment their eyes were always straying over my shoulder in search of a prettier face. Now Mr Arthur looks only at me, and such compliments as he pays me are quite unconventional.

'You know,' he said yesterday, 'it's a pleasure to hear you talk, Miss Pirbright. You've the softest and sweetest voice I ever heard.'

'How kind of you. But surely you know plenty of ladies who speak equally well or better.'

He laughed. 'We don't go in for a lot of elegant talk where I come from. Hark at me, for instance, as Lancashire as cotton. And when we do try to sound grand, it comes out just a bit like this.' He said the last words in a mock-refined accent I really cannot reproduce on paper, but the effect was very comic.

He is pleasingly complimentary, too, in noticing what I wear. To-night at dinner I wore a new gown of fawn tussore. The material had been chosen by Mama, and I was not sure that I liked it. In any case I dislike the present style of evening dress, which bares the shoulders and most of the arms. It is a style only becoming to plump ladies, I feel, and makes me feel conscious of the 'salt-cellars' at the base of my throat and the regret-table lack of dimples in places where dimples are so much admired. But Mr Arthur came out with one of his forthright compliments.

'That's a nice bit of stuff, Miss Amy, and very well cut. You've a good dressmaker, I can see that—if you don't mind my saying so.'

I murmured something about not caring very much for the colour.

'Aye, well, tussore takes dye badly, it's best left in its natural shade. But I tell you what—and you're welcome to snub me if I'm talk-ing out of turn—I'd like to see you in some of the Indian silks we've just got in, brand new stock. Some of them'd look a treat on you. There's a beautiful shade of old rose, and a dark peacock-blue with a fine sheen on it. With your lovely skin you'd set them off perfectly.'

I eyed him keenly, wondering how much deliberate flattery there was in his words. 'Thank you, Mr Arthur. I have always thought my skin very colourless and uninteresting, not at all what is admired. It is nice to know that someone does admire it.' Now carry on with the flattery, sir, I thought. But he said, 'I don't like young women to look like milk-maids or Dutch dolls. I like a fine fair skin, like a true lady's, and that's what you've got.'

The fine fair skin was suffused with a painful blush, not at all becoming to it, I knew. But he seemed not to notice, turning to his plate as though he had not just paid me the compliment of my life. And I believed, I hoped, he meant it.

After that he began to talk with real enthusiasm, I could tell, of the various materials handled by his house, their quality and character-istics, and from that to the sundries, bonnets, gloves, bags, scarves, artificial flowers and fruit, buttons and general haberdashery. As it hap-pened I am very familiar with all these things from shopping at Pir-brights, and find them very commonplace, so I could only make occasional sounds demonstrating interest; I hope he thought them enough. Clearly he will make a worthy successor to his father, in time to come. I drew him gently away from the subject with questions about his home; he talked just as fluently of Manchester, its mills and dread-ful slums, its prestigious daily paper, the *Manchester Guardian,* the cel-ebrated Hallé Concerts, which seem to be rather like our 'Monday Pops', the elegant Portico Library.

'Is Manchester a pleasant place to live in?' I asked, and fancied he gave me a curious thoughtful look, as he answered that the Brearleys' home was in a suburb on the south side of the city, a new and handsome house with extensive grounds and stabling. Nobody would think of living anywhere else, he added; it was up to Sydenham and Dulwich, any time, and had the Cheshire countryside beyond. 'Manchester muck makes Manchester brass, they say, but there's a lot more to us than that.'

I had been aware of Mama watching us while this conversation was taking place, and listening, I have no doubt, with a sort of extension of the ear peculiar to mamas, making it possible for them to engage in a lively conversation with their neighbours at table while taking in all the important things said by somebody several places distant. I thought she must be pleased to see a young man paying attention to me at last, and congratulating herself on the choice of the fawn tussore. Papa, too, smiled and seemed even more than usually full of good nature.

APRIL 5TH

The Brearley family have left. Without them the house seems strangely quiet, though I confess I am just a little tired and glad we are alone again. Not once in the past two days have I had a chance to slip up to the old nursery and confide in you, dear Journal. I am so unused to society; perhaps I should put my mind to mixing more with other people. Tennis parties I detest, but I suppose I might be passable at croquet. I wish I had not given up sketching.

I feel oddly flat and lifeless. If the Brearleys were to return tomorrow I would gladly accompany them to the dullest museum in London, whatever that may be.

APRIL 9TH

I have been too restless these last few days to write anything. Mama has several times asked me if I were quite well. I have begun this entry before breakfast to make sure that I do not spend another day without committing my thoughts and experiences to paper—for what they are worth. I imagine some girl of the future reading you, Journal, and remarking on what a singularly useless life I led. If only . . .

At that point I broke off. Sarah appeared, sent upstairs to tell me that the parcel post had brought something for me. I hastened down to find Mama and Papa in the morning-room.

Mama pointed to a large parcel. 'I believe you should open this yourself, Amy,' she said with a smile. 'I have had one too.'

With the aid of a table-knife I removed the wrappings. From layer after layer of paper, very neatly and professionally used, there emerged a bolt of silk, the colour of a peacock's plumage, seeming to vary as one turned it about from rich turquoise to sapphire, and from that to the colour one sometimes sees in the deep-sea waves. I knew at once that it was the Indian silk Mr Arthur had mentioned to me.

Mama and Papa were watching me. I said, 'How very beautiful!'

'Very,' Mama agreed. 'I might be envious of you, dear, if I had not received this.' She picked up a bolt of grenadine, of the best quality, I could see, of the soft snuff-brown which is her favourite colour and suits her fair complexion and pretty greying hair better than any. 'From Mr Arthur,' she said, 'with a very nice letter of thanks to us for entertaining him and his parents, and hopes that you and I will accept these small presents for our summer wardrobe. Wasn't it thoughtful of him?'

'Coals to Newcastle, as you might say,' Papa put in. 'But thoughtful, very. I couldn't have chosen better myself.'

'Of course,' Mama said, holding up the silk and glancing from it to me and back again, 'it's a colour you've never worn, dear, and rather novel, for anyone of your age, but I can tell it will suit you. Do you like it, really?'

I said that I did, and that it was very kind of Mr Arthur to send me a length of material as well as Mama. I think I knew, and I'm sure Mama and Papa did, that Mama's was the duty gift, and mine the one the sender thought more important. Papa said jokingly that he felt left out, and might at least have been sent a handkerchief.

'You must write the letter of thanks, of course,' Mama said.

'Why me? You were the hostess, Mama.'

'I'm sure Mr Arthur would rather hear from a young lady than her old mama—don't you agree, William?' she said, looking what I can only call coy.

So I must abandon you, Journal, and write a very careful letter to Mr Arthur. I have never written to a gentleman before in my life.

APRIL 28TH

Mr Arthur is coming to London on business. His parents will not be accompanying him. I am glad I have had the silk made up, and so successfully.

MAY 1ST

Dear Journal, it has happened, and I don't know whether to laugh or cry. Mr Arthur has asked Papa for his permission to propose marriage to me.

Papa said yes, of course; I think he knew quite well what was coming, he and Mama have both worn such an air of secrecy recently, and I have known they were talking about me as soon as I came into a room and the conversation stopped. I thought Papa seemed just a little nervous when he gave me the news.

'Amy, my dear,' he said, 'you'll give this very serious thought, won't you. It's not every day a girl gets a proposal from a decent, honourable young man with a fine future before him. I know Walter Brearley and I know his shop, and believe me young Arthur's got a rich inheritance there. It may all be a bit sudden, seeing it's only a month since you first met him, but you won't turn him down because of that, will you? He talked to me very sincerely, Amy. Take my advice, and your mother's, and listen to him.'

I did listen, as Arthur sat beside me on the sofa in the drawing-room, and told me that he had wanted me for his wife since the first time we had met. 'I knew you were what a man doesn't meet every day, Miss Amy—a proper lady, more so than some I know with a handle to their name. And then, your father and mine are in the same line of business, and you understand the life I live. I'm asking you to share it, and I want you to believe I'll do my best to make you very happy. You'll have a home as good as the one you've been used to, and everything you want that I can give you. Won't you say yes?'

I said yes. And Arthur kissed me, very respectfully, on the cheek, and we went arm-in-arm to tell Papa and Mama.

Tomorrow we are going to Regent Street to choose the ring.

Oh, Journal, I am so confused; grateful—*very* grateful to dear Arthur, for rescuing me from the dusty Shelf all young women dread, and for being so kind and thoughtful in every way. With him I can look forward to what I long for. Lovely children. He is, as Papa says, the right man for me—who could be righter? I can hardly believe all this is true.

And yet, I *did* expect to feel more, when I used to dream romantic dreams of my future husband. More . . . what?

I expect I am a complete goose to entertain such thoughts. I must consider myself a very, very lucky girl. Girl, indeed! Lucky woman of twenty-seven.

MAY 27TH

The day of our engagement party has come. Beautiful weather, the garden in perfection with early roses and azaleas in their full glory, a marquee on the lawn in case the house should become uncomfortably hot with the press of people. For almost all who were invited have accepted, yet I know they have done so with the expectation of a vulgar spectacle, Trade flaunting itself and its moneybags. They will be disappointed: Papa has hired the best caterers in the West End. There will be waiters, charming floral arrangements, Chinese lanterns in the trees, the best wines and food, everything tasteful as well as luxurious. I shall wear my dress of Indian silk which I have had made close-fitting, long-sleeved, and without crinoline, in the Rossetti style to which Sir Edwin drew my attention. Mama and the dressmaker think it horrid, but I feel it suits me very well. Across my forehead will be the ribbon circlet Arthur has so cleverly designed to disguise the height of my brow. I suppose I may say that this is the greatest day of my life.

Letty and her husband and little Amelia are coming, and I don't know how many of our relations; I only hope they will behave themselves with so much wine to be had. I shall be very careful of it myself.

A coiffeur is coming to do my hair, as Sarah's efforts may be all very well for everyday but not for such an occasion as this. I shall rest after luncheon, to look as well as possible this evening.

MIDNIGHT

What a strange, unexpected turn of events!

The reception went off very well, Mama in white kid gloves receiving everybody as though she did it every day of her life, and Papa being expansive to many people he knows sneer at him when not enjoying his hospitality. I felt I looked in high fettle (for me) especially with the very slight, discreet touch of colour Mama added to my cheeks. Arthur was most complimentary. I thought he looked superb in evening dress, with a single diamond pin in his shirt-front.

Supper was over, the gaiety at its height and many of the guests what Papa calls 'flown', when, as Arthur and I and my parents were taking tea at a small table in a corner of the drawing-room, the head waiter from the catering firm appeared suddenly, looking important.

'I beg pardon for interrupting you, sir and madam, but it has just been brought to my notice that there is an intruder on the premises.'

'Oh, indeed? A thief?' Papa said.

'Very probably, sir. He was found in the marquee by one of our men during the clearing-away. I took the liberty of bringing him in.'

'Oh,' Mama said nervously, 'if he is at all dangerous I think the police should be called. We, er . . .'

But the man had already snapped his fingers, and at the summons another waiter approached from the double doors, dragging by the hand . . .

A child. A boy, aged about nine, I thought; thin, pale, shabby, with big frightened dark eyes.

'Why, what's this?' Papa exclaimed, and Mama gasped.

'In the marquee, sir and madam,' the head waiter repeated, 'that's where we found this young ruffiner, lurking. No doubt after the guests were gone he planned to break into the house and admit his accomplices.' I thought that the man had certainly read a good deal of sensational literature. 'Small,' he went on, 'they likes 'em small to put through pantry winders and down cellar gratings. That's how they gets in, where grown men can't. Confess it now, you varmint,' and he shook the boy's shoulder violently. 'May be the police won't be so hard with you, if you tell 'em who your mates is.' I saw Mama wince at his shaking of the child, and Arthur was half-way to his feet. But the boy neither quailed nor tried to escape.

'I was not going to break in,' he said, in a sweet, singularly clear voice, 'and I haven't any mates. I just wanted to see the—the assembled company.'

'Bless us,' said Mama, 'how the child speaks.'

The head waiter gave the slight shoulder another jerk. 'Madam may be taken in by soft talk, but I ain't, my bucko—I know your sort, you're taught all kinds of tricks to deceive people. Bill, go and fetch a constable.'

'Just a minute,' Papa said. 'I think we should give this dangerous villain a chance to explain himself. Well, boy?'

The child made a slight formal bow to him. 'Sir, I saw the lights from our house—that is next door, you know. I had never seen anything like them, and I thought some grand fête must be in progress. So I got through the hedge and had a good look.'

'A pretty story,' said the head waiter. The boy shot him a proud glance.

'It's true. Then I went into the big tent because I thought it was something to do with soldiers—like the Field of the Cloth of Gold. But there were only tables and plants in pots. Then the man came in and caught me. And now if you please I should like to go home, for my father will be anxious if he finds me out of bed.'

His captor was looking uncertain, as well he might with a prisoner who spoke more purely and beautifully than any of us, myself included. I said, 'What is your name?'

'James Lindsay, ma'am. And my father is Captain Robert Lindsay.'

I whispered to Papa, 'The little house next door.' It was such a little house that one hardly noticed it, compared with the size of Lamorna Towers; it had once been a staff cottage, but for some reason had been separated from the grounds and a hedge planted in between. It stood right back from the road in a narrow strip of garden which was uncultivated, so far as I remembered.

Papa answered, 'Yes. Tenants in there—I told Greenway he could let it to anyone respectable.' To the child he said, 'All right, my boy. It's about time you went back to your father. One of the servants will take you.'

'No,' I said suddenly, 'I will.' They looked at me in astonishment as I rose and went to the boy, meaning to take him by the hand; but with a most manly and courteous gesture he slipped his arm through mine.

Arthur rose too. 'I'll come with you, of course.' And leaving my astonished parents and the flustered waiters, we, an oddly-assorted trio, set off. As James was so much shorter than I it was very uncomfortable to walk linked with him, but I knew that he felt it to be the right way to escort a lady, and would not humiliate him by drawing my arm away. Arthur said nothing; he seemed to find the situation beyond understanding, and he had drunk quite a quantity of champagne. Perhaps it seemed to him an example of the way Londoners carried on. We walked through the May dusk, beneath the strings of many-coloured Chinese lanterns that had attracted James, down the drive to the road. I asked James to tell me about the Field of the Cloth of Gold.

'It was where the two kings met, ma'am, Henry the Eighth and Francis the First of France. They arranged it to fix a peace between the two countries, you see, Henry took his Court to France and they lodged in great tents all gilded and decorated with heraldic pictures, and there were almost three thousand horses for the tournaments.'

Arthur said, 'You seem to know a great deal of history, young man.'

'Oh, I do, sir,' James replied. 'Military history, that is. My father is a soldier, and I intend to be one, too.' He sounded perfectly matter-of-fact, not boasting at all, and as composed as though the scenes in the marquee and the house had never taken place. He sounded, in fact, grown-up; too grown-up for his size and years. I felt a twinge of pity and curiosity about him.

'I am not partial to Henry the Eighth, myself,' he informed us. 'He was ill-tempered and cruel. Did you know he had two of his wives killed?'

We said we did.

'I suppose,' James reflected, 'it was not quite so bad to have your head cut off, if the executioner was good at his work. But it must have been quite frightful to be burned.'

As he said that a kind of shock, or shudder, went through me, something like the feeling electric galvanism is supposed to produce, very unpleasant indeed. Arthur felt the convulsion of my arm against his own. He said (and I had never heard him speak sharply before), 'That's enough, lad. We don't talk of such things before ladies.'

'I'm sorry, sir.' James subsided into silence as we turned up the path that led to the cottage. There was a light in the downstairs window at the front. Even before we reached the door it opened.

I shall not write any more tonight. It is very late, past one, and I feel completely worn out, as though I had run a very long way.

MAY 28TH

I saw him first against the lighted room, a tall dark shape. He stepped forward, crying, 'Jamie!' and the boy left us and went to him.

'I'm sorry, father, if you missed me.'

'I did. Where have you been?' The voice was very faintly Scots, educated Scots.

I said, 'I'm afraid it was our fault, Captain Lindsay. Your son saw the lanterns in the trees, and wandered into our garden.'

'I see. And you are Mrs . . . ?'

'Miss Pirbright.'

'It was very kind of you to bring him back.'

'We could do no less. This is my fiancé, Mr Brearley.' The two men murmured acknowledgments. Captain Lindsay had moved back within the radius of the lamp inside the room. The first thing I saw in him was an instant look of James, something impossible to define. He was much older than one would have expected to be the father of a young child—forty, at least, perhaps more, very thin, haggard, almost, dark and pale, a small moustache above an unsmiling mouth. I thought his look was accusing, though goodness knows it was not we who had enticed James into our grounds. I said, 'Goodnight, then. Goodnight, James,' suppressing an urge to say that it would be perfectly all right if he were to come to visit us. Something told me that neither James's father nor Arthur would have been pleased with that.

When the door had shut and we were walking back I sensed even more clearly that Arthur was in less than a good humour. Being Arthur, he did not sulk, but came frankly out with it.

'I didn't think you ought to encourage that sort of person, Amy. For all you know that boy *was* sent to do a bit of thieving . . .'

'No!'

'Or at least to scrape up an acquaintance with you, for what he could get out of it.'

'With me? He didn't even know who I was, or anything about us. That was perfectly clear.'

'He knew you were the folk at the big house, didn't he? I don't want you taken advantage of, Amy, now or any time.'

It was a temptation to snap back that as yet he had no rights over me, that if I wanted to be taken advantage of I would be, that it was ridiculous to think of that polite, too-learned little boy being a burglar's assistant. Then, walking beside Arthur in the late-evening peace, I reflected that men are, they say, always to some degree little boys, and that this particular one had had his treat spoiled. It had probably been in his mind to take me out into the gardens after the guests were gone, and saunter beneath those pretty lights, among the sleeping flowers, and perhaps speak to me more tenderly than Northern restraint would let him do by day. Instead, he had been made escort to a small child who had decidedly not been invited to our fête, and who monopolized my attention, even to linking arms with me, as Arthur should have done. Of course he was annoyed and disappointed.

So I smiled up at him, and began to talk of our wedding, which is to be in July; not a fashionable month, outside the London season, but such as the Pirbrights have very little to do with that sort of fashion. Very soon he cheered up and was my good-tempered Arthur again.

I have risked annoying him even more; I shall not tell him what I did this afternoon. He had business engagements all day, so that I was left to myself, apart from the attention of Mama's dressmaker who seems to need far more fittings than I should have thought even the Princess Royal had when she married Prince Frederick of Prussia.

All last night, and this morning, I was unable to get out of my head the picture of James, so very slight and ill-nourished in looks, like the Oliver Twist Arthur had imagined him to be. Surely he was not properly fed? Nothing had been said of his mother—surely she would have come out to greet him, with his father?

And—yes, I remembered all too vividly the father's face, the hollows under the high cheek-bones accentuated in the lamplight. Surely he would not be offended if I made a neighbourly gesture . . .

I asked in the kitchens what had been left from the party. Cook said, with a shrug, that them caterers had took away whole hampers-full, but that there was a bit saved in the pantry. This, I knew very well, was the servants' perquisite, the right to left-over dainties from upstairs.

Very tactfully, I said, 'Do you think, Cook, you could spare enough—a few little bits—just to make up a basket for a poor family? I feel so sorry for them, and I very much doubt whether anybody from the church pays them visits.'

'Lor, Miss Amy, 'course I could! When did you ever know me speak against good works? Blessed are they that hunger and thirst after righteousness, *I* say. Take what you like, and welcome. I'll get you a basket and a cloth.'

I was not sure about James's appetite for righteousness, but I was pretty sure that he would not be able to resist the hoard I found in the pantry. Far from being a bit, it covered two tables and a shelf. I collected some chicken in aspic, a little cold Scotch salmon, tartlets of all kinds of jam and conserves, a slice of rich fruit-cake, and, to balance all this richness, some plain rolls of new bread.

The cottage looked far more dilapidated than it had done in the dusk. None of the outside wood could have been painted for years, an upstairs window had a pane missing, the lace curtains looked grimy. The garden, too, was utterly neglected, a wild straggle of plants run to seed and overgrown with weeds. Suddenly I felt depressed. I wished I could turn back, but somebody might well be watching from a window. I knocked. Even the knocker seemed ready to fall off.

It was a full minute before the door opened. There stood not James, but his father.

I had been so confident that the child would answer the door that I must have looked foolishly dumbstruck. We stood in silence on each side of the threshold. The man was as haggard and shabby as he had appeared the night before, or more so, and I saw what I had not seen then—that his left sleeve was empty from above the elbow. He was regarding me with a look of utter dislike. Under that icy stare my eyes dropped. I muttered, 'I thought that James . . .'

'James is at school. What do you want?'

'I am Miss Pirbright. We met last night . . .'

'I know who you are.'

All my instincts told me to turn on my heel and go before I could be insulted. But pride won. I said, 'I thought James might like a few little things left over from the party. It seems a pity to waste them, and we have no children in the house to eat them up.'

'Then I suggest you take them to an orphanage or a church mission. My son has no need of charity.' His hand was on the door, ready to close it.

I felt a tide of anger sweep through me. Papa says I only lose my temper once a year, and when I do the heavens fall. I said (only I sounded to myself to be shouting), 'Your son is a charming little boy who was unfairly treated last night on my father's premises, by someone who was not one of our servants. I brought him back myself rather than let him risk any more such mistakes. I wanted him to have these as a very small reward for behaving so well in unfortunate circumstances, and if you refuse to give them to him, with my love, I shall most certainly not take them to an orphanage or church mission, you may do that yourself, sir, or whatever you please.' I slammed the basket down on the ground between us.

A layer of ice melted from the dark stare, and the grim lines of Captain Lindsay's face relaxed very slightly. He bent and picked up the basket—how awkward everything must be, with only one hand!—and said, expressionlessly, 'You had better come in.'

I went in. Too late I realized that I had committed an awful social *faux pas* in visiting a man alone, without a maid. For there was no sign of female presence about the small room into which the front door opened directly. It was gloomy, cold, and almost as bare as a cell. There was a table with an ancient-looking cloth on it, two upright kitchen chairs, a small, cheap horsehair sofa, such as one sees outside second-hand shops, and on the floor a small square of worn drugget laid over bare boards. I have never before been in such a room, even when I visited those cottagers during my spell of Good Works; at least their humble homes showed some sign of an attempt to decorate bareness with little personal touches, a picture of the Queen, a china figure won at a fair. Here there was nothing: except, hung from a nail on the wall above the fireplace, a sword.

My face must have given away my feelings, but Captain Lindsay politely took no notice. Instead, he drew out a chair and gestured to me to be seated.

'I spoke hastily just now,' he said, as though it pained him to apologize. 'You must forgive me, Miss . . . Pirbright. I am a shade sensitive to any suggestion of my son being patronized. I see now that such was not your intention.'

Priggish, formal beast! I thought. What an unpleasant father for that nice child.

'No, it was not,' I answered. 'I hope I never patronized anyone in my life. I was not brought up to that sort of behaviour. You may be interested to know, Captain Lindsay, that my father is a draper, though we do live in a big house and keep servants. We are not at all grand, in fact, as you may have thought we were. I expect you come from a family far above ours, for it's quite clear that James is a true gentleman.' I may have emphasized 'James', being still in a temper with the man.

Captain Lindsay had been standing over me, but now he sat down at the table, facing me. Suddenly he smiled, and the smile quite transformed his grim face into sweetness and—yes, a kind of handsomeness. One could see that he had once been dashingly good-looking, before—whatever had happened to him.

'And I have behaved quite unlike a true gentleman. Quite right, madam. I am a boor, you must think by now. To make a lady explain herself as frankly as you have done was inexcusable. Please forgive me. This time I mean it.'

His voice was quite strongly Scots now that he was not speaking as though quoting Queen's Regulations. I smiled back, my temper quite gone.

'Of course I forgive you, sir. I realize what it must have looked like, marching here with a basket of foodstuff. I did try to do church work, once, but I never seem to get these things right, and I certainly haven't today. Did James tell you what happened last night?'

'No. This is the first I've heard of unfair treatment.'

I told him about the marquee, and James being dragged before my parents. He listened attentively, then said, 'James would not have told me such a thing; it would have sounded to him like telling tales.'

'Yes, I can imagine that. Well, as we walked here he talked to us, and I . . . I liked him so much. I thought him so clever and yet so modest and gentle, and . . . I wanted to see him again. That's all.'

He said nothing, but sat silently studying me. Then he said, 'I should tell you about us, James and me. I would not be telling many people.' He went on to explain, very crisply and without dwelling on detail, that he came of a Highland family with a tradition of soldiering, and had willingly embarked on it as a career, after his elder brother, who by family custom should have been the soldier, elected to farm the estate instead. Little was said about this brother, but I gathered there had been faction between the two young men. Fortune took him to India, where our Empire was threatened by native unrest. While he was serving there he met the beautiful daughter of an English gentleman and a high-caste Indian girl, and married her against the furious written commands of his father.

When the marriage was known in Scotland legal processes were set up to cut him out of any share in what should have been his and his brother's, his father having strong objections to 'niggers inheriting a good Scots name'. There was nothing Robert Lindsay could do without taking at least a year's leave from his regiment, and abandoning his wife and baby son to the dangers around them. When the threatened

Mutiny at last broke out, in '57, he was obliged to leave them with Indian relatives and follow his Commander-in-Chief, Sir Henry Lawrence. He heard no more of them until the whole ghastly revolt had been bloodily quelled, and he had lost his left arm at the Siege of Delhi.

'It was not easy; for a long time I was in a hospital—if you could call it a hospital—and when I was able to leave my wife's relatives had vanished. I traced them months later. My wife had been murdered, with so many other women looked on as white. Jamie was living with a native family; he was almost as much Indian as British.

'The army had no more use for me, so I came home,' he said bleakly. 'I had my wound pension, nothing more. There was no welcome for us in Morayshire.'

And so Sydenham, I thought, an almost derelict cottage; the man hedged about with fierce pride like a hedgehog's quills, the child . . .

'James is at school?'

'Alleyn's School. One of the best in England.'

Of course. What bit of money there was must be spent on Jamie and the education of a gentleman. 'He told me he intends to be a soldier,' I said.

'That will never be. He has a brain far beyond that. It did little for me,' and he glanced down at the empty sleeve. 'So, now I have told you more than I am used to tell anyone. Will you take tea with me?'

I knew it would please him if I said yes, and watched him put a blackened little kettle on a scarcely less black fire, take out china, spoons and a tin caddy from a corner cupboard, and set about a process that belonged only to servants, in our house. When it was ready I suggested, as casually as I could, that we might sample the jam tartlets in the basket. To my surprise he agreed, and seemed to enjoy one. I wondered what they lived on, those two.

As we were drinking the second cup of the cheap bitter tea, James let himself in. He looked from one to the other of us with a bright face.

'Oh,' he cried, ''Tis the fairy Lady of Shalott!' I might have known he would be full of quotations.

'No,' I said, 'only me, dropped in to see you both.'

'Ah, but last night you looked like her, in your green gown, as though you had just left the web and left the loom and taken three paces through the room . . .'

'Well, perhaps I had, and if so I was lucky to find you and your father instead of Sir Lancelot, whom I have always found a very tiresome character.'

Captain Lindsay said abruptly, 'I thought you were in fancy dress last night.'

'Goodness, no. It is a style favoured by artists—not fashionable at all, but I like it. Sir Edwin Bracegirdle suggested it to me,' I said, not altogether truthfully. I was a little piqued at his implication that I had looked ridiculous. 'The material is a very fine silk from India.'

I thought his brow darkened, and realized how tactless I had been; his dead wife must be for always associated in his mind with Indian silks. But he said, not angrily, 'It reminded me for a moment of someone or something. What have you been doing today, Jamie?'

James went to his father, whose arm came round him. Seen together, so close, they were very alike. 'Latin, father, mostly. And some geography, the Scandinavian countries. And history.'

'I should think you hardly need lessons in that.'

'Oh, but I do,' James answered seriously. 'I am very careless about facts if they don't interest me. Were you like that, when you were at school in Scotland?'

'We had to mind our facts there, laddie, or we got the tawse.'

'What was that?'

'A leather strap across our hands, back and front. If you got it too often you had to find someone to write your letters home for you. Now would you not like to see what Miss Pirbright has very kindly brought for your tea?'

James unpacked the basket, almost shining with pleasure. 'Oh, how simply ripping!' It amused me to hear slang on his lips. He laid out the tartlets in a ring, put the cake in the centre, then unwrapped the savouries. His face fell. 'We have not enough plates . . .'

'Who needs plates?' I said. 'This cloth Cook put over them is quite big enough to cover the middle of the table, and perfectly clean. Let's make a sort of indoor picnic, and eat with our fingers.' Joyfully James agreed, spreading the cloth and laying the food out with mathematical neatness. I put the kettle back on the low fire and slipped an extra spoonful of tea into the pot, while father and son were talking to each other; I resolved that more and better tea would find its way into the cottage, somehow or other. The milk in the jug was blue, the thinnest of skimmed stuff; I poured most of it into their cups.

James fell on the food with schoolboy gusto, and his father ate as though he were not used to good food, yet would not let the fact be seen by strangers. I sat with my elbows on the table, inelegantly, watching them. I would like to have had a banquet cooked and set before them, a great fire of logs made up, the room transformed into a place of cheerful comfort, the miserable horsehair sofa turned into a jolly, plump, velvet-upholstered one, where I could sit in the middle with an arm round each of them. A great warm tide of feeling washed over me, bringing tears to my eyes that I must not let fall.

James said, with his mouth full, 'I think you *are* a fairy lady, Miss Pirbright.'

'Far from it, I fear, James.'

'Yes. You spread bare tables with magical feasts.'

This was so exactly what I had been thinking of doing that I wondered if he could possibly have read my mind. I wondered, too, what his father's thoughts were, as I caught the dark eyes resting broodingly on me. Fear of patronage, of being treated like the deserving poor by the rich neighbour, even if she *were* a draper's daughter. Regret that he had told me even so much of his story? Jealousy, in case I might lure

James away from him. I felt the piercing look even though I kept my face turned from him. At last, determined not to be misunderstood, I met his gaze with mine, and found I could not drop my eyes, caught and held as they were by others dark as night yet clear and brilliant as a Highland stream—or what I imagined a Highland stream to be, for the land of brown heath and shaggy wood which had always charmed my imagination existed for me only on paper, within the works of Scott, not in my experience. Yet here was just such a romantic figure as I had sighed over in the poems, a soldier wounded in the wars, exiled from his country, reduced almost to beggary, yet with a haughty unbroken spirit and a tender heart for his motherless child . . .

I don't know how long I would have gone on like this, musing and gazing, with scraps of sonorous verse chasing through my mind, if James had not politely handed me the last of the cake. 'You must have it, Miss Pirbright, for a handsome husband or ten thousand a year.'

I came down to earth with a bang.

'Thank you, James, but I couldn't possibly eat any more.'

'Oh. But then you already have a husband. To be, that is,' added the pedantic child.

'Yes. I am to be married soon.'

'Will you still live next door to us?'

'No. We shall be living near Manchester.'

'In the county of Lancashire, on the banks of the Irwell, the Medlock, the Irk and the Tib. A centre of the cotton industry, for which its damp climate makes it suitable,' James recited.

'Goodness, is all that true? What a lot you know, James.'

'I don't think it sounds very agreeable.'

'Agreeable or not, I shall have to live there.' And entertain Arthur's friends and the Brearley clan, and listen to talk about advertising campaigns and new stock lines and sales policy; and be a good wife to Arthur and the mother of his children.

I pushed back my chair and rose. 'I'm afraid I must go now.' I collected the basket and went to the door, James beside me, thanking me again in his charming way. Captain Lindsay seemed to be murmuring a speech of thanks, but I wanted to hurry away, not to talk further. At the door I turned and offered him my hand. He held it very tightly, as someone in pain might, and looked down at me with that unfathomable, uncomfortable gaze, seeming to fight for words. At last he said, 'Do I not . . . have we not met before?'

'Never. I'm sure I should have remembered.'

'But . . . I know you.'

'You have probably seen me in the gardens or walking out.'

As I reached the end of the path I turned and saw them still at the door. James was waving vigorously, Captain Lindsay standing motionless, looking after me.

JUNE 2ND

These have been strange, not altogether happy days. I have taken to writing in you, Journal, here in my bedroom, since now I am an engaged woman, Mama says, it seems just a little foolish for me to sit in the old nursery. I shall soon, she says, be thinking of a nursery of my own. I have looked round it and wondered what I should take: the toy theatre, Dobbin, the dolls' house? No doubt Arthur would be only too ready to supply splendid new toys from Pratt's, and I suppose the old and the new would mix. There are some beautiful new dolls from Paris, with china heads and the sweetest expressions.

I should be so excited by all this, but it is a little disturbing that when I try to visualize my children I can only see James's face. This is ridiculous, of course. How could I, with my mousy hair and greenish eyes, ever produce a child like that, even allowing for Arthur's being dark-haired? He is so rosy-cheeked and English-looking, whereas poor little James, now that I know about his parentage, could not possibly be anything but Anglo-Indian.

The evening following my visit to the cottage was rather uncomfortable. I felt that I should tell Arthur and my parents where I had been, but could not bring myself to do it. The place and its occupants were constantly in my mind, making me rather absent in my manner. Papa asked whether my wits had gone wool-gathering. Mama said, 'It was that champagne. I told you we should have had a nice cider cup.'

'Aye,' said Arthur, 'I'd a bit of a head on me this morning. It was good stuff.'

I started to protest that of course it was not the champagne, then thought it better to let them believe it was. While we played a hand of whist (which is so fashionable now but so intensely boring) my thoughts were not on the cards but on the problem of how I could visit the Lindsays again without reviving the Captain's suspicion that I was there to dispense charity. They need supplies of tea, of basic foods, proper milk instead of that skimmed stuff—and coal and lamp-oil and goodness knows what else, if one looked round that cottage thoroughly. Yet it is not my place to supply these things, and certainly not my parents'. The Lindsays are nothing to us but neighbours, and not really quite neighbours in the usual sense.

Yet in the Biblical sense they are. 'Thou shalt love thy neighbour as thyself.' In that meaning, everyone is our neighbour . . .

'Do you know you've just revoked, partner?' Arthur asked.

'Oh. Oh dear, I'm sorry. What can I have been thinking of?'

What, indeed?

'That funny little boy,' Mama said, some time later, as we were drinking coffee. 'I quite forgot about him until this moment. Did you get him home safely, and are they respectable people?'

Arthur shrugged, leaving me to answer.

'The cottage is in a very bad state,' I said. 'Don't you think you could have it put to rights, Papa? The child looks very fragile, and . . . I thought his father appeared not strong.'

'Oh? Greenway's said nothing to me, and they pay their rent regular, so far as I know. What's the matter with it—rats, drains, damp?'

'I really don't know, Papa—we were only there for a moment, weren't we, Arthur.' (Now I have started lying by omission.)

'Well, well, I'll send him round to have a look.'

So that is the most I can do for the Lindsays. I have had a wild thought of asking them here. But Captain Lindsay would be too proud to come, and somehow it would be all wrong.

Later, after Papa and Mama had retired, Arthur asked me to stroll with him in the gardens, as the night was so warm and pleasant. As we walked he put his arm round my waist; I guessed this was what he had intended the night before. We had never touched so closely. The nearest we get to proximity within doors is to sit next to each other on the drawing-room sofa, and of course Arthur is permitted to kiss my cheek in the morning and at night. Now, when we reached the little leafy arbour at the end of the long path that borders the rose garden, he led me into it and drew me down on to the rustic bench, took me in his arms, and began to kiss me.

I had never been kissed like that before; I did not know such things happened, and was indignant with Arthur for taking such a liberty. I pulled back from him sharply.

'Don't you like it, Amy?' he asked, surprised.

'No. It is detestable. I would prefer you not to do it again.'

'Oh. Well, I know I've kept pretty cool so far, but a man does expect . . .'

'Expect what?'

'Well . . . it's difficult talking about it, dear, but when we're married things will have to be . . . that is, we'll . . . Oh, dash it, Amy, don't you know what I'm talking about?'

I did not; I do not. Neither Mama nor Miss Tomkins nor anyone else has enlightened me about the mysterious processes attending marriage and birth. My wide reading has made none of it clear to me, and to tell the truth I have never wished to know until the time was ripe. I know that men and women are differently made, of course; I could hardly help it, with classical statues and pictures in the art galleries to inform me. But what has that to do with Arthur wanting to kiss me in that . . . well, improper way?

By this time I was feeling sorry for poor embarrassed Arthur, and so embarrassed myself that I felt the best thing would be to pretend none of it had ever happened. I rose, saying briskly, 'Let's continue our walk, the night-scented stock should be delicious.' No more was said, and in the house Arthur gave me the usual kiss on the cheek as we said goodnight. It was all I could do not to recoil.

What ails me? Am I unnatural in some way—not fit for marriage? Or is something the matter with Arthur, to make him behave like that? I am glad he is going back to Manchester tomorrow; I need time to think.

JUNE 3RD

This morning, after a great effort of will, I went to Mama and summoned up all my courage to tell her what was troubling me so much. She listened to my halting speech, saying only, 'Mm,' now and then. It was easy for neither of us, but hardest for me. At last I got to the end of what I wished I had never begun.

It was a few moments before she spoke.

'Amy, dear, all this is my fault.'

'No, Mama.'

'Yes. You see, I was brought up to think a girl should know nothing before she got married. I knew nothing myself, and it was a shock to me, I can tell you. I ought to have had the sense, with you girls . . . but

Letty always seemed as though she could deal with anything, and you—well, you weren't so concerned with young men, and all that sort of thing . . .'

'And you thought I'd never get married—wasn't that it, Mama?'

'Yes, I suppose it was, dear. You always had your head in a book, and you were full of such fancies—I *did* think you might turn out to be a maiden lady.'

'Well, that sounds better than spinster. But since I am to be married, don't you think I ought to know something now, Mama? Please won't you tell me?'

She sighed deeply. 'I don't know how I can, Amy. You see, you are so romantic, and life isn't really like romance. All that poetry . . . it isn't true. There are other things, *physical* things, which we have to endure . . .'

'But Arthur, Mama. I am going to marry Arthur. Surely I should not find him repulsive?'

'If you had, you would hardly have become engaged to him, would you?'

'No. But that was before . . . last night.'

'Oh, dear. But you do like him? I remember an old saying—"We should let our likings ripen before we love."'

'Of course I like him. He's nice, and kind, and good-looking.'

'And with such prospects! He'll make you a wonderful husband, my dear. Depend upon it, once you're married, everything will be all right.'

'Was it all right for you, Mama?'

There was just the least pause before she said, 'I married a good man. So will you. That is quite enough for happiness.'

I thanked her for listening and trying to help. But I wish she could have helped more.

There is another fitting for my wedding-dress tomorrow, and after that Mama and I are going to the West End to shop for my trousseau. I am to have two small bridesmaids, and Letty as a matron of honour. You may like to know the details of The Dress, which Miss Farrier is very proud of. She based it on a plate in the *Domestic Magazine*. It is of white silk, trimmed with white crêpe and Brussels lace; a low, square-cut bodice, with a little lace pelerine buttoned in front, from bust-line to throat. The skirt is bell-shaped, of course, but not too full, trimmed with two rows of crêpe ruches and a deep flounce.

My veil is of Brussels lace, very long, reaching to the floor behind, with a wreath of orange blossoms. The bridesmaids and Letty are to wear white tulle, with rose-coloured slips underneath, and veils of tulle with wreaths of red and white roses, the pelerine of tulle à la Mary Stuart. Arthur's gift to them will be a pearl bracelet each.

He said before he left that his parents have promised to put down the money for a house, as their wedding present to us. This seems hugely generous, to my mind.

As I was making out a shopping list just now I caught myself humming. At first I could not think what the tune was, then it came to me; an old song Letty's nursemaid used to sing.

O Madam, I will give to you the keys of Canterbury,
    And all the bells of London shall ring to make us merry,
If you will be my bride, my sweet and only dear,
    And walk along with me anywhere.

He offers her a new gift in every verse, a gown made of silk, horses white as milk, a fine ivory comb, but she refuses all of them until at last he offers his heart. I tried to remember all the verses, forgot some, and came back to the one I knew, the keys of . . .

Canterbury. As I said it, I felt a sensation as though a great bell had pealed out only a few inches from my ear, deafening and dumbfounding me. I have never swooned in my life, but I believe I almost swooned just now.

JUNE 4TH

I have been in the strangest mood today, so restless and nervous that Miss Farrier spoke to me quite severely, for her, when I could not stand still for the fitting. I feel—not quite ill, but disturbed and apprehensive, as though something terrible were drawing near and I could not stop it. I have begun a letter to little Amelia, to enclose with her birthday present, and another to Letty, but I found myself writing such nonsense that I gave up. I wish Letty were here, perhaps I should go to Dorking and see her, but Mama would think it very strange, and Letty is so caught up with her own concerns now that she might not have time to talk about my troubles.

Troubles? What troubles have I, with my wedding only six weeks away?

The air is close today, as though thunder were not far off, and the sun has not shown itself. I have taken a headache powder, but there is still a beating in my temple.

I have made up my mind. I shall go to the cottage this afternoon.

JUNE 5TH

I walked up the path under a lowering grey sky. The birds were quiet, the gardens very still, as though nothing were growing. Through the trees I could see the windows of Mama's bedroom, the curtains drawn, for this was the time she took her long nap. She would have stared to see me leave the house in an old dress of plaid cotton, one that had been my favourite years ago and had never been cut up or thrown away. I was determined not to look opulent, or anything other than myself.

He opened the door at once. This time there was no stare of hostility.

'Come in,' he said, 'I have been waiting.'

'But—how could you know I would come?'

'I have been waiting since the last time.'

We seated ourselves at the table, as we had sat before. It held a pile of books, some of them open. He shut them, saying, 'I try to help James with his work.'

'Yes.'

In the silence we looked at each other, his grave gaze dwelling on my worn old gown, which must have appeared very much at home in that humble room, I studying his face, much younger-looking now that his expression was no longer stern and angry. I thought that he was perhaps younger than I had first guessed him to be, and that the lines on his face came as much from the suns of India as from age. There was little grey in the thick dark hair, which my hands itched to reach out to and stroke.

As they do at Quaker meetings I spoke as the spirit moved me, without thought. 'I cannot rest. I have thought of you constantly. I am almost ill with thinking of you. If you look on me as lost to all shame in saying so, then I'm sorry, but I can do nothing else.'

He shook his head.

'Last time,' I said, 'you asked me if we had met before, and I said no. Now I have come to think we must have done. But I truly cannot remember where. It was not in the street, or at some party or dance, for I have *talked* to you—and I don't mean the other day. Perhaps my memory is going, or something is happening to my mind, for I have begun to remember things without knowing what they are.'

'What things?'

'Well . . . the night I brought James back, he was talking about the burnings in Tudor times. I felt an awful shudder of fear, as though I had . . . experienced death by burning, or feared it. Since then even gazing into a fire has made me uneasy.'

A faint shiver went through him. 'Yes. What else?'

I told him about the strange sensation which had come over me when I recalled the song about the keys of Canterbury, and about the figures my hand had drawn by itself. And of what I have not confided to you, Journal, that when I sat down to make a rough sketch of my wedding-dress to send to Letty, the same outlines began to appear on the paper, which I hurriedly screwed up and threw away. And of a dream, the sort I used to have so often, in which I almost *saw* the person I was to lose by waking.

He listened, nodding now and then.

'What is the matter with me?' I asked him. 'Am I mad?'

'No, unless I am, too.'

'You mean you remember such things?'

'No. But I have the Sight, as some have in the Highlands, and I have seen you; your face, yet not your face as it is now, but other features disguising your spirit. Time and again I have seen it, and known you, as sometimes in dreams we meet people who have other faces, yet whom we know to be themselves.'

'What—did you know of me?'

'That you were bonny, and brave. That you risked your freedom for your safety, and your life for mine. I had a name for you: *mo nighean donn.*'

'What does that mean?'

'In the Gaelic, my brown girl.'

'Nut-brown maid! That was what someone used to call me—I remember it now—but so far off, so very far off. Are you sure we're not dreaming? Have I been searching for you, all this time?'

'And I for you, *mo chridhe.*'

Our hands were clasped now, on the table top. I saw how sunbronzed it was, that solitary hand, and felt how strong. I said, 'Some sort of miracle must be at work. How . . . how long do you suppose we have known each other?'

'How can I tell? There are mystics in India who could tell you more. Perhaps we have met a thousand times, perhaps only a few. It may be that in some of our lives we missed each other. The wonder is that we have met now.'

I had been thinking, confusedly. 'But what about Heaven, and Hell? Where were we, after we died, as we must have done?'

'All this is beyond my understanding. God has disposed of us as He thought fit. Let us not trouble ourselves with that now.'

He stood up and drew me to him, more tightly than one could have thought possible for a man with one arm. Suddenly, all that I had asked Mama, and that she had not been able to tell me, was clear, clearer than if I had attended a lantern-lecture on the subject. I clung to him and kissed him again and again, hungry for him, with a hunger I had known long, long ago. He understood my body's language, and I his, and when he asked a question with his eyes, mine answered yes.

The small bedroom was cold and bare, yet to me it was a palace of delight. Paradise on earth. There was no mystery any more, only the great and wonderful mystery of our knowing each other at last.

I turned over to look at him. His face was young and relaxed and utterly peaceful, as they say the faces of the newly dead are. I stroked his cheek. He opened his eyes and smiled, and drew my hair across his lips. Somewhere on the floor was a chenille snood; I hoped I would be able to find it, and put my hair up as though it had never been taken down. Then I suddenly came back to reality, and I sat up.

'Arthur!' I said.

'Who, my dearest?'

'Arthur, my fiancé. What am I going to say? What am I going to do? They would never believe me, if I told them. They would think . . . oh, horrors!'

There was a shadow of doubt and fear in the dark eyes, so brilliant with love a moment before. 'You'll go back to him?'

'No, of course not, never. How could I leave you now? Besides . . . I am hardly what he bargained for; I suppose he would regard me as ruined. But I shall have to say something—to him, and my parents: tell them I can't marry him.'

Robert frowned. 'You know I am a very poor man, dearest. How can I keep you? Yet I can never let you go again. We have acted very rashly. Perhaps I *have* ruined you.'

'I would rather be ruined by you than married in St Paul's by any-body else. You said that God had disposed of us in the past, and He'll do so now, according to His will. No, leave it to me. I must go, before James comes home.'

I write all this down hardly believing a word of it. Yet it happened, beyond doubt, this afternoon which transformed my life. One of the strangest of all these strange things was that he did not know my Christian name; I told him what it was at a moment when he could hardly call me Miss Pirbright. He said, 'Amy. Aimée. Well-beloved.' It had never sounded so pretty to me before as it did spoken by that soft Scots voice.

I am very happy. But not looking forward to what I shall have to tell Mama and Papa. It is almost dinner-time now. How can I break it to them so suddenly? No, I shall behave as calmly as I can this evening, and pray very earnestly before I sleep tonight that I may be given the wisdom and the strength to say what I must.

I dread hurting them, and Arthur. But I dread hurting Robert more.

JUNE 6TH

This has been the most difficult day of my life. I hope never to have to spend such another.

After thinking very, very carefully I decided to tell Mama when she was by herself, rather than wait until Papa—poor Papa! came home. About eleven in the morning I knew that she would be writing letters in the pretty little room she calls her boudoir, and I went there.

She looked up brightly as I entered. 'Ah, my dear. Would you like to help me begin writing the invitations? I've made a list of everybody I can think of, and goodness, what a long one it is, not to mention all the Brearleys' relations. Do you think Aunt Belle would be very offended if we left her out? She is so much given to spasms, and it would be most inconvenient if she went and had one in church. Can you remind me of Arthur's sisters' married names, by the way?'

I went and sat on the little chair by her desk, the one with the embroidery in Berlin wool. The pattern jumped out at me as if stitched in phosphorus; I think I shall always remember some of its detail.

'Mama,' I said, breathing very deeply to keep calm, 'do you mind not beginning the invitations now?'

'Oh. But with only six weeks to go, dear—'

'I know. But . . . Mama, I have something very difficult to tell you. I don't know how to begin. Can you help me?'

Her pretty colour faded a little. 'You're not ill, Amy?'

'No, very well, never better. Mama, I cannot marry Arthur.'

She put her hand to her heart.

'I cannot marry Arthur. I have discovered that I don't love him enough to marry him. I am very, very sorry, Mama, more sorry than I can say.'

Her lips moved, but no words came.

'You remember the other day we had a difficult little talk? I tried then to ask you how it felt to love a man enough for marriage. Well, now I have found out. Mama, I have met someone I truly love.'

'I don't understand you, Amy.'

'The little boy who was in the marquee that night—that Arthur and I took home—his father and I felt an instant attraction to one another. I have seen him since, and . . . and it is more than attraction, it is love. I know now what love is, and why a man and woman wish to belong to each other.' (Robert and I had agreed that I should make no mention of the strange bond of recognition that was between us. They would neither understand nor credit it, and I should probably be regarded as mad, as well as bad.)

Mama said, through stiff lips, 'What an impossible story. How can you tell such lies, Amy? You don't know this man. *When* have you seen him again?'

'Yesterday afternoon and once before that. We had a long talk. He feels as I do.'

Her chin was trembling. 'You've been deceiving us.'

'No, Mama, truly. I had no intention of deceiving you, or upsetting things, as I know I have done. It was simply love at first sight—I can't help it. Say what you like to me, I'm sure I deserve it, but I can never, never marry Arthur now.'

At that she broke, weeping dreadfully, as I had never seen my calm dignified mother weep before. Through her tears she gasped out how impossible it would be to cancel the wedding—the invitations—the dresses; what would people say, what would they think? 'Poor Arthur, what has he done to deserve it? And Papa—this may very well kill him. It may kill *me,* and then you will have got rid of both of us and will be free to go your own way, you wicked girl.'

I put my hand on her knee, but she shook it off. 'Mama, don't say such bitter things, or we shall both be sorry. Let me get you your smelling-salts, and Susan will make us some tea.'

Over the rest of the day I will draw a veil.

Mama retired to bed after the scene in the boudoir. I had hoped she would stay there, so that I could face Papa by myself, but when he arrived home she was sitting in the drawing-room, wearing a black dress, her hands folded, not speaking to me at all. Papa took one look at her and asked, 'What's wrong, Amy?'

'I have to tell you something, Papa. Shall we have dinner first?'

'If you think that's best.' I could see that he was puzzled and worried, but he made a good show of eating, while Mama merely pecked, saying Yes and No to his remarks, nothing at all to mine. It was a great relief when we moved from the table, and tea was served by the fire.

Then I told him.

It was easier than telling Mama, perhaps because he had not been involved in the practical arrangements for the wedding. But not easy to watch his face change from its usual good-humoured expression to utter despondency. When I came to the end of the sorry tale I could almost have cried out that it was all untrue, or that it didn't matter, and I would marry Arthur to please him. But things had gone too far for that.

He said heavily, 'If it had been anybody but you telling me, Amy, I wouldn't have believed this. I don't know what to say. I'm very, very disappointed in you.'

I realized then what I had been too selfish and blind to realize before—that the Brearleys had been invited here on purpose. He must have been introduced to Arthur in Manchester, and been taken with the idea, the faint hope, that this might be the answer, the salvation of his spinster daughter. It had come so near to that, and now that hope was dashed, all his care for nothing.

I kept saying I was sorry, over and over again.

Mama spoke for the first time. 'We shall never hold our heads up after this.'

'Well, never mind that, Alice. The question is, do you know what you're doing, Amy?'

'No, Papa. I don't know anything, only what's happened.' And I was not going to tell them all of that.

'Are you going to marry this man?'

'I don't know. We haven't discussed it.' I must have sounded as silly as I now felt.

Papa turned the bell-handle which summoned the servants. 'I want to see him, and we may as well get it over.'

'See Robert?'

'We'll not have any first names used.' To the manservant who answered the bell he said that he wished Captain Lindsay to be fetched from next door, at once. Then we all sat, silent and miserable, until the door opened and Robert was shown in.

I saw with relief that he appeared very different from the man I had seen in his own cottage. The lines of stress had not come back to his face, so that he looked younger and altogether more comely. He wore a suit of tweed, obviously very good, though far from new; I guessed it was his best, made for him long before. He looked every inch a Scottish gentleman, who might just have strolled in from the heathery moors beyond his estate. I saw Papa and Mama take swift note of the missing arm, of the soldierly bearing, and of the beautiful, educated voice with its Highland tinge.

'I am glad you sent for me, Mr Pirbright. I would have presented myself without asking, but I thought it best to wait for a summons.'

I could see that they were surprised. I guessed they had expected some fortune-hunting, raffish half-pay officer, down-at-heel and probably given to drink and the horses, a figure of caricature.

'What's this I hear from my daughter?' Papa asked.

'Whatever Miss Pirbright has told you is perfectly true, sir.'

'*Is* it. So you and she have decided between you to break off her forthcoming marriage, all for some preposterous whim you've taken? It's not even as though you'd been properly introduced—'

'Or moved in the same circles,' Mama put in.

'Just because my daughter took your child home after her engagement party, and you spoke to her for perhaps a minute, with her fiancé present—you can't tell me that's a foundation for a disgraceful upheaval like this?'

'You ought to be ashamed,' Mama said.

'I am not at all ashamed,' Robert answered. 'I fell in love with Miss Pirbright at once, and she with me, she gives me to understand. It may be unusual and unconventional, but such things happen.' He smiled at me. 'I regret very much all the trouble it has caused you, and if Miss Pirbright wishes to change her mind and continue with her marriage arrangements I shall naturally release her from any obligations to me. Indeed, she has none.'

'Do you want to be bought off?' Papa asked brutally. 'I'm prepared to discuss it.' The look Robert turned on him was steely, and I gasped.

'Well, then, are you proposing to marry her?'

'If she will have me.'

'And how do you—disabled, out of work, I dare say—propose to keep her as she's been accustomed?'

'I have not yet given my mind to that, sir.'

'Well, you had better do so, hadn't you? And look here,' Papa's face was growing redder and redder, 'I don't want you to see her, talk to her, communicate with her, until I've some guarantee that you can take care of my daughter. Six months, I'll give you. We'll postpone the wedding, eh, Alice? Not cancel it, then something at least can be saved from all this mess. Now, those are my terms, and I want no arguments from either of you.'

Robert and I looked at each other. I was helpless to make any objection or suggestion. Papa was right, of course; it was all madness. Robert gave me the slightest nod, and I knew I must say yes to whatever Papa proposed. For all my twenty-seven years— soon to be twenty-eight—I am as dependent on him as though I were still a child, with only the legacy of three hundred pounds, left me by a godfather, to my name. I could not earn my own living for one day.

Robert stood there, straight as a guardsman, as he had stood from the beginning of the interview. I wanted to run to him, hide my face against his breast, make my parents see that we are one now, indivisible, and that our sudden discovery of each other is not to be dismissed as 'this mess'. But I took strength from him, enough to enable me to say, 'I will do whatever you wish, Papa.'

Robert said, 'That is perfectly fair. I will not approach Miss Pirbright again for six months. Perhaps it will be easier for us all if I take another lodging.'

Mama looked relieved; I think she had visions of my slipping out by night for stolen meetings. My heart sank at the thought of distance lying between us, but I knew that it was the best thing.

There seemed nothing else to be said. Robert made a small courteous bow towards them both, and another to me; he had better sense than to attempt an embrace, nor did I wish it. I said, 'Give my love to Jamie.'

'Thank you. I will.' And he was gone.

My thoughts are in such turmoil I can write no more. I am sorry and ashamed, and glad and proud, all at once. If I could go back to the night of my engagement party knowing what I know now, I would still have taken James home.

Nobody has yet asked me how far our relationship has gone; I suppose it would not occur to them that there has even been time for what has happened, or that their virtuous daughter could behave so outrageously. Well, I have no regrets for the seal we have set on our love.

I will be strong, I swear it to myself. I will live through the separation, and wait, and hope . . .

So long as I do not quicken with Robert's child.

For the past eleven months I have not written in you, Journal. You have remained shut by your gilt clasp in the drawer of my escritoire. Now the escritoire stands in a very different room from the one you saw the last time I opened you; a high light room with windows that look on glorious scenery, rolling pastures, hills, a line of dark forest, the distant shine of loch-water. I am no longer the Amy Pirbright whose Journal you were, but Mrs Robert Lindsay.

How wonderfully Providence has worked for us! I will not fill these pages with a detailed account of the long, difficult time I spent after Robert had left the cottage, without any trace. I confess that at one desperate time, soon after he had gone, I longed so terribly for news that I walked to Alleyn's School and enquired, feeling like a spy, whether James Lindsay was still a pupil. They told me he was, so at least I knew that Robert was not far away. I knew he would be too honourable to approach me, and thereafter I made no more secret enquiries.

I wrote to Arthur, as kindly and apologetically as I could. He came south, of course, for a further explanation, baffled by the whole matter, and dreadfully disappointed. If he had not been so nice about it, anxious to do what he could to mend things, ready to take the blame, it would all have been easier to bear. As it was I let Mama and Papa do most of the talking, for I knew they would comfort him as much as they could with assurances that I would come to my senses in time and the wedding would take place. Privately I told him, very gently, that he was not the man for me. When he returned to Manchester I think he had a very fair idea of the truth of that. I hope he will make some lucky girl a good husband, and knowing his good sense I think he will.

I was, I admit, highly nervous for the first month after Robert left. Then I knew that what I had feared would not happen. I set myself to pass the time as well I could, applying myself to sketching, reading anything which might throw some light on the mystery of my recognition of Robert, and his of me (but nothing did). It is amazing how calm we can be when we must, when no amount of agonizing will do any good. I think I must have learned Stoicism in my former lives.

After the first few weeks Mama stopped reproaching me, urging Arthur's virtues and painting rosy pictures of the life I could now be leading. I think she knew that none of it was having the least effect. Letty came, and tried a little sisterly persuasion, pointing out the joys of marriage, but it was as though she and I had never shared any secrets, for I could find nothing to say to her.

It was on a dark morning in December that Susan knocked at the door of the old nursery, where I was sorting out toys to send to the church's Christmas bazaar. There was a gentleman downstairs, she said, with the mistress, and I was wanted.

I suppose I knew before I even entered the morning-room. Robert was there, even more a country gentleman than he had seemed last time I saw him. A handsome Inverness cape graced his shoulders; he might have stood for a fashion-plate representing what the well-dressed man is wearing out of town. More importantly, he looked better, healthier, a little more substantial than the battered warrior I had known, and when I entered he gave me a smile that was all unclouded welcome. To Mama he said, 'May I?' and when she nodded he stepped forward; I was enfolded in the cape and in his arm, back where I belonged, his lips briefly, sweetly, on mine.

Mama, very subdued in manner, left us alone, and he told me the story she had already heard. After leaving the cottage in June he had thought long and hard what to do for the best. 'It came to me that a man may have too much pride—what I had not done for Jamie, I did for you.' Which was to go to Scotland, and re-visit his family home.

His father had died, some three years before. No word of it had reached him because he had not kept in touch with the family. There was a legacy for him—not large, but handsome enough. In the will his father stated that it only came to him because of the death of his wife, in the knowledge that only one half-caste child had come of the marriage. 'It went against the grain to accept it, knowing that, but I'd no choice.' The years had mellowed his brother Ian, and the cause of their dispute, the handsome Jean Campbell, had long since married someone else. The Glenmhor estate had flourished and grown, by now, to more than a hundred acres of fertile lowland, producing fine cattle, short-horned and polled, oats and barley for the whisky whose manufacture was the chief local industry. Plenty for them both, said Ian, and better to take his brother into the business rather than an outsider.

'It could have happened long before,' said Robert. 'The unco' thing is that I cannot even remember the colour of Jean Campbell's eyes.'

'But you remember the colour of mine?'

'Very well: true cairngorm colour. I have not forgotten anything about you.'

'Jamie?' I asked, 'Has he not forgotten me?'

'He talks of you all the time. He's waiting for you now, Amy. And so am I.'

Papa proved a thorough sportsman, not harking back to the breaking of my engagement. It was clear that he liked Robert, and that Mama did too. In time she would cease to compare him with Arthur, and even cease to find him a little strange and alarming.

Because of the lingering scandal of the jilting of Arthur, which had provided gossip for the neighbourhood, we were married very quietly by special licence, only my parents, Letty, Edward and Amelia being present, Amelia wearing her prettiest frock and a garland of flowers in honour of being my bridesmaid. Robert and I spent Christmas, the happiest of Christmases, at Lamorna Towers, then travelled northwards, hundreds of miles, first by train, then carriage, until we came to our Highland home, and Jamie.

As time goes on and we grow even closer to each other, we remember things from those other times—fleeting things that never make up a whole picture, any more than scraps of glass from a kaleidoscope could show you a pattern: ships and landscape, castles and hovels, cruel faces and beautiful ones, battles and courtly dances. One day when I was wearing a long string of amber beads, reading, absent-mindedly playing with the necklace, Robert said, 'Do you know why you are doing that?'

I looked down, seeing only the honey-coloured smoothness of the amber. 'No—what?'

'You are remembering telling your beads, in a time when you were a Catholic.'

My child is to be born soon after the turn of the year. Robert says he cares not at all whether it is a son or a daughter, so long as it is well and bonny. I asked him the other day what names he would choose. What I pleased, he said. His mother had been Morag, but he would not wish that on our daughter.

'Anne,' I said suddenly.

'Why Anne?'

'I don't know. She was . . . I remember something to do with her being like a lily, I think. But not who she was, or anything more. Sometimes I see the emeralds I told you about—I think a man wore them who was part of her story.'

'Do you still see the Great Ruby?'

I shook my head. 'No. When I have, it has changed into something else, a place that is all red, ceiling and walls. What can that have been?'

'I see it too. But what does it matter to us, *Eilidh mo chridhe*?' I have been Eilidh, not Amy, for a long time now, ever since Ian misheard my name and thought it was Ailie. I like the Gaelic name best. It seems like a dream now that I was ever Amy, or lived at Lamorna Towers. Perhaps some day those other lives, too, will slip into the past. The one I have met and lost through the long centuries is mine at last, and God willing I shall never let him go.

This exclusive edition has been typeset for

THE REINCARNATION LIBRARY

in 11 point Fairfield LH Light

with Rococo Ornaments Two MT and display in Nuptial Script,

and printed by offset lithography on archival quality paper

at Thomson-Shore, Inc.

The text and endpapers are acid-free

and meet or surpass all guidelines

established by the Council of Library Resources and

the American National Standards Institute™.

Text design by Margaret M. Wagner

Cover design by Marshall Lee

Æ